ILLEGAL

Jennifer opened the door and looked up—and up.

Thegun Thegun Nug towered over her; behind him stood the other Foitani. Close up, the huge blue aliens really were intimidating. Without intending to, she took a step back. "What can I do for you?"

"You can come with us," Thegun Thegun Nug said.

"I'd sooner talk here," she answered.

"It was not a conditional request," Thegun Thegun Nug said. Only then did she notice he held something in his hand.

The something sparked.

That was all Jennifer remembered for a long time . . .

By Harry Turtledove
Published by Ballantine Books:

EARTHGRIP

Harry Turtledove

A Del Rey Book
BALLANTINE BOOKS · NEW YORK

A Del Rey Book
Published by Ballantine Books

Library of Congress Catalog Card Number: 91-92193

ISBN 0-345-37239-5

Manufactured in the United States of America

First Edition: December 1991

Cover Art by Barclay Shaw

To Jim Brunet . . .
there is some truth
in what he says.

THE G'BUR

1

THE PRINCE OF T'Kai let the air out of his book lungs in a hiss of despair. "Of course we will fight," K'Sed told the four human traders who sat in front of his throne. "But I fear we are done for." His mandibles clattered sadly.

The humans looked at one another. No one was eager to speak first. K'Sed watched them all, one eyestalk aimed at each. Jennifer Logan wished she were anywhere but under part of the worried alien's gaze. Being back at her university library was a first choice, but even her cabin aboard the merchant ship *Flying Festoon* would have done in a pinch.

At last Bernard Greenberg said, "Your Highness"—the literal translation of the title was *One With All Ten Legs Off The Ground*—"we will do what we may for you, but that cannot be much. We are not soldiers, and there are only the four of us." The translator on his belt turned his Spanglish words into the clicking T'Kai speech.

K'Sed slumped on his throne, a brass pillar topped by a large round cushion on which his cephalothorax and abdomen rested. His walking-legs—the last three pairs—came within centimeters of brushing the carpet and giving the lie to his honorific. His two consorts and chief minister, who perched on lower toadstool seats behind and to either side of him, clacked angrily. He waved for silence.

Once he finally had it, he turned all his eyes on Greenberg. Even after most of a year on L'Rau, the master merchant found that disconcerting; he felt as if he were being measured by a stereopantograph. "Can you truly be as weak as you claim?"

3

K'Sed asked plaintively. "After all, you have crossed the sea of stars to trade with us, while we cannot go to you. Are your other powers not in proportion?"

Greenberg ran a hand over his bald pate. Just as he sometimes had trouble telling the crablike G'Bur apart, they only recognized him because he wore a full beard but had no hair on his crown.

"Highness, you have exposed the Soft One's cowardice!" exclaimed K'Ret, one of K'Sed's consorts. Her carapace darkened toward the green of anger.

"Highness, do not mistake thought for fear." That was Marya Vassilis. She was the best linguist on the *Flying Festoon*'s crew and followed the T'Kai language well enough to start answering before the translator was done. "We do not want to see the M'Sak barbarians triumph any more than you do. Where is our profit if your cities are overthrown?" She tossed her head in a thoroughly Greek gesture of indignation.

"But by the same token, Highness, where is the Soft Ones' profit if they die fighting for T'Kai?" put in B'Rom, K'Sed's vizier. He was the most cynical anthropod Jennifer had ever known. "For them, fleeing is the more expedient choice."

"Manipulative, isn't he?" Pavel Koniev murmured. The other humans glanced at him sharply, but he had turned off his translator. "Get us to feel guilty enough to do or die for T'Kai."

One of K'Sed's eyestalks also peered Koniev's way; Jennifer wondered if the prince had picked up any Spanglish. But K'Sed made no comment, turning all his attention back to Greenberg. "You have not yet answered my question," he pointed out.

"That, Highness, is because the answer is neither yes nor no," Greenberg said carefully. K'Ret gave a derisive clatter. Greenberg ignored it and went on, "Of course, my people know more of the mechanic arts than yours. But as you have seen on all our visits, our only personal weapons are stunners that hardly outrange your bows and slings."

"That might serve," K'Sed said. "If a thousand of the savages suddenly fell, stunned, as they charged—"

Greenberg spread his hands in regret. "A hundred, perhaps, Highness, but not a thousand. The guns have only so much strength in them. When it is gone, they are useless, except as clubs."

Without flesh surrounding them, it was hard for K'Sed's eyes to show expression, but Jennifer thought he gave Greenberg a baleful stare. "And your ship?" the prince said. "What excuse will you give me there?"

"It is armed," Koniev admitted. K'Sed hissed again, this time with a now-we're-getting-somewhere kind of eagerness. Koniev, who was weapons officer when the *Flying Festoon* was offplanet, went on, "The weapons, unfortunately, function only out in space, where there is no air."

"No air? There is air everywhere," K'Sed said. T'Kai astronomy was about at the Ptolemaic level. The locals believed the humans when they said they came from another world; they and their goods were too unlike anything familiar. Not all the implications, though, had yet sunk in.

"I think we are all looking at this problem in the wrong way," Jennifer said.

Her crewmates all looked at her in surprise. Her silence through the uproarious meeting up to this point was very much in character. It wasn't just because she was only twenty-two and an apprentice. Had she been twice as old and a master merchant—not that she ever wanted to become a master merchant—she would have acted the same way.

"Tell us," Greenberg urged, in a tone that said he thought she was so quiet because she didn't operate in the same world as everyone else. "What have you seen that we've missed?" She flushed and did not answer. He growled, "Come on. His Highness doesn't care how pretty you are. Don't keep him waiting."

"I'm sorry, Master Merchant," she said, flushing even harder. It wasn't her fault she'd been born blond and beautiful. She rather wished she hadn't been; it kept people from taking her seriously. But Greenberg was right—to the T'Kai, she was as hideous and alien as the rest of the Soft Ones. The master merchant's glare forced more words from her. "We know, don't we, that there isn't much we can actually do against the M'Sak—" Her voice was small and breathy, barely enough to activate the translator.

"*We* don't know that," B'Rom said, not deigning to turn even one eyestalk Jennifer's way. "You Soft Ones keep saying it, but we do not know it."

The interruption flustered her. She took a while to get going again. At last she said, "Maybe the M'Sak also doubt we are as harmless as we really are—"

Sixteen eyestalks suddenly rose to their full length; sixteen eyes bored into Jennifer's two. She stopped, glancing toward Greenberg for support. He nodded encouragingly. "I think you have their attention," he said. He was fond of understatement.

"But what do I tell them now?" she asked.

"I haven't the slightest idea," he told her. "How do you think we'd look tricked out with a paint job and enough false legs and teeth to impersonate four *f'noi*?" The *f'noi*, which looked like an unlikely cross between a tiger and a lobster, was the worst predator this continent knew.

"You're baiting me!" Jennifer said. From some people, they would have been fighting words. She wished she could sound fierce instead of disappointed.

Marya Vassilis stepped into the breach. "We don't yet know your barbarous foes well," she reminded the prince and his retinue. "You will have to advise us on how we can best appear terrifying to them."

"Maybe even the sight of your ship will be enough," K'Sed said hopefully. "I do not think any Soft Ones have traded directly with the M'Sak."

"Why should they?" observed D'Kar, K'Sed's other consort, with what the translator rendered as a scornful sniff. She wore gold bands round all her walking-legs and had two rows of yellow garnets glued to her carapace. "The M'Sak are such low wretches, they surely have nothing worth trading for."

"Let them eat cake," Koniev quoted. No matter how well the computer translated, it could not provide social context. *A good thing, too*, Jennifer thought as the talk at last turned serious.

When they got back to the suite the humans had been modifying to their comfort for the past several months, Jennifer flopped down on her air mattress and put a reader on her nose. The mattress, a washbasin, and a chemical toilet were great improvements over the local equivalents. T'Kai sleeping gear, for instance, resembled nothing so much as a set of parallel bars.

Greenberg said something to her. Her attention was on the

reader, so she didn't pay much attention. He coughed. She looked up. Her eyes took several seconds to focus on the real world.

"Thanks for the notion that got us going there," he repeated.

"Oh. Thank you very much. I wasn't sure what would come of it, but . . ." She hesitated. As often happened, the hesitation became a full stop.

"But anything was better than staying stuck where we were," Greenberg finished. "Yes." He was resigned to finishing sentences for her by now.

She went back to the reader, but still felt his eyes on her. She was used to looks from men, but on this cruise Greenberg and Koniev both seemed to have taken to Marya, though she was fifteen years older than Jennifer and lovely by the canon of no human world. To Jennifer, that was more a relief than anything else.

Greenberg said something to her. Again, she noticed that he said it, but not what it was. He repeated himself once more. "What are you reading?"

"Heinlein—one of the early Future History books." She'd loved Middle English science fiction ever since she was a child. It was all English, he'd taught her the ancient speech so young that she read it as fluently as she did Spanglish. She was also still young enough to think that everyone ought to love what she loved. "Would you like to borrow the fiche when I'm through with it?" she asked eagerly.

"More of your dead languages?" he asked her. She nodded. "No, thank you," he said. His voice was not ungentle, but her face fell. He went on, "I'm more interested in what's really here than in some ancient picture of a future that never happened."

"It's not so much the future he creates, but the way he does it," she said, trying to get across the fascination that rigorous world building had for her.

He shook his head. "I haven't the time or the inclination for it now. Illusions are all very well, but the M'Sak, worse luck, are real. I just hope illusory threats can chase them away. I have the bad feeling they won't. There's going to be some very real fighting before long, I'm afraid."

Jennifer nodded. As the meeting with the prince and his court was breaking up, a messenger had come in with bad news: C'Lar, one of the northern towns of the T'Kai confederacy, had fallen to the M'Sak. The T'Kai and their neighbors had been peaceful for several generations now. As K'Sed himself was uneasily aware, they were no match for the vigorous barbarians now emerging from the northern jungles.

But K'Sed intended to try, and nobody on the *Flying Festoon* had even brought up the idea of backing the other side. For one thing, T'Kai objets d'art brought the crew a tidy profit, trip after trip; that would vanish with a M'Sak conquest. For another, the M'Sak were not nice people, even for crabs. Their leader, V'Zek, seemed to have taken Chingis Khan lessons—he was both ruthless and extremely able.

Jennifer worried about that until the Heinlein story completely occupied her, but it was a distant sort of worry. If worse came to worst, the *Flying Festoon* could always lift off and leave.

K'Sed, of course, would not be so lucky.

V'Zek came down from his shelter and stepped away from it to watch the full moon rise. Many of his warriors felt anxious away from the trees they were used to, but he took the southlands' open spaces as a challenge, and he never met a challenge any way but claws-first.

Thus he did not pull in his eyestalks when he was away from the posts that held up his shelter and the web of ropes that imitated the closely twined branches of the jungle. And, indeed, there was a certain grandeur in seeing the great yellow shield unobscured by twigs and leaves.

He stretched his eyestalks as far as they would go, a grasping-claw's length from his cephalothorax. He drew a knife and brandished it at the moon. "Soon everything you shine on will be mine."

"The Soft Ones may perhaps have something to say about that, my master," a dry voice beside him observed. He hissed in surprise. He had not heard Z'Yon come up. The shaman could be eerily quiet when he chose.

"Soft Ones," V'Zek said, clicking his scorn. "They did not save C'Lar, nor will they save T'Kai when we reach it. I almost wonder if they exist at all. So much open space makes people imagine strange things."

"They exist," Z'Yon said. "They are one of the reasons I sought you out tonight. What do you plan to do about them?"

The chieftain clacked discontentedly. Since C'Lar fell, he had known the Soft Ones were real, but had tried to avoid thinking of them. Z'Yon was useful, because the shaman made him look at hard questions. "I will deal with them, if they care to deal with me," V'Zek said at last. "Some of their trinkets are amusing."

He thought of the mirror some grandee had owned in captured C'Lar. It was his now, of course. He admired the perfect reflection it gave. It was ever so much clearer than the polished bronze that was the best even T'Kai made. He had not known what a handsome fellow he was.

But Z'Yon would not leave off. "And if they do not?"

"Then I will kill them." V'Zek was very straightforward. That made him a deadly dangerous warleader—he saw an objective and went right after it. It also suited him to lead the M'Sak, whose characters were mostly similar to his own, if less intense. Z'Yon, though, did not think that way: another reason he was valuable to his chieftain.

The shaman let V'Zek's words hang in the air. V'Zek suspected his carapace was turning blue with embarrassment. Who knew what powers the Soft Ones had? "No rumor has ever spoken of them as killers," he said, the best defense of his belligerence he could come up with.

"No rumor has ever spoken of anyone attacking them, either," Z'Yon pointed out.

V'Zek knew that as well as the shaman. He changed the subject, a chiefly prerogative. "Why else did you want to see me?"

"To warn you, my master." When Z'Yon said that, V'Zek grew very alert. The shaman had smelled out plots before. But Z'Yon went on in a way his master had not looked for. "When the moon comes round to fullness again, unless I have misreckoned, the great f'noi that lives in the sky will seek to devour it." The M'Sak were not as intellectually sophisticated as the T'Kai, but their seekers-after-wisdom had watched the heavens through the trees for many years.

The chieftain cared nothing for such concerns. A superstitious chill ran through him; he felt his eyestalks contract of themselves. "It will fail?"

"It always has," Z'Yon reassured him. "Still, you might spend some time warning the warriors this will take place, so they are not taken by surprise and perhaps panic-stricken."

"Ah. That is sensible. Claim yourself any one piece of loot from my share of the booty of C'Lar." V'Zek was open-clawed with his gifts; who would stay loyal to a chieftain with a name for meanness?

Z'Yon lowered and raised his eyes, a thank-you gesture. "I wish I could have told you sooner, my master, but the campaign has disrupted my observations, and I did not become certain enough to speak until now."

"It is of no great moment." V'Zek settled back on his walking-legs. "Fifty-one days should be adequate time to prepare the fighters. By then, if all goes well, we will be attacking the city of T'Kai itself."

"Yes, and that is why you will need to harden the warriors' shells against fear. Think on it, my master: When the *f'noi* in the sky wounds the moon with its claws, what color does the moon turn as its blood spreads over it?"

V'Zek thought. He had seen such sky-fights a few times, watching as Z'Yon and the other shamans beat drums to frighten away the sky-*f'noi*. "The color of bronze, more or less . . ." The chieftain paused. "You are subtle."

"You see it too, then: When the heavenly *f'noi* attacks the moon, it will become the color of the T'Kai banners. That is an omen which, without careful preparation, common warriors might well see as disturbing."

"So they might." V'Zek opened and closed his upper grasping-claws while he thought, as if he wished to rend something. His left lower claw was never far from the shortspear strapped to his plastron. "Suppose the omen means that T'Kai will fall to us. Suppose that, till the evil night, you put that meaning about."

"Shall I consult the moltings, to seek the true significance of the phenomenon?"

"For your own amusement, if you like." That lower claw moved closer to the shortspear; Z'Yon felt his small, fanlike tail, of itself, fold under the rear of his abdomen. He did not need the reflex to know he was afraid; he felt the fear in his wits as well as his body. His chieftain went on, "Of course, you will present it to our warriors as I have given it to you now."

"Of course, my master." Z'Yon backed out of V'Zek's presence. When—actually, just before—he had gone a seemly distance, he turned and hurried away.

V'Zek let the slight breach of etiquette pass. He glowered up at the moon. Nothing would interfere with his plans for conquest: not the Soft Ones, whatever they really were, and not the moon, either. *Nothing*.

Having made that vow to himself, he returned at last to his shelter. The ropes and poles were a poor substitute for the fragrant, leafy branches he was used to. He let out a resigned hiss and wondered again how the southrons bore living away from the forests. Maybe, he thought, they were such skillful artificers exactly because they were trying to make up for what they lacked.

The why of it did not matter, though. They had been making their trinkets and trading them back and forth for so long that they forgot claws had any other uses. C'Lar had fallen even more easily than V'Zek had expected.

He composed himself for sleep. C'Lar was only the beginning.

Up on the battlements, Marya giggled. Jennifer took the reader off her nose for a moment so she could watch T'Kai's army march out of the city. The host looked martial enough to her, if uncertainly drilled. She asked, "What's funny?"

"It's just that I've never seen such a lot of tin openers on parade," Marya said.

Bernard Greenberg said, "They're on the big side for tin openers," but now he smiled, too. Marya had a point. Being armored themselves, the G'Bur had developed an assortment of weapons reminiscent of those of Earth's Middle Ages: halberds, bills, and partizans. All of them looked like big pieces of cutlery on long poles. On L'Rau, piercing and crushing took the place of slashing.

Pavel Koniev swung a wickedly spiked morning star, but his expression was sheepish. He said, "When the locals gave me this, I had visions of smashing the M'Sak army single-handed.

But if they're all toting polearms, I won't be able to get close enough to them to do any good.''

Jennifer went back to her reader; if not being described in Middle English, archaic weapons held little interest for her. Greenberg was saying, ''It's a personal defense weapon, like the shortspears they carry. If you're close enough to have to use it, odds are we'll be in a lot of trouble.'' Out of the corner of her ear, she heard him click off his translator, in case one of the natives nearby was eavesdropping. He also lowered his voice. ''We probably will be.''

Marya and Koniev followed the master merchant's example. Jennifer would have, but she was engrossed in her Heinlein again. Marya said, ''They seem willing enough to fight—which is more than I can say for their prince.''

''I'm afraid he knows more than they do,'' Greenberg said. Down below, a couple of K'Sed's warriors were clicking and clacking at each other loud enough to draw even Jennifer's notice. They had gotten the heads of their weapons tangled and were holding up their whole section. Greenberg went on, ''They're amateurs—smiths and taverners and carapace-painters and such. The M'Sak are professionals.''

''We're amateurs, too,'' Koniev said.

''Don't remind me,'' Greenberg told him. ''I'm just hoping we're amateurs at a higher level, so we can match up against G'Bur professionals.''

''A higher level indeed,'' Marya said. ''With the *Flying Festoon* and our drones and such, we'll be able to keep track of the barbarians and their route long before they know where we are.''

Greenberg said, ''That will be for you to handle, Jennifer.''

''Huh?'' Hearing her name brought Jennifer back to the here and now. She lowered the reader from her nose and got the local sun full in the face. Blinking, she said, ''I'm so sorry. What was that?''

''The drones.'' Greenberg sounded as if he were holding on to his patience with both hands.

''Oh, yes, the drones. Of course,'' Jennifer said. Unfortunately, she hadn't the faintest idea of what he wanted her to do with them. She knew he could tell, too. Her cheeks grew hot. When she wasn't preoccupied by her Middle English science fiction, she wanted to do well.

"I'll handle the drones, Bernard," Koniev said, seeing her confusion. "I've had experience with them."

"I know you have. That's why I'm giving them to Jennifer," Greenberg said. "She has to get some herself."

Koniev nodded. So did Jennifer; Greenberg had a way of making sense. Then she saw a sparkle of irony in Marya's dark eyes. She flushed all over again. Another reason Greenberg might want her back aboard the *Flying Festoon* was to keep her out of trouble. It didn't occur to her to wonder whether that meant trouble with the M'Sak or trouble with him.

Just then, K'Sed came over to the four humans. The prince of T'Kai had gone martial to the extent of carrying a ceremonial shortspear that did not look sharp enough to menace anything much more armored than a balloon. "Let us see what we can do," he said. For a moment, only Jennifer's translator picked up his words. Then the other traders switched theirs back on. The machines' flat tones did not make him sound martial.

Greenberg said, "Your Highness, we admire your courage in going forth to confront your enemies. Many princes might stay within the walls and try to withstand a siege."

"If I thought I could, Soft One, I would. But V'Zek, may his clasper's prongs fall out, would swallow my cities one by one, saving T'Kai for the last. Maybe the town can hold against him, maybe not. But the confederacy would surely die. Sometimes a bad gamble is all there is."

"Yes," Greenberg said.

"I thank you for making it better than it might be. Now I join my troops." K'Sed gestured jerkily with the shortspear and headed for the way down. That was neither stairs nor ramp, merely a double row of posts driven into the wall. With ten limbs, the G'Bur needed nothing more complex. Humans could use the posts, too, though less confidently.

"More to him than I thought," Koniev said as he watched the prince descend.

"He's brave enough, and bright enough to see what needs doing," Greenberg agreed. "Whether he has the skill and the wherewithal to do it is something else again. Maybe we can help a little there."

"Maybe." Marya sounded about as convinced as K'Sed but, like the prince of T'Kai, was ready to get on with it. "Shall we go down? Otherwise they'll leave without us, which won't make them like us any better." She lowered herself off the edge of the wall, grunted when her feet found purchase, and then rapidly climbed down.

Jennifer stuck her reader in a pocket and followed Marya's lead. She didn't think about what she was doing until her boots kicked up gravel in the courtyard below. Then she started to put her reader back on.

Greenberg came down beside her. He wiped his hands on the sides of his coverall and shook his head. "I don't like that. Hell of a thing for a spacer, isn't it—a bad head for heights?"

"It would be a nuisance, wouldn't it?" Jennifer said. "I just don't notice them."

"Nothing seems to get to you, does it?" Greenberg said. She shrugged and started to walk with the rest of the humans toward the T'Kai army. The warriors milled about under their standards: bronze-colored pennons bearing the emblem of the confederacy T'Kai ruled—a golden grasping-claw, its two pincers open. Greenberg coughed. "You won't be marching with us," he reminded her. "You're going back aboard the *Flying Festoon,* remember?"

"Oh, that's right," she said, embarrassed. She'd forgotten all about it. The ship sat a few hundred meters away, its smooth silver curves contrasting oddly with the vertical dark stone curtain of the walls of T'Kai. Willingly enough, Jennifer hurried toward it.

Bernard Greenberg watched Jennifer head back to the *Flying Festoon.* Her curves contrasted oddly with the jointed, armored G'Bur all around her. He sighed. Try as he might, he could not stay annoyed with her. He walked on over to where K'Sed was haranguing his army.

The prince was less optimistic than most human leaders would have been, were they facing his predicament. Even his peroration sounded downbeat. "Warriors of T'Kai, we are fighting for our freedom and our lives. Fighting is our best chance to keep them; if we do not fight, we will surely lose them. So when the time comes, let us fight with all our strength."

He got no cheers, but the soldiers began tramping north, the humans with them. Heavy wagons drawn by *t'dit*—large, squat, enormously strong quasi crustaceans—rumbled in a long column between troops of warriors. Choking clouds of dust rose into the sky.

"I wish I had a set of nose-filters," Koniev said, coughing.

"Get used to it," Greenberg waved his hand at the ground over which they were walking—bare dirt, sparsely sprinkled with small bushes here and there. Most of them, now, were sadly bedraggled. "No grasses, or anything like them," the master merchant went on.

"So?" Koniev said indifferently.

Greenberg stared at him. "So?" he echoed. "Next trip in, we'll have a load of grain genetically engineered to take advantage of the gap in the ecosystem—grain is just grass with big seeds, after all. I've had people working on that for a long time, but always on a shoestring, so it's taken a while. T'Kai would pay plenty for a new food crop like that . . . if there's any T'Kai left to sell it to in a couple of years. The M'Sak won't give a damn about it—what forest nomads would?"

Marya knew about the grain project. "We're not just trying to save T'Kai out of altruism, Pavel," she said.

"Well, I was hoping not," he said. "Where's the profit in that?"

Greenberg clapped him on the back. He had the proper merchant's attitude. Now if only Jennifer could find a fraction of it in herself . . .

Quiet and smooth, the *Flying Festoon* rose into the air. The ground screen showed G'Bur with eyestalks that seemed more than fully extended, G'Bur pointing grasping-claws at the trade-ship, a few G'Bur running like hell even though starships had been visiting L'Rau every few years for a couple of generations now.

Jennifer noticed the excited locals only peripherally. The novel she was reading interested her much more than they did. Only when the *Flying Festoon* reached the five thousand meters she had preset did she reluctantly lower the reader and get around to the job she had been assigned.

Three drones dropped away from the ship and slowly flew off: northeast, due north, and northwest. One of them, Jennifer thought, ought to pick up the advancing M'Sak army. When it

did, she would have more to handle. Until then, she could take
it easy. She got out the reader and put it back on. The novel
engrossed her again.

Prestarflight writers, she reflected, had one thing wrong about
trading runs. Nobody in a novel ever complained about how
boring they were. But then, she supposed, nobody set out to
write a deliberately boring book.

Not for the first time, she wished she'd never gotten involved
with real traders. But it had seemed such a good idea at the
time. A whole little academic community specialized in comparing the imagined worlds of Middle English science fiction
with the way things had actually happened. She'd always intended to join that community and, at the end of her sophomore
year, she'd had a notion original enough to guarantee her tenure
before she turned thirty—no mean trick, if she could pull it off.

She had reasoned that her competition—ivory-tower types,
one and all—hardly knew more about how things really worked
outside the university than the old SF writers had. If she spent
a couple of years on real fieldwork and coupled that unique
perspective with a high-powered degree, what doors would not
open for her?

And so she'd taken a lot of xenanth courses her last two years.
Some of them, to her surprise, were even interesting. When the
crew of the *Flying Festoon* decided to carry an apprentice, there
she was, ready and eager.

Here she was still, bored.

She read for a while, took a shower she did not really need,
and programmed the autochef for a meal whose aftermath, she
realized with remorse, she would have to exercise off. She did,
until sweat stuck her singlet and shorts to her. Then she took
another shower. This one, at least, she had earned.

After all that, she decided she might as well check the drones'
reporting screens. Night had fallen while she was killing time.
She did not expect to find anything exciting, the more so as the
drones would be only halfway to the jungle home of the M'Sak.

For a moment, the regular array of lights twinkling in the
blackness did not mean much to her. *A town*, she thought, and
checked the map grid to find out which one it was. COORDINATES
UNMATCHED, the screen flashed.

"Oh, dear," she said, and then, finding that inadequate, followed it with something ripe enough to have made Bernard Greenberg blink, were he there to hear it.

She sent the drone in for a closer look. Then she called Greenberg. He sounded as if he were underwater—not from a bad signal, but plainly because she had awakened him. "I hope this is important," he said through an enormous yawn.

Jennifer knew him well enough to translate that: *it had better be* sounded in her mind. "I think so," she said. "You do want to know where the M'Sak are camped, don't you?" The silence on the comm circuit lasted so long, she wondered if he had fallen asleep again. "Bernard?"

"I'm here." Greenberg paused again, then sighed. "Yes, you'd better tell me."

V'Zek peered into the night. The tympanic membrane behind his eyestalks was picking up a low-pitched buzz that would not go away. Scratching the membrane with a grasping-claw did not help. The chieftain summoned Z'Yon. His temper rose when the shaman clicked laughter. Laughing around V'Zek was dangerous, laughing at him insanely foolhardy.

"Well?" V'Zek growled. He reared back so the other M'Sak could see his shortspear.

Z'Yon opened the joint between his carapace and plastron to let the chieftain drive home the spear if he wanted. V'Zek thought the gesture of ritual submission insolently performed, but his anger gave way to surprise when the shaman said, "I hear it, too, my master. The whole army hears it."

"But what *is* it?" V'Zek demanded. "No sky-glider makes that sort of noise."

Z'Yon opened the edges of his shell again, this time, V'Zek judged, in all sincerity. "My master, I cannot say. I do not know."

"Is it a thing of the T'Kai?" V'Zek was worried. He expressed it as anger; no chieftain could show anything that looked like fear. "Can they smite us with it? Have you heard of their possessing such?" He looked as if he wanted to tear the answer from Z'Yon, with iron pincers if his own were not strong enough.

"Never, my master." Now the shaman truly was afraid, which made his overlord a trifle happier. Z'Yon spoke more firmly a moment later. "My master, truly I doubt it is a T'Kai thing. How could they conceal it?"

"And more to the point, why? Yes." V'Zek thought, but came up with no alternatives that satisfied him. "What then?"

"The Soft Ones," Z'Yon said quietly. "Traveling through the air, after all, is said to be their art, is it not?"

The suggestion made sense to V'Zek. He wished it had not. When the other choice was thinking them creatures of near—or maybe not just near—supernatural powers, he had preferred to doubt that such things as Soft Ones even existed. After C'Lar, he could not do that any more. So he had thought of them as skilled artificers—their mirrors and such certainly justified that. But then, the T'Kai confederacy was full of skilled artificers. The difference between those of his own race and the strangers seemed one of degree, not of kind.

The T'Kai, though, he knew perfectly well, could not make anything that buzzed through the air. If the Soft Ones could . . . It had never occurred to V'Zek that the line between skilled artificers and creatures of near-supernatural powers might be a fine one.

Someone cried out in the camp, a shout of fear and alarm that tore the chieftain from his uncharacteristically philosophical musings. "There it is! The sky-monster!" Other yells echoed the first. Warriors who should have been sleeping tumbled out of their tents to see what the trouble was. Panic ran through the camp.

"By the First Tree, I see it myself," Z'Yon murmured. V'Zek aimed his eyestalks where the shaman's grasping-claw pointed. At first, he saw nothing. Then he spied the little, silvery box his army's campfires were illuminating. The buzzing came from there, sure enough. No, no T'Kai had made the thing, whatever it was. Every line, every angle screamed its alienness. V'Zek wanted to run, to hide himself under the leaves and branches of the forests of M'Sak, to imagine himself undisputed lord of all creation.

He did not run. He filled his book lungs till they pressed painfully against his carapace. "Warriors!" he bellowed, so loud and fierce that eyestalks whipped toward him all through the camp. "Will you flee like hatchlings from something that does you no harm?"

"How much you take for granted," Z'Yon said, but only V'Zek heard him.

He knew the shaman was right. He ignored him anyhow—he had only this one chance to rally the army to him before it fell apart. He cried out again. "Let us try to make it run off, not the other way round!" He snatched up a fair-sized stone, flung it with all his might at the thing in the sky, and wondered if he would be struck dead the next moment.

So, evidently, did his followers. The stone flew wide, but the thing floating in the air took no notice of it and did not retaliate. "Knock it down!" V'Zek shouted, even louder than before. He threw another stone. Again the buzzing device—creature?—paid no attention, though this time the missile came close to it.

Crazy confidence, fueled mostly by relief, tingled through V'Zek. "You see? It cannot harm us. Use arrows, not stones, and it will be ours!" He had led the M'Sak many years now, almost always in victory. As they had so often before, they caught fire from him. Suddenly the sky was full of rocks and arrows, as if the fear the northerners had felt were transmuted all at once to rage.

"My master, you have magics of your own," Z'Yon said, watching the frenzied attack on the sky-thing. V'Zek knew the shaman had no higher praise to give.

Praise, however, won no battles. The M'Sak roared as one when a stone crashed against the side of the sky-thing. It staggered in the air. V'Zek ached to see it fall, but it did not. An arrow hit the thing and bounced off. Another, perhaps shot by a stronger warrior, pierced its shiny skin. It lurched again.

Despite that, its buzzing never changed. And after a little while, it began to drift higher, so that not even the mightiest male could hope to hit it.

"A victory," V'Zek shouted. "We've taught it respect."

His warriors cheered. The thing was still there; they could see it faintly and still catch its sound, though that was muted now. But they had made it retreat. Maybe it had not been slain or broken or whatever the right word was, but they must have hurt it or it would not have moved away at all. The panic was gone.

But if V'Zek had managed to hold his army together, he still felt fury at the buzz which remained, to his way of thinking, all too audible. The sky-thing showed no sign of departing for good. It hung over the camp like, like—on a world where nothing flew and only a few creatures could glide, he failed to find a simile. That only made him angrier.

"What's it doing up there?" he growled. At first it was a rhetorical question. Then the chieftain rounded on Z'Yon. "Shaman, you lay claim to all sorts of wisdom. What *is* it doing up there?"

Z'Yon was glad he had been working through that question in his own mind. "My master, I do not think it came here merely to terrify us. Had that been the aim, it would be more offensive than it is. But for its, ah, strangeness, in fact, it does not seem to seek to disturb us."

V'Zek made an irregular clicking noise. The sky-thing was disturbing enough as it was. Yet Z'Yon had seen a truth: it could have been worse. "Go on," the chieftain urged.

"From the way it hangs over us—and keeps on hanging there—my guess is that somehow it passes word of us to the Soft Ones and, I suppose, to the T'Kai as well. I say again, though, my master, this is only a guess."

"A good one," V'Zek said with a sinking feeling. Hanging there in the sky, that buzzing thing could watch everything he did. At a stroke, two of his main advantages over T'Kai disappeared. His army was more mobile than any the city-dwellers could patch together, and he knew with no false modesty that he surpassed any southron general. But how would that matter, if T'Kai learned of every move as he made it?

He clicked again, and hissed afterward. Maybe things could not have been worse after all.

B'Rom peered into the screen Greenberg was holding. "So that is the barbarians' army, is it?" the vizier said. "Does their leader camp always in the same place within the host?"

"I'd have to check our tapes to be sure, but I think so," Greenberg answered cautiously; B'Rom never asked anything without an ulterior motive. "Why?"

The chief minister's eyestalks extended in surprise. "So I can give proper briefing to the assassins I send out, of course. What good would it do me to have them kill some worthless double-pay trooper, thinking all the while they were slaying the fierce V'Zek?''

"None, I suppose," Greenberg muttered. He had to remind himself that the M'Sak had not invaded the T'Kai confederacy for a picnic. Drone shots of what was left of C'Lar said that louder than any words.

B'Rom said, "Do you think our agents would be able to poison the barbarians' food, or will we have to use weapons to kill him? We would find fewer willing to try that, as the chances for escape seem poor."

"So they do." The master merchant thought for a moment, then went on carefully, "Excellency, you know your people better than I ever could. I have to leave such matters of judgment in your hands." He knew the translator would spit out the appropriate idiom, probably something like *in the grasp of your claws.*

The minister went click-click-hiss, sounding rather, Greenberg thought unkindly, like an irritated pressure cooker. "Do not liken me to the savages infesting our land." He glared at Greenberg from four directions at once, then suddenly made the rusty-hinge noise that corresponded to a wry chuckle. "Although I suppose from your perspective such confusion is only natural. Very well, you may think of yourself as forgiven." He creaked again and scurried away.

No doubt he's plotting more mischief, Greenberg thought. That was one of the vizier's jobs. The old devil was also a lot better than most G'Bur—most humans, too, come to that—at seeing the other fellow's point of view, very likely because he believed in nothing himself and found shifting position easy on account of that.

The T'Kai army moved out. Greenberg, Marya, and Koniev tramped along with the G'Bur. Even the locals' humblest tools would have fetched a good price on any human world. The waterpots they carried strapped to their left front walking-legs, for instance, were thrown with a breathtaking clarity of line the Amasis potter would have envied. And when they worked at their art, the results were worth traveling light-years for.

The T'Kai treated their land the same way. The orchards where they grew their tree-tubers and nuts were arranged like Japanese gardens, and with a good deal of the same spare elegance. The road north curved to give the best possible view of a granite boulder off to one side.

Greenberg sighed. The M'Sak cared little for esthetics. They were, however, only too good at one art: destruction. The master merchant wished he had a warship here instead of his merchant vessel. He wished for an in-atmosphere fighter. Neither one appeared.

"I didn't think they would," he said, and sighed again.

"Didn't think what would?" Marya asked. He explained. She said, "How do the M'Sak know the *Flying Festoon* isn't a warship?"

"Because it won't blast them into crabcakes, for one thing."

"Will it have to? They've never seen it before. They've never seen anything like it before. If a starship drops out of the sky with an enormous sonic boom and lands in front of them, what do you think they'll do?"

Greenberg considered. As far as he knew, no offworlders had ever visited the M'Sak. He laughed out loud and kissed Marya on the mouth. She kissed him back, at least until a couple of G'Bur pulled them apart. "Why are you fighting?" the locals demanded.

"We weren't," Greenberg said. "It's a—"

"Mating ritual," Marya supplied helpfully.

The G'Bur clacked among themselves. The translator, doing its duty, laughed in Greenberg's ear. He didn't care. He thought what the G'Bur did to make more G'Bur was pretty funny, too.

Jennifer put down the reader. Naturally, Greenberg's orders had come just when she was getting to the interesting part of the book. She wished this Anderson fellow, who seemed to have a feel for what the trader's life was like, were on the *Flying Festoon* instead of her. As he was about a thousand years dead, however, she seemed stuck with the job.

She had all three drones over the M'Sak army now, flying in triangular formation. They stayed several hundred meters off the ground. That first night had not been the only time the barbarians attacked them, and they thought of more ploys than Jennifer had. One M'Sak climbed a tall tree to pump arrows into a drone she'd thought safely out of range. Greenberg would not have thought well of her had it gone down.

She made a sour face. She did not think Greenberg thought well of her, anyway. Too bad. No one had held a gun to his head to make him take her on. Just as she had to make the best of boredom, he had to make the best of her.

The M'Sak were approaching a wide, relatively open space with low bushes growing here and there. When L'Rau got around to evolving grasses, that kind of area would be a meadow. It would, Jennifer thought with a faint sniff, certainly be more attractive as a broad expanse of green than as bare dirt and rocks punctuated by plants.

But even as it was, it would serve her purpose. She did not want the M'Sak distracted from her arrival by anything.

She told the computer what she wanted the *Flying Festoon* to do. She was smiling as she picked up the reader again. She doubted the M'Sak would have trouble paying attention to her.

These days, V'Zek and his army almost ignored the drones that hung over them. Their buzzing still reached the chieftain's tympanic membrane, but he no longer heard it unless he made a deliberate effort. If the things were spying on him for the Soft Ones, then they were. He could do nothing about it, now that the drones kept out of missile range.

The M'Sak marched in a hollow square, with booty and prisoners inside. The army was smaller than it had been when it entered T'Kai territory, not so much from casualties as because V'Zek had left garrisons in the towns he had taken. He intended to rule this land, not just raid it. When the T'Kai finally came out to fight, he would still have enough warriors to deal with them.

"For that matter, they may just yield tamely," the chieftain said to Z'Yon, who was ambling along beside him. The shaman was not a large male, nor physically impressive, but had no trouble keeping up with the hulking youths who made up the bulk of V'Zek's army.

Z'Yon did not answer for a moment; he was chewing a *f'leg*-fruit he had snipped from a bush as he walked past. When he was done with it, he said, "I have to doubt that. The confederation is stronger to the south. I think they will try to meet us somewhere there."

"I begin to wonder. The southrons are such cowards," V'Zek said derisively.

"Such what?"

"Cowards," V'Zek said, a little louder. The noise from the sky was louder, too. The chieftain turned his eyestalks that way, wondering if the drones were dropping lower again for some reason of their own. If they were, he would have his troopers drive them up again—they should not be allowed to think they could get gay with the bold M'Sak.

But the sky-things were where they had always been.

"Don't take the T'Kai too lightly," Z'Yon warned. He also had to raise his voice. V'Zek felt his eyestalks shrink back toward his shell. That was not a thin buzz coming from the sky now; it was a roar. It got louder and *louder* and LOUDER. V'Zek's walking-legs bent under it, as if he had some great weight tied to his carapace.

Z'Yon pointed with a grasping-claw. V'Zek made an eyestalk follow it. Something else was in the sky that did not belong there. At first he thought it just a bright silver point, as if a star were to appear in daylight. But it got bigger with terrifying speed—it became a shining fruit, a ball, and then, suddenly, the chieftain realized it was a metal building falling toward him. No wonder his legs were buckling!

He no longer heard the noise of its approach, but felt it as a vibration that seemed to be trying to tear his shell from his flesh. He looked up again, willing one eye to follow the sky-building as it descended. Would it crush him? No, not quite, he saw.

The roar continued to build, even after the thing was down on the ground in front of the M'Sak host. Then all at once it ended, and silence seemed to ache as much as clamor had a moment before.

"The Soft Ones!" Z'Yon was shrieking.

V'Zek wondered how long the shaman had been talking, or rather, screaming. "What about them?" he said. His own voice echoed brassily on his tympanic membrane.

"It's their ship," Z'Yon said.

"Well, who cares?" the chieftain growled. Now that the accursed noise had stopped, he was able to think again, and the first thing he thought about was his army.

When he looked back over his cephalothorax and tail, he let

out a whistle of fury. His army, his precious, invincible army, was in full flight, dashing in all directions.

"Come back!" he bellowed. He chose the one line that had even a tiny chance of turning the warriors. "The prisoners are escaping with our loot!"

That made eyestalks whip around where nothing else would have. He saw he had not even been lying: captives from C'Lar and other towns were scuttling this way and that, with baskets on their carapaces and in their grasping-claws. He sprang after one and swung down his axe. It bit through the poor fellow's shell, which was softened by recent privation. Body fluids spurted. The prisoner fell. V'Zek slew one of his own soldiers, one who was running.

The chieftain reared back on his hindmost pair of legs, waved the dripping axe on high. "Rally!" he cried. "Rally!" A few officers took up the call. V'Zek fought and killed another would-be fugitive. The warriors began to regroup. They had feared their master for years, the unknown from out of the sky only for moments.

Then an even louder voice came from the sky-thing, roaring in the T'Kai dialect, "Go away! Leave this land! Go away!"

V'Zek understood it perfectly well. Most of his soldiers could follow it after a fashion; the M'Sak language and that of the southrons were cousins. The chieftain thought the sky-thing made a mistake by speaking. Had it remained silent and menacing, he could not have fought it, for it would have given him nothing to oppose. This way—

"It's a trick!" he shouted. "It's the accursed T'Kai, trying to run us off without fighting us!"

"Doing a good job, too!" one of his fleeing soldiers cried.

The fellow was too far away for him to catch and kill. V'Zek had to rely on persuasion instead, a much less familiar technique. Still, with the full power of his book lungs, he said, "It hasn't harmed us. Will you run from noise alone? Do you run from thunder and lightning?"

"Not bad," Z'Yon said beside him. Then he, too, raised his voice. "If this is the best the T'Kai can do, you warriors should be ashamed. Our master has the right of it: a good thunderstorm back home is more frightening than this big hunk of ironmongery ever could be. If it smites us, that is the time to worry. Till then, it's only so much wind.''

As an aside to V'Zek, he added, "If it smites us, I suspect we'll be too dead to worry about anything." But only the chieftain heard him; Z'Yon knew what he was doing.

Long-ingrained discipline, the fear of losing plunder, and the sky-thing's failure to do anything more than make threatening noises slowly won the day for V'Zek. The M'Sak reclaimed most of their captives and most of their loot. They re-formed their ranks and, giving the building that had fallen from the sky a wide berth, resumed their march south.

V'Zek wanted more than that. He wanted revenge for the sky-building's nearly having put paid to his whole campaign. He sent a squad of halberdiers against it. Their weapons were good for cracking shells; he wanted to see what they would do against that gleaming metal skin.

He never found out. The sky-thing emitted such a piercing screech that he, no short distance away, drew in his eyestalks in a wince of pain. His warriors dropped their polearms and fled. Most returned to their troop, but two dashed straight for Z'Yon: the shaman was the army's chief healer.

Z'Yon examined them, gave them a salve, and sent them back to the comrades. When he turned back to V'Zek, his hesitancy showed the chieftain he was troubled. "The salve will soothe a bit. It will do no more. Their tympanic membranes are ruptured.''

"Deafened, are they?" V'Zek glowered at the flying building. He only glowered, though. If the thing really could be dangerous when provoked, he would not provoke it. He had more important things to do than pausing for vengeance in the middle of his attack on T'Kai.

But once he had broken the confederacy, he told himself, the Soft Ones—or whoever was in charge of the sky-thing—would pay for trying to thwart him. Anticipating that was almost as sweet as wondering how many days he could keep Prince K'Sed alive before he finally let him die.

Browns and greens chased each other across K'Sed's carapace as he looked at the M'Sak army in the vision screen. His eye-stalks pulled in a little. He noticed and lengthened them again, but Greenberg caught the involuntary admission of fear. "They are still advancing," the prince said. The translator's flat tones could not sound accusing, but the master merchant knew what he would have felt in K'Sed's shoes.

Not, he thought, that the prince wore any. He shoved the irrelevance aside. "So they are, Highness," he said. If K'Sed felt like restating the obvious, he could match him.

"You said your ship would frighten them away," K'Sed said. "Were I not used to it, the sight and sound of a ship falling from the sky would be plenty to frighten me away."

"Yes, Highness," Greenberg agreed. "I thought that would be true of the M'Sak as well." Out loud, he did not draw the obvious conclusion: that the invaders, or at least their leader, were braver than K'Sed. He hoped the prince would not reach that conclusion for himself. K'Sed was demoralized enough already.

His next words showed that to be true, but at least he was thinking in terms of the nation he led, rather than personally. "I wish we could fortify a strongpoint and force the M'Sak to attack us on ground of our own choosing. But I fear they would only go around us and keep on ravaging the countryside." Refugees from the north had spread lurid tales of the destructiveness of the M'Sak, tales that did not shrink in the telling. Sadly, recon photos confirmed them.

"Your Highness, I fear you are right." Anything that kept K'Sed focused on dealing with his problems seemed a good policy to Greenberg.

"And after all," the prince said, mostly to himself, "the savages are still some days' journey from us."

"So they are." Greenberg chose his words with care, not wanting to let K'Sed delude himself that he need do nothing, but not wanting to alarm him further, either. "And remember Your Highness, that we still shadow their every move. When our forces close with theirs—" not, Greenberg made sure, *when they attack us* "—we will know their every move. They cannot take us by surprise."

"That is true." K'Sed brightened a little. "We will be able to ready ourselves to meet them. I shall remind my officers of this."

As soon as the prince was gone, Greenberg called Jennifer.

He'd grown to expect to have to wait for her to answer the signal. When she finally responded, he said, "From now on, I want to hear everything the M'Sak do. *Everything*, do you hear? We can't afford to let them get any kind of edge at all."

"I understand," she said after another pause. "I'll do the best I can."

"Keep the reader off your nose for a while, can you?" he said.

Still another pause, this time a hurt one. "I said I'd do my best, Bernard."

"All right." Against his best intentions, Greenberg felt guilty. "It's important, Jennifer. Try to remember that. A whole civilization could be riding on what you spot."

"I'll remember," she said. He had to be content with that.

"We draw closer, my master," Z'Yon said. As the M'Sak moved further from their home, the land grew strange. These cool uplands—with only those trees that yielded nuts and tubers, and those in the neat orchards—were daunting. Even the shaman felt under his shell how far away the horizon was.

V'Zek rarely showed worry. This time was no exception. He made his eyestalks long as he peered south. The smellpores around his eyes opened wider; he seemed to be trying to sniff out the T'Kai. At last he said, "It will be soon."

Two of his eyes stayed where they were. The other two broke from their southward stare to glance up at the three drones that still shadowed his army, and at the flying building as well. The latter was just a silver dot in the sky now, but V'Zek knew its true size. He wondered absently how far up it was, to look so small. However far that was, it was not far enough.

Without his willing it, his grasping-claws clattered angrily. "They watch us," he said. His voice reminded Z'Yon of the hunting call of a *f'noi*.

"They are not very brave, my master," the shaman said, trying to ease the chieftain's gloom.

But V'Zek burst out, "How brave need they be? Knowing how we come, they can meet us at a spot of their own choosing. And when at last we fight them, they will see every move we make, as we make it. They will be able to respond at once, and in the best possible way. How can we gain surprise in a fight like that?''

"Warrior for warrior, we are better than they," Z'Yon said. But he knew, as did V'Zek, that that only meant so much. Fighting defensively, the T'Kai might hold their casualties close to even with those of the invaders. A few engagements like that, and the M'Sak were ruined. Unlike their foes, the T'Kai could levy fresh troops from towns and countryside. The M'Sak had to win with what they had.

The shaman turned one cautious eye toward his chieftain. He was in luck: V'Zek paid him no attention. The chieftain's eyestalks were all at full length, his eyes staring intently at one another—a sure sign of furious concentration.

Then V'Zek let out a roar like a f'noi that had just killed. "Let them see whatever they want!" he cried, so loud that half the army looked his way. He took Z'Yon's upper grasping-claws in his and squeezed till the shaman clattered in pain and feared for his integument.

V'Zek finally let go. He capered about like a hatchling, then, as if whispering some secret bit of magical lore, bent to murmur into the shaman's tympanum, "They cannot see into my mind."

Pavel Koniev leaped aside. The halberd's head buried itself in the ground where he had stood. The G'Bur hissed with effort, using all four grasping-legs to tug the weapon free. It lifted.

Too slow, too slow—before the local could take another swing with the long, unwieldy polearm, Koniev sprang close. The G'Bur hissed again, dropped the halberd, and grabbed for his shortspear. By then Koniev had jumped onto his back. He swung the mace up over his head.

The circle of spectators struck spearshafts against carapaces in noisy tribute to his prowess. The claps and whoops that Greenberg and Marya added were drowned in the din. Koniev scrambled down from the G'Bur and gave him a friendly whack where a grasping-leg joined his shell. "You almost split me in two there, N'Kor, even though that halberd just has a wooden head."

"I meant to," N'Kor said. Luckily, the soldier did not seem angry at having lost. "I thought it would be easy—I flattened you often enough when we started our little games. But you're learning, and you Soft Ones dodge better than I dreamed anything could. Comes of having just the two legs, I suppose." With their wide, armored bodies and three walking-legs splayed off to either side, the G'Bur were less than agile.

Of course, Greenberg thought as Koniev repeated his moves slowly so the locals could watch, the G'Bur weren't very fragile, either. A practice halberd would bounce off a carapace with the equivalent of no more than a nasty bruise, but it really might have done in Pavel.

"A good practice," Koniev was saying to N'Kor. "With the M'Sak so close, we need all the work we can get."

N'Kor made a puzzled noise that sounded like brushes working a snare drum. "But you have your little belt weapons that bring sleep from far away. You will not need to fight at close quarters."

"Not if everything goes exactly as it should," Koniev agreed. "How often, in a battle, does everything go exactly as it should?"

This time, N'Kor's clattering was a G'Bur chuckle. "Next time will be the first. As I said, for a trader you are learning."

"Hmm," was all Koniev said to that. He wiped sweat from his face with a yellow-haired forearm as he walked over to the other two humans. "What are they doing?" he asked Greenberg; the master merchant always kept the vision screen with him.

"Making camp, same as we are," he answered after a brief look at it.

"How far away are they?" Marya asked.

She and Koniev waited a moment while Greenberg keyed new instructions into the vision screen. The M'Sak camp vanished, to be replaced by a map of the territory hereabouts. Two points glowed on the map, one gold, the other menacing scarlet. "Fifteen kilometers, more or less," Greenberg said, checking the scale along one side of the screen.

"Tomorrow," Marya said thoughtfully. Her dark eyes were hooded, far away. Greenberg suspected he bore a similarly abstracted expression. He had been in plenty of fights and skirmishes, but all of them out of the blue, leaving him no time for anything but reaction. Deliberately waiting for combat was, in a way, harder than taking part.

Because humans needed less room than G'Bur, the tents they set up were dwarfed by the locals' shelters. But their three stood out all the same, the orange nylon fiery bright when compared to the undyed, heavy fabric that was the standard tent-cloth on L'Rau.

Marya opened her tent flap. She hesitated before going through and looked from Greenberg to Koniev. Daylight was fading fast now, and campfires were not enough to let the master merchant be sure she flushed, not with her dark skin. Had it been Jennifer, there could have been no doubt.

"Come in with me," Marya said quietly.

Now the two men looked at each other. "Which one?" they asked together. They laughed, but without much mirth. Till now, they had never had any trouble sharing her affection . . . but there might not be another night after this one.

Marya knew that, too. "Both of you."

Greenberg and Koniev looked at each other again. They had never done that before. Koniev shrugged. Greenberg smiled.

"Come on, dammit," Marya said impatiently.

As the closing tent flap brushed him, Greenberg reflected that he had already decided it was no ordinary night.

In the *Flying Festoon*, Jennifer read fantasy and wished she were with the three traders. She had heard them all together when she called to ask if they'd come up with any new notions on how to use the starship in the upcoming battle. They hadn't; flying low and creating as much confusion as possible was the best thought they'd had. Jennifer got the idea their minds were elsewhere.

They could have invited me down, she thought. There would have been nothing to landing the *Flying Festoon* outside the T'Kai camp and then finding the brilliant tents the humans used. Except for Prince K'Sed's huge pavilion, they were the most conspicuous objects in camp.

But they had not asked her to come down, and she would not go anywhere she was not asked. She felt the hurt of that implied rejection, and the sadness. The three of them had a world in which she was not welcome. *Maybe it's just because I'm younger than any of them*, she told herself. She did not believe it. No matter what courses she had taken, she was not a trader. Greenberg must be sorry he had ever chosen her.

She gave herself back to her fantasy novel. It reminded her that she had a place of her own, too, in an intellectual world where she was up and coming, not all too junior and none too skilled. It also reminded her, unfortunately, that the nearest center of that world was some light-years away.

She began a fantasy of her own, one where she saved the *Flying Festoon* from hideous danger in space. The traders were ready to go into cold sleep and unfurl the light-sail for a sublight trip back to civilization that would surely last centuries. Somehow, armed with no more than a screwdriver and determination, she saved the hyperdrive.

She managed to laugh at herself. Even before spaceflight, that would have made god-awful science fiction. Here and now, it was simply ridiculous. If anything went wrong, the best she could do was scream for help; all other alternatives were worse.

She turned down the temperature in her cabin till it was just above chilly, then dug out blankets and wrapped them tight around her. She finally fell asleep, but it was not the sort of warm embrace she wanted to enjoy.

II

"THEY AREN'T FOUR times our size, are they?" Prince K'Sed spoke with a certain amount of wonder as he studied the drawn-up ranks of the enemy.

"You knew that, Your Highness," Greenberg observed, hoping to hearten the T'Kai leader. "You've received M'Sak ambassadors often enough at your court."

"Ambassadors are different from soldiers," K'Sed answered. Now he could see the M'Sak were G'Bur much like the ones he commanded, but it did not seem to hearten him.

Eyeing the force ahead, Greenberg understood why the prince remained apprehensive. The ranks of the M'Sak were grimly still and motionless, while the T'Kai milled about and chattered as if they were still on march or, better image yet, gabbing about this and that while they tried to outdo one another in the marketplace. For the most part, they *were* merchants, not soldiers, by trade. The M'Sak, unfortunately, were soldiers.

The master merchant slowly realized that went deeper than the discipline the northern warriors showed. Everything about them was calculated to intimidate. Even their banners were the green of an angry G'Bur, not the unmartial bronze under which the T'Kai mustered. Greenberg wondered how many such clues he was missing but that were playing on the psyches of K'Sed and his army.

And yet, the T'Kai owned an edge no soldiers on L'Rau had ever enjoyed. "They cannot hide from us," he reminded K'Sed. "We will know all their concealed schemes and be able to

33

counter them.'' Only once the words were out of his mouth did
he stop to think the one might not be the same as the other.

Something of an odd color moved with a peculiar sinuous
motion through the ranks of the T'Kai. V'Zek wondered if the
southrons had lured ghosts to fight for them. Trying to suppress
superstitious dread, he put the question to Z'Yon.

"Anything is possible, my master, but I have detected no
signs of this," the shaman said. "I think you are seeing instead
a Soft One."

V'Zek gave a clattery shudder of disgust. The Soft One moved
like—like— V'Zek took a long time to find a comparison. Finally he thought of water pouring from a jug. That did not make
him feel much better. Live things had no business moving like
water pouring from a jug.

He waved to his drummers. Their thunder signaled his warriors forward. He spent only moments worrying about being
watched from the sky. Once it was pike against pike, things
would happen too fast for that to matter. And he felt fairly sure
the sky-things could not read his thoughts. If they could, reading
his hatred would have burned them down long since.

"They're advancing," Jennifer reported.

Greenberg's voice was dry as he answered, "I'd noticed. Let's
check the screen and see what they're up to." After a pause, he
spoke again. "Two lines, no particular weighting anywhere
along them I can see. Whatever cards he's holding, he doesn't
want to show them yet."

"No," Jennifer agreed. She paused herself, then added,
"Maybe we shouldn't have let him get used to the idea of having
the drones up there."

"Maybe we shouldn't. Why didn't you say something about
that sooner?"

Jennifer hated blushing, but couldn't help it. Luckily, the link
with Greenberg was voice-only. "I just thought of it now."

"Oh," Greenberg said. "Well, I didn't think of it at all, so
how am I supposed to criticize you? We're all amateur generals
here. I just hope it doesn't end up costing us. Do you suppose
we shouldn't have shown the northerners the *Flying Festoon*,
either?"

"We'll find out soon enough, don't you think?"

"Yes, I expect we will. This is a tad more empirical than I'd really planned on being, though. Wish us all luck."

"I do," Jennifer said. "You three especially, because you're on the ground."

The master merchant did not answer. Jennifer sighed. She sent the *Flying Festoon* whizzing low over the battlefield. The roar of cloven air filled the cabin when she activated the outside mike pickup. Then she shut it off again and turned on the ship's siren. It reverberated through the hull, even without amplification, and set her teeth on edge.

She studied the pictures the drones gave her. After reading about so many imaginary battles in Middle English, she fancied herself a marshal. She soon discovered the job was, as with most jobs, easier to imagine than to do. She found no magic strategic key to V'Zek's maneuvers. If anything, she thought him over-optimistic, advancing as he was against a strong defensive front: the T'Kai right was protected by a river, the left anchored by high ground and a stand of trees.

She wondered if he knew something she didn't, and hoped finding out wouldn't be too expensive.

B'Rom sidled up to Greenberg crabwise—an adverb the master merchant applied to few G'Bur but the vizier. "Soon now," B'Rom declared. The translator should have given his clicks, hisses, and whistles a furtive quality, but that, sadly, was beyond its capabilities.

"Soon what?" Greenberg asked, a trifle absently. Most of his attention was on the forest of oversized cutlery bearing down on the T'Kai. The *Flying Festoon*'s histrionics left his ears stunned. He hoped the M'Sak were quaking in the boots they didn't wear.

Then his head whipped around, for B'Rom said, "Soon the assassination, of course. What better time than when the savages are in the midst of their attack?"

"None, I suppose," Greenberg mumbled. His hand eased on the stunner. Maybe he wouldn't have to use it after all.

The racket overhead was appalling and confusing, but V'Zek was proud of the way his warriors pressed on toward the waiting

enemy. The Soft Ones had blundered in showing their powers
too soon. That relieved V'Zek: ghosts or spirits never would
have made such a foolish mistake. The Soft Ones were natural,
then, no matter how weird they looked. V'Zek was confident
he could handle anything natural.

A warrior whose carapace was painted with a messenger's red
stripes rushed up to the chieftain. V'Zek's eyestalks drew together in slight perplexity—what could be so urgent, when the
two armies had not even joined? Then the fellow's left front
grasping-claw pulled a war hammer from its concealed sheath
under his plastron. He swung viciously at the M'Sak chieftain.

Only V'Zek's half-formed suspicion let him escape unpunc-
tured. He sprang to one side. The hammerhead slammed painfully against him between right front and rear grasping-legs, but
the chisel point did not penetrate. By the time the would-be
assassin struck again, V'Zek had out his own shortspear. He
turned the blow and gave back a counterthrust his enemy beat
aside.

Then half a ten M'Sak were battling the false messenger.
Before their chieftain could shout for them to take him alive, he
had fallen, innards spurting from a score of wounds. "Are you
all right, my master?" one of the soldiers gasped.

V'Zek flexed both right-side grasping-legs. He could use
them. "Well enough." He looked closely at the still shape of
his assailant. The curve of the shell was not quite right for a
M'Sak. "Does anyone know him?"

None of the warriors spoke.

"I suppose he is of T'Kai," the chieftain said. The soldiers
shouted angrily. So did V'Zek, but his fury was cold. He had
wanted the southrons for what they could yield him and his
people. Now he also had a personal reason for beating them.
He reminded himself not to let that make him break away from
his carefully devised plan. "Continue the advance, as before,"
he ordered.

"Some sort of confusion for a moment there around the chieftain." Jennifer's voice sounded in Greenberg's ear. With the
M'Sak so close, he had put away the vision screen. He let out
his breath in a regretful sigh when she reported, "It seems to
be over now."

"Damn." Marya and Koniev said it together. All three humans were on the right wing—the right claw, they would say on L'Rau—of the T'Kai army, not far from the river. Since V'Zek led the invaders from their right, he was most of a kilometer away, out of their view.

Closer and closer came the M'Sak. They were shouting fiercely, but the din from the *Flying Festoon* outdid anything they could produce. "Shoot!" cried an underofficer.

G'Bur held bows horizontally in front of themselves with their front pair of grasping-claws, using the rear pair to load arrows—sometimes one, sometimes a pair—and draw the weapons. The M'Sak archers shot back at the T'Kai, lofting arrows with chisel-headed points to descend on their foes' backs.

Every so often, a warrior on one side or the other would collapse like a marionette whose puppeteer had suddenly dropped the strings. More commonly, the shafts would skitter away without piercing their targets. Exoskeletons had advantages, Greenberg thought.

An arrow buried itself in the ground less than a meter from his left boot. He shuffled sideways and bumped into Marya, who was unconsciously moving away from an arrow that had landed to her right. Their smiles held little humor. She said, "Shall we give them something to think about?"

Greenberg and Koniev both nodded. The three humans leveled their stunners at the M'Sak. The gun twitched slightly in the master merchant's hand as it fed stun charges one after another into the firing chamber.

One after another, M'Sak began dropping; pikes and halberds fell from nerveless grasping-claws. The invaders' advance, though, took a long moment to falter. Greenberg realized the M'Sak, intent on the enemies awaiting them, hadn't noticed their comrades were going down without visible wounds.

Then they did notice, and drew up in confusion and fear: for all they knew, the felled warriors were dead, not stunned. Greenberg took careful aim and knocked down a M'Sak whose halberd had a fancy pennon tied on below the head—an officer, he hoped. "Good shot!" Koniev cried, and thumped him on the back.

"I only wish we had a couple of thousand charges instead of

a hundred or so," Marya said, dropping another M'Sak. "That would end that, and in a hurry, too."

By no means normally an optimist, Greenberg answered, "We're doing pretty well as is." The M'Sak left was stalled; had they been humans, the master merchant would have thought of them as rocked back on their heels.

The officers who led the T'Kai right did not have that concept—or heels, for that matter—but they recognized disorder when they saw it. "Advance in line!" they ordered.

The T'Kai raised a rattling cheer and moved forward. They chopped and thrust at their foes, who gave ground. For a heady moment, Greenberg thought the M'Sak would break and run.

They did not. Faced by an assault of a sort with which they were familiar, the invaders rallied. Their polearms stabbed out at the T'Kai, probing for openings. The opposing lines came to close quarters. For a long time, motion either forward or backward could be measured in bare handfuls of meters.

The humans stopped shooting. They had to be careful with charges, and friend and foe were so closely intermingled now that a shot was as likely to fell a T'Kai as an M'Sak. If the enemy broke through, stunners could be of value again. Without armor, the humans were useless in the front line.

Koniev laughed nervously as he watched the struggle not far away. He said, "I never thought there would be so much waiting *inside* a battle."

"I notice you're still holding your stunner, not your mace," Marya said.

Koniev looked down as if he had not been sure himself. "So I am." The mace was on his belt. He touched it with his left hand. "If I have to use this thing, odds are we'll be losing. I'd sooner win."

Greenberg's own personal defense weapon was a war hammer. He had almost forgotten it; now he noticed it brush against his thigh, felt its weight on his hip. He nodded to himself. He would just as soon go on pretending it wasn't there.

"The savages are mad, mad!" Prince K'Sed clattered, watching the M'Sak swarm up the slope toward his waiting soldiers. "All the military manuals cry out against fighting uphill." Like a proper ruler, he could stand on any walking-leg. He had studied the arts of war even though they bored him, but had never expected the day to come when he put them to practical use.

B'Rom clicked in agreement. "No law prevents our taking advantage of such madness, however." He turned to the officer beside him. "Isn't that so, D'Ton?"

"Aye, it is." But the general sounded a little troubled. "I had looked for better tactics from V'Zek. After all, he—" D'Ton had at least the virtue of knowing when to shut up. Reminding his prince and vizier that the enemy had won every battle thus far did not seem wise.

"Let us punish him for his rashness," B'Rom declared. D'Ton looked to K'Sed, who raised a grasping-claw to show assent.

The general scraped his plastron against the ground in obedience. He had no real reason not to agree with the prince and vizier. Knowing when and by what route the M'Sak were coming had let the army choose this strong position. Not taking advantage of it would be insanely foolish. He filled his book lungs. "Advance in line!"

Lesser officers echoed the command. Cheering, the prince's force obeyed. They knew as well as their leaders the edge the high ground gave them. Iron clashed and belled off iron, crunched on carapaces, and sheared away limbs and eyestalks.

With their greater momentum, the T'Kai stopped their enemies' uphill advance dead in its tracks. The two lines remained motionless and struggling for a long moment. Here, though, the stalemate did not last. The T'Kai began to force the M'Sak line backward.

"Drive them! Drive them! Well done!" D'Ton shouted. V'Zek truly had made a mistake, he thought.

Prince K'Sed, gloomy since the day he learned of the M'Sak invasion, was practically capering with excitement. "Drive them back to M'Sak!" he cried.

"Driving them back to level ground would do nicely," B'Rom said, but as he spoke in normal tones, no one but K'Sed heard him. The T'Kai warriors picked up the prince's cry and threw it at the foe. "Back to M'Sak! Back to M'Sak!" It swelled into a savage chant. Even B'Rom found a grasping-claw opening and closing in time to it. Irritated at himself, he forced the claw closed.

* * *

"Hold steady! Don't break formation! Hold steady!" V'Zek heard the commands echoed by officers and underofficers as the M'Sak gave ground. He wished he could be in the thick of the fighting, but if he were, he could not direct the battle as a whole. That, he decided reluctantly, was more important, at least for the moment.

"Back to M'Sak! Back to M'Sak!" The shout reached him over the din of battle and the yells of his own warriors.

"Amateurs," he snorted.

"They aren't fond of us, are they?" Z'Yon observed from beside him.

"They'll be even less fond of us if they keep advancing a while longer." *And*, V'Zek thought but did not say, *if my own line holds together*. He would never have dared try this with the T'Kai semirabble. Even with good troops, a planned fighting retreat was dangerous. It could turn unplanned in an instant.

But if it didn't . . . if it didn't, he would get in some fighting after all.

Being a trader was different from what Jennifer had expected. So was watching a battle. It was also a good deal worse. Those were real intelligent beings trying to kill one another down there. Those were real body fluids that spurted from wounds, real limbs that lay quivering on the ground after being hacked away from their former owners, real eyestalks that halberds and bills sliced off, real G'Bur who would never walk or see again but who were in anguish now and might well live on, maimed, for years.

She tried to detach herself from what she was seeing, tried to imagine it as something not real, something only happening on the screen. Koniev or Marya, she thought, would have no trouble doing that; about Greenberg she was less sure. She knew she had no luck. What she watched was real, and she could not make herself pretend it was only a screen drama. Too many of these actors would never get up after the taping was done.

So she watched and tried not to be sick. The really frustrating thing was that, in spite of having a full view of the whole battlefield, she could not fathom what, if anything, V'Zek was up to. The T'Kai right wing was holding; the left, by now, had actually advanced several hundred meters.

This, she thought with something as close to contempt as her mild nature allowed, was the sort of fighting that had made V'Zek feared all through the T'Kai confederacy? It only showed that on a world with poor communications, any savage could build up a name for himself that he didn't come close to deserving.

F'Rev had no idea what the battle as a whole looked like. The commander-of-fifty had his own, smaller problems. His troop was in the T'Kai center. The line he was holding had stretched thin when the army's left claw drove back the barbarians: it had been forced to stretch to accommodate its lengthened front.

Now it could not stretch any further. He sent a messenger over to the troop on his immediate right, asking for more warriors.

The messenger returned, eyestalks lowered in apprehension. "Well?" F'Rev growled. "Where are the reinforcements?"

"He has none to send, sir," the messenger said nervously. "He is as thin on the ground as we are."

"A pestilence!" F'Rev burst out. "What am I supposed to do now?"

V'Zek's guards almost killed the red-striped messenger before he reached the chieftain—after one try on their master's life, they were not about to permit another. But when the fellow's bona fides were established, he proved to bring welcome news.

"There's a stretch in the center, three or four troops wide, my master, where they're only a warrior or two thick," he told V'Zek.

Z'Yon, who heard the gasped-out message, bent before V'Zek so that his plastron scraped the ground. "Just as you foretold, my master," the shaman said, more respectful than V'Zek ever remembered hearing him.

The chieftain knew he had earned that respect. He felt the way bards sometimes said they did when songs seemed to shape themselves as they were sung, as if even the sun rose and set according to his will. It was better than mating, purer than the feeling he got from chewing the leaves of the *p'sta* tree.

Neither moment nor feeling was to be wasted. "Now we fight back harder here," he told the subchiefs who led his army's right claw. "We've drawn them away from their strongpoint; now we'll make them pay for coming out."

"About time," one of his underlings said. "Going backward against these soft-shells was making my eyestalks itch."

"Scratch, then, but not too hard. I want you to hold their left in place, make it retreat a little if you like, but not too far."

"Why not?" the subchief demanded indignantly.

"Because that would only hurt them. I intend to kill." V'Zek was already running full tilt toward the center. Here indeed was his chance to fight.

"The M'Sak aren't giving up any more ground on the left," Jennifer reported into Greenberg's ear. "I suppose the T'Kai charge has run out of steam now that they're down onto flat ground." A moment later she added, "The barbarians are shifting a little toward the center, or at least V'Zek is moving that way."

"Anything serious there, do you think?" the master merchant asked.

After her usual hesitation, Jennifer said, "I doubt it. What can he do that he hasn't already failed with on the left? He—" She stopped again. When she resumed, all she said was, "My God."

This time, Greenberg did not blame her for halting. He could not yet see what had gone wrong, but he could hear that something had. He snapped, "What is it, Jennifer?"

"They found a soft spot in the line somehow—the M'Sak in the T'Kai line, I mean." Another wait, this time for Jennifer to collect herself. "Hundreds of them are pouring through. They're turning in on the T'Kai left wing and—rolling it up, is that the phrase?"

"That's the phrase," the master merchant said grimly.

Along with Koniev and Marya, he ran to try to stem the rout. Long before he reached the rupture point, he knew it was hopeless. No mere thumb could repair this dike. The few M'Sak the humans dropped did not influence the battle in the least.

From the *Flying Festoon*, Jennifer said, "I'm sorry I didn't notice anything going wrong."

"I don't think there was anything *to* notice, Jennifer," Koniev told her. "V'Zek didn't find that soft spot in our line—he made it. He lured the left out till the T'Kai got overextended, and then—and now—''

"And now," Jennifer echoed ruefully. "A few minutes ago, I was thinking V'Zek a fool of a general for letting himself get driven down the slope. He must have done it on purpose. That makes me the fool, for not seeing it."

"It makes all of us fools," Greenberg said.

"But he shouldn't have been able to do it," Jennifer protested. "Humans are a lot more sophisticated than any G'Bur, let alone barbarians like the M'Sak. We had the drones watching every move he made, too."

"He managed, though, in spite of everything," Greenberg said. "And that makes him a very nasty enemy indeed."

No one argued with him.

"We are undone!" K'Sed cried. It was not a shout of panic, but rather of disbelief. "They tricked us!" The M'Sak surged against his line and pushed it back. Maybe, he thought much too late, he should not have called for pursuit down off the slope the T'Kai had held. Then, perhaps, he would not have had these screaming, clacking savages in his rear, rolling up his warrior like a moltling folding a shed piece of grasping-claw.

"I did not know trickery was against the rules," B'Rom said. The vizier made as much a point of pride at being unimpressed with everything as V'Zek did with being unafraid. He went on, "After all, we tried to do the same to the M'Sak with what we learned from the Soft Ones."

"The Soft Ones!" K'Sed shouted. "They tricked us, too! They said we would win if we fought here. This whole botch is their fault."

"Oh, twaddle, Your Highness."

K'Sed stared at B'Rom. Under other circumstances, that would have been lese majesty enough to cost the vizier his shell, one painful bit at a time. But now—K'Sed mastered his anger, though he did not forget. "Twaddle, is it?"

"Certainly." Whatever his shortcomings in behavior, B'Rom was no coward. "They told us nothing of the sort that I recall. They said this was a good place to fight, and it is. You can see that with three eyes closed, as can I. But they are traders, not generals—that, unfortunately, is not a deficiency from which V'Zek suffers.''

"Unfortunately.'' K'Sed could play the game of understatement, too. Staying detached was not easy anymore, though, not when the line was unraveling like a poorly woven basket and the guards were almost as busy behind the prince as in front of him. He did try. "All these unfortunate things being true, what do you recommend now?''

One of B'Rom's eyestalks pointed behind him and to the left. "Running for the forest yonder seems appropriate at the moment, wouldn't you say? We'll save a remnant that way, rather than all staying in the trap.''

"Our right—''

"Is on its own anyway.''

K'Sed hissed in despair. B'Rom had a way of being not just right, but brutally right. With a more forceful prince, he would have been killed long since. K'Sed wished he were that sort of prince. The T'Kai confederacy could use such a leader, to oppose V'Zek if for no other reason. He was as he was, though; no help for it. "Very well. We will fall back on the forest.'' He hoped all the practice he'd put in with the shortspear would stay with him.

Chaos also gripped the T'Kai right claw, if in a less crushing embrace. Still under assault from the M'Sak before them, the T'Kai warriors could do nothing to rescue their cut-off comrades. In fact, the northerners pouring through the gap where the center had been tried to roll them up and treat them like the left.

"Here they come again!'' Marya shouted. The humans expended more precious stun charges. M'Sak fell. Others advanced past them. Dying in battle, even strangely, held few terrors for them. They did not know the stun guns were not lethal, but they had seen enough to be sure the weapons were not all-powerful.

Pavel Koniev perturbed them more than the stun guns could when he sprang out and shrieked "Boo!'' at the top of his lungs. The cry was as alien to their clicks, hisses, and pops as his fleshy body was to their hard integuments. Not even their stories held ghosts as strange as he.

But the M'Sak were soldiers, and they were winning. As with the *Flying Festoon*, the mere appearance of the unknown was not enough to daunt them. They rushed forward, weapons ready. The humans snapped shots at them. As with any hurried shooting, they missed more often than they wanted to. And they had time to press trigger buttons just once or twice before the M'Sak were on them.

Marya's scream made the shout Koniev had let out sound like a whisper. The warrior in front of her was startled enough to make only a clumsy swipe with his partizan. She ducked under it, stunned him at close range, then dashed up to crush the brain-nodes under his suddenly flaccid eyestalks.

Koniev did not use his stunner. He killed his foe with exactly the same move he had practiced on the way north. Then, orange body liquids dripping from his mace, he stood on the fallen M'Sak's carapace and roared out a challenge to the local's comrades. The challenge went unanswered.

Greenberg did not find out till later how his friends fared. At the time, he was too busy staying alive to pay them much attention. He threw himself flat to avoid a halberd thrust, then leaped up and grabbed the polearm below the head to wrestle it away from the M'Sak who wielded it.

That was a mistake. G'Bur were no stronger than humans, but their four grasping-limbs let them exert a lot more leverage. Greenberg found himself flung around till he felt like a fly on the end of a fisherman's line. He lost his grip and fell in a heap. The M'Sak swung up the halberd for the kill.

Before he could bring it down, he had to parry a blow from a T'Kai. The soldiers from the southern confederacy were frantically counterattacking. Greenberg scrambled to his feet. "Thanks!" he shouted to the warrior who had saved him. He doubted the local had done so out of any great love for humans. But if the right wing of the T'Kai army was to escape as a fighting force, it could not let itself be flanked like the luckless left. Greenberg did not care about why the local had rescued him. Any excuse would do.

The M'Sak gave ground grudgingly, but they gave ground. More and more of them went off to finish routing the left—and to plunder corpses. That was easier, more profitable work than fighting troops still ready to fight back. The T'Kai right broke

free of its assailants and retreated south and east along the bank
of the stream that protected its flank. The three humans trudged
along with it.

Jennifer turned on the *Flying Festoon*'s spotlight. A finger of
light stabbed down from the sky. The ship descended, its siren
wailing. She wished it were a rocket like the ones she read
about—then it might incinerate thousands of M'Sak with its
fiery blast. Sometimes mundane contragravity was too safe to
be useful.

By then, the M'Sak took the starship for granted. They ignored it until it came down on top of several of them and smashed
them into wet smears beneath it. The rest scattered. Jennifer
ordered the air lock open. Her comrades laughed in delight as
they scrambled inside. "It's a weapon after all!" Greenberg
shouted.

"Why, so it is," Jennifer said. "Do you want to start squash-
ing them by ones and twos?"

After a moment, Greenberg shook his head. "Not worth it, I
don't think—might as well go smashing cockroaches with an
anvil."

"All right," she said. She looked in the viewscreen. "They
are running away."

"Good. That will let this half of the army get loose." Greenberg ran a grimy forearm across his face. He was swaying where
he stood. "I don't believe I've ever been this tired in my life. I
think we'll spend the next couple of nights in the ship."

"All right," Jennifer said again. She stifled a small sigh. With
everyone else aboard, she wouldn't get much reading done.

Jennifer walked along the wall of the little town of D'Opt.
Her reader was in her pocket; Bernard Greenberg walked beside
her. They both looked out at the M'Sak who ringed the place.
Jennifer wished the barbarians seemed further away. D'Opt was
barely important enough to rate a wall; its four meters of baked
brick sufficed to keep out brigands. Keeping out V'Zek and his
troopers was likely to be something else again.

Walking-claws clattered on the bricks, close by her. She turned
her head. So did Greenberg. He had the higher rank, so he spoke
to K'Sed. "Your Highness."

The prince did not answer for some time. Like the humans, he was looking out at the encircling enemy. At last he said, "I wish we were back in T'Kai City."

"So do I, Your Highness," Greenberg said. Jennifer nodded. T'Kai City's walls were twice as high and three times as thick as those of D'Opt, and made of stone in the bargain.

"You Soft Ones could have done more to help us get there," K'Sed said—crabbily, Jennifer thought. She supposed the prince was not to be blamed for his bad temper. K'Sed had certainly had a hard time of it. Skulking through the woods and fleeing for one's life were not pastimes for which princes usually trained.

But Greenberg said, "Your Highness, were it not for us, you would have no army left at all, and the M'Sak would be running loose through the whole confederacy. As is, you are strong enough still to force them to concentrate against you here."

"But not strong enough to beat them," K'Sed retorted. "That only delays matters, does it not? Had we fought them somewhere else, we might have won."

The unfairness of that almost took Jennifer's breath away. For once, she did not hesitate. Before Greenberg could reply to the prince, she blurted, "But you might have lost everything, too!" *You likely would have lost everything*, she said to herself.

"We'll never know now, will we?" K'Sed sounded as if he thought he had scored a point. "And after the fight, you did little to keep the barbarians off us."

"We did what we could, Your Highness," Greenberg said. "I am sorry the M'Sak did not oblige us by holding still to be smashed one at a time."

His sarcasm reached the prince where Jennifer's protest had failed. K'Sed bent his left walking-legs, letting that side of his plastron almost scrape the bricks—a G'Bur gesture of despondency. "I knew this campaign was ill-omened when we undertook it. Even the moon fights against us."

It was late afternoon. Greenberg and Jennifer looked eastward. She rarely gave L'Rau's moon a thought—why worry about a dead stone lump several hundred thousand kilometers away? It looked as uninteresting now as ever: a gibbous light in the sky, especially pale and washed out because the sun was still up.

"What about the moon, Your Highness?" she said.

"When it grows full, three days hence, it will be eclipsed," K'Sed told her, as if that explained everything.

"Well, what of it?" She was so surprised, she forgot to tack on K'Sed's honorific. "You must know what causes an eclipse?"

The prince was distraught enough to miss her faux pas. He answered, "Of course—the passage of our world's shadow over the face of the moon. Every enlightened citizen of the towns in the confederacy knows this." K'Sed turned one eye-stalk toward the soldiers swarming through D'Opt's narrow streets. "Peasants, herders, and even artisans, though, still fear the malign powers they believe to stalk the night."

"That is not good," Greenberg said.

Jennifer thought he'd come up with one of the better under-statements she'd heard. As low-technology worlds went, L'Rau, or at least the T'Kai confederacy, was relatively free from su-perstition. But the key word was *relatively*. And because hu-mans dealt mostly with nobles and wealthy traders, she did not have a good feel for just how credulous the vast majority of the locals were.

She had also missed something else. K'Sed pointed it out for her, literally, gesturing toward the bronze-hued T'Kai banners that still fluttered defiance at the M'Sak. "Perhaps our color is ill-chosen," the prince said, "but when the swallowed moon appears in that shade, how will the ignorant doubt it implies their being devoured by M'Sak? Truly, I could almost wonder myself." K'Sed *was* a sophisticate, Jennifer reminded herself, but even sophisticates on primitive planets found long-buried fears rising when trouble came.

"Maybe we could teach your soldiers—" Jennifer stopped, feeling Greenberg's ironic eye turned her way. She realized she'd been foolish. Three days of lessons would not overturn a life-time's belief. She asked, "Do your warriors know the eclipse is coming, your Highness?"

"Sadly, they do. We tried to keep it from them, but even the M'Sak, savages though they be, have got wind of it. From time to time they amuse themselves by shouting it up to our sentries, and shouting that they will destroy us on that night. I fear . . ." K'Sed hesitated, went on, "I fear they may be right."

* * *

"Are you sure it is prudent to warn our foes of what we intend?" Z'Yon asked, listening to the M'Sak warriors yelling threats at the southrons trapped in D'Opt.

"Why not?" V'Zek said grandly. "We spread fear through their ranks, and anticipation of disaster. Having them with their eyestalks going every which way at once can only help us. And besides, they cannot be sure we are not lying. Almost I find myself tempted to delay the assault until the darkening of the moon is past."

"That might be wise, my master," Z'Yon said.

"What? Why?" When V'Zek stretched his walking-legs very straight, as he did now, he towered over Z'Yon. His voice, ominously deep and slow, rumbled like distant thunder—*not distant enough*, the shaman thought. He sank down to scrape his plastron in the dirt. "Why?" V'Zek repeated. "Speak, if you value your claws."

"The moltings suggest, my master, that we may fare better under those circumstances."

"So you consulted the moltings, did you?" The chieftain let the question hang in the air.

Z'Yon felt its weight over him, as if it were the big metal skything that had crushed a fair number of M'Sak to jelly. "You said I might, my master," he reminded V'Zek, "for my own amusement."

"For yours, perhaps. I, shaman, am not amused at your maunderings. On the given night we shall attack and we shall win. If you put any other interpretation on what the moltings say, you will no longer be amused, either; that I promise you. Do you grasp my meaning?"

"With all four claws, my master," Z'Yon assured him, and fled.

Jennifer watched Greenberg cut another piece from the juicy, rare prime rib. "The condemned man ate a hearty meal," he said, and cocked an eyebrow at her. "Is that a quotation from your ancient science fiction?"

She paused to swallow and cut a fresh piece for herself. The *Flying Festoon*'s autochef did right by beef and nearly everything else, though Koniev swore its vodka was good only for putting in thermometers. She answered, "No. I think it's even older than that."

"Probably is," Marya agreed. "It sounds as if any society would find it handy."

"No doubt," Greenberg said. "The T'Kai would certainly think it was relevant tonight." He told the others what he and Jennifer had learned from K'Sed.

Koniev nodded slowly. "I've heard the barbarians shouting their threats. I didn't take much notice; the translator garbles them a lot of the time, anyway. But they're not bluffing, then?"

"Not even a little bit," Greenberg said. "That's why we'll stay close by the ship. We may have to pull out in a hurry, and fighting my way back to the *Flying Festoon* through a mob of panicked or bloodthirsty G'Bur is something I'd rather not even have nightmares about."

"Sensible," Koniev said. Marya nodded a moment later.

"Too bad the T'Kai won't be able to take ship with us," Jennifer said.

"Yes—a good market will close down if the confederacy goes under," Marya said. "V'Zek won't be eager to deal with us, I'm certain."

"That's not what I meant!" Jennifer said angrily. She noticed the others staring at her and realized that until now she'd never been interested enough in what they were doing to get angry. She went on, "We'll be running away while the highest culture on this planet goes under. That counts for more than markets, if you ask me."

"Of course it does," Greenberg said. "I told you as much before, when you were setting out the drones, remember? Why do you think we've put so much effort into trying to save T'Kai? No matter how much money's on the line, I wouldn't do foot-soldier duty for a people I didn't like and respect. Do the characters in your old books care that much for profit?"

She bit her lip. "No, of course not—they're supposed to be true to life, you know."

"All right, then." Greenberg sounded relieved, maybe because he wanted her to stay involved. "What we've been trying to do, then, is—"

"Wait," Jennifer told him.

He, Koniev, and Marya stared again—she hardly ever interrupted. She ignored them. She got up from the table and dashed—again something new—for her cabin. Behind her, Koniev said, "What's twisting her tail?" She ignored that, too.

She returned a couple of minutes later with her reader set to the right part of the story she'd found. She held it out to Greenberg. "Here. Look at this, please. I think it's important."

Greenberg set the reader on his nose. He took it off again a moment later. "Jennifer, I'm sorry, but I can't make heads or tails of Middle English, or whatever the right name for this is. What are you trying to show me?"

She made an exasperated noise and took back the reader. She peered into it, then returned it to him. "This story is called 'The Man Who Sold the Moon.' Do you see the circle, here and on this page?" She hit the FORWARD button. "And here—" She hit it again. "—and here?"

"The one with '6+' printed inside it? Yes, I see it. What's it supposed to be, some sort of magic symbol?"

She told him what it was supposed to be. He and Marya and Koniev all looked at one another. "This Heinlein person didn't think small, I have to give him that," Greenberg said slowly. "But I still don't quite follow how you think it applies to our problem here."

She knew she looked disappointed; she'd expected Greenberg to catch fire from her own inspiration. It was almost poetically apt, she thought: She'd planned to use trading to help her study Middle English science fiction, and now the Middle English science fiction might help her fellow traders. She did some more explaining.

Koniev said, "Where would we get enough soot, or for that matter rockets?"

"We don't need rockets," Jennifer said, "and soot wouldn't do us much good here, either. Instead . . ."

She outlined her plan and watched the three traders think it over. Koniev spoke first. "It might even work, which puts it light-years ahead of anything else we've got going for us."

"Pulling out the *Flying Festoon* will be tricky, though," Marya said.

Greenberg said, "Some of us will have to stay behind, to show the T'Kai we aren't abandoning them." He sounded unhappy at the idea, but firm. "All of us but Jennifer, I think. This is her hobbyhorse; let her ride it if she can."

"And let her—and us—hope she'll be able to rescue us if she can't," Marya said.

Jennifer gulped. If her scheme didn't work out as advertised, she'd be a long way away when D'Opt fell. Academia hadn't prepared her for having lives rest on what she did. "It will work," she said. Her nails bit into the palms of her hands. She knew she'd better be right.

V'Zek sent the T'Kai female scuttling out of his tent when the guard called that Z'Yon would have speech with him. "This is important, I take it?" the chieftain rumbled. It was not a question. It was more like a threat.

Z'Yon stooped low, but managed to keep the ironic edge in his voice. "It is, unless you would sooner not know that the great sky-thing has departed from D'Opt."

"Has it indeed?" V'Zek forgot about the female, though her shell was delicately fluted and the joints of her legs amazingly limber. "So the Soft Ones give up on their friends at last, do they?" He wished the weird creatures were long gone; without their meddling, he would have overwhelmed T'Kai without having to work nearly so hard.

Then Z'Yon brought his suddenly leaping spirits down once more. "My master, the Soft Ones themselves are still in D'Opt. They have been seen on the walls since the sky-thing left."

The chieftain cursed. "They are still plotting something, then. Well, let them plot. The moon still grows dark and red tomorrow night, and the Soft Ones cannot alter that. And our warriors will fight well, for they know the darkened moon portends the fall of T'Kai. They know that because, of course, you have been diligent in instructing them, have you not, Z'Yon?"

"Of course, my master." The shaman suppressed a shudder. V'Zek was most dangerous when he sounded mildest. As soon as Z'Yon could, he escaped from the chieftain's presence. He wondered how many eyestalks he would have been allowed to keep had he not followed V'Zek's orders in every particular. Surely no more than one, he thought, and shuddered again.

V'Zek watched the shaman go. He knew Z'Yon had doubts about the whole enterprise. He had doubts himself. The Soft

Ones alarmed him. Their powers, even brought to bear without much martial skill, were great enough to be daunting. He would much rather have had them on his side than as foes. But he had beaten them and their chosen allies before, and after one more win they would have no allies left. For a moment, he even thought about trading with them afterward. He wondered what they would want for the weapons that shot sleep as if it were an arrow.

But even more, he wondered what they were up to.

The guard broke his chain of thought. "My master, shall I fetch back the female?"

"Eh? No, don't bother. I've lost the mood. After we win tomorrow, we'll all enjoy plenty of these southron shes."

"Aye, that we will!" The guard sounded properly eager. V'Zek wished he could match the fellow's enthusiasm.

Jennifer looked at L'Rau in the viewscreen. The world was small enough to cover with the palm of her hand. Away from the *Flying Festoon*, the ship's robots were busy getting everything into shape for tonight. She'd had to hit the computer's override to force it to make the gleaming metal spheroids do as she ordered.

At last, everything was the way she wanted it. She still had a good many hours of waiting before she could do anything else. She got into bed and went to sleep.

Her last fuzzy thought was that Heinlein would have approved.

L'Rau's sun set. Across the sky, the moon rose. The shadow of the world had already begun to crawl across it. The M'Sak raised a clamor when they saw the eclipse. Their tumult sounded like thousands of percussion instruments coming to demented life all at once.

The translator could handle some of their dialect. Most of their threats were the same stupid sort soldiers shouted on any planet: warnings of death and maiming. But some M'Sak showed imaginative flair, not least the barbarian who asked the defenders inside D'Opt for the names of their females, so he would know what to call them when he got to T'Kai City.

The hubbub outside the walls faded. An enormous G'Bur

came out from among the soldiers. This, Greenberg thought, had to be the fearsome V'Zek. "Surrender!" he shouted up at the T'Kai. He used the southern speech so well, the translator never hiccuped. "I give you this one last chance. Look to the sky—even the heavens declare your downfall is at hand."

Prince K'Sed waved a grasping-claw to Greenberg. The master merchant stepped out where the M'Sak could see him; he hoped the sight of a human still had some power to unsettle them. "You are wrong, V'Zek," he said. The translator, and amplifiers all along the wall, sent his reply booming forth, louder than any G'Bur could bellow.

"Roar as loud as you like, Soft One," V'Zek said. "Your trifling tricks grow boring, and we are no hatchlings, to be taken in by them. As the sky-*f'noi* makes the moon bleed, so we will bleed you tonight, and all T'Kai thereafter." The M'Sak warriors shouted behind him.

"You are wrong, V'Zek," Greenberg repeated. "Watch the sky if you doubt me, for it too will show T'Kai's power."

"Lie as much as you like. It will not save you." V'Zek turned to his troopers. "Attack!"

M'Sak dashed into archery range and began to shoot, trying to sweep defenders from the walls. The T'Kai shot back. Greenberg hastily ducked behind a parapet. He was more vulnerable to arrows than any local.

"What if you are wrong, Soft One, and your ploy fails?" Only B'Rom would have asked that question.

"Then we die," Greenberg said, a reply enough to the point to silence even the cynical vizier. B'Rom walked away; had he been a human, he would have been shaking his head.

Arrows ripped through the T'Kai banners above the master merchant. He glanced up. The grasping-claw that stood for the confederacy had a hole in it. Not liking the symbolism of that, he looked away.

Shouts and alarmed clatterings came from the wall not far away. The translator gabbled in overload, then produced a word Greenberg could understand. "Ladders!"

Though poles set into a wall sufficed for the G'Bur, when such aids were absent the locals, because of the way they were built, needed wider and more cumbersome ladders than humans used. That did not stop the M'Sak from slapping them against

the walls of D'Opt and swarming toward the top. In fact, it made
the defenders' job harder than it would have been in medieval
human siege warfare—being heavier than scaling ladders made
for humans, these were harder to topple.

Without exposing more than his arm, Greenberg expended a
stun cartridge when the top of a ladder poked over the wall. The
barbarian nearly at the level of the battlements tumbled back
onto his comrades below. They all crashed to the ground. Cheering, the T'Kai used a forked pole to push over the suddenly
empty ladder.

"Good idea!" Koniev shouted. He imitated Greenberg. Another set of crashes, another overturned ladder.

"I'd like it better if I had more than—" Greenberg checked
the charge gauge, "—half a dozen shots left."

"Eight here," Koniev said. Marya was somewhere off around
the wall's circuit. Greenberg hoped she would not stop an arrow.
For that matter, he hoped he would not stop one himself.

"Ladders!" The cry came from two directions at once. The
master merchant looked at the moon. L'Rau's shadow covered
more than half of it, but totality was still close to an hour away.
"Ladders!" This shout was further away. *Click-pop-hiss-click*:
By now, Greenberg had heard the T'Kai word often enough to
recognize it in the original, even if he needed electronics to
reproduce it.

"Lad—" This time, the cry cut off abruptly after *click-pop*—
an arrow must have found its mark. The M'Sak were throwing
everything they had into this attack. Greenberg worried. Jennifer hadn't counted on the possibility of D'Opt's falling in a hurry.
Neither had he. If that was a mistake, it was likely to be his last
one.

"Forward!" V'Zek roared. "Forward!" He wished he could
have gone up the first ladder and straight into D'Opt. Waiting
behind the scenes for his warriors to do the job was the hardest
part of being chieftain. He corrected himself: no, the hardest
part was knowing he needed to hold back, and not giving in to
the urge to go wild and slaughter.

If he suppressed that urge all the time, he wondered, would
he be civilized? He found the idea ridiculous. He would only be
bored.

He cast two critical eyes on the fighting, turned a third to Z'Yon, who was clipping a wounded M'Sak's shell so no sharp edges would further injure the soft tissues inside. His fourth eye, as it had been most of the night, was on the moon. The fully lit portion grew ever smaller.

"You were right, shaman," he said, an enormous concession from him. But even a chieftain felt small and insignificant when the natural order of the world turned upside down.

Z'Yon did not answer until he had finished his task—had his prediction been wrong, he would have dared no such liberty. What would have happened to him had he been wrong was unpleasant to contemplate anyhow. He hoped he sounded casual rather than relieved when he said, "So it seems."

"The warriors truly know the meaning of the prodigy," V'Zek went on. "They fight bravely. I think they will force an entrance into the town not long after the whole moon goes into the jaws of the *f'noi* in the sky. You did well in instructing them and insuring that they would be of stout spirit for the battle."

"I did as you commanded, my master." Z'Yon's eyestalks tingled in remembered fright. A ladder went over, directly in front of the shaman and his chieftain. Injured M'Sak flailed legs in pain. One lay unmoving. "They fight well inside D'Opt, too."

"Doubtless their leaders and the Soft Ones have filled them with nonsense so they will not despair at our might," V'Zek said scornfully. "And see over there!" He pointed with a grasping-claw. "We've gained a stretch of wall! Surely the end cannot be far away."

"Surely not, my master." Z'Yon wished he had not taken omens with the moltings; he would have had no qualms now about being as excited as V'Zek. He tried to stifle his doubts. He had been wrong before, often enough.

The last bit of white disappeared from the moon. V'Zek shouted in a voice huge enough to pierce the tumult. "Now we hold the moment between our claws! Strike hard and T'Kai falls. The sky gives us victory!"

"The sky gives us victory!" the warriors cried, and redoubled their efforts. The dim red light made seeing hard, but cries of alarm from the walls showed places where the M'Sak were gaining fresh clawholds. Z'Yon decided he had been wrong again after all.

The last bit of white disappeared from the moon. "Now's the time, Jennifer," Greenberg said quietly into his comm unit. "Get things rolling, or the T'Kai have had it."

The pause that followed was longer than speed-of-light could account for. The master merchant started to call down curses on Jennifer's head. He wished he could take her damned reader and wrap it around her neck. He was starting to get more creative than that when she said, "Initiated."

He checked his watch. The delay had been less than fifteen seconds. All she'd done, obviously, was start the program before she answered him. He felt ashamed of himself. The fighting had screwed up his time sense.

He hoped he hadn't waited too long. T'Kai warriors fought desperately to keep the M'Sak from enlarging the two or three lodgments they had on top of the wall and to keep them from dropping down into D'Opt. If the southerners broke now, nothing could save them. But if he'd told Jennifer to start before the eclipse was total, odds were her scheme would have been wasted.

Too late for it's now, anyhow. He wondered how long things would take at the *Flying Festoon*'s end. When he judged the moment ripe, he started the tape that was loaded into his translator. The amplifiers around the wall made all the battle din, all V'Zek's shouts, seem as whispers beside his voice. "The very heavens proclaim the glory of T'Kai! Look to the sky, you who doubt, and you will see the truth writ large on the face of the moon itself!"

The message repeated, over and over. In the spaces between, the master merchant heard what he most hoped for: quiet. T'Kai and M'Sak alike were peering upward with all their eyes.

"Hurry up, Jennifer, dammit," Greenberg muttered. He made sure the translator could not pick up what he said.

". . . Look to the sky, you who doubt, and you will see the truth writ large on the face of the moon itself!" That roar might have been enough to frighten the M'Sak troops, had they not heard it before. More Soft One trickery, V'Zek thought, and handled as ineptly as the rest of their stunts.

Nevertheless, he looked. He could not help it, not with that insistent great voice echoing and re-echoing on his tympanic membrane. The moon remained dim and bronze—alarming, but alarming in a familiar way.

V'Zek laughed, loud and long. The last bluff had failed. No one but the *f'noi* in the sky could harm the moon, and from the *f'noi* it always won free in the end.

"Lies!" V'Zek shouted. "Lies!"

And as he watched, as he shouted, the moon changed.

A light-sail is nothing more than a gauze-thin sheet of aluminized plastic, thousands of kilometers across. When fully extended, it holds photons' energy as a seaboat's sail traps the wind. As it needs no internal power source, it makes a good emergency propulsion system for a starship.

Normally, one thinks only of the light-sail's catching photons. No one cares what happens to them afterward. Jennifer did not think normally. A corner of her mouth twisted—on that, no doubt, she and Greenberg would agree. She'd realized the light-sail could also act as a mirror, and, with the ship's robots trimming it, a mirror of very special shape.

She'd been ready for more than a day. She was, in fact, reading when Greenberg called her, but she wasted no time getting things under way. The adjustment was small, tilting the mirror a couple of degrees so the light it reflected shone on L'Rau's moon instead of streaming past into empty space.

As soon as she was sure the robots were performing properly, she went back to rereading "The Man Who Sold the Moon."

The wait seemed to stretch endlessly. The M'Sak were not going to pause much longer, Greenberg thought, not with their chieftain screaming "Lies!" every few seconds. Then golden light touched the edge of the moon, which should have stayed bronze and faint upwards of another hour.

The light stayed at the edge only a moment. Faster by far than L'Rau's patient shadow, the radiant grasping-claw hurried to its appointed place in the center of the moon's disk, so that it became a celestial image of the emblem of T'Kai.

The warriors of the confederacy suddenly pressed against their foes with new spirit. The humans had promised a miracle, but few, Greenberg knew, believed or understood. Asking a planet-bound race to grasp everything starfarers could do was asking a lot. But since the prodigy worked for them, they were glad enough to accept it.

As for the M'Sak— "Flee!" Greenberg shouted into the translator. "Flee, lest the wrath of heaven strike you down!" The barbarians needed little urging.

"Hold fast!" V'Zek shrieked. A warrior ran by him. The warrior also shrieked, but wordlessly. All his eyes were on the moon, the horrible, lying moon. V'Zek tried to grab him. He broke away from the chieftain's grip and ran on. V'Zek swung a hatchet at him, but missed.

The chieftain's mandibles ground together in helpless fury. Moments before, he had led an army fine enough to satisfy even him. Now it was only a mob, full of fear. "Hold fast!" he cried again. "If we hold, we will win tomorrow."

"They will not hold," Z'Yon said softly. Even the shaman, curse him, had three eyes on the sky. "And tomorrow, there will be ambuscades behind every tree, every rock. We daunted T'Kai before. Now we will be lucky to win back to our own forests again."

V'Zek's eyestalks lowered morosely. The shaman was likely right. The M'Sak had gone into every fight *knowing* these effete southrons could never stand against them. And they never had. But now—now the T'Kai, curse them, *knew* the very heavens fought for them. Worse, so did his own warriors.

He turned on Z'Yon. "Why did you fail to warn me of this?"

"My master?" Z'Yon squawked, taken aback. Too taken aback, in fact, for he blurted out the truth. "My master, I did tell you the moltings indicated the need for caution—"

"A pestilence on the moltings!" Before V'Zek was aware of willing his grasping-claw to strike, the hatchet he carried leaped out and crashed through Z'Yon's shell, just to the left of the shaman's center pair of eyestalks. Z'Yon was dead almost before his plastron hit the ground.

V'Zek braced and pulled the hatchet free. Killing Z'Yon, he discovered, solved nothing, for the shaman's words remained true. There was no arguing him out of them any more, either.

And a little while later V'Zek, like his beaten, frightened warriors, fled north from D'Opt.

Until the sky-*f'noi* began to relinquish its grip on the moon, the hateful emblem of T'Kai glared down at them. Forever after, it was branded in their spirits. As Z'Yon had foretold—another bitter truth—few found home again.

L'Rau's sun grew visibly smaller, visibly fainter in the holovid tank as the *Flying Festoon* accelerated toward hyperdrive kick-in. Jennifer waited eagerly for it to disappear. Civilization lay on the other side of the starjump. "Back to the university," she said dreamily.

Bernard Greenberg heard her. He chuckled. "I won't miss L'Rau myself, I tell you that. Anytime you have to bring off a miracle to get out in one piece, you're working too hard."

He spoke to her differently now; he had ever since she'd brought the *Flying Festoon* back to the planet. He'd kissed her then, too, where before he'd hardly seemed to notice her as anything save a balky tool. *But I'm not balky any more*, she realized: she'd proven herself a part of the crew worth having. A kiss of acceptance was worth a hundred of the sort men tried to press on her just because of the way she looked.

"Speaking of miracles, that eclipse was visible over a whole hemisphere," Koniev said. "I wonder what G'Bur who've never heard of T'Kai made of it." He took a sip of ship's vodka. For once he was not complaining about it—a measure of his relief.

"Giving the next generation's scribes and scholars something new to worry about isn't necessarily a bad thing," Marya said. She moved slowly and carefully, but X-rays said she had only an enormous bruise on her shoulder from a slingstone, not a broken collarbone. Left-handed, she raised her glass in salute. "Speaking of which, here's to the scholar who got us out." She drank.

"And with a profit," Koniev said. He drank.

"And with a civilization saved and a market for our next trip," Greenberg said. He drank.

Jennifer felt herself turning pink. She drank, too. After that, even her ears heated. "Speech!" Marya called, which made Jennifer swallow wrong and cough.

"A pleasure to pound your back," Greenberg said gallantly.

"Are you all right now?" At her nod, he grinned. "Good, because I want to hear this speech, too."

"I—don't really have one to make," she said with her usual hesitancy. "I'm just glad it all worked out." A moment later, she added, "And very glad to be going home."

"Aren't we all?" Greenberg said. Koniev and Marya lifted their glasses again, in silent agreement. The master merchant also drank. Then he asked, "What are you going to do, once you're back?"

"Why, go back to school, of course, and work on my thesis some more," Jennifer said, surprised he needed to ask. "What else would I do?"

"Have you ever thought about making another run with us?"

"Why ever would you want me to?" Jennifer said. She was not altogether blind to what went on around her, and a long way from stupid; more than once, she suspected, Greenberg must been been tempted to leave her on L'Rau.

But now he said, "Because nothing succeeds like success. This little coup of yours will win you journeyman status, you know, and a share of the profits instead of straight salary. And with your, uh, academic background—" Jennifer guessed he'd been about to say "odd academic background," but he hadn't— quite. "—you'd be useful to have along. Who knows? You might come up with another stunt to match this one."

"You really mean it, don't you?" She had trouble believing her ears.

"Yes, I do," Greenberg said firmly.

"We'd like to have you along," Marya agreed. Koniev nodded.

"Thank you," Jennifer said. "Thank you more than I can say." She went over and kissed Greenberg. She found she didn't mind at all when his arm slipped around her waist. But she still shook her head. "Once, for me, is enough. I feel very certain of that. The university suits me fine."

"All right," Greenberg said. "I'll see you get rated journeyman anyhow. You've earned it, whether you choose to use it or not."

"Thanks," she said again. "That's very kind. I won't turn you down. Not, mind you, that I ever *will* use it."

"Of course not," Greenberg said.

She looked at him sharply. As a master merchant, he was used to—and good at—manipulating people to get his way. *Not this time, you won't*, she thought.

THE ATHETERS

III

THE TALL FUR crest above Gazar's eyes rippled slightly. With Atheters, Jennifer thought, that was supposed to mean they were going to get down to serious business. She hoped so. Gazar had shown her nothing but junk—well, not junk, but certainly nothing worth taking offworld—for the past two hours.

As the Atheter merchant rummaged through his wicker basket, Jennifer wondered, for far from the first time, what she was doing sitting cross-legged on a fat tree branch dickering with an alien who looked like a blue plush chimpanzee with a prehensile tail. She'd firmly intended to teach Middle English literature after a single trading run gave her a taste of the life Middle English science fiction writers tried to imagine.

That had been two trips ago, now. She still hadn't quite worked out why she'd signed up for her second trip. Had she really been *that* depressed about not getting the first teaching job she'd applied for?

She stopped the useless worrying as Gazar's big golden eyes—his least-chimplike feature—went wide. He'd found what he was looking for, then. With a fine dramatic sense, he held whatever it was concealed between his six-fingered hands. He started squawking. The translator Jennifer wore on her belt turned his words into Spanglish. "Here, my fellow trader, is something not many will be able to show you."

"Let me see—" Jennifer's soft, breathy voice didn't activate the translator. She tried again, louder. "Let me see it, please." The machine let out a series of raucous squawks and shrieks.

"Here." Crest erect with pride, Gazar opened his hands.

"This is carved *omphoth* ivory, which of course means it is very, very old."

"Why 'of course'?" Had Gazar not made an issue of it, Jennifer would have taken him at his word. The ivory of the figurine was yellowed, the carving in a style unlike anything she had seen on Athet: it was vigorous, exuberant, unsophisticated but highly skilled. Back in civilization, collectors would pay a lot for it.

"Surely any nestling knows—" Gazar began. Then he let out a high-pitched screech that reminded Jennifer of forks on frying pans. To him, it was laughing. He was, in fact, laughing at himself. "But why should you, from the treeless wastes between the stars? 'Of course' because as soon as my earliest ancestors bravely crossed the Empty Lands into this forest, they began to hunt the *omphoth* that roamed here. No *omphoth* has been seen alive in more than a thousand winters."

"Oh." Jennifer was glad the alien would not notice her distaste. Humans, she was sure, had exterminated a lot more species than the Atheters, but they had also learned not to sound proud of it. Maybe, she thought, Gazar had an excuse. "Were these *omphoth* fierce animals, then, that killed and ate your people?"

"They were worse!" Gazar's tail writhed like a fat, pink worm, a sure sign of agitation. "They ate the trees! Fruit, leaves, branches, everything!"

That hit him where he lived, all right, Jennifer thought, in the most literal sense of the word. Atheters were arboreal by evolution and by choice. They only came down from their precious trees for stones and for copper and tin ores. Their domestic animals were as tree-bound as they were. No wonder they called the savannahs that alternated with their rain forests "the Empty Lands."

"No wonder you hunted them, then," Jennifer said soothingly. "What would you want in exchange for this figurine?"

"Ah, so here at last is something that interests you, then? I was beginning to think nothing did." Atheters understood sarcasm just fine. Gazar's tail twitched again, a different motion from the one it had made before; he was deciding how greedy he could be. "You must understand, of course, that because there are no more *omphoth*, the object is irreplaceable, and so doubly precious.''

"I suppose so," Jennifer said. The flat tones of the translator made sure she sounded indifferent. She'd hoped Gazar wouldn't think of that.

"Oh, indeed!" Always raucous, his screeches were nearly apoplectic now. "In fact, I would not think of parting with it for less than half a dozen scalpels, two dozen *swissarmyknives*"—the Terran name came out in one squawked burst— "and, let me see, two, no, three bottles of the sweet tailtangler you humans brew."

He meant Amaretto, Jennifer knew. The Atheters were crazy about it. She also knew he had decided to be very greedy indeed. She gasped. The translator turned the noise into a scream of rage worthy of—what was that ancient mythical ape's name?— King Kong, that was it. That was how Atheters gasped. They were a noisy species. Jennifer said, "Why not ask for our ship, while you are at it?"

Gazar's grin exposed formidable teeth. "Would you sell it to me?"

"No. Nor will I give you everything that in your extravagance you demanded. Are you trying to empty all our stores so that we cannot deal with anyone else here?" The haggling went on for some time. It started to grow dark outside. Gazar's hut of woven branches. Eventually they agreed on a price. Jennifer rummaged in her backpack. "Here are your two scalpels and fourteen knives. I will come back tomorrow with the bottle of tangletail," she said.

"I trust you so far," Gazar agreed.

"Now I must go back to my ship, while there is still some light." Jennifer stood up. She was not very tall by human standards, but she had to stoop to keep from bumping the ceiling of the hut.

Gazar scurried around to open the door for her, a courtesy she'd read of but one long obsolete on civilized worlds, where doors were smart enough to open themselves. "Until tomorrow," the Atheter merchant said.

"Yes." Jennifer started down the chain ladder the crew of the *Pacific Overtures* used to reach the lower branches of the big trees on which the locals lived. The Atheters carved what they reckoned hand-, foot-, and tailholds into the forest giants' trunks, but for humans, who unfortunately lacked both opposable big toes and any sort of tails, prehensile or otherwise, ladders were infinitely preferable.

Gazar peered anxiously after her. "Be careful down there," he called. "The *omphoth* may be gone, but there are all manners of dangerous beasts."

"I have my weapon that throws sleep," she reminded him. He smiled a big-toothed, reassured smile, then started screaming at the top of his lungs for customers. His shrieks were just a tiny part of the din; living as they did in an environment where they could rarely see far, Atheters advertised with noise.

Jennifer was relieved to descend to the relative quiet of the forest floor. She took out her stunner; she knew Gazar hadn't warned her just for politeness' sake. The ground featured not just the usual assortment of large mammaloid carnivores, but also poisonous lizardy things that struck from ambush out of piles of leaves. The thick boots she wore to protect herself against them were one more reason not to use the locals' routes up and down trees.

Being under those trees, Jennifer discovered, had other risks she hadn't thought of. Something whistled past her face, so close she could feel the breeze it raised, and smacked to earth just in front of her feet. She sprang back in alarm. Without her willing it, her finger went to the stunner's firing button.

But, she saw, it was only one of the big, knobby, hard-skinned fruits that fell from the Atheters' trees. As she looked around, she saw two or three more similar fruits and a couple of scraggly saplings that were not doing at all well as they tried to grow in the gloom cast by their elder relatives.

"A stupid seed," she muttered. Then she shivered. Stupid the seed certainly was, but had it fallen in a spot half a meter different, it would have smashed her skull. As she walked on, she cocked her head to look up every so often. Not just seeds fell from the Atheters' tree, but also rubbish the locals threw out.

After a few hundred meters, she emerged from the forest into a large clearing, almost big enough to be an independent patch of plain. In the middle of it, sunset gleamed off the metallic bulk of *Pacific Overtures*. Jennifer blinked; after forest twilight, the crimson sun-reflections from the ship were dazzling.

She hurried toward it. Less than a hundred meters away, she stumbled over something and nearly fell. As she caught herself, she saw she'd tripped on a stump completely overgrown by grass and low bushes. It had been a big tree once; now it was just a menace to navigation.

She sighed with animal pleasure the moment she got inside *Pacific Overtures*. After the humid heat of the jungle, conditioned air was a blessing. She shook back her long, blond hair, frowned at how heavy and limp with sweat it was. As she had before, she thought about cutting it short. But it helped the Atheters tell her apart from the other humans on *Pacific Overtures*, so she supposed it was worth the bother.

She was into the common room before she realized how much like a trader she was starting to think. Annoyed, she kicked at the carpet.

The scuffing noise made Sam Watson look up from the spice cones he was grading. His eyes lingered. That annoyed Jennifer all over again; hot, grubby, and none too clean, she felt anything but attractive. Men, though, usually seemed to think otherwise.

The once-over ended soon enough not to be offensive. "How'd you do?" Watson asked. "Get anything interesting?"

"As a matter of fact, I did." She took the ivory figurine from her beltpouch and set it on the table in front of him. "Have you ever seen anything like this before?"

He reached for it, then paused. "May I?" At her nod, he picked it up. He was a medium-sized, medium-brown man in his mid-thirties, five or six years older than Jennifer. She suspected he wore his bristly handlebar mustache for the same reason she kept her hair long: to give aliens something by which to recognize him. She couldn't think of any other reason for him to want a black caterpillar in the middle of his face.

The caterpillar twitched as he pursed his lips. "Can't say as I have," he said slowly. "That's an old, old style of carving."

"I thought so, too, though I hadn't seen it before," she nodded. "Gazar—the merchant I got it from—says the animal whose ivory it comes from is a thousand years extinct."

"I wouldn't be surprised, though I've never met a merchant, human or otherwise, who wouldn't stretch things for the sake of profit. Still, it's a pretty piece." He handed it back to her. "If it really is as old and rare as all that, it might even be museum quality."

"Do you think so?" Jennifer felt her pulse race, as if Watson had said a magic word. In a way, he had. Private collectors had only private wealth with which to buy. Museums could draw on the resources of whole planets. If they started bidding against one another, they could make a trader rich for life.

"*Might* be, I said." Watson jabbed a rueful thumb at his spice cones. "One thing certain—none of these is. Some will help make prime Athet brandy, some good brandy, and the rest rotgut. They'll all turn a profit, but no big deal."

"I suppose not." Jennifer daydreamed about what she could do with a really big profit. Heading the list, as always, was setting up—and then occupying—an endowed chair. She smiled, imagining the Jennifer Logan Endowed Chair for the Study of Middle English Science Fiction—maybe even of Middle English Literature, for her interests had broadened since she left the university. "But I'd need to find the *omphoths*' graveyard for that," she murmured.

Watson scratched his head. "The which? For what?"

"Never mind, Sam." Jennifer felt herself flushing. After so many years of ancient literature, she often found herself speaking a foreign language even when she used perfectly good Spanglish.

"All right." Watson shrugged. He was a pragmatic type who did not waste his time worrying about what was of no immediate use to him. That made him narrow, but within his limits acute. "Now that we know your ivory exists, we'll have to see if we can get more. Don't forget to tell Master Rodriguez about it."

"I won't. When do you suppose she'll be back?"

Watson shrugged again. "She's got some sort of complicated deal brewing with the treelords, so she may be gone days yet. Who can say?" He gave a wry chuckle. "Whatever she's up to, it's a lot bigger than the trinket exchange level we humble journeymen operate at."

"I suppose so." Jennifer still had mixed feelings about her rank. If she hadn't made journeyman at the end of her first run, she wouldn't have had anything to fall back on when her try at a real job went up in smoke. Maybe she would have tried again instead of signing up for another trip.

Watson, she knew, would have told her it was much too late to worry about such things now. He would have been right, too. That didn't stop her.

Now he glanced longingly back toward his spice cones. "I'd better finish these, so I can see exactly what I've got. Congratulations on the ivory. I'm most sincerely jealous."

She smiled. "Thanks." She headed on to her own cubicle and shut the door behind her. The figurine went into her strongbox. She walked down the hall to take a fast shower. Then she did what she did during most of her free time: she got out her reader and went from modern times back to the days before English changed to Spanglish. She might not be teaching the ancient literature, but she still loved it.

This new tale wasn't science fiction but, she discovered as she read, it did show respect for rational thought. She laughed a little, quietly, at a pleasant coincidence between past and present. Even across a gap of a thousand years, such things turned up now and again. They only made her enjoy her reading more.

Master Merchant Celia Rodriguez called a crew's meeting two afternoons later. Jennifer made sure she was in the common room at the appointed time; Master Rodriguez's tongue could degauss computer chips when she got annoyed. The other five merchants who made up the rest of *Pacific Overtures'* crew were equally punctual, no doubt for the same reason.

Jennifer loathed meetings, feeling they wasted time in which she could be doing something useful instead. Sitting through a great many of them had only made that feeling stronger. She got ready to look interested while she thought about her ancient scientific detective.

Celia Rodriguez's first words, though, made her sit up and take notice. "The civilization in this whole tract of forest is in deep trouble." Master Rodriguez's take-it-or-leave-it delivery was a good match for her looks: she was about fifty, heavyset, with blunt features and iron-gray hair she wore short. She badly intimidated Jennifer. Most loud, self-assured people intimidated Jennifer.

"What do you mean?" demanded Tranh Nguyen. He was

also a master merchant, though junior to Rodriguez. "Judging from the records of earlier trade missions here, technology is improving, the standard of living is up, and population per tree keeps increasing." A couple of others, Sam Watson among them, nodded agreement.

"You're right," Rodriguez answered at once. "None of that matters at all, though, because the forest itself is dying back. Dim lights!" she told the ship's computer, and the common room went dark.

"First image," she commanded. The computer projected a map onto the wall next to her. "The green shows the extent of this tract of forest at the time of the first landing on Athet, 250 years ago. Second image." The borders of the green patch changed shape. "This is about a hundred years ago. Note the losses here, here, and here. Note also that the open space in which we are sitting appears during that interval."

Jennifer thought of the stump she'd tripped over. That had seemed just one of the small things that made up a day. Now it looked more like a symptom of a much bigger problem.

So it proved. "Third image," Rodriguez said. The map changed again. "This is where we are today. See how much bigger this clearing has grown, and the appearance of these two further west. See also where grassland has replaced forest here, and in this sector. The next map is an extrapolation of where these trends will lead if they keep on for another two hundred years. Fourth image."

The new map that appeared beside the master merchant brought gasps of surprise and dismay from her colleagues. The broad expanse of forest that had dominated this part of the continent was gone, only a few small outcrops surviving like islands in a sea of grass.

"This, of course, spells catastrophe for the Atheter civilization here," Master Rodriguez said. "The locals are so tied to their arboreal life-style that they have a great deal of trouble adapting to life on the ground. Their most likely response to the failure of the trees would be to try migrating to the next big forest tract, a couple of hundred kilometers away. That tract is already settled; I doubt its inhabitants would welcome newcomers with open arms."

"Have you shown the treelords these maps?" Tranh Nguyen asked.

Rodriguez shook her head. "I prepared them last night, after our meeting. The treelords realize they have a problem, but not its extent. As you said before, they can support more people per tree than they once could, which has helped mask there being fewer trees in which to support them. But now they have begun to notice."

"What do they want us to do, then?" Nguyen went on, having the seniority to ask the questions the whole crew was thinking.

"We've spent 250 years building up our image here as the wise, powerful traders from the stars. Now they want us to live up to it." Master Rodriguez's smile was ironic. "They want us to make the forest grow bigger again. Not much, eh?"

This time, several people spoke at once. "How do they propose to pay for it?" It was the first question that flashed through Jennifer's mind, though she did not speak aloud. Her own smile was rueful. Yes, she thought like a merchant now, sure enough.

"I don't know," Rodriguez said. "I don't know if we can, for that matter, but even trying will be expensive. And Athet has never been what you'd call a high-profit world. For something of this scale . . ." She let the words hang.

"I don't like the idea of standing by and watching a civilization fall," Suren Krikorian said. He was a journeyman hardly senior to Jennifer, but came from a wealthy family—he did not need to worry about the consequences of speaking his mind.

"Neither do I," Celia Rodriguez replied. "I don't like the idea of bankrupting myself either, though. Even a preliminary study on the local problem will keep us here a lot longer than we'd planned, and that will be expensive. If we don't have something to show for it when we get back to *our* civilization, we'll all be badly hurt."

Krikorian scowled but did not answer. The master merchant was right, and everyone knew it. Jennifer suddenly got up and hurried away from the table. She remembered to say "Excuse me" just as she left the common room, but so softly she was afraid nobody heard her.

"I trust this will be interesting," Rodriguez said when she got back. By her tone, she did not trust any such thing.

Jennifer felt herself flush. "I—I hope so, Master Merchant," she said, wishing she could push arrogance into her voice whenever she needed it. She held up the *omphoth*-ivory figurine. "I—I was just thinking that if the Atheters have more pieces of this quality, they would help pay us for our time here."

Celia Rodriguez's voice changed. "May I see it, please?" Jennifer brought it to her. She examined it closely, then asked, "May I show it to the rest of our group?" Jennifer nodded. "Opinions?" the master merchant asked as she handed Tranh Nguyen the piece.

The merchants passed it from one to another. Finally, Sam Watson returned it to Jennifer. "Enough like this, and staying here may well be worth our while," Nguyen said. No one argued with him.

"I only hope there *are* enough pieces," Jennifer said. "The trader from whom I got this one told me that the animals from which the ivory came have been extinct for a thousand years."

"Have they?" Now calculation was in Rodriguez's voice, and something else as well—the purr of a predator that had just spotted dinner. "Then with a little luck, we may be able to clean out the whole supply. We'll sell a few pieces when we get back to civilization, leave the rest with our brokers while half a dozen other ships scurry out here to try to get in on the good thing. And when they come back empty—why, then we'll sell more, at four times the price."

Everyone in the common room grinned at Jennifer. She smiled back, a little uncertainly—attracting attention, even favorable attention, made her nervous. It did, however, beat the stuffing out of the other kind, she thought.

Gazar's crest rose. His tail thrashed. "Your people will be buying many *omphoth*-ivory pieces, you say?"

Jennifer nodded. "As many as they can. If you want more, if you want more to sell to us, now would be a good time to get them, before you have to compete with the lure of offworld goods."

"And if I do get them, you will trade those offworld goods to me?" The Atheter's golden eyes were big and yellow as twin full moons.

"Certainly," Jennifer said. "Provided, that is, that you remember the favor I have done you and keep your demands within the bounds of reason.''

Gazar winced. ''Now I understand why your teeth are so small, merchant from the stars—your sharp tongue long ago sliced off their points.'' He displayed his own formidable set of ivory.

''From you, I will take that as a compliment,'' Jennifer chuckled.

''I meant it as one,'' Gazar said. ''You must understand me, even with advance notice I doubt I will be able to get a great many pieces. *Omphoth* ivory has become rare enough over the years that most of it, now, is in the treasury of one treelord or another. Still, some may be persuaded to fall from the branch.''

''I hope so.'' Jennifer paused. ''Speaking of falling from the branch, I almost had my head smashed in by a falling fruit the other day.''

''I'm glad you escaped. Still, that shows the folly of going down to the ground, does it not?''

''Not what I meant.'' Jennifer reminded herself not to be annoyed. Just as she was a product of her environment, so Gazar was of his. ''I would have thought that you treefolk would take care to harvest those fruits for yourselves, and not let the ground creatures have the benefit of them.''

The Atheter made a horrible face. ''Not even the crawlers in the leaves would want them. Our trees are wonderful. They are our lives, they are our livelihoods, they are our homes. But we do not eat their fruits. They taste dreadful.''

''Oh. All right.'' Jennifer thought for a moment. ''But you have many different kinds of large trees in this forest. Surely some must be of use to you.''

''A few,'' Gazar said grudgingly, as if making an enormous concession. ''Most, though, are truly foul—better for weapons, as you saw, than for food.''

''You know best, I'm sure.'' Jennifer stood up, as well as she could inside Gazar's shop. ''I'll come back again in a few days. I hope you'll have found some *omphoth* ivory by then.''

''So do I,'' Gazar said. ''My mate is pregnant with a new set of twins, and I expect we will need a larger house after they are born. The more offworld goods I get from you, the sooner I can buy it. Maybe I will buy a slave or two as well.''

Jennifer was glad Atheters had trouble reading human expressions; she was afraid her revulsion showed on her face. *You are not here to reform these people*, she told herself. Until they industrialized, they probably would have slaves, and there was nothing she could do about it. No, not quite nothing—trading with them was bound to spur their own technology, which might hasten the day when slavery grew uneconomic here.

As she walked back to *Pacific Overtures* this time, she kept a wary eye on the treetops. When a big fruit crashed down into the bushes, maybe fifty meters off to her left, she almost jumped out of her skin. No missiles came any closer than that, though, for which she was duly grateful.

Back at the ship, she gave herself the luxury of a few seconds of gloating. A small private hoard of *omphoth* ivory couldn't help but improve her credit rating when she got back to civilization. A large private hoard would be nicer yet, but she knew she lacked the resources to get her hands on one.

Maybe next trip out, she'd score that really big coup . . . She stopped in dismay. That was thinking too much like a trader to suit her. If she got a decent stake out of this run, she'd be able to afford to look for an academic job.

"And if I land one," she said aloud, "I'll never again go to a world that doesn't have an automated information retrieval system."

Pleased at that promise to herself, she dug out her reader and returned to twentieth—or was it nineteenth?—century London. The more stories she read about this detective, the more she wanted to read. That surprised her; the fellow who wrote them had also turned out a lot of bad science fiction. But the detective and his amanuensis lived and breathed. These tales were what the writer should have been doing all along, instead of wasting his time on things he wasn't good at.

She put down the reader and fought back angry tears. What was she doing aboard *Pacific Overtures* except wasting her time on things she wasn't good at?

Tranh Nguyen made as if to bang his head against the corridor wall. "I don't know why the forest is shrinking," he growled. "As far as I can tell, the soil in the grasslands is the same as the soil where the trees still grow. It has the same mineral content, the same little wormy things crawling through it, the same everything.''

"Not the same everything." Celia Rodriguez shook her head. "It doesn't have trees on it any more. We still have to find out why."

"Excuse me," Jennifer said—softly, as usual—as she tried to get past them.

Neither master merchant paid any attention to her. Tranh Nguyen said, "I know we have to, but I'm not sure we can. I do what the computer tells me to do, I compare the results of one sample to those from another, but if nothing obvious shows up, I'm stuck. I can't make the intuitive leap—I'm a trader, after all, not an agronomist who might see more than is in the computer program.''

"Excuse me," Jennifer said again.

"An agronomist!" Rodriguez clapped a hand to her forehead. "As if we could afford to haul an agronomist all the way out here! As if we could find an agronomist crazy enough to want to come! We have to be able to do this kind of work for ourselves, because if we don't, no one will."

"I know that as well as you do," Tranh Nguyen said. "Why carry the big computer library, except to make sure we can do a little of everything? A *little* of everything, though, Celia, not everything. We may really need a specialist here. Right now, I'm stymied."

"Excuse me," Jennifer said one more time.

Celia Rodriguez finally noticed she was there. She stepped out of the way. "Why didn't you say something?" she demanded.

Jennifer shrugged and walked by. She was often effectively invisible aboard *Pacific Overtures*. She much preferred that to the way things had been on her last trading run, when two male journeymen, neither of whom she wanted in the least, had relentlessly hounded her through the whole mission.

Sometimes she wished she were chunky and hard-featured like Celia Rodriguez instead of slim and curved and possessed of an innocent look she could not get rid of no matter how hard she tried. She would have enjoyed being valued for herself instead of just for her blue eyes. She'd never found a tactful way

to say that to the master merchant, though, and so sensibly kept
her mouth shut.

She let herself into her cubicle and closed the door after her.
That cut off most of the noise from the corridor, where Rodriguez and Tranh Nguyen were still arguing. She carefully took
off her backpack and set it on the floor. Then, grinning, she
leaped onto her mattress and bounced up and down like a little
kid.

When she was done bouncing, she got up again and opened
the backpack. Inside, wrapped in a square of thick, native,
printed cloth that was a minor work of art in itself, lay two fine
omphoth-ivory figurines. One was a carving of an Atheter; but
for its age, Jennifer would have guessed it a portrait of Gazar.
It certainly captured the local merchant's top-of-his-lungs style—
she could practically see the fur rising on the figurine's back.

That piece was excellent, but it paled beside the other.
"This," Gazar had said, swelling up with self-importance, "is
a veritable *omphoth*, carved from its own ivory to show later
generations the sort of monsters we had to battle in those ancient
days."

To a tree-dweller, Jennifer had to admit, it must have looked
like a nightmare come to life. She thought of an elephant's
head mounted on a brachiosaur's body, though the ears were
small and trumpetlike, the tusks curved down, and the trunk—
miraculously unbroken on the figurine—seemed to be an
elongated lower lip rather than a nose run rampant. Such
details aside, the carved *omphoth* certainly looked ready to
lay waste to whole forests.

Imagining a full-sized one, Jennifer had trouble seeing how
the Atheters ever could have killed it. When she had said as
much to Gazar, he'd burst into epic verse in a dialect so antique
that her translator kept hiccuping over it. Apparently a band of
heroes had gone out into the Empty Lands, brought back an
immense boulder, somehow manhandled it up into the treetops,
and then dropped it on an *omphoth*'s head.

"Thus was the first of the monsters slain," Gazar had de-
claimed, "giving proof—could be done again." Jennifer remembered staring at her translator; the machine wasn't
programmed to produce rhymes like that.

Now, though, she was more interested in the statuette than in the poetry its model had inspired. No matter how many tree-lords ransacked their collections for Celia Rodriguez, she did not think the master merchant would come up with a finer piece.

How much would the *omphoth* be worth? Enough to set up an endowed chair of Middle English literature? Jennifer knew she was dreaming. The whole hoard *Pacific Overtures* was bringing back might be worth something close to that, but her few private pieces wouldn't come close.

She sighed, rewrapped the figurines, and put them in her strongbox. One of these days, she told herself—most likely, just about the time when she would start forgetting her Middle English.

No, that was unfair. She loved the old language—although perhaps it wasn't older, she thought, surprised, than Gazar's hunting epic—and kept fresh her command of it. Fiche and a reader even a journeyman could easily afford.

She settled in with her scientific detective. This tale, part of what was called his memoirs, had to do with horse racing. Jennifer had seen a great many alien beasts on her trading runs, but never a horse. She had to struggle to work out from context what several of the words in the story meant; she was always rediscovering how large a vocabulary Middle English had. Even so, as she usually did, she got the gist of the piece and smiled at finding an exchange that had passed straight into Spanglish.

" 'Is there any point to which you would wish to draw my attention?'

'To the curious incident of the dog in the nighttime.'

'The dog did nothing in the nighttime.'

'That was the curious incident,' remarked Sherlock Holmes.''

She finished ''The Silver Blaze,'' loaded the fiche *Oxford English Dictionary* into the reader so she could look up a few words that had completely baffled her. But her mind kept going back to the dog that had not done anything. She frowned, trying to figure out why.

Then her eyes got wide. She reached under the bunk for her strongbox. She got out the two figurines she had just bought from Gazar. She looked from one of them to the other, then slowly nodded. This had to be how Holmes felt when all the pieces fell together. She quoted him again. ''When you have eliminated the impossible, whatever remains, *however improbable*, must be the truth.''

"Excuse me, Master Merchant." Jennifer had to say it three times before Celia Rodriguez noticed her. She didn't mind; she was used to that.

Finally Rodriguez looked up from her computer screen. "You want something, Jennifer?" She sounded surprised. Jennifer didn't mind that, either. She usually kept a low profile.

"Yes, I think so, Master Merchant. That is, I think I may know why this forest is shrinking."

Rodriguez slammed a meaty hand down on the panel in front of her. "Well, if you do, that's more than anyone else does. And I haven't seen you doing anything in the way of trying to find out, either. So how do you know? Divine inspiration?"

"No. I—I—'' Jennifer had to work to keep her voice audible in the face of such daunting sarcasm. "I—I got the idea from a Middle English book I was reading."

The master merchant groaned. "Jennifer, I don't begrudge anyone a hobby. Tranh Nguyen keeps trying to beat the computer at chess. He'll keep trying till he's 105, if he lives that long. Me, I like to knit. That's even useful, every now and then. I've traded things I've made for more than they're worth. You have your ancient books. They're harmless, I suppose. But what can they possibly have to do with why this forest tract on Athet is getting smaller?"

"It's—a way of thinking. But never mind that now. You're right, Master Merchant, I haven't done much work on the problem till now. I'm sorry. But can you tell me if you have maps that show the boundaries of the forest from a long time ago? Long before we first landed here, I mean: back when the Atheters were first settling this territory."

"I think so, yes." Rodriguez fiddled with the computer. A map appeared on the screen, replacing the chart she had been studying. "As best we can tell now, this is the size of the forest about fifteen hundred local years ago. It started declining then, slowly at first, but more and more rapidly in the past millennium. The process was well under way when humans came here, for reasons we still can't fathom—no great climatic changes, no shifts in the nature of the soil, nothing."

The master merchant checked herself, glanced sourly at Jennifer. "Oh, I'm so sorry. Now you know why, out of your antique books. Enlighten me, please."

Jennifer took a deep breath. If she was wrong now, the fitness report Rodriguez turned in on her would make it next to impossible for her to fly again. After not getting a fair shot at one career, the prospect of washing out of another frightened her more than she was willing to admit, even to herself.

"I think it was—" She spoke so softly that Rodriguez had to lean forward to hear what she was saying. She involuntarily yelped, "—the *omphoth*."

"The *omphoth*?" The master merchant looked disgusted. "You come in here, waste my time with this foolishness when I have serious work to do? The *omphoth*," she said, as if to an idiot child, "have been extinct for a thousand years. You were the one who found that out. How can something that isn't here any more have anything to do with conditions now?"

"By not being here," Jennifer said. Rodriguez snorted and turned back toward the computer screen. "No, wait!" Jennifer said desperately. "The forests really started shrinking a thousand years ago—you said so yourself. And the Atheters here finished wiping out the *omphoth* a thousand years ago. Don't you think there's a connection?"

"Coincidence," Rodriguez snorted. But she did look at Jennifer again. Now she might have been talking to a clever child. "Be reasonable. The Atheters got rid of the *omphoth* because they kept eating up the forest. So why is it shrinking now that they're gone?"

"Yes, they ate the trees," Jennifer agreed. "They even ate the horrible fruits that the Atheters can't stand, that none of the animals that are still around want anything to do with. What happens to the fruits that fall to the ground now?"

"They sprout, of course."

"Yes." Jennifer nodded eagerly. She was so full of her idea, she was almost fluent. "They sprout. They sprout under the trees that dropped them in the rain-forest gloom. Not many grow up, and the ones that do only grow up in the same place trees had always been."

"So what do the *omphoth* have to do with any of that? If they eat those fruits, they digest them, don't they? That gets rid of them a lot more thoroughly than trying to grow in the shade.''

"They digest the fruit, yes, but what about the seeds inside?" Jennifer asked. "Lots of plants on lots of worlds disperse their seeds by passing them through animals' guts. I looked that up when I first wondered if there was any connection between the *omphoth* disappearing and the forest shrinking back."

"Do they? Did you?" Now, at last, Celia Rodriguez began to seem interested.

"Yes. It makes sense here, too, in ecological terms. It really does, Master Rodriguez. The *omphoth* ate fruit nothing else here likes at all. Doesn't that probably mean they and the trees evolved together? The trees provided them a special food and in return they disseminated the seeds inside. And so when they disappeared, the seeds didn't get disseminated any more, and that's what I think has made this tract of forest get smaller."

"Hmm." The master merchant pulled out her lower lip, then let it snap back with a soft plop. "You've done your homework on this, haven't you?"

"Of course I have, Master Rodriguez." Jennifer knew she sounded surprised. If she was good at anything, it was research.

"Hmm," Celia Rodriguez said again. "Well, what do we do even if you're right? The *omphoth* are extinct. We don't have a time machine to bring them back."

"Ooh." It was like a blow in the belly—Jennifer hadn't thought that far ahead.

But once the master merchant had an idea, she was not one to let go of it. She said, as much to herself as to Jennifer, "They're extinct here, anyhow. But this isn't the only tract of rain forest on Athet, not by a long shot. It's just the one off-worlders do the most business with. Maybe others have relatives of the *omphoth* still running around loose."

"It shouldn't be hard to find out," Jennifer said.

Celia Rodriguez barked a couple of syllables' worth of laughter. "No, not hardly," she agreed. "Even with our translators barely working, the way they act when they're still picking up new languages, the locals won't be in much doubt about whether they have *omphoth* around."

Jennifer thought of something else. "I hope the main hold is big enough to carry one. More than one, I mean, if we intend to establish them here.''

"First things first." The master merchant laughed again. "Hope the stunners are strong enough to put them under. Otherwise I suppose we'll have to herd them across the however many hundreds or thousands of kilometers it is from where they are to here. And for that—" Rodriguez's tone was still bantering, but Jennifer had no doubt she meant what she said "—for that, I would definitely charge extra."

Something went crashing through the undergrowth far below the branch on which Gazar's establishment was perched. Then the something—Jennifer and Gazar both knew what it was; nothing else made that much racket—let out a bellow that sounded like a cross between a kettledrum and a synthesizer with a bad short in its works.

Gazar made a ghastly face. "Now I know why our heroic ancestors slew all the ancient *omphoth*—in the hope of getting a good night's sleep. The cursed beasts are never quiet, are they?"

"They don't seem to be," Jennifer admitted. The cries of the newly released animals could be heard even inside *Pacific Overtures*.

Out along the branch, Atheters shouted and screeched. Jennifer's translator screeched, too, protesting the overload. It did manage to pick up one call. "Come on out, Gazar, and look at the *omphoth*! Here it comes!"

"Why should I want to see the creature that torments my rest?" Gazar grumbled, but he went. Jennifer followed more slowly, the hobnails in the bottom of her boots helping to give her purchase on the branch.

Young Atheters squealed and clung to their mothers' fur as the *omphoth* lumbered by underneath. It took no notice of the excited locals in the tree; its attention was centered solely on food. It pulled up a bush, spat it out—it was still learning what was good in this new forest and what was not.

"It doesn't look the way an *omphoth* is supposed to," Gazar complained; having found that figurine for Jennifer, he fancied himself an expert. "It doesn't even have tusks."

He had a point, she supposed. The new beasts were not identical to their exterminated cousins. Not only were they tuskless, but their lower-lip trunks were bifurcated for the last meter or so of their length. They hardly had any tails, either, and their claws were smaller than those of the *omphoth* this forest had once known.

But in the one essential way, they were like the *omphoth* of old: they were ravenously fond of the big, knobby fruits the various trees here produced. The *omphoth* under Gazar's tree bent its head down so its forked trunk could grab fruit that had fallen to the ground. Wet chewing noises followed.

Then the *omphoth* reached up almost as high as the branch on which Jennifer was perched. If the baby Atheters had squealed before, they shrieked now. Jennifer could not blame them. The sight of that open pink maw only a few meters away made her want to shriek, too. The *omphoth* had dreadful breath.

It was not interested in snacking off the locals, though. All it wanted to do was pluck more fruit from any branch it could reach. Finally it stripped those branches bare and stamped away to look for more fodder.

Gazar turned around to display his hindquarters at it, a gesture of contempt he had never been rude enough to use on a human. He caught Jennifer's eye. "Some treetowns are even less happy with these beasts than ours," he said. "I only hope they are not so shortsighted as to try to get rid of them."

"Why would they do that?" Jennifer exclaimed in horror. "The *omphoth* are saving the forest for you."

"Saving the whole, aye, but damaging the parts. We have laws against building on branches lower than a certain height." Gazar blinked. "I suppose one reason we have those laws is the *omphoth* of long ago. I never thought about it till now. But not every treelord enforces those laws—without *omphoth*, they matter little. Now there are *omphoth* again, and they've already wrecked some houses that were low enough for them to reach."

"Oh. I'm sorry to hear that," Jennifer said. "Your people had better know, though, that we won't be around to get more *omphoth* for them if they go and kill these. You need to build up the herd, not destroy it."

"The treelords know that," Gazar said, still sounding a long way from happy at the prospect. "Armed males travel through the trees to guard the beasts from harm."

"I should hope so," Jennifer said. After all the trouble the crew of *Pacific Overtures* had gone through in stunning and transporting the great beasts, the idea of having them hunted down was appalling.

She took her leave from Gazar and climbed down the chain ladder to the ground. The *omphoth* was nowhere to be seen, although she could still hear it somewhere off deeper in the forest. She was glad it was not between her and *Pacific Overtures*.

Immense footprints and crushed bushes showed the beast's path. So did a huge pile of steaming, stinking, green dung. In the dung Jennifer saw several teardrop-shaped seeds.

She smiled. These particular seeds got no great advantage from their trip through the *omphoth*'s gut. But *omphoth* also wandered out to the edges of the savannah country surrounding the forest. Seeds deposited there would be more likely to thrive. With luck, the forest would grow again.

Her smile grew broader. All too often preindustrial races wanted nothing more from traders than help in war against their neighbors. This time, though, the crew of *Pacific Overtures* had really accomplished something worth doing. They'd turned a profit on the deal, too. Jennifer had learned to think well of the combination. She hurried toward the ship.

An *omphoth* came out of the forest. Sam Watson stepped up the gain on *Pacific Overtures'* viewscreen. He and Jennifer watched the beast's pupils shrink in the sudden bright sun. It didn't seem to like the feeling much. With a bellow, it drew back into the shelter of the trees.

Watson yawned and stretched. "I'll almost miss the big noisy things," he said.

"Yes, so will I, but not their racket," Jennifer said.

"No, not that. Maybe the next ship in can see if coffee does for Atheters what it does for us. I suspect a good many of them will need it, though they're not what you'd call a quiet race themselves."

"Hardly." Thinking of Gazar, Jennifer knew that was, if anything, an understatement. After a moment, she went on, "Maybe we should have done some tests with the coffee in the galley. If it worked, they'd have paid plenty for it."

"Too late to worry about it now, what with us upshipping tomorrow. I wonder how much the ivory will end up bringing. The way Master Rodriguez has things lined up, we may take a while selling everything, but we'll get a lot when we finally do. It's especially nice," Watson added, "that the new kind of *omphoth* we've introduced here doesn't have tusks; the Atheters won't have the incentive of hunting them to carve more trinkets for traders."

"That's true," Jennifer said. "I wouldn't feel right if we'd brought them here just to have them killed off."

"No." Sam gave Jennifer an admiring look. She hardly noticed it; she was used to admiring looks from men, and used to discounting them, too. But this one proved different from most. "That was a lovely piece of analysis you did, Jennifer, working out the connection between the extinction of the old *omphoth* and the trouble the forest was having."

She felt her cheeks heat with pleasure. "Oh. Thank you very much."

"I ought to thank you, for bumping up our profits, and I suppose for the Atheters, too. How did you ever work out that the *omphoth* passed the seeds through their intestinal tracts and then out again?"

"That? It was—" Jennifer paused, knowing he wouldn't understand—he was just a merchant, after all, not a scholar of Middle English. She found she didn't care. "It was alimentary, my dear Watson."

THE FOITANI

IV

ALI BAKHTIAR GLANCED toward the clock. A dark, arched eyebrow rose. "Isn't your first class at 0930, Jennifer? You're going to be late."

"I'm almost ready." Jennifer made sure one last time that she had all her notes. She took a couple of deep breaths, as if she were going to start lecturing then and there. "I hope the hall's well miked. My voice just isn't big enough to carry well by itself."

Bakhtiar smiled encouragingly. "You'll do fine." When he looked at the clock again, the smile faded. "But you'd better get moving."

"Here I go." Jennifer ran a hand through her long, blond hair. "Do I look all right?"

"That is a foolish question. You know you look wonderful." He stepped forward to kiss her; his hand slid down her back to cup her left buttock. He pulled her closer. The kiss went on and on.

Finally she twisted away. "You were the one who said I'd be late," she reminded him. She knew her looks drew men to her; she found that a nuisance as often as she enjoyed it. Living with Ali Bakhtiar the past year had at least given her an anchor. Seeing her on his arm kept a fair number of other men—not all, but a fair number—from pestering her. Even so, there were times when she wished she was still trading with aliens, to whom she was as peculiar as they were to her. It made life simpler.

But as she strode out of the apartment she and Bakhtiar shared, that sometimes-wish vanished. This would be her third semester of teaching Middle English science fiction at Saugus Central University. She still had trouble believing that, after close to ten years traveling the wilder reaches of the local arm of the galaxy, she actually had the academic job she'd wanted all along.

Sometimes you'd rather be lucky than good, she thought as she hurried toward and then across the university campus. She'd been about to set out on yet another trading run when word of the opening at Saugus Central came over the data net. The post would have been long filled by the time she got back, which meant she would have left on one more mission still, just to put more credit in her account. By the time the next job opening appeared, she might have been nearing master-trader status. Master trader was all very well—after some years of trading, she knew it was a title that had to be earned—but she much preferred putting *assistant professor* in front of her name.

Saugus was a good planet for hurrying. The weather here in the foothills was cool and crisp, the gravity was only about .85 standard, and the air held a little more oxygen than human beings had evolved to breathe. The clock in the classroom said 0929 when she stepped through the door. She grinned to herself. Being late on the first day didn't make a prof look good.

She got to the podium just as the clock clicked to 0930. "Good morning. I'm Dr. Logan," she said—she didn't believe in wasting time. "This is Middle English 217: Twentieth-Century Science Fiction." Someone got up and left in a hurry. *In the wrong room,* Jennifer thought. Other students tittered.

"Can you all hear me?" Jennifer asked. Everyone nodded, even the students in the back of the hall. The miking was all right, then. Her voice was so light and breathy that it needed all the help it could get.

"All right. This course is part language, part literature. As you'll have noticed when you were registering, beginning and intermediate Middle English are prerequisites. Don't forget, the documents we'll be reading are a thousand years old. If you think you'll be able to get through them with just your everyday Spanglish, or even with an ordinary translation program, you can think again."

Someone else, a girl this time, walked out the door shaking her head. Jennifer felt the eyes of the rest of the class upon her. Most students muttered their notes into recorders with hush-mikes. A few stroked typers or scribbled on paper in the ancient fashion; in every class, she'd found people who remembered better when they wrote things down.

A couple of male students hadn't started taking notes at all. She could tell what was in their minds as well as if she were telepathic. It annoyed her. No only were they boys by her reckoning, but she'd been places and faced challenges they could hardly imagine. She knew they didn't care what she'd done. To them, she was only an attractively shaped piece of meat. That annoyed her even more.

She sighed to herself and went on, "That's not to say you won't find words—a lot of words—that look familiar. A lot of Spanglish vocabulary can be traced back to roots in Middle English. That's especially true of Middle English science fiction. Many, in fact most, of our modern terms relating to spaceflight come from those first coined by science-fiction writers. Remarkably, most of those coinages were made before the technology for actual spaceflight existed. I want you to think for a moment of the implications of that, and to think about the leap of imagination those writers were taking."

Some of them made the mental effort, she saw. She knew they were doomed to failure. Imagining what humanity had been like before spaceflight was as hard for them as willing oneself into the mind of an ancient Sumerian would have been for an ordinary citizen of the twentieth century.

She held up a sheet of paper. "I want to talk about the books we'll be reading this semester," she said. The back door to the lecture hall opened. She frowned. This was one of the times she wished she had a deep, booming voice. She hated latecomers interrupting her when she'd already started lecturing. She began, "I hope you'll be on time for our next—" but stopped with the complaint only half-spoken. The new students were not human.

The whole room grew quiet when the three of them walked in. They were dark blue and on the shaggy side. The door was more than two meters high, but they had to stoop to get under the lintel. The door was more than a meter wide, but they had to turn sideways to go through it. Their faces had short muzzles and impressive teeth.

"What species are they?" a student in the front row asked

the fellow next to her. He shrugged and shook his head. Likely neither of them had ever been off Saugus before, Jennifer thought.

She knew the aliens' race. Of all the places she would never have expected to meet Foitani, though, a Middle English class on a human-settled planet of no particular importance to anyone ten light-years away came close to topping the list. Maybe, she thought, they were looking for the engineering department instead. She called, "How may I help you, Foitani?"

The three big blue creatures cocked their heads to one side, listening to the translators each wore. One of them answered, speaking softly in his own rumbling language. His translator turned the words to Spanglish. "Apologies for tardiness, honored instructor. We concede the fault is ours; we will yield any forfeit your customs require."

"We will," the other two echoed.

"No—forfeits—are necessary," Jennifer said faintly. "May I direct you to the class you are seeking?"

The Foitan who had spoken first bared his teeth—or possibly hers; the differences between Foitani sexes did not show on the outside. Jennifer knew the gesture was the Foitani equivalent of a frown, but it made the alien look as if he intended to take a bite out of someone. She wished for the trader's stunner she seldom wore any more. The Foitan said, "Have we interpreted your symbology inaccurately? This hall is not for the teaching of Middle English two-one-seven?"

"You're enrolled in my class?" Jennifer heard herself squeaking, but couldn't help it. It wouldn't matter anyhow; translators were fine for meaning, but they filtered out tone of voice.

"So we ought to be," the Foitan answered, his own translator sounding grave as usual. "Our funds were accepted, our names inscribed in your computer banks. I am Thegun Thegun Nug; here beside me stand Aissur Aissur Rus and Dargnil Dargnil Lin."

Jennifer shoved notes aside. "Enrollment," she muttered. The list appeared on the screen set into the top of the podium. Sure enough, the three Foitani were on it. Human names came in such bewildering variety that she hadn't especially noticed theirs. "Very well," she said, "sit down—if you have the reading knowledge of Middle English this course requires."

The Foitani sat. They weren't so much bigger than the average human as to make human furniture impossible for them—just enough bigger to be intimidating, Jennifer thought. Aissur Aissur Rus said, "We will meet the language requirements of the course, honored instructor. We are Foitani, after all. We are practiced in dealing with languages far more ancient and different from modern speech than your Middle English."

She knew that was true. "Very well," she said again, and began talking about the books she would be assigning. Never had she had such perfect attention from students on the first day of class. After the ostentatious if somber politeness of the Foitani, it was as if all her human students feared they would be torn limb from limb if they got out of line.

Because she didn't have to pause even once, she got through all the material she'd planned to present in spite of the delay the Foitani had caused. Only after the three big aliens left the hall did the rest of the people there start chattering among themselves. Even then, their voices were low, subdued.

Jennifer went back to her office to see how the campus computers were doing on a couple of her pet research projects. The new printouts had some important data, but didn't interest her as much as they should have: With three Foitani—Foitani!—enrolled in her course, she had trouble getting excited about revised charts of de Camp's use of the colon rather than the comma to introduce quotations, or on a fresh stemma tracing the spread of the word "thutter" from Anderson to writers of the next generation like Stirling and Iverson.

After lunch, she taught one course in modern Spanglish literature and another in composition, neither of which excited her very much but both of which helped pay her half of the rent for the apartment she shared with Ali Bakhtiar. She told herself she would have gone through them without much thought no matter what; with three Foitani in her morning class to think about, she knew she wasn't giving the afternoon sessions her full attention.

When she got back to the apartment, Bakhtiar was already there. His last class—he taught imaging, both tape and film—got out half an hour before hers. All she wanted to do was exclaim about the Foitani. He listened, bemused, for several minutes; she was not usually the sort to gush. At last, he held up a hand. "Wait one second, please. Why are you so excited about having these three aliens in your class?"

"That's what I was telling you," Jennifer said. "They're Foitani."

"So I'd gathered," he answered with a wry quirk of that eyebrow. Sometimes she thought he practiced in a mirror, but she'd never caught him at it. "But who are the Foitani?"

She stared at him. "You really don't know?"

"Why should I?" he asked reasonably. "How many species of aliens do we know? Several hundred without hyperdrive, several dozen with it. That's on top of Allah only knows how many human-settled worlds. So why should I remember anything in particular about this one bunch?"

Jennifer knew he was right—humanity had spread too widely, learned too many things, for any one person to keep track of more than a tiny fraction of all there was to know. But somehow Bakhtiar's complete ignorance of the Foitani badly irked her. She wanted to exclaim over them and have him exclaim right back. How could he do that if he had no idea why she was exclaiming in the first place?

He saw something was wrong; after all, he had lived with her for a year. Spreading his hands to placate her, he said, "Tell me about them, then, if they're that important."

"Well, for one thing, we've only known they aren't extinct for about the past fifty years," Jennifer said. "They used to rule a big empire in toward the galactic center, a good many thousand years ago. Then they started fighting among themselves; I don't think anybody knows why. They kept right on doing it, too, till they'd wrecked just about all the worlds they lived on."

"Wait a minute." A light came on in Bakhtiar's eyes. "Didn't they run a holovid special on that three or four years ago? Secret of the lost race, or something like that? I remember watching it, but I'd forgotten the name of the race."

"I suppose they may have," Jennifer said. Three or four years ago, she'd been dickering with the Atheters over the price of *omphoth* ivory. "But yes, those were the Foitani. *Are* the Foitani," she corrected herself.

"Why have they enrolled in your Middle English class? What do they think they're going to get out of it?"

"I haven't the slightest idea," Jennifer said. "Of course, I don't know what about a third of my human students are going to get out of the class either, except for four units of credit."

Several years of trading missions among the stars had let her forget the time-serving students, the ones who took a course because they needed to fill a breadth requirement or because it happened to fit their schedules. The ones she'd remembered were the ones like herself, who enrolled in classes to learn something and worked hard at everything, for pride's sake if for no other reason. Saugus Central University had plenty of those. Unfortunately, it had plenty of the other sort, too, as she'd found to her dismay.

Ali Bakhtiar said, "Well, it's nice you had something out of the ordinary to liven up your day. Let's go have dinner, shall we?"

"Foitani in a Middle English class is more than something out of the ordinary," Jennifer said. But Bakhtiar was already walking into the kitchen and didn't hear her—the apartment wasn't miked. Glaring at his back, Jennifer followed him.

She wanted to talk more about the aliens after dinner, but he turned on a battleball game and was lost to the world for the next couple of hours. Battleball required the biggest, strongest bruisers humanity produced. The Foitani, Jennifer suspected, could have torn most of them in half without working up a sweat—assuming Foitani sweated in the first place.

She didn't care about battleball one way or the other. She sometimes watched because Ali liked it so much; it gave them something to do together out of bed. Tonight she didn't feel like making the effort. She went into the bedroom to work on the computer for a while.

When she found herself yawning, she shut down the machine. She needed a few seconds to return from the distant past's exciting imagined future to her own thoroughly mundane present. Somehow hardly anyone in Middle English science fiction ever got bored or had to go to the bathroom at an inconvenient time or worried about her credit balance.

As *she* went off to the bathroom, Jennifer reflected that her own credit balance was in pretty good shape. Thanks to the *omphoth* ivory, she had a good deal more to her name than if she'd landed the first academic job she'd tried for. And she had no business being bored, not with three Foitani to wonder about.

She hoped the Foitani would get around to explaining just what they were doing in a Middle English course. She didn't know enough about their customs to risk asking straight out, but she'd die of curiosity if they kept quiet all semester.

She spat toothpaste foam into the sink. In the front room, Ali Bakhtiar yelled, "Reload and spin, fool, before he gets you!" The battleball game was in the last five minutes, then. Jennifer made a sour face. If Ali thought battleball more interesting than the Foitani, that was his problem.

Even when she got into bed, the big blue aliens would not leave her mind. Thegun Thegun Nug, Aissur Aissur Rus, and—what was the third one's name? Dargnil Dargnil Lin, that was it. She wondered if they were males or females. She thought of them as males, but that was only because they were large and had deep voices: anthropocentric thinking, the worst mistake a trader could make.

But she wasn't a trader any more. She was doing what she'd trained to do—what she'd always wanted to do, she told herself firmly.

Ali Bakhtiar came to bed a few minutes later. Her back was to him. She breathed deeply and steadily. He stroked her hair and slid his hand down to the curve of her hip. Most of the time, she enjoyed making love with him. Tonight, though, she was still annoyed at him for not caring more about the Foitani. She kept on pretending to be asleep. If Bakhtiar tightened that hand so she'd have to notice it, he'd get all the fight he wanted and then some.

He didn't. He took it away, muttered something grumpy under his breath that she didn't quite catch—*just as well, too*, she thought—and rolled onto his stomach. Moments later, he was snoring. As if to punish herself for feigning sleep, Jennifer lay awake for the next hour and a half.

The Foitani pulled their weight in the Middle English class. However they did it, they stayed up with the reading. They were certainly more familiar with human customs than Jennifer was with theirs; they asked good, sensible questions and seldom needed anything explained more than once.

Little by little, they started becoming individuals to Jennifer. Thegun Thegun Nug seemed to be senior to the other two; they deferred to him and let him speak first. Aissur Aissur Rus thought for himself. His interpretations of what he'd read were most apt to be off-base, but also most apt to be interesting and original. Dargnil Dargnil Lin, by contrast, was conservative: steady, sound, not likely to go far from the beaten path but perfectly reliable on it. The studies all three of them turned in were among the better ones she got from the class. No doubt they'd linked their translator programs with the printer, but humans whose first language wasn't Spanglish did that, too.

Jennifer spent the first couple of weeks in the course on stories that dealt with alien contact. Experience had taught her that students enjoyed the theme, enjoyed seeing how wildly wrong most ancient speculation was. That some writers came within shouting distance of what the future really looked like also piqued their interest.

"Remember, science fiction wasn't supposed to be prophesy," she said. "Trying to foretell—to guess—the future is a much older set of thought processes. Science fiction was different. Science fiction was a literature of extrapolation, of taking something—some social trend, some new technology, even some ideology—that existed in the writer's time and pushing it farther and harder than it had yet gone, to see what the world would look like then.

"Of course, a lot of it became trivial even within a few years after it was written. Social trends, especially, changed so fast that they rarely lasted long enough to be carried to the extremes writers imagined. As humans have always been, in the twentieth century they were sometimes radical, sometimes reactionary, sometimes sexually permissive, sometimes repressive. They'd go through two or three of these cycles in a person's lifetime, as we do today.

"Some writers, though, chose harder questions to ask: how humanity would fit into a community of intelligent beings, some quite different from us; how we should treat each other under changed circumstances; what the relationship between government and individual should be. That's why writers like Anderson, Brin, and Heinlein can still make us think today, even though the worlds they imagined didn't come true."

Somebody stuck up a hand. "Why are the videos from that time at an intellectual level so much lower than the books?"

"That's a good question," Jennifer said approvingly. "The answer has to do with the economics of book and video distribution back then. Books made money with much smaller audiences than videos did, so they could target small segments—in the case of science fiction, generally the better-educated section—of the population, and present sophisticated ideas to them. Videos needed mass appeal. They borrowed the exotic settings and adventure of written science fiction, but seldom attempted to deal with serious issues."

"Another question, please, honored professor?"

"Yes, go ahead, Aissur Aissur Rus." Jennifer was always curious to hear what the Foitani would ask. Aissur Aissur Rus had a special knack for coming up with interesting questions.

He did not disappoint her now. "Honored professor, I taste the intellectual quality of the authors you mention, which is indeed praiseworthy. Yet others—Sturgeon, Le Guin—seem to write more pleasingly. Which carries the greater weight?" His bearlike ears twitched. Jennifer thought that meant he was pleased with himself.

"Before I answer, Aissur Aissur Rus, may I ask a question in return?" Jennifer said. He waved a hand back and forth in front of his face. She knew that meant yes. She went on, "How have you learned Middle English well enough to have a feel for its style?" Not many human undergrads, even with computer aids, developed that kind of sensitivity to a language not their own.

Aissur Aissur Rus said, "To prepare us for this class, honored professor, our people used a Middle English/Spanglish program, a Spanglish/Raptic program—Rapti, you should know, is a world that once lay at the edge of Foitani space—and finally one from Raptic into our own tongue. Eventually our machines acquired sufficient vocabulary and context cues to abandon the two intermediate programs; they began to read directly from Middle English into our speech. From that point, it was not hard for us to learn Middle English directly."

"I see," Jennifer said slowly. And indeed she did see how, but not why. What good was ancient science fiction to the Foitani? She almost asked straight out. Before she did, though, she felt she had to deal with Aissur Aissur Rus's question. "In their own time, the writers you named—and some others like them—were often very highly esteemed indeed, exactly because they were such fine stylists. And to say they did not address serious issues is not true, either. But they are less often read now because their concerns are not as relevant to us today as those of other authors. Do you see?"

"Yes, I taste the distinction you are cooking, but I am not sure it is valid," Aissur Aissur Rus said. "Again I ask, which carries the greater weight, abstract artistic excellence or utility?"

"That is a question humans have asked for as long as they have examined their own art," Jennifer said with a smile. "No one has ever come up with a definitive answer."

"Questions have answers," Dargnil Dargnil Lin said reprovingly.

"That may be so, but often only on a case-by-case basis—and with something as subjective as artistic elegance, one man's answer is another man's error," Jennifer said.

"Before the Suicide Wars, the Great Ones would have known." Even through the translator's flat tones, Dargnil Dargnil Lin sounded sure of that.

"If the Great Ones were as great as that, why did they fight the Suicide Wars?" Aissur Aissur Rus asked. Jennifer did not think the remark had been meant for the class to hear, but the translator sent it forth all the same.

Thegun Thegun Nug said, "Enough. We interrupt the discourse of the honored professor." All three Foitani visibly composed themselves to listen. Jennifer found she had no choice but to go on with her lecture. *One day*, she told herself, *I will ask my questions of them*. It would not be that day, though.

"It's so frustrating," she said to Ali Bakhtiar when she got home from her last class. "They're good in class. They're *very* good. But *what are they doing there*?"

"I haven't the faintest idea," Bakhtiar answered, as he had every time she raised the issue. Now his patience showed signs of wearing thin. "I wouldn't lose sleep over it, either. If they want to spend good money to hear you talk about your musty old books, that's their problem, not yours."

"Musty old books? Problem?" Jennifer didn't know where to start being indignant at all that.

"You look silly standing there with your mouth hanging open," Bakhtiar said.

If she'd had her stunner on her belt, she would have given him a dose big enough to keep him out the rest of the night—and maybe for the week after that. Her mouth *was* open, she realized. She shut it. She wasn't indignant any more; she was furious. Usually anger made her come to pieces. Now she knew what she had to do. When she spoke again, her voice was even tinier than usual. "I'll start looking for my own apartment."

Ali Bakhtiar stared at her. "Don't do that!" he said in alarm. She watched his face, the way his eyes moved up and down her. The alarm wasn't for her, at least not the part of her that dwelt behind her eyes. It was concern that he wouldn't be able to sleep with her any more. As if to prove it, he reached out to take her in his arms.

She took one step back, then another. He followed. "You leave me be," she said. She hated her voice for quavering. Her eyes filled with angry tears. She hated them even more.

"You're just upset," Bakhtiar said smoothly. "If it'll make you feel better, I'll apologize. Come here, Jennifer; it's all right." He put his hands on her shoulders.

A moment later he reeled away, right hand clutching left wrist. Jennifer hoped she hadn't broken it. She'd never needed unarmed combat on any of the worlds she'd visited, but all traders learned it, to protect themselves from aliens and humans both. Now she was using it for the first time, not a five-minute walk from the peaceful campus where she'd wanted to spend her days in quiet research. She'd already learned life didn't always work out the way one thought it would.

She walked past Ali Bakhtiar to the phone. He flinched back from her as if she'd suddenly sprouted fangs and talons; his eyes said he'd never seen her before. Maybe he hadn't, not really— maybe all he'd paid attention to was the small, shapely body, the blond hair that fell to the small of her back, the blue eyes and clear features. She started getting angry all over again.

She keyed the number of a friend, a colleague in the dead languages department a few years older than she. "Ella? It's Jennifer. Is there any chance I could sleep on your couch for a few days? I've had a fight with my boyfriend and I'll be moving out of here as soon as I can."

"I don't see any reason why not," Ella Metchnikova answered, her almost baritone contralto booming in Jennifer's ear. "Come on over."

"Thank you, Ella dear. I will." Jennifer hung up, threw some books, disks, and papers into an attaché case, then tossed the case, a change of clothes, and her toothbrush into a blue plastic shopping bag. She paused at the door to look back at Ali Bakhtiar. "I'll be out of here just as quick as I can get a place. If you mess with my things, even a little bit, I won't hit you in the wrist next time. I promise you that."

Then she had an afterthought. She went past Bakhtiar again, this time into the bedroom. It spoiled her grand exit, but she did not care for melodrama in her own life anyhow. She found her stunner and dropped it into the bag, too. One more trip by her lover—her former lover, she amended to herself—and she was gone.

Ella Metchnikova lived only a few blocks away. Her apartment building—and her apartment—were nearly clones of the one in which Jennifer had lived; the same construction company must have put up both of them.

Ella was large and blustery. She hugged Jennifer when she came in, kissing her on each cheek. "You have my sympathy, if you want it," she said. "More likely you think you're well rid of him, and if you think that, you're probably right. Let me give you something more practical instead." She took a glass from the refrigerator and handed it to Jennifer.

Jennifer sipped cautiously. Ella had handed her glasses before. Sometimes they were tasty, sometimes anything but—one of Ella's hobbies were reconstructing drinks nobody had drunk for hundreds of years. There were often good reasons why nobody had drunk them for hundreds of years.

This one wasn't bad—smooth, a little sweet, not alcoholic enough to scorch her throat or make her eyes water. As she was supposed to, she asked, "What's it called?"

"A Harvey Wallbanger," Ella said. "Orange juice, ethanol, and a liqueur called Galliano that I just found a bottle of last week. I thought it was long since extinct, but somebody still makes it. Can't imagine why. It's death by itself—think of high-proof sugar syrup with yellow food coloring. But it is good for something, you see."

"Yes, so it is." Jennifer took a larger sip, then another one. Warmth spread from her stomach. "Thanks for taking me in on short notice."

"On no notice, you mean." Ella laughed. A moment later, the laugh got louder. "I didn't know anybody on this planet could blush."

Jennifer's cheeks only grew hotter. "I can't help it if I'm fair."

"I know you can't. I can't help laughing about it, either. Have you had dinner?"

Jennifer let Ella mother her. It took her mind off the sudden crash of her relationship with Bakhtiar and off the hideous nuisance of moving—although her trader training would come in handy there, for she was used to packing quickly and thoroughly. Her trader training kept coming in handy all sorts of ways, something she'd certainly not expected when she signed up as an apprentice. All she'd wanted was something out of the ordinary on her resumé.

After dinner, she accessed the realty data net to see what sort of apartment she could find. The results of the search annoyed her: with the semester well begun, the units nearest the campus were full up. "Nothing closer than three kilometers," she complained.

"Maybe I ought to take that one," Ella said, looking over her shoulder. "You could have this place. I need the exercise more than you do." She sighed. "No, it wouldn't do. Knowing me, I'd take the shuttle in instead of walking. Oh, well."

Still grumbling, Jennifer electronically arranged to move into the nearest apartment she'd found, though she put in a withdrawal option in case something closer to the university opened up before she took possession of the new place. She'd enjoyed walking to work. She could afford the penalty she'd have to pay if she used the option.

"When does it come vacant, three days from now?" Ella asked.

"That's right. I hope I won't be too much a bother till then," Jennifer said. She'd already started thinking about what she could give Ella to repay her kindness.

"Tonight's not a problem, and neither is tomorrow. But the

day, or rather the night after that—well, I'd invited Xavier over, and . . . you know what I mean," Ella said.

"Oh, yes," Jennifer said quickly. Ella and Xavier had been lovers for a long time. Jennifer didn't know how long, but it was longer than she'd been on Saugus. "I'll find someplace else to be, even if I have to sleep in the office that one night. It has a couch, of sorts, that wouldn't be too bad, really. And I'll be going into the new place the next day, so I won't cramp you any more after that."

"You're sweet, Jennifer. Sometimes I think you're too sweet for your own good. That's why you surprised me when you said you were breaking up with Ali. What touched that off, if you don't mind my asking?"

Jennifer started to explain about the Foitani. Before she'd gone three sentences, she ran into the same wall of incomprehension with Ella that had driven her out of the arms of Ali Bakhtiar. Even though humans had spread over several thousand light-years, most of them, if they traveled at all, went from one human-settled planet to another and had only sketchy dealings—if any—with the many other species who shared the galaxy with them. Ella knew a lot more about ancient distilling techniques than she did about the Foitani.

When Jennifer was done, her friend shrugged and said, "It doesn't seem like much of a reason to me, but you know best how *you* feel. And it sounds like something else would have happened if this hadn't."

"I suppose so," Jennifer said. "I guess I knew I was more or less marking time with Ali." She ruefully shook her head. "I hadn't expected to get my nose rubbed in it this way, though."

"You never do," Ella said. "I remember this fellow I was seeing about ten years ago . . ." The tale that followed went on for some time and was more lurid than the fiction Jennifer was used to reading.

When she tried to sleep in Ella's front room, Jennifer tossed and turned. She was still upset. Moreover, the couch was harder and narrower than her big bed. The room wasn't as dark as her bedroom, and the noises of ground traffic outside were louder. Someone in an apartment across the courtyard had a clock that chimed the hours. She listened to it announce midnight, then, a year or so later, one o'clock. Finally she slept.

Ella's alarm screamed like a banshee—worse than an Atheter, Jennifer thought fuzzily as her panic at the hideous noise faded and she realized what it was. Ella was either a serious sleeper or selectively deaf, because the clock squalled on and on until at last she yelled for it to shut up.

Jennifer winced at her red-tracked eyes after she got out of the shower. She felt as if she had a hangover, without even the remembered pleasure of getting drunk the night before. Moving as if underwater, she dressed in her one clean outfit—making a mental note to wash the shirt and skirt she'd worn yesterday— dove into a cup of coffee, gulped down a fruit bar, and headed for the university.

The caffeine and the thought of the material she was going to present made her more lively by the time her Middle English class rolled around. She was beginning a new unit today, which also pleased her; she felt as if she was turning over a whole new leaf in her life. That absurd jingle left her chuckling to herself as she strode into the lecture hall.

The chuckles disappeared before she reached the podium. She fixed the class with as steely a gaze as she could muster— not very steely, she knew down deep, but she did her best. In what she hoped was a stern voice, she demanded, "Who hasn't kept up with the reading for today?"

A few luckless souls, lazy and honest at the same time, raised their hands. "You'll have to do better than that," she told them. "You knew when you enrolled—you certainly knew when you saw the syllabus—your work load would be heavy here. You have to stay with the lectures if you expect to get full benefit from the course."

Thegun Thegun Nug and the other two Foitani had kept their big, thick-fingered hands down. Jennifer was sure it wasn't because they didn't want to admit they'd fallen behind. She almost used them as an example, to say to the rest of the class, *See, if they can keep up, you ought to be able to.* Only the thought that they might not want to be singled out held her back.

She said, "We're not going to look at imaginary aliens for a while. Instead, we'll consider science fiction's examination of a problem that was pressing for several generations: the risk that mankind would annihilate itself over local disputes on Earth before it acquired the technology to get off the planet."

All three Foitani sat straighter in their slight, too-small chairs. She thought of the history of their race and shivered a little: a species didn't have to be planet-bound to do a pretty fair job of annihilating itself.

"For those of you who did read the lesson," she went on, "we'll discuss *A Canticle for Leibowitz* first. Ever since it was written, many people have named it the best science fiction novel of all time. The section I want to examine now is the middle one, the one called 'Fiat Lux.' "

"What is the meaning of this heading?" Aissur Aissur Rus asked. "Our translator program broke down on it, making obscure references to ancient wheeled conveyances and soaps. This does not seem appropriate to the content of the book."

"It sure doesn't." Jennifer wondered how any program could come up with anything so farfetched. "Maybe the problem is that the heading isn't in Middle English but rather Latin, a still older human speech. 'Fiat Lux' means 'let there be light.' "

"Ah." That wasn't Aissur Aissur Rus; it was a human student. Several others also made notes. Jennifer silently sighed. *Lazy*, she thought. They should have had no trouble accessing the meaning of the phrase. Not only was Latin still used liturgically, it was an important ancestral tongue to Spanglish.

" 'Fiat Lux' is particularly interesting for its blend of historical analogy and extrapolation," she said. "The role of the church in the piece is based on what the church actually did after the collapse of the Roman civilization earlier in Earth's history; the Romans, by the way, were the people who used Latin.

"But the civilization which Miller envisioned collapsing after nuclear war was his own, which had already become highly dependent on technology. As civilization restored itself, as it began to discover once more how the world worked, it also began to discover that it was in fact rediscovering, was only finding out what its ancestors had already known. Miller effectively paints into his book the intellectual turmoil this realization would create—"

Jennifer stopped there. She hadn't intended to, but one glance at the Foitani would have distracted anybody. They weren't making a racket, they weren't even jumping up and down, but they had come to full alert for the first time in her presence. When a large creature—three large creatures—with spiky ears and good teeth comes to full alert in a human's presence, the human comes alert, too. Three million years of biological programming was screaming *Wolves!* in her ears.

She needed only a moment to collect herself. Thanks to her time as a trader, she knew how to break free from the prejudice of shape. A small part of her mind noted that she was thanking her time as a trader rather often these days. That annoyed her, all the more so as she'd wished she was on a nice, quiet university campus while it was going on.

She said, "Is there a question?" Her voice was still light, but steady enough.

She'd expected the Foitani to be bursting with questions. They surprised her. They started when she spoke to them, then looked at each other, as if she'd caught them picking their noses—if doing that was bad Foitani manners.

Finally Thegun Thegun Nug said, "No, no questions at this time, honored professor. We were merely interested in the analogies between the world this author draws and the experiences of our own people."

"Very well, I'll go on," Jennifer said. The translator's tone was as bland as ever, but she knew she'd heard a lie just the same—or at least, not all of the truth. Something more than interest in analogies had stirred up the Foitani there. But if they didn't care to talk about it with a human, what could she do?

Distractedly, she got through the rest of the day's presentation. The discussion was less lively than she'd hoped, not least because the Foitani had stopped taking part. They paid close attention to everything she and the humans students said, though: their ears kept twitching. Maybe that was a reaction they couldn't control.

When Jennifer got back to Ella's apartment, she wanted to talk about the aliens' extraordinary reaction to *A Canticle for Leibowitz*. Ella didn't want to listen. Ella was planning tomorrow's extravaganza with Xavier and wanted to talk about that. Jennifer, who was sick of men in general and Ali Bakhtiar in particular, made a poor audience.

After she and her friend discovered they weren't going to communicate that evening no matter how hard they tried, Jennifer began playing with the computer and de Camp's colons again. She wondered if some of the works where commas appeared instead were the work of overzealous copy editors. Off-hand, she couldn't think of a single twentieth-century author who had a good word to say for copy editors.

The next day in class, she talked more about *A Canticle for Leibowitz*, comparing it to other works that looked at the aftermath of atomic war: *Davy, The Postman, Star Man's Son*. "This subgenre of science fiction was played out by the end of the twentieth century," she said. "By then it had become plain that such a conflict would not leave the survivors, if there were survivors, in any condition to recover as quickly as earlier writers had imagined."

Again, the Foitani stirred. Again, Jennifer thought they would say what was in their minds. Again, they did not. She almost asked them straight out. Unfortunately, that seemed to lie in the unpleasant middle ground between foolhardy and suicidal. The Foitani had been willing, even eager to talk before. Why not now, with a topic that really hit them where they lived? Jennifer had no answers. Grumbling to herself, she finished her presentation and stalked out of the lecture hall.

She went through her other two classes on automatic pilot. Still on automatic pilot, she started back toward her own apartment. After a couple of hundred meters, she muttered, "Idiot!" under her breath and turned toward Ella's building. After another fifty meters, she said, "Idiot!" again, much louder this time. A student close enough to hear gave her a curious look. Her cheeks flamed. That seemed only to interest the student more—he was a young man. Jennifer spun away and tramped with grimly determined stride back to her office.

It wasn't the ideal place to spend a night. The "couch of sorts" was considerably more disreputable—and shorter—than the one in Ella's apartment. But the rest room was only a couple of doors down the hall. For one night, it would do. *Tomorrow*, Jennifer thought, *I'll be in my own new apartment*. That made the idea of one uncomfortable evening—even the thought of a dinner at the university cafeteria—bearable.

The dinner turned out to be bearable, too. Jennifer's best guess was that the university food service would soon fire whoever was responsible for cooking something edible. She took her Coke—what else, she said to herself, would a professor of

Middle English drink?—out into the evening twilight and walked across campus slurping on it.

Once back in her office, she dutifully set to work. No one yet had come up with a computer program for grading essays. She scribbled marginal comments in red ink. At least Spanglish orthography corresponded to sound; she didn't have to deal with the erratic spelling that had plagued Ancient and Middle English.

Twilight faded to darkness around her. At just after 2100, a security guard phoned. "Sorry, Professor Logan," he said when he saw her face. "Just checking—the IR telltale showed somebody was in there. As long as it's you, there's no problem."

"I'm so glad," she said, but he had already switched off.

She tried to recover her train of thought. This student actually showed some grasp of how Piper had put together his future history, and she wanted to make sure she cleared up the gaps in the girl's understanding.

Just when she had reimmersed herself in the essay, the phone chimed again. This time, it was Ali Bakhtiar. "What do you want?" Jennifer said coldly.

Bakhtiar flushed. "I want to apologize again," he said. "I've just met your Foitani, and they're at least as impressive as you said they were. At least." He looked more than a little shaken. He didn't look shaken very often.

"Wait a minute. You *met* them? How did you meet them?"

"They came over here looking for you. They said they wanted to talk with you about the class. They didn't seem much interested in taking no for an answer, if you know what I mean. Finally I convinced them you'd moved out. I sent them on to your friend with the deep voice—Ellen Metchnikova, is that right?"

"Ella," Jennifer corrected absently. "Oh, God. She's not going to be very happy to see them. She has company tonight."

"I gathered that," Bakhtiar said. "I called her place to warn you they were coming, and she didn't much want to talk. She kept the vision blank, too. She snapped out where you were and switched off. So now you know."

"Oh, God," Jennifer said again. Ella would be a long time forgiving her for this, if she ever did. "Thanks, Ali, I guess. Better to know they're on the way."

"Listen, is there any way you could forget about moving out and come back here?" Bakhtiar said. "I really am sorry about what I said before, and I—"

"No, Ali," Jennifer said firmly. She'd already done all the thinking she needed to do about that one. "I'm sorry, too, but I don't think we were going anywhere anyhow. Just as well to break it off now. I hope we can still be friends, but that's it."

Bakhtiar scowled. "I hate when women say that. Anyway, though, I thought you ought to know about these creatures of yours. Good luck with them."

"They're not my creatures," Jennifer said, but Bakhtiar, like the security guard, didn't wait on the line to give her the last word. Shaking her head, she stared down at the essay on Piper. "Where was I?"

Just when she thought she remembered, the phone chimed again. She muttered something under her breath and jabbed a thumb at the ACCEPT button. The vision screen did not light. *Ella,* she thought, and Ella it was. "Jennifer, three blue behemoths are on their way to visit you."

"Thanks, Ella. Ali just phoned to warn me he'd sent them to your place. I'm sorry about that," Jennifer added.

"You ought to be," Ella snapped. "I don't like being interrupted when I'm right on the edge, and I especially don't like being interrupted twice."

"Oh, dear." Jennifer swallowed a giggle.

"If you weren't my friend . . . Well, these Foi-whatevers look big enough to have you for breakfast instead of talking, if that's what they want. Maybe you should keep your door locked after all."

"Don't be silly, Ella. Go back to Xavier, and I hope nobody interrupts you any more."

"Better not," Ella said darkly. "Good-bye." As it was the first one she'd got in three calls, Jennifer cherished that good-bye. She went back to work on the essay, hoping to finish grading it before the Foitani arrived.

A few minutes later, the elevator down the hall beeped. *The Foitani,* Jennifer thought. She put aside the paper; maybe it was never going to get finished. As it went back onto the pile, her brows came together. To get into the building this late, you were supposed to have an authorization card for the elevator to read.

Then she shrugged. Maybe the Foitani had ridden up with someone who had a card. They knew her name, after all; a little explaining would be all they'd need.

Someone knocked on the door—knocked so high up on the door that it could only have been a battleball centerliner or a Foitan. She hadn't heard footsteps in the hall, but then the Foitani didn't wear shoes. They were very smooth and quiet for beings so large, as if they were closer to their hunting ancestors than humans were.

Jennifer opened the door and looked up and up. Thegun Thegun Nug towered over her; behind him stood the other two Foitani. Close up, they really were intimidating. Without intending to, she took half a step back before she said, "Hello. What can I do for you this evening?"

"You can come with us," Thegun Thegun Nug said.

The flat tone of his translator made Jennifer unsure just how he meant that. "I'd sooner talk here," she answered.

"It was not a conditional request," Thegun Thegun Nug said. Only then did she notice he held something in his left hand; anthropocentrism made her automatically look toward the right first.

The something sparked. That was all Jennifer remembered for a long time.

When she woke up, she was on a starship. The realization filtered in little by little, with her returning consciousness. Perhaps it took longer than it should have, for she had a headache like a thousand years of hangovers boiled down into a liter. Her trading stunner would quietly put a person out for an hour or two and leave her feeling fine when she woke up. Whatever the Foitani used didn't work that way. Oh my, no. The first time she tried to sit up, her head felt as if it would fall off. She rather wished it would, so she could forget it for a while.

After a bit, she began to notice things other than her pounding skull. The gravity was a good deal higher than Saugus's comfortable .85. It wasn't a planet's g-field, either. She didn't know how she knew the difference—no star traveler had ever succeeded in putting it into words—but she knew. The air was more than conditioned; it had the perfect flatness a good recycling plant gives.

Everything pointed to its being a Foitani ship, too. The chamber that held her was bigger and had a higher ceiling than humans were likely to build. Even the plain, foam pad on which she lay was outsized. The light from the ceiling panel had an oranger cast than humans would have used.

She looked around; she had to close her eyes several times at the pain that turning her head cost her. But for the bare mattress, the only things in the chamber with her were three plastic trash bags. She crawled over to them, moving slowly and carefully because of both the higher gravity and her headache. The trash bags held everything she'd had at her office, from her toothbrush to her computer to the complete contents of her desk, right down to paper clips and small change.

With a gasp of delight, she found her stunner. The delight quickly disappeared. Given that she was on a Foitani ship which she had no idea how to fly, how much good was the stunner likely to do her? She would have traded it in an instant for a year's supply of tampons. Since no one appeared with the trade offer, she clipped the stunner onto her belt.

Then she looked around for a place to relieve herself. Somehow, no one in her Middle English novels ever worried much about that. Neither had she, until she went on her first trading run. Squatting in the bushes brought her down to basic reality in a hurry.

She picked the corner farthest away from the foam-rubber mat. If the Foitani didn't come in and give her somewhere better to go before she had to empty her bladder, they could clean up after her themselves.

She was uncomfortable but not yet urgent when a door appeared in the far wall of her chamber: one second it wasn't there, the next second it was. Thegun Thegun Nug stepped inside. Of itself, her hand reached for her stunner. "That will do you no good," the Foitan said.

Suddenly she wasn't so sure. Maybe she couldn't fly this ship herself, but if she knocked Thegun Thegun Nug out and threatened to start carving him into strips a centimeter wide, his henchbeings might be persuaded to turn around and take her back to Saugus. Since that was the best notion she had, she pressed the trigger button.

Thegun Thegun Nug bared his teeth, but uncooperatively refused to fall over in a large, blue heap. "I said that would do you no good," he told her. "Your weapon makes me itch, but it does not make me sleep. Foitani stunners use a different ray."

Jennifer's gonging head gave anguished testimony to the truth of that. Back to her next priority, then. "Take me to whatever you people use for a toilet."

Thegun Thegun Nug took her. He even walked out of the room and left her alone. "My folk do not require privacy for this function, but we have learned humans prefer it." The door in the wall did not disappear, though.

"Thank you so much," Jennifer said, acid in her voice. "Why couldn't you have left me with my privacy back on Saugus, instead of kidnapping me?"

Her sarcasm rolled off Thegun Thegun Nug's blue skin. Through the opening in the wall, he answered, "You are welcome. And you would not have come with us of your own free will from the world you call Saugus; you were content there. But we have need of you, have need of your knowledge. Thus we took you."

"Thanks a lot," Jennifer muttered. The sanitary arrangements were simple enough: a couple of round holes in the floor, each close to half a meter wide. She squatted over one of them. When she was done, she called Thegun Thegun Nug, "Do you have anything I can use to wipe myself clean? Something soft and absorbent, I hope."

"I will see," the Foitan answered after a moment. "My species' orifices do not have this difficulty." Now the doorway vanished. The Foitan stayed away for a quarter of an hour. When he returned, he brought a length of gauzy cloth. "This is from our first-aid kit. Use it sparingly. It is all we can afford to give you."

"How long will the flight be?" she asked. Thegun Thegun Nug did not answer. She tried another string of questions. "What do you mean, you have need of my knowledge? How do you know what I know? And what kind of good is the knowledge of a professor of Middle English to you, anyhow?"

Thegun Thegun Nug chose to respond to one of those questions. "You were recommended to us by another human."

That only created more confusion for Jennifer. "I was? By whom?"

"By one with whom we have worked. He came across a situation beyond his expertise, and suggested you were the one to employ. From all we have seen of you, the probability that he is correct seems, if not high, then at least significant. He will also give you such aid as he may: he is still within Odern space."

"Odern?" The translator had left the word unchanged.

"Odern is my planet," Thegun Thegun Nug said. "It is one of the 127 worlds within our former sphere that still support Foitani life, one of the nineteen where starflight has been rediscovered. Before the Suicide Wars," he added, "we had settled on several thousand worlds; the precise number is still a matter of dispute among our scholars."

Jennifer shivered. She tried to imagine how humanity would war with ninety-five percent of its planets swept clean of life. She also wondered what the Foitani had found important enough to fight about on such an enormous scale. Humans had battled over religion with similar ferocity, but the rise of technology had weakened religion's hold on mankind. Maybe the Foitani had kept their fanaticism after they reached the stars.

Thegun Thegun Nug said, "Analysis of our rations has shown that you may safely eat them. You need have no concern on that score."

"How nice." Jennifer set hands on hips, took a deep breath. "You haven't given me a single reason why I should have the least bit of interest in doing anything for you. And I tell you this: kidnapping me like this has given me an awfully big reason not to."

"You have been on our payroll since the day we enrolled in your class, honored professor," Thegun Thegun Nug said. "We will pay standard journeyman merchant's wages, either in your currency or trade goods—your choice."

"I wasn't talking about money," Jennifer said. "And you have gall, too, putting me on your payroll for something I have less than no interest in doing."

For the first time outside the lecture hall, she succeeded in impressing the Foitan. "Money is not a sufficient inducement?" he said slowly. "I had been given to understand—and nothing I observed on Saugus diminished my understanding—that humans are a mercenary species, willing even, at times, to take arms against their own race or kin-group for the sake of profit."

"Some humans are. This human isn't. Damn you!" Jennifer heard her voice breaking, but could not do anything about it. "I was doing what I wanted to do, at last, after years of not being able to. What right do you have to take me away from that?"

"The right of species self-interest," Thegun Thegun Nug said, "which to us is paramount. I might also point out that, at need, physical coercion is available to force you to our will."

Jennifer's stomach turned to a small, chilly lump of ice. She felt her knees wobble. She was sure, though, that the more weakness she revealed to this inexorable alien, the worse off she would be. She looked up into the Foitan's round, black eyes. "How well do you think I'd do for you if you tortured me into submitting?"

"Less well than if you cooperate voluntarily, I admit. Torture, certainly, would be a last resort. I am, however, perfectly prepared to take away from you all your possessions and leave you alone in your chamber until ennui induces you to evince a more constructive attitude. My race has been waiting for twenty-eight thousand years. A fraction of another matters little to us."

She had no doubt Thegun Thegun Nug meant exactly what he said. Being bored into cooperation was attractive only in comparison to being tortured. The worst of it was, the trader part of her wanted to go along with the Foitan. *No, the traitor part*, she thought. But how many merchants had won the chance to trade with the Foitani? If she looked at it the right way—*the wrong way*, the professorial part of her insisted—that was what she'd be going, trading her knowledge for their goods, if she *did* know what the aliens thought she knew. If she couldn't skin them on that deal, she didn't deserve to be a journeyman.

"All right," she said. "If you think I'm worth risking an interstellar war to get, I'll do what I can for you—provided you let me go after I'm done."

"Certainly," Thegun Thegun Nug said at once. "As for risking war with humans, I will only say it is highly unsafe for ships flown by other species to enter Foitani space unescorted. It is not altogether safe for our own ships to fly. Many weapons from the Suicide Wars are in free orbit throughout our former domain, and hard vacuum is an excellent preservative."

"Wonderful," Jennifer muttered. Now all she had to do was worry about hitting a mine that had been floating free since the days when Cro-Magnon man chased woolly mammoths between glaciers back on Earth.

"It is not wonderful, but it is a fact," Thegun Thegun Nug said; none of the three Foitani had much of a sense of humor. "Our detectors should suffice to get us back to Odern, however."

"They'd better," Jennifer said. "If we blow up, I'll never forgive you."

Thegun Thegun Nug started to answer, then stopped and seemed to think better of it. At last he said, "Come. I will return you to your chamber."

"What happens the next time I need to relieve myself?"

"One of us will escort you here. Were our situations reversed, would you trust me unescorted on a human ship?"

Jennifer wanted to say she wouldn't trust the Foitan no matter what. That did not seem politic at the moment, regardless of how true it was. Without a word, she followed Thegun Thegun Nug out of the toilet chamber and back to her own. She thought hard about annoying her captors with toilet calls at every hour of the day and night. With some species, she might have tried it. Her best guess, though, was that the Foitani would simply stop coming after a while, leaving her to foul her chamber. She decided not to risk it.

Aissur Aissur Rus brought her a plastic pouch of food a couple of hours later. She looked at it without enthusiasm. It resembled nothing so much as dry dog food. "This will nourish you, and should cause no allergic responses," the Foitan said.

Of the three aliens, Jennifer thought Aissur Aissur Rus the most open. Hoping he would answer where Thegun Thegun Nug had not, she asked, "Why did you people grab me? What do you think I can do for you, anyhow?"

"As a matter of fact, taking you was my idea," he said.

She stared at him. After liking him the best, hearing that jolted her. "What is it you want from me?" she repeated.

"One of your human sages once said, 'I am a midget, standing on the shoulders of giants.' When we Foitani of the present days look at the deeds of the Great Ones before the Suicide Wars, we are midgets trying to see up to the shoulders of giants. Perhaps you can help us do that. If not, perhaps you can help us see around the giants' bodies to a new way."

Jennifer frowned. Thegun Thegun Nug had evaded her questions. Aissur Aissur Rus seemed to answer openly enough, but the answer did not mean anything to her. "Go away and let me eat," she told him.

"I did not know you required privacy for that," he said.

"I don't require it, but I'd be grateful. I have a whole lot of things I need to sort out in my mind right now. Please."

Aissur Aissur Rus studied her. The Foitan's eyes had no sclera, no iris, no pupil. They were completely black and completely unreadable. At last, without a word, he made the doorway appear in her wall, walked through it, and made it disappear after him.

She ate. The coarse, crunchy lumps in the plastic pouch tasted like what she thought dog food ought to taste like; they came from something that had been meat quite a while ago. She made herself go on eating till she was full.

When she was done, she looked up at the ceiling and said, "I would like something to drink, please." The Foitani had to have electronic eyes and ears in the chamber.

Sure enough, Aissur Aissur Rus brought her a jug a few minutes later. "This is pure water," he said. "You may drink it safely."

"Thank you," Jennifer said. "May I also have water for washing?"

"Perhaps when you go to the toilets, so it will run down into a disposal hole," Aissur Aissur Rus said. "How often do you usually wash? The human custom is once a day, is it not? I suppose that might be arranged."

"You might have thought beforehand about what I'd need," Jennifer said.

"We are not used to considering the needs of other species. It is not the Foitani way, and does not come easy to us."

"Really? I never would have noticed."

Irony bounced off Aissur Aissur Rus as if he were iron-plated. When he saw Jennifer had no more to say, he turned and left as abruptly as he had before. She drank the jug dry. The water was cold, and had the faint, unpleasant untaste of distilling. It did help to ease her headache.

The jug was made of soft plastic. She flung it against the wall nonetheless. It denied her the good satisfying crash she craved, falling to the ground with a dull thump. She walked over to it and kicked it as hard as she could. That helped, but not enough. She found a pen, drew a couple of black circles on the side of the jug to stand for Foitani eyes. She kicked it again.

"Better," she said.

V

JENNIFER'S COMPUTER INSISTED the flight to Odern lasted twenty-three days and some hours after the aliens snatched her away from Saugus. She thought it felt more like twenty-three years. By the time the ship landed, she wished all the Foitani had succeeded in blasting themselves to hell and gone—and then another twenty kilometers farther, for luck.

For one thing, her period arrived while she was in space, with no possibility of privacy whatever. She didn't much feel like explaining to the aliens how her plumbing worked, but she didn't have much choice, either, not if she wanted to keep her clothes clean. This time, they gave her all the absorbent cloth she wanted without arguing; menstruation, evidently, was one aspect of humanity about which they hadn't informed themselves.

"You wanted me, you got me—just the way I am," she told Thegun Thegun Nug.

"As you say." The Foitan hesitated. "You are certain you are not wounded?"

"I'm certain."

"As you say," Thegun Thegun Nug repeated. Though his translator sounded flat as ever, he did not seem convinced. *Squeamish, are you?* Jennifer wondered. She wished she could break out in green, smelly spots, just to revolt him.

For another, she got thoroughly sick of kibbles and water as a standard diet. "You knew you were going to kidnap me," she snarled at Dargnil Dargnil Lin. "Why didn't you buy—or even steal—something edible for me?"

"These rations are both edible and nutritious," Dargnil

118

Dargnil Lin answered primly. "They are adapted for human needs from our standard spacecraft fare."

"You mean you eat this stuff all the time when you're in space?" Jennifer asked. When Dargnil Dargnil Lin waved a hand in front of his face in the Foitani equivalent of a nod, she said, "That's the best argument against spaceflight I ever heard." Dargnil Dargnil Lin left quite suddenly. *Maybe*, Jennifer thought, *I've managed to annoy him for a change*. She hoped so.

The one good thing about the flight was that it met none of the infernal devices left over from the Suicide Wars. Having to go that far to find something good brought the rest of the journey into perfect perspective for Jennifer.

She did not even know the ship had touched down until all three Foitani appeared outside the disappearing doorway. "Come with us," Thegun Thegun Nug said.

"How can I say no?" Jennifer murmured. Not only did he have his two immense comrades to help enforce his wishes, he was also carrying that vicious Foitani stunner. Getting shot with it was better than dying, but only a little.

The Foitani led her in the direction away from the lavatory. That was her first hint something unusual had happened. Any hope she had of seeing more of the ship quickly went by the wayside; one stretch of blank corridor looked just like another. But the chamber they went into had big space suits in a rack to one side; in a human ship, that would have made it the air lock.

Thegun Thegun Nug touched a panel on the far wall. Another doorway opened. Sunlight poured in. So did fresh air. After more than three weeks of the recycled product, it smelled amazingly sweet. The doorway framed buildings and green hills. *The green hills of Odern*, Jennifer thought. She shook her head. Rhysling would not have approved.

Thegun Thegun Nug turned and went backward out the door. Since he didn't fall, Jennifer figured he was going down a ladder. Aissur Aissur Rus followed him. "Now you," Dargnil Dargnil Lin said. "I will come last." Since he also had a stunner, Jennifer did not argue.

The way down proved not to be a ladder, but rather rungs set into the side of the spacecraft. The rungs were made for people the size of Foitani, which is to say, they were much too far apart for Jennifer. She was enough meters off the concrete below to get nervous at the thought of missing one, which did nothing to improve her grip.

"Hurry, can't you?" Dargnil Dargnil Lin called from the air lock.

"No, I can't," she said through clenched teeth. By the time she reached the ground, sweat was pouring from her armpits, too. This was a lot harder than going down the wall on L'Rau. She wanted to stand where she was and catch her breath, but from the way Dargnil Dargnil Lin was descending behind her, he didn't care whether he landed on her or not. She skipped aside in a hurry.

Once on the ground, Dargnil Dargnil Lin reached up and slapped the side of the ship. The rungs vanished, leaving the side smooth once more. It had to be memory metal, Jennifer thought. On human worlds, the stuff was a toy. The Foitani would appear to have exploited the technology more intensively.

As soon as the rungs disappeared, her captors seemed to forget all about her. They faced the low, rounded, green hills behind the spaceport, bowed themselves almost double. Still bowed, they began a slow, mumbling chant. Their translators picked up some of it for Jennifer. "Great Ones, look kindly on us. We return to Odern our homeworld, faithful always to our mission to regain the glory you once knew. Though earthgrip holds you now, we shall redeem you. May your glory return speedily, Great Ones, speedily. So may it be."

"You worship the Foitani who lived before the Suicide Wars?" Jennifer asked when Thegun Thegun Nug and his companions decided to notice her again.

"Not worship so much as respect," Aissur Aissur Rus said, "and truly the deeds of the Great Ones deserve—no, demand— respect. The more we learn of them, the more we seek to emulate them, to restore our sphere to the grandeur it once knew."

To bring about the conditions that caused the Suicide Wars, whatever those were, Jennifer glossed mentally, with a slight internal chill. Aloud, she said, "Then you don't really believe the Foitani you call the Great Ones live inside those hills?"

"Not now," Aissur Aissur Rus said. Before Jennifer could do more than start to frown, the Foitan went on, "But once they did. Those are not natural hills. Once a city stood there. We've mined it for millennia.''

Jennifer glanced over to the hills once more, this time with fresh eyes. They still looked big enough and permanent enough to have been in place for millions of years. And this was after—how long had Thegun Thegun Nug said?—twenty-eight thousand years, that was it, of neglect and erosion. She tried to imagine the towers that must have existed before earth and plants and time had their way with them, tried and failed.

"Odern was but a minor world in our former sphere," Aissur Aissur Rus added. "Others have remains far grander and far better preserved. But most of those worlds are dead, of course."

"Of course," Jennifer echoed softly. That internal chill grew and spread as she thought about what living as the scattered survivors of the galaxy's biggest slaughterhouse had to be like for the Foitani. No wonder they didn't have much of a sense of humor.

"Now come with us," Thegun Thegun Nug said. "We have reported our success to our kin-group chiefs. They and we will presently acquaint you with the other human in our employ."

The other human—Jennifer had forgotten about him. Of itself, her hand went to the stunner she still wore on her belt. It was no more than an annoyance to the Foitani, but the first time she saw this other human, she intended to flatten him—and to kick him while he was down, too.

The spaceport tarmac was full of big, blocky-looking Foitani ships. A couple of kilometers away, almost hidden by one of them, she saw a vessel that had to be human-built. It was the sort of medium-sized, medium-slow ship a trader who worked solo might fly. "He'll be *so* low, all right, when I'm through with him," she said under her breath.

Like the ships, the spaceport buildings were on what was to her a heroic scale. Foitani who carried things that looked a lot more lethal than stunners stood outside doorways. They touched their left knees to the ground as Thegun Thegun Nug and his comrades went by. Even from that position of respect, their fathomless black eyes bored into Jennifer. She wondered if she really did prefer these dispassionate stares of suspicion to the longing glances human males so often sent her way. Maybe not, she decided.

Inside the administrative center or whatever it was, Foitani tramped purposefully down corridors wide and tall enough to echo. Some were armed like the guards outside; others spoke into computers. They all went about their business with the serious intensity that seemed a hallmark of the species.

Thegun Thegun Nug stood outside a place marked by writing in the angular Foitani script. He spoke to the air. Jennifer did not know what he said; somewhere between the ship and here, he and his fellows had turned off their translators. The air answered, as unintelligibly. Thegun Thegun Nug spoke again. One of those unnerving now-you-see-it, now-you-don't doors opened in front of him.

Jennifer had never been inside a spaceport operations center, but every third holovid drama seemed set in one, so she had some idea what they were like. This was definitely the Foitani version of such a nerve center. Big, blue aliens talked into microphones, listened to oddly shaped headsets that accommodated their erectile ears, and watched holographic displays. For a few seconds, no one paid any attention to Thegun Thegun Nug and his comrades.

Then a Foitan spotted Jennifer. He waved her captors toward what looked like another blank wall. By now she had learned blank walls didn't necessarily stay blank among the Foitani. Sure enough, this one didn't. A door appeared, this time opening onto what had to be the local equivalent of a boss's office. For one thing, it boasted carpeting, the first Jennifer had seen on Odern. For another, the desk behind which a Foitan stood seemed about as long and wide as the flight deck of an ancient aircraft carrier.

"You will pay your respects to Pawasar Pawasar Ras." Thegun Thegun Nug turned his translator back on as soon as the office door disappeared behind his party. He pointed to the Foitan behind the desk.

Jennifer nodded. "Hello, Pawasar Pawasar Ras." *If I had a stepladder, I'd spit in your eye.*

"I greet you, human," Pawasar Pawasar Ras said; Jennifer suspected that meant he was too important an executive to be bothered with remembering her name. "I trust your journey here was of adequate comfort."

You're pretty trusting, then, aren't you? was what she wanted to say. Since the Foitani who had kidnapped her already knew exactly how she felt about that, she kept her mouth shut.

Dargnil Dargnil Lin nudged her. A nudge from a Foitan was almost enough to knock her off her feet. "Answer the honored kin-group leader when he questions you," Dargnil Dargnil Lin said.

"I survived the journey," she said. Let this honcho make what he wanted of that.

Pawasar Pawasar Ras said, "You are doubtless of the opinion that you have seen a sufficiency of our kind." Jennifer's eyes opened wide: this was the first Foitan she'd met who had any of what humans reckoned common sense. Maybe it was rare enough in his species to make possessing it an automatic ticket to an important job like his. He went on, "Accordingly, I will let the human who has been working in cooperation with us explain the predicament he and we have encountered."

He touched something on his desk. A door appeared in a different wall of the office. Jennifer waited grimly. Whoever had set her up for this would have a lot more explaining to do than Pawasar Pawasar Ras thought. He might even find himself in a brand new predicament of his own.

A man dressed in trader coveralls came through the doorway. Jennifer stared. She'd expected to know the fellow who had betrayed her. She'd never expected he'd be someone she liked. "Bernard!" The academic part of her dredged up a stupid Middle English joke. "What's a nice guy like you doing in a place like this?"

Bernard Greenberg looked sheepish, although the top of his head was devoid of wool. "Hello, Jennifer," he said. "I'm sorry. I didn't think they'd just up and grab you."

"Well, they bloody well did," she said, then added bitterly, "Were you so angry at me for going off to the university instead of staying a trader that you decided to get even? This isn't even; this is overkill."

"No, no, no." He plucked at his salt-and-pepper beard in distress. "It's not like that, Jennifer; really it's not. I thought they'd consult you. When they told me they were going to bring you here, I tried as hard as I could to talk them out of it. But their ship had already left for Saugus by then, and even if it hadn't, it's not easy to talk a Foitan out of anything. You may have noticed that.''

"Now that you mention it, yes," she said with a sidelong glance at Thegun Thegun Nug. She studied Bernard Greenberg and decided she'd made a mistake. "I should be the one who says she's sorry, Bernard. It's not your fault—not all your fault, anyway. I just hit out at the first thing I could reach without climbing onto a box." She looked at Thegun Thegun Nug again. His translator was working, but it he caught what she'd meant as well as what she'd said, he gave no sign of it.

Pawasar Pawasar Ras said, "Enough, if you please; this is not an appropriate time or place for social intercourse. Human Bernard, be so good as to define the problem for your colleague here." *He knows* Bernard's *name*, Jennifer thought with what she knew to be a completely irrational stab of jealousy.

"If I could define the problem, honored kin-group leader Pawasar Pawasar Ras, I wouldn't need a colleague," Greenberg answered. Pawasar Pawasar Ras bared his teeth. Jennifer knew that was only a Foitani frown, but it carried more impact than anything a human could do. Greenberg turned back to Jennifer. "You know the Foitani are past-worshipers and scavengers both."

She nodded. "Given what they did to themselves so long ago, it's hardly surprising."

"No, it isn't. The local population on Odern has mined the planet pretty thoroughly, when you consider how much of what used to be here has to have rusted away or whatever over the past umpty-thousand years."

Not enough, Jennifer thought. By the way Greenberg's mouth narrowed and lengthened ever so slightly—it wasn't a smile; it wasn't even close to a smile—Jennifer knew he'd picked up what she was thinking. No nonhuman would have noticed a change in his expression. She said, "I'm still not clear what this has to do with me."

"Scavenging turned into a whole different game for the local Foitani when they reinvented the hyperdrive," Greenberg said. "They had some idea which stars held planets their species had settled once upon a time. When they went out to look at those planets, they found that a lot of them were dead. Some had no Foitani left, some had no life at all—sterile. Fission bombs, diseases, asteroid strikes, poison gas—I don't know what all. The old imperial Foitani—"

"The Great Ones," Pawasar Pawasar Ras corrected.

"The Great Ones, I mean—well, they seem to have had a more advanced technology than we do now. They were great at killing, that's certain. And on a lot of those dead worlds, the toys they left behind survived in much better shape than on a place like Odern, where everything got reused over and over again as the world was sliding into barbarism. Now, on one of the planets that used to be part of the empire, they've come across something they can't handle."

"They said that themselves," Jennifer said. "They didn't explain it, though—they haven't explained much of anything. So what exactly are you talking about?"

"They've found an artifact they cannot try to use and stay sane. If they're within ten or twelve kilometers of it, they can't help trying to use it, either, whatever the hell it is. I've seen dozens of the poor bastards who tried. They aren't pretty. The ones on the fringes of the effect around the thing can fight the compulsion, but if they get too close, they're doomed. Finally they lost enough people to make them fortify the whole area. But they were still curious, so they hired a non-Foitan—me—to see what he could find out."

"And you went crazy, too," Jennifer said, "or you never would have given them my name."

Pawasar Pawasar Ras's eyes swung sharply toward Greenberg when Thegun Thegun Nug's translator turned that into the local language. "Does the other human speak accurately, human Bernard? Has the Great Unknown"—even with the translator, Jennifer could hear the capital letters—"affected your psychological integrity?"

"I do not think so, honored kin group leader Pawasar Pawasar Ras," Greenberg answered. Jennifer had finally managed to get his goat; he gave her a dirty look as he went on, "You may have noticed that humans use irony more than Foitani do."

"This practice of saying one thing while meaning another is rank, manifest foolishness," Pawasar Pawasar Ras said.

"As may be," Greenberg answered mildly; he sounded used to soothing Pawasar Pawasar Ras every so often. He turned back to Jennifer: "I couldn't find anything about this artifact that would make anybody go insane, human or Foitan. If it's not a physical effect, what's left? Best bet, I figured, was something cultural. I've been a trader a long time; I know something about that sort of thing. But you know more. Not only do you have your trader background, you've got a working knowledge of all the hypothetical cases your old-time writers invented. And the more I dealt with this thing, the more hypothetical everything about it looked, if you know what I mean. So I mentioned your name to the Foitani.''

The worst part was, it made sense. Jennifer tried to stay angry, but failed. She let out a long sigh. ''And they took the ball and shot it toward the far goal,'' she said. ''That does seem to be the way they do things.''

''It certainly does.'' Greenberg cocked his head at her. ''Shot the ball toward the far goal? I didn't know you followed battle-ball.''

''An acquired taste. It's wearing off, believe me. Now that I'm here, there isn't any good way back without going along, is there?'' She turned to Pawasar Pawasar Ras. ''All right, where next?''

''To the world Gilver,'' he answered with almost robotic literality. ''This is the world upon which the Great Unknown is situated.''

''Any chance for research first?'' she asked: she *was* an academic before anything else. ''You've been studying your ancestors ever since the, ah, Suicide Wars. Did they leave behind any records that might help you understand this thing?''

''That is an intelligent question.'' Pawasar Pawasar Ras's ears twitched, so he was genuinely pleased. ''We have not found any data related to the world Gilver that pertain to it. Dargnil Dargnil Lin here can assist you in examining our data bases, if you think that would be valuable. He is expert in the ancient archives.''

''I would like to see them, yes,'' Jennifer said. She wondered if Dargnil Dargnil Lin was an exception, or if steady, solid, serious types among the Foitani gravitated toward jobs like archivist as they did with humans.

''See to it, Dargnil Dargnil Lin,'' Pawasar Pawasar Ras said.

''It shall be done, honored kin-group leader,'' Dargnil Dargnil Lin replied.

Striking while the iron was hot and the big boss in a cooperative frame of mind, Jennifer said, "I saw Bernard Greenberg's ship here at this spaceport, honored kin-group leader." If she was going to butter up Pawasar Pawasar Ras, might as well get him good and greasy. "May I stay aboard it? A human ship truly would be a more proper base for me." *And thanks to you, I'll never, ever keep a dog.*

"If the human Bernard does not object, you may do this," Pawasar Pawasar Ras said.

"I don't object," Greenberg said at once.

"Then you may make those arrangements, human," Pawasar Pawasar Ras said to Jennifer—he still didn't have her name. Though Foitani eyes were next to impossible to read, she felt his gaze intensify as he went on, "Do not think this will permit you two humans to plan a joint escape. Aside from the dangers inherent for non-Foitani flying through space once in the Great Ones' sphere, we have our own tracker and explosive device secured in the—the—what is the name of your ship, human Bernard?"

"The *Harold Meeker*, honored kin-group leader," Greenberg said.

"Yes, the *Harold Meeker*. Very well, then, human, ah—"

"Jennifer." *Took him long enough to ask*, Jennifer thought.

"Yes, Jennifer. You may proceed, then, human Jennifer, with your researches for a period not to exceed, ah, twenty Odern days, Dargnil Dargnil Lin to assist you as necessary. Then you and human Bernard shall travel to Gilver to continue in the attempt to analyze the Great Unknown. Thegun Thegun Nug, Aissur Aissur Rus, Dargnil Dargnil Lin, and I shall accompany you there."

Jennifer had expected the other three Foitani to go offworld with her if she left Odern. They were plainly her keepers. But Pawasar Pawasar Ras surprised her by including himself. From what she knew of big-wheel executives, they didn't often inflict themselves on actual research sites. "Why you?" she asked him.

"The Great Unknown is my project," Pawasar Pawasar Ras said, as if that explained everything. To him, it seemed to. To Jennifer, it showed the Foitani definitely were not human—not that she hadn't noticed that already.

* * *

Jennifer finished a salami sandwich. The meat was greasy, the bread bland. The mustard was tangier than she cared for. She washed down the sandwich with a glass of *vin* extremely *ordinaire*. After Foitani rations, it all tasted wonderful. "Thank you, Bernard," she said. "I just may live. I may even decide I want to."

"Sorry there isn't more and better," Greenberg answered. "I've been in Foitani space long enough that I'm starting to run low myself."

"And I'll make you run out all the faster. I'm sorry."

"Don't be. You always did apologize too much; do you know that? If I hadn't opened my big mouth, you'd still be happily back on Saugus. Sharing real food with you is the least I can do to pay you back. We won't starve on what the Foitani eat—"

"However much we wish we would," Jennifer finished for him.

He studied her, one eyebrow raised. After Ali Bakhtiar's virtuoso displays of superciliosity, this was amateur night. The master trader said, "You've changed a bit since we flew together a few years ago. Then you wouldn't have interrupted or made sour jokes."

She shrugged. "I've finished growing up. I find I can manage all right for myself. Now to business, if you don't mind, because I don't want to spend one more second here than I have to. First off, is your ship bugged?"

"I assume so. Pity we don't know some arcane foreign languages we could use to talk privately," Greenberg said. Jennifer gave a rueful nod. Nobody bothered to learn to speak foreign languages these days, not with oral translator programs so widely available. She supposed she could make a stab at speaking Middle English, but the Foitani were more likely to understand her than Greenberg was.

"What is this Great Unknown thing, anyway?" she asked.

"If I knew, I would tell you," he answered. "If I knew, we could go home, come to that. But I don't know. I just hope we'll be able to find out. I keep worrying about what the Foitani may do if we can't—and we may not be able to. Nobody who isn't a Foitan has any real notion of what their ancestors were capable of, back before the Suicide Wars. I told you, though, it's pretty clear they were technologically ahead of where we are now."

"That won't help us understand them." Jennifer slowly shook her head. "They may have been ahead of us technically, but socially! Think of spending however many thousands of years they took to build up their empire, and then to blow it to bits, and themselves with it." She shook her head again, this time in horror. The Foitani seemed to have lived out every human's darkest nightmares.

Greenberg said, "To this day, they don't know why they started to fight. But once they got going, they did a good, thorough job, which is typical of the species. Pawasar Pawasar Ras says they undoubtedly intended to kill themselves off altogether; in a crazy sort of way, he thinks less of them for failing."

"The worst part of it is, now that I've been around Foitani a while, I can almost see the logic in that." Jennifer started to say something more, but found herself yawning instead.

"You may have more privacy aboard one of their ships, or in the spaceport," Greenberg said. "You'll certainly have more room. This isn't a big ship at all."

"If you want me to leave, I will. Otherwise I'd sooner stay here," Jennifer said. "I don't need a whole lot of privacy from you, do I? After all, we've flown together before."

"I'll set you up with a foam pad in the storeroom." Greenberg spread his hands. "I'm sorry, but that's the best I can do if you want any room to yourself."

"Drag the pad in here tonight, would you? After getting lifted the way I did, just being close to somebody human will feel good. I don't think you're going to molest me."

Greenberg grinned lopsidedly. "Tempting as the notion is—no." He rummaged in a compartment, pulled out the promised foam pad. Except for being smaller, it was identical to the one on which she had awakened inside the Foitani ship. Greenberg rummaged some more, let out a grunt of triumph. "I thought I had a spare pillow in here. And here's a blanket, too."

Jennifer took them. "Thanks. But do you know what the biggest pleasure being aboard your ship will be for me?" With waiting for Greenberg to reply, she went on, "Having a toilet that fits my behind."

He laughed at that. "Yes, I've seen what the Foitani use. They'd be especially bad for you, wouldn't they?" He waved toward the refresher cubicle. "Help yourself."

"I don't mind if I do." She hesitated, then asked, "You wouldn't by any chance have tampons or anything like that?"

"I don't know if there are any in the sanitary supplies or not. I never needed to find out until now."

"Well, if you don't, I suppose I can improvise something or other. I did it once; I can do it again."

When she got out, Greenberg went in. She stripped down to her underpants, gave her grimy outfit an unhappy look, and then brightened—the *Harold Meeker* would be able to get clothes *clean*, not just stir the dirt around as she had been doing. She slid under the blanket.

Greenberg surprised her by stooping next to the foam pad and reaching out to touch her shoulder. She stiffened. Was he going to make advances now? She'd made love with him a few times on their first trip together, on the way home from L'Rau. But this was *not* the right time, not for her. She tried to figure out how to tell him that without hurting him or making him angry.

But all he wanted was to apologize again. "Jennifer, I'm so sorry. You should be back on your campus, doing what you wanted to do."

"It can't be helped," she said. Her dreams of elaborate revenge had collapsed when she found out how the Foitani learned of her, and from whom. While they lasted, though, they'd helped sustain her. With nothing in their place, she felt very tired. "Just let me sleep."

"Fair enough." Greenberg rose; Jennifer's eyes closed even as he did so. She heard cloth whisper when he pulled off his coveralls, then the muffled sound his body made pressing against the sofa bed. He must have touched the light switch, for the darkness behind her eyelids got blacker. "Good night," he said.

She thought she answered him, but she was never sure afterward.

Dargnil Dargnil Lin stood in front of a workstation. It had all the elements of the ones with which Jennifer was familiar— holoscreen, mike, keyboard, and printer—yet was in aggregate nothing like them. The Foitani had their own engineering traditions, which owed nothing to those of mankind.

"I suppose you will want to begin with our records pertaining to the Great Unknown," Dargnil Dargnil Lin said.

"I'd rather have more background first, if I could," Jennifer answered. "Can you show me something basic and general about your race as it was before the Suicide Wars?"

"Your time for research is limited." The translator was expressionless as always, but Jennifer thought she heard a sniff in the Foitan's voice. She looked up at him without saying anything. He bared his teeth at her. She kept waiting. At last he said, "Let it be as you wish, then." He spoke to the workstation. The screen lit. Dargnil Dargnil Lin said, "This is a history such as our adolescents use."

"Good." The video had more text to it than a comparable human one would have used, and Jennifer could not read the Foitani written language. But there were still plenty of pictures, and Dargnil Dargnil Lin's translator turned the sound track into Spanglish for her. She watched and listened and spoke low-voiced notes into her computer.

On a historical star atlas, she watched the empire of the Great Ones spread. The sound track attributed their unbroken run of success to their inherent superiority over all the races they encountered. She wondered whether the species was biologically programmed to think that way, the Foitani of Odern were imitating their ancestors, or if they were projecting their own attitudes back onto the Great Ones.

A few minutes of watching made her toss out that last possibility. The Foitani of long ago had definitely been in the habit of killing off races that proved obstreperous. They did not bother to hide or even to go out of the way to justify genocide; they simply went about it, with second thoughts as few and far between as if they were swatting flies.

"Can you stop the tape for a moment?" Jennifer said. Dargnil Dargnil Lin could. Jennifer asked him, "Would your people act that way again if you were strong enough?"

"Probably," he said. "We have not reached the heights the Great Ones achieved, however, and races such as your own appear more potent than any they faced. Thus we have had to begin to learn to treat with other species rather than simply rolling over them. It is not easy for us."

Jennifer bit back the sardonic retort that automatically came to mind. The Foitani could not help being what they were. Expecting aliens to act like humans was the easiest way for a trader to get into trouble. Moreover, mankind could not boast a spotless record among the stars, though humans had perpetrated their worst acts of savagery on themselves.

The same seemed true of the Foitani. The screen Jennifer was watching suddenly turned a dazzling white. She staggered back, hands to her eyes, as if caught by the blast of a real explosion. When she looked again, a phrase in the Foitani written language filled the screen. "The Suicide Wars," Dargnil Dargnil Lin read for her.

"I'd suspected that, yes," Jennifer murmured. Far more rapidly than it had grown, the Foitani empire crumbled. Most of the stars that had filled the holovid map went dark. A handful, scattered at random across two or three thousand light-years, kept glowing red. An even smaller handful burned with a yellow light.

"Those yellow dots are the worlds of our species that have relearned starflight," Dargnil Dargnil Lin said. "On the red, Foitani also survive, but in a state of savagery."

"But *why* did it happen?" Jennifer asked. "What made you fight like that?" The tape hadn't offered a clue; its narration merely recorded the event without analyzing what had brought it on.

"I cannot answer for certain, nor could anyone else on Odern," Dargnil Dargnil Lin said. "There are speculations, but who can truly hope to see into the minds of the Great Ones? Only when we can match their deeds will we be worthy to comprehend their thoughts."

Jennifer's mouth twisted in discontent. The Foitani were too busy venerating their past to try seriously to understand it. "May I speak without causing offense through ignorance of your customs?" she asked, one of the standard questions every trader learned.

"Speak," Dargnil Dargnil Lin said.

"If the Great Ones were as magnificent in every way as you make them out to be, why did they ever go and fight the Suicide Wars in the first place?"

"For reasons of their own, reasons which surely reflected their greatness," Dargnil Dargnil Lin answered. Jennifer filled her lungs to shout at him; that was less than no answer, for it shunted aside thought rather than inspiring it. But the Foitan was not through. "Some among us have speculated that the Great Unknown contains the full and proper response to your question, and that our failure to grasp merely reflects our degeneracy in comparison to our ancestors."

"That's—" Jennifer stopped. How did she know it was nonsense? She was no Foitan—*thank God*, she added to herself. She tried again. "That's interesting. What evidence do your scholars apply in support of it?" The idea of the Foitani of Odern as decadent descendants of the true race had a nasty appeal to her, not least because it made their behavior in snatching her the product of debased minds.

Dargnil Dargnil Lin said, "I will show you a tape and let you draw your own conclusions."

"Show me several tapes, ones with differing points of view. How can I decide what is true on the basis of a single report?"

"You are a scholar," Dargnil Dargnil Lin said, as if reminding himself. "Very well, let it be as you wish." For the next several hours, Jennifer viewed records of the Foitani discovery of the Great Unknown, and of speculations about it. When she was through for the day, she mentally apologized to the big, blue aliens. She'd thought them too staid to produce much in the way of crackpottery. Now she knew better. Given the proper stimulus, they could be as bizarre as any human ever born.

The Great Unknown was proper enough. She studied orbital views of it, then pictures taken at long range from the ground, and finally close-ups. "Those were obtained by remote-controlled cameras," Dargnil Dargnil Lin said of the last batch. "We have a great store of data, as you see. They do not lead us toward understanding, however."

The old Foitani seemed to have gone in for monumental architecture in a big way. Massive colonnades led toward an enormous column that leaped most of a kilometer into Gilver's sky. No weeds, no undergrowth marred the Great Unknown or its precinct, even after twenty-eight thousand years. Nor had Gilver's tectonic forces damaged either tower or colonnades. They might have been raised yesterday rather than in the late Pleistocene.

"Why didn't this thing get bombed along with the rest of the planet?" Jennifer asked.

"Something else we do not know," Dargnil Dargnil Lin said.

"For your knowledge base, though, you should also observe some of the first of our people to come close enough to the artifact to feel its effect." He spoke into the microphone again.

After a few seconds of viewing, Jennifer had to turn away. Greenberg had been right; the Foitani who got too close to the Great Unknown weren't pretty. They hadn't just been damaged—they'd been destroyed. They drooled and shook and sucked on their toes and relieved themselves wherever they happened to be. Their muzzled faces gave not the slightest indication of surviving intelligence, nor could Dargnil Dargnil Lin's translator make sense of the shrieks and growls that sprang from their throats.

"This happened to *all* your people who got too close?" Jennifer said, gulping.

"All. The precise radius at which the Great Unknown began to grip them varied with the individual, but within it no one was safe."

"Hmm." Jennifer thought for a while. "And we know this didn't happen with Bernard. Does it happen to Foitani from worlds other than Odern who come to Gilver?"

"We do not know," Dargnil Dargnil Lin said. "We do not want to find out. To an alien such as yourself, all who still inhabit the Great Ones' sphere may rightly be known as Foitani. Well and good. But those who spring from other worlds are untrustworthy at best and outright abomination at the worst. Only we of Odern are the true descendants of the original race."

"Oh, my aching head," Jennifer said softly.

"Your head still distresses you? Perhaps it is an aftereffect of the ray Thegun Thegun Nug used to stun you. I hope you have an analgesic available."

"Never mind," Jennifer said, not surprised the translator had been too literal. All the surviving Foitani had been separated from one another for more than twenty thousand years. No wonder they'd have trouble getting along. After so much time, they wouldn't even all be of the same species any more. She asked, "When you deal with these other Foitani, what language do you use?"

"That of the Great Ones, so far as we understand it. It is the only speech we have in common, after all. Some worlds, among which Odern takes the lead, also use this tongue in everyday life in place of our former degenerate jargons. Others barbarously insist on maintaining the primitive languages they employed before coming into contact with more civilized Foitani.''

"All right; thanks. I think I've seen enough for today, if that's all right with you." What with the spectacle of completely deranged Foitani and the realization that the Foitani of Odern were just one small part of a much bigger puzzle, Jennifer was sure she'd seen enough.

Bernard Greenberg clapped a rueful hand to his forehead when she told him what she'd learned. He said, "I should have thought of that. It's too easy to forget how long they spent isolated on their own planets."

"With luck, it won't matter," Jennifer answered. "After all, the Foitani from Odern are the only ones who know about Gilver, so they'll be the only ones we have to worry about."

"I suppose so," Greenberg said. "But if they learned of the place from records they dug up, there's always the chance some other bunch will, too."

Jennifer had tried not to think about that. "Bite your tongue."

The more she researched the Great Unknown, the more she concluded that was a good name for it. Fusion bombs had all but sterilized Gilver. They'd fallen all around the mysterious artifact, but not a single one had landed inside what she'd taken to calling the radius of insanity. The planet's ecosystem was still struggling to repair itself; parts of that continent had become almost lush with greenery. Within the radius of insanity, nothing grew. Mere life, apparently, was not allowed to disturb the Great Unknown.

"I can imagine achieving that effect for a limited time, with periodic maintenance," Dargnil Dargnil Lin said when Jennifer asked him about it. "But to continue since the Suicide Wars . . . no, human Jennifer, it is but another of the wonders the Great Ones left behind for us to marvel at."

Jennifer was sick of marveling at the Great Ones. She wanted answers, and the Foitani records on Odern held precious few of them. "I never would have believed it," she said when her last allotted research day was done, "but I'll be glad to go to Gilver, just to try and figure out what's really going on."

"More power to you, if you can do that on Gilver," Greenberg answered. "If you think Odern is boring, you haven't seen anything yet."

"I haven't seen anything of Odern, except the spaceport and the library. Neither one of them is likely to drive Earth or Redford's Star off the tourist itineraries."

He smiled at her. "You've changed; do you know that? You're not nearly the same person you were when you flew with me aboard the *Flying Festoon*."

Jennifer mentally prodded herself. "It hasn't been that many years, Bernard. I don't feel different in any particular way."

"You are, though. Back then, when anybody said anything to you, you were as like as not to pull back into your shell and not even answer. You don't back away any more; you're a lot surer of yourself than you used to be."

"Am I?" Jennifer thought about it. "Well, maybe I am. I'm older now, after all. I was just a student when I took my first trading run." She laughed, mostly at herself. "All I wanted to do was get something out of the ordinary on my vita. I did that, all right. I've been to places most Middle English professors would run screaming from. Come to think of it, I wouldn't blame them. If I thought it would do any good, I'd run screaming out of here."

"It wouldn't do any good. But Odern is lively, next to Gilver. Here at least you have a whole planet full of people doing all the normal things people do. There are only two kinds of people—well, Foitani, but you know what I mean—on Gilver. They have soldiers, to guard something nobody else is supposed to know about, and they have scholars, to try to understand something they don't dare approach. Aissur Aissur Rus is from Gilver—he was the head of the research team there."

"I like him better than a lot of the others," Jennifer said.

"Yes, he's sharp," Greenberg agreed. "He thinks for himself, and that's unusual among the Foitani. They usually just go around trying to figure out what the Great Ones would have done. I suppose that's one of the reasons he got the job. Nobody here had any idea what the Great Ones were doing with the Great Unknown, so they had to get someone who could put his own slant on things. But that's not the point I was trying to make. Aissur Aissur Rus was so glad to get away from Gilver that he volunteered to be part of the team that brought you back here."

"That's great," Jennifer said. "But he's going back there, with us, isn't he?"

"So he is, but I don't think it's because he really wants to. The Foitani run more toward a strong sense of duty than we do."

"After what they put themselves through with the Suicide Wars, it sounds like a survival characteristic for them. To pull themselves back up after something like that, they'd have to have been able to stick together."

"I suppose so." Greenberg yawned. "We'd better get some sleep. If your research is done, we'll probably be leaving for Gilver early tomorrow, or maybe even late tonight. The Foitani don't believe in wasting time. They could be in here any minute now, to install the course tape and the electronic countermeasures they hope will get us there without being blasted by something leftover from the Suicide Wars."

"Of course, they have their own bomb aboard already," Jennifer said.

"There is that, yes. But we don't have to worry about it as long as we're good little boys and girls." Greenberg's voice was dry.

"That's great," Jennifer said again. She walked into the refresher cubicle. When she came out, Greenberg went in. She undressed, lay down on the foam pad—it never had gotten moved to the storeroom—and pulled the blanket up over her. She closed her eyes, but discovered that, though she was tired, she wasn't ready to sleep. The faint ammoniacal smell of the foam pad reminded her of the one she'd had on the Foitani ship, which in turn made her feel all over again how very much alone she was. But for Greenberg, she was the only human for too many hundred light-years. The *Harold Meeker*'s temperature was perfectly comfortable. She shivered under the blanket even so.

Greenberg came out of the refresher. He yawned again, stepping toward his sofa bed. If he had any worries like Jennifer's, he didn't show them. She suspected they were there; back aboard the *Flying Festoon*, he'd been good at keeping things to himself so his worries wouldn't worry others. It was one of the several traits for which she admired him.

She nodded to herself. "Bernard," she called softly, "do you really feel like sleeping right away?"

He stopped in midstride. His voice was controlled and careful when he answered, "Does that mean what I think it means?"

She nodded again, this time for him. "I think it means what you think it means."

"Jennifer, any man who didn't want to go to bed with you the minute he set eyes on you would need his vision correction adjusted. You know that," Greenberg said. Jennifer did know it. The knowledge had not always brought happiness; men found it too easy to separate her body from her, to want the one without caring about the other. But Greenberg was going on: "We have enough other things to worry about right now, so I want to know if you're sure. If it's going to complicate our lives a lot, it's more trouble than it's worth."

"If you have the sense to say something like that—and I was sure you did—then we should be able to manage, don't you think?"

"I hope so," he answered. He pulled off his shorts. The cabin of the *Harold Meeker* was small; two quick steps brought him to the foam pad. He got down beside her. She wadded up the blanket, threw it against the wall. He smiled. "I forgot just how lovely you are. I'd sort of kept from looking at you a lot—I didn't want to make a nuisance of myself, or more of a nuisance than I've already been for getting you dragged to Odern in the first place."

"That's foolish," Jennifer said. "It's not as if we haven't seen each other before. Trading ships are like that. And we're friends already, and more than friends, even if it was a while ago now."

"Quite a while ago now—getting close to ten years, isn't it? I didn't want to impose, and you were still upset about being here. But—" He didn't go on, at least not with words.

Jennifer savored what he was doing. She remembered from the *Flying Festoon* that he was seldom in a hurry—a rare virtue in men, she'd since found. Since he was about twenty years older than she was, she wondered if it was just that he was more thoroughly mature. More likely, it was that he was simply himself. Whatever it was, she enjoyed it.

Some considerable while later, she arched her hips so he could slide down her underpants. "Be careful with them," she said. "I only have the two pairs, and yours aren't made for the way I'm put together."

"I like the way you're put together."

"I noticed." Her hand closed on him.

"And I'll be careful," he promised. "How's that—and that—and that?"

Her underpants had only gotten as far as her knees, but she didn't care. "Mmm. That's—nice. Oh, yes. Right there, right there—"

The communicator buzzed harshly. "Oh, no," Jennifer said. Greenberg was a good deal more eloquent than that. The communicator ignored both of them. It kept on buzzing.

"Open your ship at once, humans. This is Pawasar Pawasar Ras speaking. I shall brook no delay." The electronic translator's tone was flat, but the words could hardly have been more peremptory. Pawasar Pawasar Ras went on, "We need to install important gear aboard the *Harold Meeker* immediately. Refusal to open the ship will be taken as evidence of conspiracy against the Foitani species."

"What do you suppose they do to conspirators against the Foitani species?" Jennifer asked.

Greenberg stroked her one last time. "I'm tempted to find out." But the moment was broken, and they both knew it. He got up from the foam pad and called out, "We will open the ship in a moment, Pawasar Pawasar Ras. You roused us from our rest, that's all."

"What rest?" Jennifer said. Then she giggled. "I was certainly roused, though."

"Shut up," Greenberg said over his shoulder as he dressed. She put her clothes back on, too. He ordered the air lock open. The alien, faintly spicy smells of Odern's air filled the cabin.

Two Foitani technicians came in. They filled the cabin, too, to overflowing. They installed their gadgetry, then ran some checks to make sure their artificial-intelligence system meshed with the *Harold Meeker*'s computers. One of them wore a translator. He said, "If you try to disable this system, you will also disable your own electronics. If by some accident you do not do that, you will remain altogether vulnerable to weaponry from the days of the Suicide Wars. I tell you this for information's sake. You may die if you like, but you should be aware of how and why this will come to pass."

"Thank you for being generous enough to warn us," Greenberg said.

"You are welcome." Like most Foitani, the technician was irony-proof. "You will lift off as soon as is practicable, which is to say, at once."

Greenberg drew himself to attention and spoke to the air: "Commence lift-off sequence."

"Automatic checklist commencing," the ship's computer answered.

"Wait for us to leave this cramped vessel, you fool," the Foitani technician exclaimed. "We are not ordered to fly to Gilver." For once, Jennifer saw an agitated Foitan.

"Sorry. Computer, cancel lift-off sequence," Greenberg ordered. He turned back to the technician. "You did tell me to lift off at once, did you not?"

"Yes, but—" The Foitan gave up. Along with his companion, he hastily departed from the *Harold Meeker*.

Greenberg grinned at Jennifer. "The best way to confuse them is to take them perfectly literally when they don't want you to. Only trouble is, they're so literal-minded themselves that you don't get as many chances as you'd like." The grin changed shape, just a little. "Which is true of other things as well. Where were we when we got so rudely interrupted?"

Jennifer stepped close to him, took his hand, and guided it. "I think," she whispered, "you were right about here."

The trip from Odern to Gilver was about as long as the one from Saugus to Odern had been. Other than that, the two journeys held no similarity. This time, Jennifer had pleasant human company aboard a human ship. All the facilities were designed for her species; she'd been glad to discover that the *Harold Meeker*'s sanitary supplies did include tampons.

She studied the material Dargnil Dargnil Lin had taken from Odern's library. The Foitani of Odern did very much seem to be spiritual descendants of their long-destroyed imperial ancestors: they were stern, humorless, efficient, and basically unwilling to recognize other species as anything but creatures to be exploited. *I can testify to that*, she thought.

Nothing in the data gave her any great insight into the Great Unknown. If the Foitani thought she'd step off the *Harold Meeker* with the answer to their problem all wrapped up with a bow around it, they were going to be disappointed. She took malicious glee at the idea of disappointing them, glee tempered only by the realization that disappointed Foitani were also liable to be dangerous Foitani.

The idea of stepping off the *Harold Meeker* without the answer made something else occur to her. "What became of the *Flying Festoon*, Bernard?" she asked. "Why aren't you still flying it?"

"I sold it after that first trip you took with me," he said, shrugging. "Marya and Pavel both reached master status after that run and they wanted commands of their own. I could have kept it and hired on some less experienced crewfolk, I suppose, but I didn't feel like it. So I sold it and got this smaller ship. I'm a jack-of-all-trades and I like my own company pretty well, so I thought I'd make a few runs by myself. I was turning a profit till this mess with the Foitani blew up. If we can figure out the Great Unknown, I'll make one yet. So will you."

Jennifer sighed. She'd been a trader long enough that turning a profit was important to her, too. She wondered if it was important enough to mean she had to satisfy the Foitani after all. Maybe it was. If they kept their bargain and let her take her pay in trade goods, she was more confident than ever that she could squeeze them till their black, ball-bearing eyes popped.

But she was not just a trader; and she didn't want to be a full-time trader. She spent a lot of time with her reader in front of her face, going through Middle English science fiction both to keep her grasp of the language sharp and to see if any of the science-fiction writers, with their elastic minds, had imagined a race analogous to the Foitani. That was a better hope than wading through the xenanthropology manuals: a glance there had told her what she already knew, that none of the other races with which humanity was acquainted resembled the blue-skinned aliens at all. Besides, Middle English was more fun to read than the manuals.

"Any luck?" Greenberg asked hopefully when she came up for air one day about halfway through the trip to Gilver.

She had to shake her head. "Nothing so far."

"Keep looking. I know how I used to sneer at you for reading that stuff, but the ideas you got from it really came in handy on L'Rau."

"I used ancient literature to help me on Athet, too: Sherlock Holmes it was that time, not properly science fiction at all. As somebody—Niven, I think it was—said back in the twentieth century, abstract knowledge never goes to waste."

Greenberg knew something about the twentieth century, but not enough. "Niven? I thought he was an actor, not one of your writers." The misunderstanding took several minutes to clear up. Finally Jennifer projected pictures of both men. "No, they're definitely not the same fellow," Greenberg admitted.

"There, you see?" she said. "They—" She stopped with a squawk, grabbing for the back of the sofa bed—the *Harold Meeker* was lurching under her feet as if caught on the ground during an earthquake. She felt the hair on her arms and at the back of her neck prickle up in alarm. Ships in hyperdrive had no business lurching. What was there to run into?

The viewscreen had been dark all through the journey; in hyperdrive, what was there to see? It was dark still, but dark in a different way, dark with the velvety blackness of space. A couple of stars gleamed, like tiny jewels set on the velvet.

Greenberg and Jennifer stared at each other. "Status report!" he snapped.

"Ship has returned to normal space," the computer answered. "Reason unknown."

They looked at each other again, this time fearfully. If they couldn't get back into hyperdrive, the way home was laser driver, light-sail, and frozen sleep. Inside human space, that was feasible; every human planet listened for rescue beacons and maintained rescue ships. Starting out from somewhere in the middle of the Foitani sphere, though, they could travel for ten thousand years before they ever got back to the edge of human space.

"Condition of hyperdrive engine?" Greenberg said urgently.

After a moment, the computer reported, "All systems appear to be performing satisfactorily. The hyperdrive, however, is not functional."

Greenberg made hair-tearing gestures. Jennifer stifled a nervous laugh—she wondered if he'd really pulled his hair before he went bald. Just then, what looked like a supernova blossomed in the viewscreen. Jennifer threw up her hands to protect her eyes. "Radiation!" the computer screeched. "Protective screens—" There was a pause of several seconds. "—holding."

The flat voice of a translator came from the comm speaker. "Foitani ship *Horzefalus Kwef* to human ship *Harold Meeker*. You may proceed in normal operation."

"First tell us what the hell just happened," Greenberg said. His own voice was shaky; Jennifer blamed him not at all.

"We have successfully destroyed a hyperdrive trap that dates from the days of the Great Ones. As soon as a ship is forcibly returned to normal space, a normal-space missile left behind in the area homes on it. That missile is now detonated. You may proceed."

For the third time in a couple of minutes, Jennifer and Greenberg stared at each other. She was not surprised that he found words first: "There's no way you can pull a ship straight out of hyperdrive like that!"

"On the contrary," the Foitan aboard *Horzefalus Kwef* answered, "there is a way. You have just seen it demonstrated. Our science has not succeeded in reconstructing what that way is. I gather from what I infer to be your surprise that human science has not either. But the Great Ones knew. I tell you once more, you may proceed. Failure to do so will be construed as lack of good faith."

"We're going, we're going," Greenberg said. He gave the computer the necessary orders. The *Harold Meeker* had no trouble returning to hyperdrive. Greenberg gaped at the blank black viewscreen and shook his head. He spoke to the computer again. "Save multiple copies of all data pertaining to this incident."

"It shall be done," the computer said.

Jennifer said, "Just knowing that a hyperdrive trap is possible is going to drive human engineers crazy for years. Nobody's ever even imagined such a thing. And you'll have the only tapes of one in action." The *Harold Meeker* was his ship; they were his tapes. Trading Guild regs spelled that out in words of one syllable; she was just a passenger here.

"*We'll* have," he corrected. "I wouldn't try to go all regulation on you. You wouldn't be in this mess if it weren't for me. And besides . . . those tapes have enough money in them for a lot more than two people."

"You don't have to do that," she said. "I didn't go into trading for the money. And all the same, I'm a long way from broke."

"You're also a long way from home, and that's my fault. Computer, log that any profits from tapes of the hyperdrive trap will be divided equally between journeyman trader Jennifer Logan and me."

"Logged," the computer said.

Jennifer saw that any further protest would be worse than useless. "Thank you, Bernard."

He brushed that aside. "Let's just see if we can get back to human space to turn the tapes into money. Right now, I have to say that's rather less than obvious."

Some people would not have been generous at all. That wouldn't have bothered Jennifer; the tapes belonged to Greenberg because he was shipmaster. Some people would have been generous and then expected something—probably a lot—in return. Very few people were like Bernard Greenberg, to be generous and then act as if nothing had happened. She thought that was wonderful, and knew he wouldn't want her to say so.

The rest of the trip to Gilver was uneventful. The only misfortune that took place was running out of human-style food and having to go over to Foitani rations. Jennifer crunched away at her kibbles with a singular lack of enthusiasm. "No, a plural lack of enthusiasm," she said a few meals later, "because there are lots of ways I don't like them."

Greenberg answered with a snort. Wordplay wasn't one of his virtues, or vices. People had been arguing about that since the days of Middle English, and longer. Puns were part of why Jennifer enjoyed Middle English science fiction in the original; Robinson, among others, was untranslatable into Spanglish because of them.

The hours followed each other, as hours have a way of doing. At last the computer announced that the *Harold Meeker* had reached Gilver's star system. The viewscreen went from blank blackness to velvety blackness; Gilver's sun blazed in the center of it. Gilver itself, a bright blue-green spark, shone in one corner. The computer swung the ship and boosted toward the planet on normal-space drive.

Alarms went off. "Missiles incoming!" the computer shouted. "Firing laser driver. Many hostile targets, converging on ship from many directions. Maneuvering to position laser driver. Firing . . . Maneuvering . . ."

"Human ship *Harold Meeker* to *Horzefalus Kwef*," Greenberg called urgently. "What the bloody hell is going on? I thought you people said Gilver was a dead world except for the Great stinking Unknown. Where are all these ancient missiles from the time of the Great Ones coming from?"

While he and Jennifer waited for an answer, the ship's weaponry blasted three missiles. But more bored in. Then those, too, began winking off the screen, some just vanishing, others exploding in spheres of radioactive fire. Jennifer found herself wondering about the *Harold Meeker*'s shielding and wishing she were wearing something more protective than thin synthetic underwear and cotton coveralls cut down to fit her. A lead suit of mail might have been nice.

At last the *Horzefalus Kwef* deigned to reply. "Human ship, these missiles are not of Great One manufacture. We are under attack by elements of a fleet from the Foitani planet Rof Golan. These Foitani are vicious and treacherous by nature. They must somehow have stolen information that led them to Gilver. We shall endeavor to protect your feeble ship as well as—" The transmission cut off.

"Did they get hit?" Jennifer asked. She half hoped the answer would be yes. The *Horzefalus Kwef* might be protecting them from the Rof Golani ships, but if it was gone they could try to head back to human space. The Foitani electronics aboard gave them some chance of making it in one piece.

But after checking the telltales, Greenberg said, "No, they're still there. The other ships are jamming their radio traffic. There they go, down toward the surface of the planet. I think we'd better follow them."

Regretfully, Jennifer decided he was right. The screen and radar plot showed explosions and missiles all around the ship. The *Harold Meeker* was not built for war. The Rof Golani spacecraft plainly were; they had more acceleration and maneuverability than a peaceful ship would ever need. By the way it performed, *Horzefalus Kwef* seemed a match for them. Staying close to it seemed the best bet for survival.

Unintelligible words came from the speaker: a Foitani voice, but not one always calm and self-contained like those of the Foitani from Odern. This one screeched and cried and yelled. "What do you suppose he's saying?" Jennifer asked.

"Nothing we want to hear, and you can bet on that," Greenberg answered. He studied the radar plot. "There goes one of the bastards! And that wasn't a missile from *Horzefalus Kwef*, either. Our paranoid friends' ground installations have paid off after all."

"They certainly don't think much of other Foitani, do they?" Jennifer agreed. "And they do think this Great Unknown thing is worth protecting. They didn't want to get caught flat-footed if another Foitani world somehow found out about Gilver."

"Somebody has, all right," Greenberg said.

The viewscreen blazed white. Alarms yammered, then slowly quieted. "We cannot sustain another hit so close without serious damage," the computer warned. A moment later, it added, "Entering atmosphere."

Atmospheric fliers swarmed up from the base on Gilver. With the fight so close to the planet, they were of some use against spacecraft. Jennifer found herself cheering when one of the attacking ships blew up in a burst of supernova brilliance. She stopped all at once, surprised and a little angry at herself. "I never thought I'd be yelling for the miserable folk who kidnapped me," she said.

"When they're helping to save your one and only personal neck, that does give you a different perspective," Greenberg answered.

"So it does," she said, glad he understood and also impressed that he could preserve his wry slant on things when they might turn to radioactive incandescence in the next instant.

Horzefalus Kwef managed to get a signal through. "Human ship *Harold Meeker*, land between the two westernmost missile emplacements at our base. Dive below us now; we will provide additional cover for you."

Deceleration compensators whined softly to themselves as the computer guided the *Harold Meeker* toward the designated landing site. The base was on the night side of Gilver. Not too far away, a large circle of ground was illuminated bright as day; at its center, the white tower that was the heart of the Great Unknown stabbed outward toward the stars.

Jennifer caught her breath at the beauty of the scene. She knew then that the esthetic sense of Odern's Foitani was different from her own, and also, she was suddenly sure, from that of their ancient ancestors. None of the pictures in their data base had been taken at night.

"Landing," the computer announced. "Recommend you do not leave the ship at the present time. The risk of radiation exposure outside appears significant."

"Did you program it for understatement?" Jennifer asked. Greenberg chuckled softly and shook his head.

Having nothing else to do, they spent their first hour on Gilver making love. Just as they were hurrying toward the end, a missile made a ground hit close enough to shake the ship. Jennifer laughed softly.

"What is it?" Greenberg gasped above her.

"Stupid twentieth-century joke," she answered, clutching him to her. "Did the earth move for you, too?" Then, for a while that could never be long enough, all speech left her.

Afterward, as he was dressing, Greenberg said, "Now I know you were really meant to be a scholar and not a trader."

"Why, Bernard?"

"Because who but a born scholar would come up with thousand-year-old jokes at a time like that? And thousand-year-old stupid jokes—you were right."

"I told you as much aboard the *Flying Festoon.* You didn't believe me then; I guess that's why you upgraded me from apprentice to journeyman."

"Partly I didn't believe you, I suppose. But there was more to it than that. You showed me you were a good trader. You got done what needed doing. You didn't seem to do it the way anybody else would, but it works for you, and that's the only thing that counts in the long run."

"I was using ancient literature as my data base instead of traders' manuals. No wonder things I tried looked strange to you."

"That's not all of what I meant, either," he said. "Most traders—just about all traders—push hard at everything they do. Pushing is part of being a trader. You're not like that. You're more reserved, shy almost. You were shy then—less so now, I think. But you still got a lot of business done."

"It's how I am," Jennifer said.

"I like how you are." His eyes softened as he smiled at her. The communicator had developed a way of spoiling tender moments, almost as if it were a baby that resented anyone else's getting attention. It did not break the pattern now. "*Horzefalus Kwef* to human ship *Harold Meeker*. We have beaten the Rof Golani pirates away. You may emerge and join our scientific team."

"Then again, we may not," Jennifer said, irked at getting interrupted yet again.

The communicator was silent only a moment. Then the Foitan on the other end said, "Our weapons are trained on you. You will emerge and join our scientific team."

This time, the look Greenberg shot Jennifer was reproachful. She felt suitably reproached; she'd known since her first contact with the species that the Foitani were humorless. Greenberg said, "Thank you, *Horzefalus Kwef*. Let us put on our suits, if you don't mind—the computer says it's 'hot' out there. Then we will emerge and join your scientific team." Sighing, he walked over to the air lock. Sighing even louder, Jennifer followed.

VI

THE PLANET GILVER had obviously had little to recommend it even before the Foitani from Rof Golan attacked. Back in what on Earth was still the Pleistocene, the Foitani had done a much more thorough job on it during their Suicide Wars. They'd eliminated their own species from the planet, and come too bloody close to destroying the whole ecosystem. Life still clung to Gilver. It no longer thrived there.

Jennifer found depressing a landscape that showed more slagged desert than forest and grassland. When she looked east rather than west, though, she looked toward a landscape with no life at all: the precinct surrounding the Great Unknown was sterile as an operating theater. The column at the heart of the Great Unknown speared the sky, though the research facility of the Foitani from Odern was more than fifteen kilometers away. That seemed to be far enough to keep the big, blue aliens safe from the hideous insanity that plagued them closer to the gleaming white tower. Their instruments wandered the precinct of the Great Unknown and probed what they could; the Foitani themselves were barred.

"The instruments don't pick up any too much, either," Jennifer complained.

Aissur Aissur Rus said, "If instruments provided the data we need, we would not have been required to requisition your services."

She gave the Foitan reluctant credit for not being mealy-mouthed, but said, "If I'm going to do you any good at all"—

and if I'm ever going to get out of here, she added mentally—"I'll have to examine your Great Unknown for myself."

"By all means," Aissur Aissur Rus said. "The human Bernard is already proficient with our ground vehicles. Before you enter the precinct of the Great Unknown, you would be wise to acquire a similar proficiency. Bear in mind that, should difficulty arise, you will have to effect your own rescue, as we shall be unable to come to your aid."

She had to admit that made sense. The ground vehicle proved simple to operate. It was a battery-powered sledge, tracked for good ground-crossing capability, and steered with a tiller. The size of the tiller was her only problem; she had to stand up to shift it from side to side.

She and Greenberg rode separate sledges into the area surrounding the tall, white pillar. The Foitani had not argued about that; they believed in redundancy, too. The vehicles purred forward side by side.

The radiation level had gone down in a hurry; the Foitani from Rof Golan had thrown neutron bombs, no doubt to make their own planned landing easier. Jennifer wasn't sorry it hadn't worked. One set of Foitani at a time was plenty.

After they'd gone four or five kilometers, she said, "We have more privacy here than we did on the *Harold Meeker*. Whatever we do, the Foitani aren't going to come after us to stop us."

"True enough," Greenberg said, "but what do you want to bet these chassis have explosives in them along with the motors?"

She thought it over. "You own a nasty, suspicious mind, and I've no doubt whatever that you're right."

They rode on. The sledges had one forward speed, slow, and one reverse speed, slower. Eventually they reached the beginning of one of the colonnaded paths that led inward to the Great Unknown's central column. The path, of gleaming gray stone, was as fresh as if it had been set in place the day before. Not even a speck of dust marred its surface. However the Great Ones had managed that, Jennifer wished her kitchen floor were equipped with a like effect.

The columns that supported the roof overhead gradually grew taller and thicker as they approached the central tower. The effect went from impressive to ponderous to overwhelming. Jennifer did not think that was merely because she was smaller than a Foitan. How any living creature could have felt anything but antlike on that journey was beyond her.

She said, "I don't like this. Why would the old-time Foitani want to make themselves into midgets? I've seen pictures of our own old monumental architecture—the pyramids of Egypt, the freeways of Los Angeles—but none of it, not even the pyramids, sets out to deliberately minimize observers the way this thing does."

"The stuff you're talking about was done in low-tech days," Greenberg said. "I suppose the effects were worked out empirically, too—on the order of, it's big, so it must be impressive. The thing to remember about the old-time Foitani is, they knew exactly what they were doing. They had all our modern building techniques and then some, and they were able to figure out just how they wanted this thing to look, too. And if it works on us, just think what it does to their descendants."

Jennifer thought about the tapes she'd seen, then quickly shook her head. She preferred not to recall the drooling, mindless Foitani who had come to the Great Unknown. She tried to imagine instead what the colonnade might have been used for, back in the days of the great Foitani empire. She pictured hundreds of thousands of big, blue aliens triumphantly marching toward the column, and hundreds of thousands more standing on either side of the path and cheering.

That wasn't so bad. Then, though, her imagination went another step, as the imagination has a habit of doing. She pictured the hundreds of thousands of triumphal Foitani herding along even more hundreds of thousands of dejected, conquered aliens of other races. She pictured those other aliens going into the base of that clean, gleaming, kilometer-high column and never coming out again.

She shook her head once more. From everything she knew about the Great Ones, that latter image had a horrifying feel of probability to it. She asked Greenberg, "Is there any way to get inside the column?"

"The Foitani have done magnetic resonance imaging studies that show it's not solid—there are chambers in there," he answered. "None of their machines found an entrance, though, and I didn't either, the last time I was here."

"Might be worthwhile blasting a hole in the side," Jennifer said.

"Might get us killed for desecration, too," he pointed out. "They've been studying this thing for a long time. If they wanted to try blasting their way in, they would have done it by now. Since they haven't, I've operated on the assumption that they don't want to."

"A shaped charge wouldn't do that much damage," Jennifer said, but then she let it go. She feared Greenberg was right. The Great Unknown was the principal monument the imperial Foitani had left behind, at least so far as their descendants on Odern knew. If they'd wanted to break into it by brute force, they probably would have done so for themselves.

Now the column was very close. Greenberg drove right up to it, halted his sledge. Jennifer stopped beside him. She craned her neck and looked up and up and up and up. The experience made for vertigo. Her eyes insisted the horizontal had shifted ninety degrees, that she was about to fall *up* the side of the tower and out into space.

She needed a distinct effort of will to wrench her gaze away and look back to Bernard Greenberg. He smiled a little. "I did just the same thing the first time I came here, only more so," he said. "The next time I looked at my watch, ten minutes had gotten away from me."

Jennifer found that she wanted to look up the side of the tower again. She ignored the impulse until it sparked a thought. "Do you suppose this is what sets the Foitani off? Maybe it just hits them a lot harder than it does us."

"I don't think it's anything so simple," he answered regretfully. "For one thing, it doesn't begin to explain why they're *drawn* here from ten kilometers away."

"No, it doesn't," she admitted with equal regret. She climbed down from her sledge. "I'm going to look around for a while."

Her shoes scuffed on the polished gray pavement. But for the faint whistle of wind between columns of the colonnade, that was the only sound for kilometers around. If Gilver boasted any flying creatures, they stayed away from the precinct of the Great Unknown. Jennifer found herself missing birdcalls, or even the unmusical yarps of the winged beasts native to Saugus.

She also found herself deliberately keeping her back to the white tower so she would not have to look up it. As deliberately, she turned round to face it. She refused to let the Foitani intimidate her.

She walked over to the tower and kicked it hard enough to hurt. Greenberg gave her a quizzical look, which she ignored. She'd booted the water-bottle the Foitani had given her all the way across her chamber. She wished the tower would fly through the air the way the water-bottle had. It stubbornly stayed in place.

"As if anything that has to do with the Foitani ever paid the least bit of attention to what I wish," she said, more to herself than to anyone else. With her pique at least blunted, she climbed back onto her sledge, turned it about, and headed back down the colonnade road toward the Foitani base outside the radius of insanity.

"What are you doing?" Greenberg called after her. "You just got here."

"I've seen all I need to see, for now," Jennifer answered, "Enough to make me certain I'm not going to turn the Great Unknown into the Great Known by walking around and peering as if I were Sherlock Holmes."

"That's the second time you've mentioned him to me. Who was he?"

"Never mind. An ancient fictional detective." Not everyone, she reminded herself, read Middle English—or even Middle English authors translated into Spanglish—for fun. She went on, "Anyway, the point is that I need more data than my eyes will give me. If the Foitani here at their base don't have those data, nobody does."

"What if nobody really does?" Greenberg asked. He was coming after her, though. The Great Unknown didn't drive humans crazy, but that didn't mean anyone enjoyed being around it, either, especially by himself.

"If they don't have the data we need, then maybe we ought to think about manufacturing some shaped charges and getting inside the column to see what's hiding there. If the Foitani want to call that blasphemy or desecration, too bad for them. They can't blame us for not coming up with answers if they won't let us ask the right questions."

"Who says they can't?" Greenberg said. Past that, though, he did not try to change her mind. She wondered if he agreed with her or if he was just waiting for her to find out for herself.

About one thing he'd been right: if the Foitani base on Gilver wasn't the dullest place in the galaxy, that place hadn't been built yet. The base was mostly underground, which had served it well when the attack from Rof Golan came. It only served to concentrate the boredom, though, because the Foitani didn't seem to care much about getting out and wandering around. There Jennifer had trouble blaming them. Gilver had not been a garden spot before the fleet from Rof Golan hit it. It was worse now.

Jennifer decided to beard Aissur Aissur Rus first. Of the Foitani with whom she'd dealt, his mind was most open. When she proposed blasting a hole in the tower, he studied her for a long time without saying anything. At last, he rumbled, "I have been urging this course on my colleagues for some time. Some say they fear the tower has defense facilities incorporated into its construction and so are afraid to damage it. Others tell me frankly they believe the demolition would be a desecration. I prefer the latter group. Its members are more honest."

"If you won't test, how do you propose to learn?" Jennifer asked.

"Exactly the point I have been trying to make," Aissur Aissur Rus said. "Now that I have your support for it, perhaps I can persuade some of my stodgier fellows to see that it is only plain sense."

"Or maybe they'll oppose you even more because you have a non-Foitan on your side," Jennifer said, thinking aloud.

"Yes, that is certainly a possibility. On the other hand, the Foitani of Rof Golan have also evidenced a strong interest in the Great Unknown. I would sooner be associated with a non-Foitan than with those savage beings who style themselves Foitani. So, I think, would others."

That righteous anger, delivered in the translator's toneless voice, made Aissur Aissur Rus seem more nearly human to Jennifer. Preferring the out-and-out infidel to the heretic, to one's own gone bad, had roots that went back to Earth and were ancient there.

"Let us take this up with Pawasar Pawasar Ras," Aissur Aissur Rus said, apparently fired with enthusiasm. "He always declined my requests when he stayed on Odern. Now that he has at last seen the Great Unknown for himself—and seen that the Rof Golani covet it—perhaps he can be made to feel as certain we can unravel its mysteries as if he were to find himself just within the radius of doom."

Radius of insanity was Jennifer's term for it, but she had no trouble following Aissur Aissur Rus. She looked up at him. He was staring away from her, staring at an empty spot a meter or so in front of the end of his muzzle. His gaze held enough intensity to make her shiver. She used once more the standard question she'd learned as a trader. "May I speak without causing offense through ignorance of your customs?"

Aissur Aissur Rus needed a moment to return to himself. Then he said, "Speak."

"Just—a feeling I had. Were you ever on the fringes of the radius of doom?"

His big, rather ursine head swung quickly toward her. "It is so. How could you have deduced it?"

"You used the comparison you made as if you understood exactly what it entailed."

Getting a Foitan from Odern to show alarm was not easy. Jennifer had seen that. Now she saw one who was alarmed and did not try to hide it. Aissur Aissur Rus's plushy blue fur rose till he looked even bigger than he was. He bared his teeth in a way different from, and more frightening than, the usual Foitani frown-equivalent. His eyes opened so wide that Jennifer saw they really did have a pale rim.

He paced up and down the chamber, working hard to bring himself back under control. At last he turned back toward Jennifer and said, "May I never have such an experience again. I knew the danger, but proved to be unfortunate. Most of us may safely work at a distance within my personal radius of doom. I went to discuss some instrument readings with a technician and found myself—"

He stopped. His fur stood on end again. He waited until it had subsided before he went on, "I found myself filled with insight such as I'd never had before. I knew—I could feel that I *knew*—exactly how to comprehend the Great Unknown. I started to go toward it, to implement my knowledge. I went by the most direct route. I threw a desk and table out of the way, tried to batter down a wall at a place where no door existed in it, kicked and clawed the technician when he had the ill luck to stand in my way. It took four of his fellows at the installation to cart me back to a safe distance, and I fought them at every step until my mind was free of the Great Unknown's thrall.''

The account of his episode of insanity was all the more chilling because it came out in the translator's flat tones. Jennifer shivered. She bore Aissur Aissur Rus no great goodwill, particularly as he'd evidently been the one who instigated her kidnapping. But she would not have wished on anyone what the Great Unknown did to Foitani.

She asked, "When you were safe again, did you recall the insight you'd had within your radius of doom?"

"No, and that may be the worst of it. I still feel that if I returned there, I would *know* again; I gather others of my kind have had a similar reaction. But none ever succeeded in communicating this knowledge, and I doubt I would prove the lone exception." He whispered something in his own language. The translator made it come out as emotionlessly as everything else, but Jennifer supplied the exclamation point: "Oh, to be wrong!"

They went to see Pawasar Pawasar Ras, who fixed Aissur Aissur Rus with a black ball-bearing stare. "You have been advocating this course for some time."

"Yes, honored kin-group leader, I have," Aissur Aissur Rus said.

Pawasar Pawasar Ras turned to Jennifer. "Why do you take his part?"

"Because if you really do want answers about the Great Unknown and nothing you've tried has worked, then you'd better try something else. If you're not serious about this project, then you can go on doing the same old things for the next twenty-eight thousand years." She threw in the number with malice aforethought. Beside her, Aissur Aissur Rus's ears twitched, but he kept quiet. She finished, "Honored kin-group leader, you were serious enough about what your people are doing here on Gilver to come here yourself. The Foitani from Rof Golan seem serious about this place, too. So why won't you do what plainly needs doing?"

Pawasar Pawasar Ras bared his teeth at her. She stood firm,

as she had with Dargnil Dargnil Lin in the library. Finally Pawasar Pawasar Ras said, "Had the Great Ones encountered your species, human Jennifer, they would have made a point of exterminating it. I must say I feel a certain sympathy toward such an attitude myself."

"I'll take that for a compliment," Jennifer answered coolly. Aissur Aissur Rus's ears twitched again. Now it was Jennifer's turn to try to stare down Pawasar Pawasar Ras. "Are you going to do what needs doing, or is this whole project just a sham?"

"Honored kin-group leader, what the human means is that—" Aissur Aissur Rus began.

"Don't soften what I said," Jennifer interrupted. "I meant it. If your people were willing to invade human space to snatch me to investigate this thing, why aren't you willing to do a proper job?"

"As we have noted, you do not think kindly of our species," Pawasar Pawasar Ras said. "Tell me this, then: why do you care whether our project succeeds or fails? Indeed, I would expect you to hope we fail, so that you might gain a measure of revenge thereby."

Jennifer looked at the big, blue alien with the same reluctant respect she'd had to give him after they first met at the Odern spaceport. "You know which questions to ask, I must say. When your people first kidnapped me, I did hope you'd fail," she answered honestly. "I've changed my mind, though, for two reasons. First, digging out the answers you need looks like the only way I'm going to get back to Saugus. And second, I just flat-out hate the idea of any job being done poorly when it could be done right."

"At last, human Jennifer, you have found a characteristic the two of us share," Pawasar Pawasar Ras said. "Very well, then, it shall be as you suggest. We shall undertake to open the tower that is the centerpiece of the Great Unknown. Should matters not go as you hope, however, remember that a share of the responsibility remains yours even if, as kin-group leader, I make the ultimate command decision here."

"You sound as if you expect the tower'll start spitting out warriors from the age of the Great Ones, or something like that," Jennifer said. "For heaven's sake, it's been sitting here ever since the Suicide Wars."

"As you did, I will give two reasons for my concern, human Jennifer," Pawasar Pawasar Ras said. "First, the Great Ones built to last, as witness the hyperdrive trap that nearly took us all on our journey here. And second, the Great Unknown remains active at least in some measure, as witness its state of preservation and the radius of doom that surrounds it. Opening the tower will be in the way of an experiment, and in a proper experiment one learns what one had not known before. I will not deny my fear at some of the things the Great Unknown may teach us."

Jennifer thought about that. A line from a Middle English fantasy writer—was it Lovecraft? Howard?—floated through her mind: *do not call up that which you cannot put down.* Maybe it was good advice.

She shook her head. If she didn't take the chance, she didn't think she'd ever see Saugus again. She was willing to take a lot of chances to get back to human space. No matter how big the tower in the middle of the Great Unknown was, she didn't think it could hold enough old-time Foitani to overrun the entire human section of the galaxy. After what Pawasar Pawasar Ras had said, she wasn't as sure of that, but she didn't think so.

"Let's go on with it," she said.

"We will need to consult with some of our soldiers," Pawasar Pawasar Ras said. "They will best be able to gauge the type and strength of explosive likely to penetrate the tower while doing the minimum amount of damage."

"Possibly Enfram Enfram Marf. He is a specialist in ordnance," Aissur Aissur Rus suggested.

"Whomever you say." Jennifer paused, wondering whether she should trot out her all-purpose question again. She decided to: "May I speak without causing offense through ignorance of your customs?"

Pawasar Pawasar Ras and Aissur Aissur Rus's translators answered together. "Speak."

"I've met a good many Foitani by now. As far as I can tell, all of you have been males. If I'm mistaken, I beg your pardon, but if I'm not, why haven't I met any of your females?"

"As this question steps along, the claws of its feet press against delicate flesh," Pawasar Pawasar Ras said.

"Shall I attempt an answer, honored kin-group leader?" Aissur Aissur Rus asked.

"Please do," his boss answered.

Aissur Aissur Rus turned to Jennifer. She was ready to hear anything—perhaps even that storks brought baby Foitani from the lettuce patch like so much airfreight. Aissur Aissur Rus said, "I know that in your species, human Jennifer, as in most, gender is fixed for the life of the individual. This is not so among us. During approximately our first thirty years of life, we are female; for the balance, we are male. Thus you will not see females in places of importance among us, as they, by their nature, cannot acquire sufficient experience to justify such placement."

"Oh," Jennifer said. That made a certain amount of sense. She decided to tweak the Foitani. "You are aware that I'm female."

"Indeed," Pawasar Pawasar Ras said, apparently relieved that someone else had done the talking about actual details. "You are, however, also of another species. The denigration implied by that far outweighs any relating to your gender."

"Oh," Jennifer said again, in a different tone of voice. The Foitani didn't need to look down their muzzles at her gender to keep her in her place.

Even Aissur Aissur Rus seemed relieved not to have to talk about gender any more. He quickly changed the subject. "Let us proceed to Enfram Enfram Marf, human Jennifer. He is our explosives expert here, as I said."

"All right." Jennifer smiled a little at finding the Foitani, for all their differences from mankind, so Victorian about the way their bodies worked. Had she not studied Middle English, she wouldn't have had a word to describe their attitude; the term had not come forward into Spanglish. Something occurred to her. "Did the Great Ones operate the same way you do, Aissur Aissur Rus?"

"Certainly." Aissur Aissur Rus drew himself up even taller than he was already, a paradigm of offended dignity. "They were Foitani and we are Foitani. How could disparity exist between us?"

"I didn't mean to make you angry," Jennifer said, on the

whole sincerely—she liked Aissur Aissur Rus best of the Foitani she'd met. "I was just asking."

"Very well, I shall assume the slight was unintentional. Now let us proceed to Enfram Enfram Marf."

The Foitani explosives expert was taller but thinner than Aissur Aissur Rus. He had a scarred muzzle that made him easy to recognize. All the Foitani seemed predatory to Jennifer; Enfram Enfram Marf seemed predatory even for a Foitan. He all but salivated when Aissur Aissur Rus explained why they were there. "I do not believe it," he said several times. "How did you persuade Pawasar Pawasar Ras to let us use the power we have? I thought he would just let us sit here forever, doing nothing."

"The opinions and suggestions of the human Jennifer aided materially in getting him to modify his previous opinion," Aissur Aissur Rus said. That made Jennifer like him even better. Plenty of humans wouldn't have shared credit with a friend from their own species, let alone with an alien they'd hijacked.

Enfram Enfram Marf turned to stare at her. "This ugly little pink and white and yellow thing?" Jennifer heard through Aissur Aissur Rus's translator. "Pawasar Pawasar Ras listened to this sub-Foitani blob where he would not hear you? Our sphere's a strange place, and no mistake."

The contempt behind the colorless words made Jennifer realize she really had been dealing with what passed for interspecies diplomats among the Foitani. If Enfram Enfram Marf thought like the average Foitan in the street, no wonder the Great Ones hadn't worried about genocide.

She smiled sweetly at the ordnance officer—she knew the smile was wasted on him, but used it for her own satisfaction—and said, "I'm female, too. How do you like that?"

Had Enfram Enfram Marf been human, he would have turned purple. He drew back a leg, as if to kick Jennifer across the room. "Wait," Aissur Aissur Rus said before the leg could shoot forward. "The human is still of use to us."

"Why?" Enfram Enfram Marf retorted. "Now that we have Pawasar Pawasar Ras's permission to open up the Great Unknown, we don't need this thing to gather data for us. We can go back to using machines; they'll be able to bring artifacts out past the radius of doom so we can properly study them."

"If all goes well, yes," Aissur Aissur Rus said. "But all may not go well. Machines are less flexible than intelligent beings, even now. Moreover, we acquired the human Jennifer not so much to gather data as to interpret it. She is expert in a peculiar form of extrapolation by storytelling that humans developed long ago, which may give her unusual insight into the reasons the Great Ones created the Great Unknown as they did.''

"How could this creature understand the Great Ones when we, their descendants, do not?" Enfram Enfram Marf demanded. But his leg returned to the floor. He bared his teeth, then went on, ''Oh, very well, Aissur Aissur Rus, let it be as you say. I shall begin calculating the proper weight, shape, and composition of the charge, based on what we know of the thickness and material of the tower's outer wall.''

"Excellent, Enfram Enfram Marf. That is what we require of you.''

"Nice to know that I'm useful,'' Jennifer remarked as Aissur Aissur Rus led her down the corridor. ''Otherwise you would have let him kick me into the middle of next week.''

Aissur Aissur Rus paused and looked down at Jennifer. After a moment, he said, "I will assume my translator should not have rendered that idiom so literally.''

"Well, no,'' Jennifer admitted.

"Good. We did not believe humans capable of time travel. We are not able to travel in time ourselves, either, though there are some poorly understood indications that the Great Ones had that ability.''

It was Jennifer's turn to stare. She had thought about pulling Aissur Aissur Rus's leg over what was indeed merely an idiom the translator program had missed—there wasn't a program around that didn't have a few of those annoying blank spots in it. Now she wondered if he wasn't telling her a tall tale to get even. The only trouble was, she didn't think Foitani minds—even that of Aissur Aissur Rus, who was the loosest, most freewheeling thinker she'd met among the aliens—worked that way.

She called him on it. "Time travel is as impossible—''

"As a hyperdrive trap?'' he interrupted. She opened her mouth, then closed it again as she realized she had no good comeback to make. She thought of herself as quicker-witted than the Foitani, but this time Aissur Aissur Rus unquestionably got the last word.

The tracked sledge delivered the explosive charge against the side of the polished white stone, then rolled off. The charge clung to the stone. The sledge stopped a couple of hundred meters away. Jennifer and Greenberg crouched behind it, on the side facing away from the stone. Greenberg spoke into his communicator. "We're under cover, Enfram Enfram Marf."

The Foitani ordnance office did not waste time replying. An instant later, a sharp, flat *craaack* rang out. It was much less dramatic than Jennifer had expected. She lifted her head. The stone panel had a neat, almost perfectly round hole in it, about a meter and a half across.

"He knows his stuff," she said, less than delighted about giving Enfram Enfram Marf any credit whatever.

"Explosives people tend to, at least the ones who live long enough to get a handle on what they're doing," Greenberg said. He spoke into the communicator again. "This was a good test, Enfram Enfram Marf. If your figures for the column are accurate, we won't have any trouble getting inside when we try this on the Great Unknown."

Again Enfram Enfram Marf did not reply. Jennifer said, "He doesn't think anyone who's not a Foitan is worth talking to."

"That's his problem. His bosses think I'm worth talking to, and they thought you were worth kidnapping so they could talk to you. I'm not going to lose a minute of sleep worrying about what the high-and-mighty Enfram Enfram Marf thinks of me."

Jennifer was sure he meant it. She admired his detachment and wished she could share it. She asked, "How do you keep from taking what aliens say personally?"

"The same way I do with humans: I try to gauge whether the person who's talking has any idea of what he's talking about. A lot of humans are damn fools, and so are a lot of aliens, Enfram Enfram Marf included. Just because he knows his explosives, he thinks he knows everything. I don't know much, but I know he's wrong."

Jennifer grinned and clapped her hands. Greenberg gave her a curious look. She wondered how she was supposed to explain to him that his line of reasoning went back thirty-five hundred years to the *Apology* of Socrates.

Before she had a chance to try, the sledge speaker spoke up

again. "Humans Bernard and Jennifer, this is Thegun Thegun Nug speaking. We shall have a charge ready for placement tomorrow. You will then proceed to begin exploration of the tower of the Great Unknown, relaying to us such data as you uncover."

To Jennifer's way of thinking, Thegun Thegun Nug had an unpleasant habit of assuming that everything would be exactly as he wished just because he said so. Greenberg did not let that bother him. He said, "Yes, we'll start exploring for you, Thegun Thegun Nug. We'll all learn something."

"That is the desired outcome," Thegun Thegun Nug agreed.

"What I want to learn is how to get out of here," Jennifer said. For all she knew, the mike was still open. Thegun Thegun Nug didn't answer her. She hadn't expected him to. He'd known all along how she felt.

The two sledges purred away from the Foitani research base toward the Great Unknown. Enfram Enfram Marf's new shaped-charge device sat behind Bernard Greenberg. Jennifer was glad it didn't rest on her sledge. She didn't quite trust Enfram Enfram Marf not to touch a button and say it was an accident. A meter-and-a-half hole out of her middle wouldn't leave much . . .

They'd only gone a couple of kilometers, barely even to the edge of the radius of doom, when a loud, warbling whistle began behind them. "What the devil is that?"

"It's a Foitani alarm," Greenberg answered.

"It sure alarms me."

Greenberg spoke into the communicator on the sledge. "Human Bernard to Foitani base: why have you switched on your alarms?" He repeated himself several times.

For a long time—more than a minute—no answer came. Jennifer began to wonder if the Foitani had forgotten about them. Then the cool tones of the translator came over the speaker. "Humans Bernard and Jennifer, this is Pawasar Pawasar Ras. I suggest you take cover as expeditiously as possible. Gilver is once more under attack from the savages of Rof Golan. Vectors of incoming ships indicate that they may attempt to land ground forces on Gilver, most probably with a view to assaulting or capturing the Great Unknown."

"We'd better head back," Jennifer said. Fliers sprang into the sky from the Foitani base. Cloven air shouted far behind them. Missiles leaped off launchers.

Then, from nowhere, a flier shrieked overhead at treetop height. A string of what might have been finned eggs fell from its belly. Had it sought the two sledges, it would have blasted them to bits. But its target was a hardpoint a few hundred meters to the west, between the humans and the base. Explosions smote Jennifer's ears. With an instinct she didn't know she owned, she threw herself off her sledge and onto the roadway, flat on her belly.

More explosions came, some distant, some close enough to lift her off the ground and slam her back down. During one brief lull, she looked over and saw Greenberg beside her. She had no idea how or when he'd got there. Then more bombs fell. Shrapnel whispered overhead.

Greenberg put his mouth next to her ear. "We can't go back," he screamed through the din.

"We can't stay here, either," she screamed back. As if to underscore her words, a fragment of bomb casing went *spaang!* off the side of a sledge.

"Then we head for the Great Unknown," Greenberg said, still at the top of his lungs.

Jennifer thought it over, as well as she could think in the midst of chaos and terror. "Sounds good," she said. "Let's do it, if the bombing ever moves away from us. It's the one place on the planet where the Foitani can't come after us."

"The ones from Odern can't, anyhow," Greenberg said. "We just have to hope that holds for the ones from Rof Golan, too."

"I wish you hadn't said that," Jennifer told him. She glanced up at her sledge. "I also wish we had more kibbles and water along." They'd planned on staying at the Great Unknown for a couple of days if they succeeded in getting into the tower, so they weren't without supplies. She looked up at the plastic bag of kibbles again and fought back a laugh. She'd never imagined a day would come when she wanted more of them than she had. She'd never imagined most of the things that had happened to her since the day the Foitani walked into her class at Saugus Central University.

More bombs struck, so close that she felt the impact with her whole body much more than she heard it. She and Greenberg clutched each other, life clinging to life in the middle of mechanized death. He shouted something at her. She knew that, but she was too stunned and deafened to tell what it was. She looked at him and shook her head.

"I love you," he said again. She still could not hear him, but his lips were easy to read.

"Why are you telling me now?" she said, slowly and with exaggerated movements of her own lips so he could follow. "We're liable to get blown to bits any minute."

He nodded vehemently. "That's just why. I didn't want to die without letting you know."

"Oh." She supposed it was terribly romantic, but she needed to be able to think about it. Thought was impossible here; she was battered and deafened and more frightened than she'd ever been in her life. Holding onto him still seemed like a good idea, so she kept on doing it.

The explosions grew more distant. Jennifer detached herself from Greenberg, far enough to peer past the front of the sledge. Dirt rose in graceful fountains all around the research base. The base fought back; close-in guns chattered maniacally, blasting bombs and incoming missiles before they struck home.

"If we're ever going to move, this is probably the time to do it," she told Greenberg. "Nobody seems to be paying attention to us."

"Let's go, then," he said. "The farther inside the radius of insanity we are, the better I'll like it." They scrambled onto their sledges and sent them dashing ahead at their best—and only—forward speed. No healthy Foitan would have had the least trouble running them down.

Greenberg looked over his shoulder. "Good thing we didn't head back to the base," he said. Jennifer looked back, too. A troop-carrier had landed right about where they would have been if they'd tried to reverse their course. Foitani—presumably Foitani from Rof Golan—leaped out of it and scrambled for cover. They started firing with automatic weapons heavier than anything a human could have carried.

"I wouldn't have wanted to meet them up close, no," Jennifer admitted. *Meet* wasn't quite the right word, she thought. The Foitani didn't look like the sort who would have waited for formal introductions before they started shooting.

The sledges crawled along. The invaders seemed too busy trying to blast the research base off the face of Gilver to bother doing anything about them. Jennifer wondered if that was too good to last. A moment later, she wished she hadn't, because it was. Something *cracked* past her ear. Then another something smacked off the rear facing of the sledge, hard enough to make it shudder under her. It kept running, though.

She turned around again. A couple of big aliens were bounding after her and Greenberg. As she'd feared, they ran faster than the sledges. Nothing grew in the area of the Great Unknown. There was no place to hide, save possibly behind the massive columns of the colonnade. The only weapon she had was her stunner, which might make a Foitan scratch but assuredly would not stop him. In any case, the soldiers' hand weapons far outranged the feeble thing.

Greenberg had seen the Foitani, too. If he felt the same choking despair that cast its pall over her, he did not show it. In fact, he stood up on his sledge—it was slow enough and smooth enough to make that safe—and jumped up and down thumbing his nose at them. That only made them run harder—and all at once, Jennifer realized he wanted exactly that. "You're a genius, Bernard!" she shouted. She stood up on her sledge, too.

The Foitani from Rof Golan kept coming. All too soon, they were only a couple of hundred meters behind the sledges. The closer they drew, the more easily Jennifer could see they were not the same as Foitani from Odern. They were taller and leaner and nearer gray than blue. Their ears were larger. So were their muzzles—and their teeth. They had red marbles for eyes, not black ones. That made them seem all the fiercer as they bore down on the humans.

Their clawed feet slapped on the smooth stone of the processionway. Jennifer heard their harsh breathing closer, ever closer. She reached into her beltpouch for her stunner, though she knew a steak knife would have done more good. She put away the stunner. If these Foitani had decided to take them prisoner instead of slaying them out of hand, she would not try to change their minds.

The Foitani caught up with the sledges. They even smelled different from the Foitani of Odern—sharper, like ripe cheese, Jennifer thought as she waited to be seized. The Rof Golani

Foitani ran past her and Greenberg, on either side of their sledges. They paid no attention whatever to the humans. Their red eyes were only on the tower ahead. Like two big machines, they pounded toward it.

Jennifer watched their backs recede ahead. "I think we may take it as proven that the Great Unknown affects more than one type of Foitani descendant," she said. She was proud of herself. The sentence came out as cleanly as if she were dictating an academic paper into the Middle English Scholars Association data net.

Greenberg gave her an odd look. "Yes, I think we may," he answered, half a beat late. "I think it's a good thing, too."

"So do I." Jennifer steered her sledge up next to his. She reached across and took his hand. Her own palm was cold and trembling. The vibration of the two sledges didn't let her tell if he also had the shakes, but he felt no warmer. After a moment, she added, "That was good thinking, luring them on into the zone of insanity. Now all they care about is the Great Unknown. Right now, they can keep it, as far as I'm concerned. I don't think I was made to be a soldier."

"Neither was I," Greenberg said. "I kept thinking about getting behind you and setting off Enfram Enfram Marf's shaped charge at the Foitani. By the time I decided it wasn't a good idea, they'd already gone by us."

"You still did better than I did," she said. "I forgot all about the stupid thing."

"That's not so good, Jennifer," he said seriously. "You should never forget about anything."

The sledges ground on toward the central tower. Jennifer kept looking back at the research base of the Foitani from Odern. The one good thing about the fighting that continued all around it was that the Foitani from Rof Golan weren't using nuclear weapons, as they had when they attacked from space. Maybe now, she thought, they were more interested in conquest than in annihilation. She hoped they would go on thinking that way; she had no confidence in the Great Unknown's ability to keep fallout from the local atmosphere.

Several other Foitani from Rof Golan strode the procession-way behind the first two. None passed the sledges, which by then were more than halfway from the outer edge of the radius of doom to the central tower. None shot at the sledges, either, for which Jennifer was duly grateful. A couple of kilometers from the tower, the sledges, slow but mechanically steady, re-passed the first two Foitani soldiers. Their gray-blue fur was damp with sweat; their tongues lolled from their mouths. They did not glance at the machines or the humans aboard them, but kept trudging toward the tower at the best speed they could muster.

The tower grew closer and closer. The two sledges stopped a couple of meters away. Greenberg climbed down from his sledge, lifted the shaped charge Enfram Enfram Marf had given him, and carried it to the side of the immense white structure. He pressed it against the stone. Jennifer wondered if it would stick, as it had against the practice slab of stone. The material of the Great Unknown seemed much more than simple white marble. But stick the charge did.

Greenberg went back to the sledge and called the research base. "We have the entry charge in place. Please advise if we should proceed, under the circumstances." Only static came from the speaker. Either no one at the base was listening, or the Rof Golani were jamming the channel. Greenberg looked at Jennifer. "What do you think we ought to do?"

"I think we ought to blow it," she said without hesitation. "We're never going to have a better chance than this. I just hope it's not all for nothing anyway—if the Foitani from Rof Golan win, what's going to happen to the *Harold Meeker*?"

"That's such a good question, I've done my best not to think about it." Greenberg made a sour face. He ran wire from the charge back to the detonator. "We have a couple of hundred meters to retreat. Let's use them." The sledges went into reverse until the wire began to grow taut.

Greenberg dismounted again and got behind his sledge. Jennifer took cover, too. She said, "I'm just glad this thing doesn't have to be set off by radio from the base, the way the practice charge did."

He let out a wry chuckle. "That would rather ruin our day's work, wouldn't it?"

"You might say so, yes," she answered, trying to match him dry for dry. She heard the slap-slap-slap of Foitani feet on the processionway. The first two soldiers from Rof Golan were getting close again. "If you're going to do it, you'd better do it now."

Greenberg glanced back toward the Foitani. He nodded. "Right you are." He brought his thumb down on the blue firing button. He grunted—squeezing the contact closed took considerable effort. Not only were Foitani stronger than people to begin with, the firing button was rigged so it could not go off by accident.

After the bombardment she'd been through, Jennifer found the detonation of the shaped charge an anticlimax. Unlike munitions makers, blasting experts do not make their devices as strong as possible, only just strong enough to do a particular job. Even in quiet circumstances, the blast would hardly have made her jump.

She looked up over the top of the sledge. Just as in the practice run, Enfram Enfram Marf's charge had blown a neat, round hole in the white stone of the tower. Blackness lay beyond it.

Greenberg looked up, too, then grabbed the communicator. "Calling the research base. I don't know whether you can see it—for that matter, I don't know if you can hear me—but we have succeeded in making a breach in the base of the column at the center of the Great Unknown."

"This is Pawasar Pawasar Ras, human Bernard," the comm answered. Jennifer jumped—she hadn't expected a reply. Pawasar Pawasar Ras went on, "I regret that our project has been disrupted by the perfidious attack from the wretched pseudo-Foitani of Rof Golan. Nevertheless, we do continue to keep you and the Great Unknown under observation. We discern no evidence of damage to the column."

Jennifer looked up over the sledge again. So did Greenberg. "I see a hole," he said. "Do you see a hole?" She nodded. "Good," he told her, then spoke into the communicator once more. "Honored kin-group leader, both of us think there's a hole in the side of that building. We're going to test it experimentally. How much do you want to bet that we get inside?"

"As a matter of fact, we may not be the first ones to do the testing," Jennifer added. The two Foitani from Rof Golan, still paying no attention to the humans or their sledges, tramped past them toward the tower.

"If you are somehow correct and there is an opening I cannot perceive, you must not permit the Rof Golani to exploit it. Use whatever means necessary to prevent their gaining entry," Pawasar Pawasar Ras said. The translator didn't let him sound agitated, no matter how upset he really was.

"How are we supposed to stop them?" Jennifer asked.

"Use whatever means necessary," Pawasar Pawasar Ras repeated.

Jennifer looked at the Foitani. Each of them was more than a meter and a half taller than she was. Each of them carried a weapon that could kill her at five times the range she could even make him itch. She looked at Greenberg. He'd been looking at the Foitani, too. Now his gaze swung back to her. She said, "Bullshit."

He nodded. "You'd better believe it." He spoke into the communicator. "Honored kin-group leader, we didn't sign up with you to commit suicide. You ought to know, though, that the Foitani from Rof Golan seem to be suffering from the same thing your people do when they get too close to the Great Unknown. They don't seem to be in any shape to relay whatever they learn to anybody."

A long silence followed. At last Pawasar Pawasar Ras said, "There may be some truth to this comment. Nevertheless—"

"No," Greenberg broke in, adding, "It's too late anyhow, honored kin-group leader. The first two Rof Golani have reached the tower."

The big, blue-gray Foitani dropped their weapons to press themselves against the smooth white stone of the wall. They were only five or six meters from the hole in its side, but gave no sign of noticing it. For several minutes, they seemed content just to stand there. Then, not getting more than a meter or so away from the edge of the wall, they began walking parallel to it, one of them behind the other.

They walked right past the hole. Their feet scuffed through the pieces of stone the shaped charge had blasted loose. They took no notice of them, either; as far as they were concerned, the area was as perfectly smooth as any other part of the processionway.

Greenberg turned to Jennifer. "I will be damned. They *can't* see that it's there."

Spanglish failed her. She fell back into Middle English. "Curiouser and curiouser." Then she said, "It makes me wonder whether the hole really is there after all."

"I can tell you two things about that," he answered. "Thing number one is that we know the Great Unknown makes Foitani crazy and we don't think it does that to us. Thing number two is, we can go and find out, so let's go and find out."

He stood up and walked toward the hole. Jennifer followed him. She saw the chunks of white stone that lay in front of it. Pretty soon, she kicked one of them. She felt it as her boot collided with it and heard it rattle away. All the same, she had the feeling she was approaching one of those holes quickly painted on the side of a mountain in an ancient animated fantasy video, the sort that would let whoever painted them go through and then turn solid again so a pursuer smashed himself against hard, hard rock. She stretched a hand out in front of her so she wouldn't hurt herself if the opening ahead proved not to be an opening.

She kicked another fragment of stone out of the way. This one clicked off the side of the tower. The noise seemed no different to her from the one the first stone had made, but the Foitani from Rof Golan hadn't noticed that one. They noticed this time. They spun around. Their red eyes blazed. They'd let their weapons fall when they came up to the column, but they still had fangs and claws and bulk. Roaring like beasts of prey, they charged at the two humans.

"Uh-oh," Greenberg said, which summed things up well enough. Running away from the Foitani didn't seem as if it would help. Greenberg and Jennifer ran for the hole instead. He shoved her in ahead of him. The rough stone at the edge of the hole ripped the knees out of her coveralls as she scrambled through. Greenberg dove after her scant seconds later, just ahead of the Foitani.

By then she had a fist-sized rock in her hand, ready to fling in the face of one of the aliens. At such a close range, she thought, she might even hurt him. Greenberg scrabbled around in the darkness for a rock for himself.

The Foitani came up to the hole and stared at it. They said something in their own language. Even without the moderating effect of the translator, Foitani from Odern sounded calm whether they were or not. As Jennifer had heard over the *Harold*

Meeker's radio, Foitani from Rof Golan yelled even when there was nothing worth yelling about. These two screamed back and forth at each other. Jennifer didn't need a translator to guess they were saying something like, "Where did the funny-looking critters go?"

Then she drew back her arm again to throw that rock, for a Foitan reached toward the hole. Those big, clawed hands came straight for her. If she waited any longer, she thought, the Foitan would pluck her straight out of her hiding place.

But his hands stopped, right where the surface of the wall had been before Enfram Enfram Marf's charge bit through it. Jennifer watched his palms flatten out against what to him was plainly still a solid surface. He turned to his comrade, gesturing as if to say, *Come on; you try it.*

The other Foitan tried it. His hands stopped where the wall should have been, too. He squawked something to his friend. Friend squawked back. They walked off, both of them shaking their heads.

Greenberg indulged in the luxury of a long, heartfelt, "Whew!" Then he said, "You don't know how glad I am that they'd put down their guns. I didn't care to find out whether bullets believed in hallucinations."

"Urk." Jennifer hadn't thought of that. After a moment, she added, "Who says I don't know how glad you are?"

Greenberg spoke into the communicator. "Research base, we are inside the central tower to the Great Unknown. I say again, we are inside." He repeated himself several times, but got no answer. He stuck the comm in his pocket. "Maybe the Foitani from Rof Golan are jamming again."

"Or maybe Pawasar Pawasar Ras and his friends can't hear you because you're calling from inside the tower and don't exist any more as far as they're concerned," Jennifer said.

He gave her a dirty look. "I was right after all when I first got to know you—reading all that ancient science fiction has twisted your mind."

"People used to say that about it then, too." Jennifer took out a hand torch and clicked it on. "As long as we're here, shall we see what *here* is like?"

Greenberg also got out a light. "We don't want to shine these out through the hole," he told her. "If the effect that keeps the

Foitani from seeing it is like a one-way mirror, bright light from this side could ruin it.''

"All right,'' Jennifer said, "but if the effect is like a one-way mirror, how come the Foitani couldn't feel their way in, either?''

"I don't know. I'm just glad they couldn't. Aren't you?''

"Now that you mention it, yes.'' Jennifer turned around and played the torch on the far wall of the chamber. However disagreeable he was, Enfram Enfram Marf had been an artist with his shaped charge: that wall, only four or five meters from the blast, was hardly even scorched. The chamber itself was bare, but for the fragments of stone from the outer wall.

"We're lucky,'' Greenberg said. "Looks like we didn't damage anything much in here.''

"We didn't, did we?'' Jennifer looked around again. "This room is so bare, it's almost as if they emptied it out on purpose, knowing this was where we'd break in.'' The words hung in the air after she spoke them. She deliberately shook her head. "It couldn't be. The Suicide Wars happened twenty-eight thousand years ago.''

"But what's been keeping the Great Unknown alive all that time?'' Greenberg said, a note of doubt in his voice. "The Great Ones had a higher technology than ours.''

"It couldn't be,'' Jennifer repeated.

What happened next made her think of the closing line of a classic Clarke story: "One by one, without any fuss, the stars were going out.'' This surprise was not on such a cosmic scale, but it more than sufficed for the occasion. One by one, without any fuss, the ceiling lights in the chamber came on.

"Oh, my,'' Jennifer whispered, and then, a moment later, "Oh, no.'' Nothing she'd seen about the empire of the Great Ones made her admire them or want them back. Much of what she'd seen had scared her spitless. And now an artifact—a big artifact—from the time of that empire was indubitably not just alive but awake. "Maybe if we leave, it'll go back to sleep,'' she said. "I think I'd rather face the Rof Golani than—this.''

"You've got a point,'' said Greenberg, who had to have been thinking along with her. But when they turned around to scramble out through the hole the shaped charge had blasted, they discovered it was no longer there. The inner wall looked as if it had stayed undisturbed for twenty-eight thousand Foitani years.

Jennifer walked over to the wall, patted it much as the soldiers of Rof Golan had from the outside. It felt as solid as it looked. "Is it real?" she asked.

"What's 'real'?" Greenberg countered. People had been wondering that since long before the days of Pontius Pilate, Jennifer thought, and generally, like Pilate, washed their hands of the question. Before she could say that out loud, Greenberg went on, "It's real enough to keep us in here, which is what counts at the moment."

"I can't argue with you there," Jennifer said. None of the walls now, so far as she could tell, held any openings. But with the Foitani, that wasn't necessarily the way things were. If the Great Ones were as adept at memory-metal technology as their distant descendants from Odern, the chamber could have had a dozen doorways, or two dozen, or three.

Bernard Greenberg evidently reached the same conclusion at the same time. He went over to the wall opposite the reconstituted one that led to the outside, began rapping on it here and there, as the Foitani did when they used their unnerving entranceways. For all the rapping, though, nothing happened.

"Try higher up," Jennifer suggested. "They're bigger than we are, so the sensitive area should be farther off the ground than if we'd built this thing."

"If humans had built this thing, it would have come with holovid instructions," Greenberg said. All the same, he raised his hand most of a meter. That produced results. In fact, it produced them twice: two doors opened up, less than a meter apart. They led into different rooms, one into a chamber much like the one in which Jennifer and he stood, the other into a long hallway.

"The lady or the tiger," Jennifer murmured. One trouble with that was that Greenberg didn't know what she was talking about. Another was that the choice was more likely to be between two tigers. She turned to Greenberg. "Which way do you think we should go?"

He plucked at his graying beard. "That room looks like more of the same. The hall is something different. Let's try it and see what happens."

"Makes as much sense as anything," Jennifer said, "which isn't much. All right, let's do it."

They stepped into the hall together. Jennifer's hand was on her useless stunner. Years of reading Middle English SF left her ready for anything, from Niven-style matter transporters to an extravaganza of lights out of the classic video *2001*. Human technology was as advanced as any in this part of the galaxy . . . except, evidently, that of the Great Ones. Not knowing what to expect left Jennifer more than a little uneasy. She reached out to Greenberg and was not surprised to find him also reaching out to her.

They didn't find themselves all at once in another part of the building. They weren't surrounded and overwhelmed by flashing lights. The hallway was just a hallway. But when Jennifer looked back over her shoulder, the door that had let them in was gone.

Every so often, Greenberg reached up to rap on the hallway wall. For more than fifty meters, nothing happened when he did; he must not have been picking the right spots. Then, with the unnerving suddenness of Foitani doors, a blank space appeared where only wall had been.

Greenberg and Jennifer both jumped. When she looked into the room that instant door revealed, Jennifer felt like jumping again. The chamber held an astonishingly realistic statue or holovid slide of a Foitan.

"He's not quite the same as the ones from Odern or from Rof Golan," Greenberg said.

"No," Jennifer agreed. The image of the Great One was a little taller than either of the descendant races she'd met. Its fur was green-blue, not the gray-blue of the Rof Golani or the plain, pure blue of the Foitani from Odern. The shape of the torso was also a little different. The legs were rather longer. The Great One might not have been of the same species as the modern Foitani; it definitely was of the same genus.

"Everything we're doing in here seems stage-managed somehow," Greenberg said. "We've known all along that this is a center for the Great Ones. What else are we supposed to learn from seeing one almost in the flesh?"

"I don't know," Jennifer answered. "Maybe that—" She stopped with a gurgle as the statue or holovid slide of the imperial Foitan turned its head and looked straight at her.

VII

WITHOUT CONSCIOUS THOUGHT, Jennifer pointed her stunner at the—no, it wasn't a statue—at the imperial Foitan and thumbed the firing button. Only later did she pause to wonder why she'd done anything so aggressively futile. If the Great One was a holovid projection or a robot simulacrum, the beam would do nothing whatever to it. Even if he was somehow alive, the most she could do was make him itch. All she knew was that she wanted a weapon, and the stunner was the best she had.

The Great One scratched vehemently, all over. "It's real," Greenberg said. He sounded as if he was accusing Jennifer.

"I'm glad you thought it couldn't be, too," she said. She put the stunner away. Enraging something with carnivore teeth and four times her weight didn't seem like a good idea.

The Foitan walked toward her. He didn't act outraged, just curious. He said something in his own language. The words didn't sound too different from the ones the Foitani from Odern used. The only trouble was that without a translator she couldn't understand any of them. She spread her hands, shook her head, and bared her teeth in a Foitani-style frown. "I wish I could wiggle my ears," she whispered to Greenberg.

A look of intense concentration came over him. His ears did wiggle, close to a centimeter to and fro. Jennifer stared at him. His smile was sheepish and proud at the same time. He said, "I haven't done that since I was a kid. I wasn't sure I still could."

Jennifer wasn't sure whether the ear wiggling did any good. The Great One stopped just in front of her and bent his knees so his eyes were on a level with hers. Those eyes were not quite the jet-black of the eyes of a Foitan from Odern; they were a deep, deep green-blue, an intensification of the shade of the Great One's skin and pelt. The color would have been stunning in human eyes. Here, it was simply alien.

"We come in peace," Jennifer said, knowing the alien would not understand. She also realized it was barely true; they'd blasted their way into the tower, and a good-sized battle was going on just outside the Great Unknown's radius of insanity. For that matter, more than a few armed Foitani from Rof Golan were inside the radius of doom, even if at the moment they were in no state to use their weapons.

Greenberg held his hands in front of him, palms out. Many races used that gesture to show they had peaceful intentions. Jennifer tried to remember if she'd seen it among the Foitani from Odern. She didn't think so. As far as she could tell, though, Foitani in general didn't have peaceful intentions all that often.

The Great One kept studying Greenberg and her. A visual examination didn't seem to satisfy the alien. The Great One sniffed at them, too, with as little regard for their modesty as a dog would have given them. Jennifer wished she hadn't spent the last several hours sweating and terrified after the Foitani from Rof Golan attacked the research base of their cousins from Odern.

Finally, to her relief, the Great One straightened up. He spoke a few words into the air. Holovid pictures of alien races appeared in front of him, one after another, as if in a video collage. Jennifer recognized a couple of species, but most were strange to her. Then the Foitan spoke again. The cavalcade of images stopped—with a pair of humans hanging in midair before the Great One.

"That's impossible," Jennifer whispered to Greenberg.

"Maybe not," he whispered back. "I've heard it claimed in traders' bars that the Foitani made it all the way to Earth. I never thought it was anything but a bar story, though."

The humans in the holovid display—a man and a woman— were a lot grimier than Jennifer had worried about being. They wore furs. The man carried a wooden spear with a stone point attached with sinews. The woman clutched a stone knife, or it might have been a scraper. They both looked scared to death.

The Great One examined them carefully as he had Jennifer

and Greenberg. He even sniffed them in the same way, as if to confirm by another sense that they were of the same type. That puzzled Jennifer. Could a holovid come with a scent attachment? She supposed so, for a race with a sense of smell more sensitive than humanity's. On the other hand—

"Bernard," she whispered, "do you think those poor cave people could somehow still be alive in here?"

He started to shake his head, then stopped. "I don't know," he said slowly. "The Foitan sure seems to be. After that, all bets are off."

Jennifer wondered if the tower was some kind of Foitani museum—or zoo. At first, no doubt because she'd seen the two humans, the idea was horrifying. Then she remembered the notion she'd had the first time she came up to the tower, of countless aliens going in and never coming out. Imagining a museum or zoo was a lot more comfortable than thinking about—what was the Middle English expression? A Final Solution, that was it.

The Foitan spoke to the air again. The humans it had called up disappeared once more, whether back into data storage or storage of a more literal sort. The Great One gave Jennifer and Greenberg another once-over. He bared his teeth at them in a Foitani frown. "Wondering what we're doing here," Greenberg guessed.

"I'll bet you're right," Jennifer said. "Earth is a long, long way from Gilver. What are the odds of cave people ending up here on their own and on the loose?" Something else occurred to her. "I wonder if the Foitan knows he's been here twenty-eight thousand years."

Greenberg hissed. "That's a real good question. I wish I had a real good answer."

"I wish I did, too."

The Foitan came out of his study. He walked over to the far wall of the chamber and rapped on it. This time it wasn't a door that opened, only a drawer-sized space. The Great One reached in, pulled something out, pointed it at Jennifer and Greenberg. By the way he handled it, the object was obviously a weapon.

"Oh, shit," Greenberg said softly. "Whether it's twenty-eight thousand years or day before yesterday, the breed doesn't seem

to have changed much some ways, does it? Oh, shit," he repeated.

Jennifer would have looked for better last words than that. But
the Great One seemed to have second thoughts. Instead of firing,
he gestured with the weapon. "I'm tired of being ordered around
by Foitani," Jennifer said. With very little choice, however, she
went down the hall in the direction the Great One indicated.

After about twenty meters, the Foitan stopped her and Greenberg. Another rap on the wall produced another doorway. The
Great One ordered the humans into the new chamber. It reminded Jennifer of nothing so much as the library setup back
on Odern: it was full of strange-looking holovid gear and computer equipment. Greenberg found another name for it. "Command post," he said.

His proved the better guess. The Great One said something.
A bank of screens came to life: the view immediately around
the tower at ground level. More than one screen showed gray-
blue Foitani from Rof Golan pressed up against the side of the
building. Some still carried the arms they had brought to Gilver
to use against the Foitani from Odern. All of them, armed or
not, had the lost-soul look of Foitani under the influence of the
Great Unknown.

The Great One had seemed almost godlike in competence and
confidence. Now for the first time Jennifer saw him discomfited.
He stared at his Rof Golani umpty-greatgrandscions as if he
could not believe, did not want to believe, his eyes. She wondered what the Great One thought of those distorted versions of
himself, versions made all the more grotesque by their obvious
insanity.

At a shouted command, the Great One shifted to a view that
had to have come from the top of the tower. Far off in the distance, Jennifer saw the spaceport by the research base of the
Foitani from Odern. She also saw atmospheric fliers, tiny specks
in the screen, diving to attack the base.

One exploded in midair. The burst of light drew the Great
One's notice. The magnification of the pickup increased. Now
small-arms flashes were plainly visible. Jennifer tried to figure
out what was going on. The Foitani from Odern—*her* Foitani—
seemed to have established a defensive perimeter against their
distant cousins from Rof Golan. As she watched, a missile

streaked out from the base to blow up a Rof Golani armored vehicle.

The Great One watched, too—in horror, if Jennifer was any judge. When the Foitan spoke again, alarms started yammering. Alarm ran through Jennifer, as well. Not so long ago, she'd scoffingly suggested to Pawasar Pawasar Ras that the tower might be full of armed Great Ones waiting to get loose. Now she didn't feel like scoffing any more.

Her own personal Great One didn't wait for any of his hypothetical relatives to arrive. Another wave of his weapon sent Jennifer and Greenberg back down the hall the way they had come. He marched them past the chamber in which they'd found him, all the way to the end of the corridor. An offhand, almost contemptuous rap on the wall produced the doorway Greenberg had found after so much effort. The Great One's weapon ordered the humans back into the room by way of which they'd entered the tower.

The Great One looked at the outer wall. Jennifer wondered if he saw it smooth and unblemished or if he could tell the hole from the shaped charge was there. Pieces of stone from the explosion still littered the floor. If the Great One saw that wall as being smooth and unblemished, he'd have the devil's own time figuring out how the broken rock got there.

Several other Great Ones came rushing into the room. They were as like the first one as so many peas in a pod—almost even down to color, Jennifer thought irrelevantly. They were all armed, too, with weapons identical to the one the first old-time Foitan carried. One of them pointed his weapon at the outer wall. Jennifer didn't see him pull a trigger or press a button, but suddenly the hole—or a hole—was visible to her again.

"Did he make a new opening, or is that the same one Enfram Enfram Marf's charge blasted?" she asked Greenberg.

"I think it's ours," he answered, his eyes wide. "What does that make the Foitan's gun, though? An illusion-piercer? An illusion-creator?"

"Whatever it is, I don't want to be on the wrong end of it. If it makes me think I'm dead, I have the bad feeling I'd really end up that way."

"Me, too." Greenberg reached out to take her hand. She

squeezed back. The contact was reassuring. She knew—she thought she knew—it was real.

A Great One stuck his head through the hole. It was barely wide enough for his shoulders to go through, but he managed to squeeze out. Jennifer wished Pawasar Pawasar Ras hadn't listened to her or to Aissur Aissur Rus. Here were the warriors of a long-forgotten day, free on Gilver once more.

One of the Great Ones pointed his weapon at Jennifer and Greenberg. He urged them toward the hole they'd made. They went. Greenberg scrambled out first. Jennifer came after him a moment later.

The Great One goosed her with his weapon to make her go faster. She squawked and almost fell as she popped out of the hole. Greenberg helped steady her, then moved her away from the opening before the next Foitan came through and stepped on her.

Imperial Foitani kept emerging. Jennifer wondered if the alarm had rung all through the tower, and how many Great Ones had been in suspended animation or whatever they used. She thought again of Pawasar Pawasar Ras's worries and how she'd pooh-poohed them. If she ever got the chance, she'd apologize to the kin-group leader.

No Foitani from Rof Golan had been within a couple of hundred meters of where the Great Ones were coming out. The gray-blue soldiers, caught in the spell of the Great Unknown, gaped as their green-blue forebears came out of what might have looked to them like solid rock.

Jennifer waited for the Rof Golani to fall to their knees and worship the returned Great Ones, or to perform some equivalent ritual. The Rof Golani pointed at the newcomers, shouting among themselves. One of them yelled something toward the revived imperial Foitani. A Great One answered. Without hesitation, the Foitani from Rof Golan began running toward the Foitani who had come out of the tower.

And, without hesitation, the Great Ones methodically began shooting them down. Most of the Foitani from Rof Golan were too befuddled to use their own weapons, but their bared teeth, outstretched claws, and bellows of fury said what they thought of the Great Ones. But that wholehearted hatred availed them

not at all, for the imperial Foitani calmly continued their mas-
sacre.

One Rof Golani somehow kept enough presence of mind to
remember he carried a weapon more lethal than those with which
he'd been born. Bullets ricocheted from the wall just above the
Great Ones' heads. Jennifer and Greenberg threw themselves
flat. A moment later, an imperial Foitan killed the only gray-
blue soldier who'd seriously tried to fight back.

Slowly, Jennifer got to her feet. The precinct that contained
the Great Unknown seemed to sway around her. Her view of
the Foitani was rocking, too. Far from reverencing the Great
Ones, the Foitani from Rof Golan had tried to kill them on sight.
The Great Ones hadn't wasted any time returning the favor,
either, and by all indications so far, they were a lot deadlier than
the Rof Golani.

An old-time Foitan walked over to the nearest Rof Golani
corpse and stared down at it. Jennifer wished she were better at
reading Foitani facial expressions. Then the Foitan removed all
doubt about what he was thinking. As Enfram Enfram Marf had
with Jennifer, he drew back his leg for a kick. Unlike Enfram
Enfram Marf, he didn't stop himself. He kicked the dead Rof
Golani as hard as he could. The body had to weigh something
close to two hundred kilos. The kick rolled it over, twice.

Several other Great Ones abused the bodies of the Foitani
from Rof Golan. One picked up the small arm the Rof Golani
had managed to fire. He examined it for more than a minute,
then threw it aside with unmistakable scorn. His own hand
weapon emitted a beam of some sort; but for being dead, the
Rof Golani looked fine.

Off in the western distance, the explosions round the research
base of the Foitani from Odern kept rumbling. Fliers clashed
above it: Rof Golani attacking, Foitani from Odern defending.
A Great One pointed his weapon at one of those fliers. It was
more than a dozen kilometers away, but it twisted in midair and
crashed to the ground with a flash of purple light.

The rest of the old-time Foitani began swatting fliers out of
the air as easily as if they'd been flies. Jennifer watched in appalled perplexity as the machines tumbled. "What's going on?"
she demanded of Bernard Greenberg, who had no more answers
than she did. "The Foitani from Odern practically worshiped

the ground the Great Ones used to live on. No matter what they said about the Rof Golani, they never said the Rof Golani hated the Great Ones, either. But they do.'' She looked at the sprawled corpses, shuddered, and looked away. "And the Great Ones hate them, too. Otherwise, they wouldn't be doing—this.'' She spread her hands in an all-encompassing gesture.

"Tell me about it,'' he said. He looked away from the carnage, too. "From what we've seen of the way Foitani treat other races, I'm glad they didn't just shoot us down without asking questions first.''

One of the Great Ones swung his head around to glare at the two humans. By the way he hefted his weapon, he wasn't far from doing what Greenberg had feared. He wrapped a hand around his muzzle so it closed his mouth, pointed first at Jennifer, then at Greenberg. *Shut up*, she figured out, and obeyed. Greenberg didn't say anything more, either.

The old-time Foitani—by now a couple of dozen of them might have been outside the tower—spread out into what looked like a skirmish line. One of them pointed west, toward the sound of fighting . . . and toward the research base of the Foitani from Odern. The whole band started moving in that direction.

By the way they set out, fifteen kilometers was a stroll in the park for them. Jennifer looked longingly toward her sledge. The Foitan who'd warned her to be quiet gestured with his weapon—*that way*. She sighed and went that way after the Great Ones.

The old-time Foitani strode along at a pace that suited them fine, which meant it was uncomfortably quick for Jennifer. She kept up anyhow, and so did Greenberg. The Great One who was covering them looked as if he'd happily get rid of them if they slowed him down.

She looked around behind her, wondering if more imperial Foitani were issuing from the central tower. They were, but by ones and twos rather than by hundreds and thousands as she'd feared. They were quite bad enough by ones and twos.

By the time the leading Great Ones neared the edge of the radius of insanity, both their human captives were panting and footsore. Another few kilometers like that, Jennifer thought, and she'd look forward to being shot. Her coveralls were soaked with sweat; it ran stinging into her eyes and dripped from her chin.

Unlike the Foitani from Rof Golan, the Great Ones seemed immune to sweat. They tramped down the processionway as if on parade. Jennifer's uneasy vision of old-time Foitani leading defeated aliens in triumph came back to her. All that made this seem different from a small-scale version of it was that they were walking away from the tower, not toward it.

Even after the processionway ended, the imperial Foitani strode grandly along. A gnarled shrub grew by their line of march. Jennifer thought nothing of that at first. Then she realized it meant they were out of the precinct of the Great Unknown, for no plants lived within it.

Ahead, the firefight between the Rof Golani and the Foitani from Odern continued. Both sides had to be going crazy, wondering what had happened to their fliers. Jennifer thought the Great Ones were crazy too. She turned her head toward Greenberg and muttered, "Do they think they're bulletproof, or what?"

"I don't know," Greenberg muttered back, soft enough so as not to earn the wrath of their watchdog. "I know I'm not, though."

Just then, the communicator in his pocket spoke up in loud, clear, translated Spanglish. "Humans Bernard and Jennifer, this is Thegun Thegun Nug. You will tell me immediately who those strange Foitani with you are. You will also tell me whether they are in any way responsible for the difficulties our aircraft have encountered over the last few minutes."

That was Thegun Thegun Nug all the way, Jennifer thought: whatever he wanted, he ordered the humans to deliver *immediately*. He also had a gift for opening his mouth at just the wrong time.

The Great One who'd kept Jennifer and Greenberg from talking with each other snarled at them and held out his hand for the communicator. Greenberg gave it to him. He held it close to his face for a moment, as if figuring out how it worked. Then he spoke into it in sharp, abrupt tones.

Silence stretched. Jennifer wondered how a Foitani translator system that was geared to handling Spanglish would deal with suddenly getting its own tongue back. After a moment, she also wondered how close the language the Foitani from Odern used really was to the speech of the Great Ones.

Evidently it was close enough, for Thegun Thegun Nug seemed to understand it. The first part of his reply came back in Spanglish. "We greet you, Great Ones, returned to the world at last after so long. We shall serve you to the best of our ability and obey you in all regards, for we—"

The translator program suddenly went out of the circuit. Thegun Thegun Nug's own voice came over the communicator. Even speaking for themselves, Foitani from Odern seldom sounded excited. Thegun Thegun Nug was no exception. "If I witnessed the Second Coming, I think I'd show a little more feeling than that," Jennifer complained to Greenberg.

"The Foitani have been waiting ten times as long as Christians," he answered. "Maybe after twenty-eight thousand years, some of the rush has gone out of it."

"Maybe," Jennifer said. But her own reference to the Second Coming rang a bell in the scholarly part of her mind. What rough beasts were these old-time Foitani, slouching out of the Great Unknown to be reborn? She looked up to the sky, which still had no fliers in it. She shivered. The old-time Foitani might be very rough indeed.

Somewhere much too close, a Rof Golani hand weapon barked. Bullets shouted past. Jennifer went flat and tried to claw holes in the ground with her nails. She couldn't call this combat, because she had nothing with which to shoot back. But by now she knew what to do when somebody started shooting at her. So did Greenberg, who might have hit the dirt a split second before she did.

One of the Great Ones was down, too, down and shrieking. His blood was even redder than Jennifer's. His comrades cried out. A couple of them stooped beside him to give what help they could. It wasn't much. His screams went on and on.

The rest of the imperial Foitani did as Jennifer and Greenberg had—they dove to the ground. But they were armed, and armed with weapons more terrible than any mere firearms. With dreadful thoroughness, they turned those weapons on one possible spot of cover after another, as far as the eye could see.

A few more bullets came their way, but only a few. They stopped all at once. The silence that settled round the Great Ones was punctuated only by the cries of their wounded comrade.

Jennifer didn't yet dare to raise her head, but she did turn to face Bernard Greenberg. "Looks like it's going to be the old-time Foitani and the ones from Odern against the Rof Golani," she said.

"I'd say the Rof Golani are in big trouble," he answered. He lowered his voice. "I'd say we are, too. I don't mean just you and me, I mean everybody."

"I know what you mean," she answered as quietly. "I've already decided I'm going to tell Pawasar Pawasar Ras that I'm sorry." But she suspected that by then, Pawasar Pawasar Ras would be happy to see the Great Ones out and loose, not afraid of them any more. Thegun Thegun Nug had all but groveled to them on the communicator, at least in the brief part of that conversation that had been in Spanglish.

The wounded Great One's shrieks shrank to gurgles. He had an amazing amount of blood in his body; the spreading puddle was a couple of meters wide. One of the other imperial Foitani spoke to him. He gasped out an answer. The second Great One touched his weapon to the wounded one's head. The wounded one jerked and lay still.

"What are they doing?" Jennifer said, more than a little sickened. "He just killed him. The old-time Foitani have to have the medical technology to save him. Otherwise, they wouldn't still be here after so long in cold sleep, if they use cold sleep. So why did he kill him instead of helping him or getting him back to the tower where he could be worked on properly?"

"Maybe he only stunned him," Greenberg said. "We don't know what all their weapons can do."

"That's true, we don't." Jennifer mentally kicked herself for jumping to a conclusion. Just because the Great Ones had done their level best to exterminate every Rof Golani Foitan within range of their weapons, that didn't have to mean they were as callous among themselves.

But everything she'd learned about the imperial Foitani argued that they might well be. Races with gentle, tender dispositions didn't make a habit—maybe even a sport—of genocide. They didn't fight Suicide Wars, either, for that matter. And the way the Great Ones tramped on and left behind the one who'd been shot argued that they had no further use for him. They were, as Jennifer had long since concluded, not nice people.

The communicator spoke up again. Jennifer caught Pawasar Pawasar Ras's name in the middle of a lot of unintelligible Foitani chatter. Her spirits rose slightly. Maybe the administrator's good sense would warn him not to trust the Great Ones too completely.

"Maybe," Greenberg said when she spoke that thought aloud; their keeper seemed more willing now to let the two humans talk. He didn't sound as if he believed it, though. He kept looking back toward where the one old-time Foitan had been shot. He obviously didn't believe the Foitan was just stunned any more either.

The sun set when the imperial Foitani were still a couple of kilometers from the research base. By the way they glared at the western horizon, they looked about ready to order it to come back up and keep lighting their way. Jennifer knew a moment's fear it might obey them, too.

But however great they were, the Great Ones had no Joshua among them. They did the next best thing: they surrounded themselves with glowing globes that filled their camp with a light about as bright as daylight.

"That's all very well if they don't have any enemies left out there," Greenberg observed, "but if they do, the only way I can think of to make themselves more conspicuous would be to paint 'shoot me' on their backs in big fluorescent letters."

In spite of everything that had happened through a long, exhausting, terrifying day, Jennifer found herself giggling. She dug out a plastic pouch of Foitani kibbles and crunched a handful between her teeth. "These things had better have all the nutrients humans need in them," she said, "because I've used up just about everything that used to be in me."

"You and me both." Greenberg pulled off his shoes and stared at his feet. "I keep waiting for them to swell up right before my eyes."

"Me, too," Jennifer said. She shed her shoes, too, and sighed in exquisite relief as she wiggled her toes. "I didn't come out here set up to hike." She swigged from her canteen. She would have killed for a cold glass of beer; warm, rather stale water was at the moment a more than adequate substitute.

Greenberg also ate some Foitani people chow. He washed it down with his own water. "Better—a little better," he said. "If they're going to the research base tomorrow, at least they won't walk our legs off, Jennifer . . . Jennifer?''

Jennifer didn't answer him. She hadn't heard him. She lay sprawled on her side in the dirt, fast asleep.

The old imperial Foitani must have eliminated or at least intimidated the Rof Golani on the ground, for Jennifer woke up the next morning. At first, she wasn't sure she liked the idea; she felt almost as bad as she had after Thegun Thegun Nug stunned her.

She grimly went through a stretching routine she hadn't used since she was in the field on her last trading run. By the time she started to sweat, some of the kinks in her legs and back began to come loose. The Great Ones watched her with impassive curiosity.

Greenberg also needed limbering up after a rugged day and a night on the ground. When he was done stretching, he looked around for a bush to go behind. But when he started to go behind it, one of the old-time Foitani growled and lifted his weapon. Greenberg sighed. ''Sorry about this, but I can't wait any longer,'' he said to Jennifer as he turned his back on her. She heard him open his fly.

''Don't turn around,'' she warned him. ''In coveralls, this is a lot more inconvenient for me than it is for you.'' As she unfastened herself and squatted, she thought again that this was a problem Middle English science-fiction writers had ignored, especially for women. She wished she could ignore it herself. She also wished she could ignore the Foitani. As they had while she was exercising, they studied her now.

Relieved—and also relieved of her dignity—she got to her feet. ''It's all right now,'' she told Greenberg.

''All right,'' he said, and turned around. ''Shall we have a lovely breakfast of dry dog food?''

''Since our other choice is leaves and whatever Gilver uses for bugs, I suppose we might as well.''

They crunched for a while. Jennifer watched the Great Ones while they watched her. They might have been sleeping on featherbeds instead of hard dirt; not a single tuft of fur seemed out of place. Some of them wore belts with pouches. They took

what looked like slabs of raw meat out of the pouches, shared
them around, and devoured them.

After a cautious pull at his canteen—who could guess when
he'd get a chance to refill it?—Greenberg said, "I meant what I
told you yesterday, you know."

"What did you tell me yesterday?" she asked, a little testily—
far, far too much had happened yesterday. When his face fell,
she remembered all at once what he'd told her. She felt herself
turn red. "I'm sorry, Bernard. I know you did."

"And so?" he said.

It was a good question. Over the years, a lot of men had said
they loved her, a lot more than she wanted to hear it from. To
many of them, it meant nothing more than that they wanted to
go to bed with her. She was already going to bed with Bernard,
and it had been her idea as much as his. She knew that said
something. But living with Ali Bakhtiar, in the beginning, had
been as much her idea as his, too.

She shook her head. "Bernard, right now I just don't know
what to say to you. I think maybe the only thing I ought to say
right now is that this isn't really the time or place to say much
of anything. You know I'm fond of you—or if you don't, I've
been doing something wrong." She smiled wryly. "But love?
I'm not even sure what love is. Let's talk about it later, when we
can think straight and feel something besides being scared out
of our minds."

"Fair enough," he said, his voice unreadable.

They had no further chance to talk about it, anyhow. The
imperial Foitani, with the gift for timing all Foitani races seemed
to share, chose that moment to break camp and start for the
research base of the Foitani from Odern. They still didn't want
the humans talking while they marched. A warning growl made
that quite clear.

The Great One who had Greenberg's communicator used it
to call the base. Jennifer heard Pawasar Pawasar Ras's name.
That was all she understood of the conversation. She wished for
some of the tricks to enhance recall that science-fiction writers
had invented: memory-RNA pills and who knew what else, all
guaranteed to let somebody learn a language in twenty-four hours
flat or your money back. Trouble was, nobody'd bothered with
such things after effective translator programs came along. Trou-

ble with that was, as she'd found more times among the Foitani than she cared to remember, take away the translator program and she was helpless without it.

Far off to the south, gunfire crackled. From several kilometers away, it sounded cheery rather than terrifying. The Great Ones grew alert when they heard it, but it wasn't close enough even for folk as aggressive as they to hose down the area with their hand weapons.

The breeze, a fickle thing, played with the marching Great Ones and wearily trudging humans, blowing sometimes from behind them but more often into their faces. The old-time Foitani ignored it; like their descendants from Odern, they were good at ignoring anything they didn't care for. Jennifer rubbed grit from her eyes as she tramped along. Stopping didn't seem like a good idea, not with that Foitan and his weapon right beside her.

She walked past a couple of emplacements the Foitani from Odern had built to protect the way to the Great Unknown. No one came out to greet the returning imperial Foitani. She looked down into one gun pit close by the side of the road. A blue Foitan lay inside, sprawled and dead.

"I hope Pawasar Pawasar Ras knows what he's doing, treating with the Great Ones," she whispered to Greenberg. She got another growl from the armed Great One for that, but no more, for it was the first thing she'd said since the day's journey began.

When the party of Great Ones came within a few hundred meters of the research base, Foitani from Odern emerged to meet them. Jennifer watched the old-time Foitani watching the blue successor race. She wondered what the Great Ones thought of them as compared to the insanely aggressive Foitani who'd developed on Rof Golan.

She still had trouble telling one Foitan from another, but thought she recognized Pawasar Pawasar Ras and Thegun Thegun Nug among the Foitani from Odern in the group that had come out of the base. All the Foitani from Odern bowed low and chanted at the Great Ones. Without the translator, Jennifer couldn't be sure, but she thought the chant was the same as the one her kidnappers had intoned when they bowed to the ancient ruins on Odern after they'd brought her there: here were the Great Ones, freed from earthgrip at last.

The gesture of submission seemed to have meaning to the imperial Foitani. They came out of the skirmish line in which they'd advanced and formed up into a single compact group. Once they were all together, they bowed, too, though not nearly so low as the Foitani from Odern had.

After that recognition ceremony, ancient and modern Foitani walked toward one another. The two groups were only a few meters apart when the breeze stopped blowing into Jennifer's face. She knew a moment's relief—*no more grit in my eyes*, she thought.

The Foitani from Odern had been moving forward with every sign of the reverence they gave to anything that pertained to the Great Ones. All at once, they stopped short. They bared their teeth. Pawasar Pawasar Ras—Jennifer was sure now it was the project leader—growled something deep in his throat.

Without any more preamble than that, the Foitani from Odern roared and charged at the Great Ones.

For an incredulous half a second, Jennifer gaped at the onrushing blue Foitani. Then Bernard Greenberg tackled her. A couple of Great Ones managed to get their weapons up before the Foitani from Odern crashed into them, but only a couple. Most had their deadly small arms torn or kicked from their hands before they could use them.

Even without weapons, the Great Ones were a match for the suddenly berserk Foitani from Odern. They smashed them to the ground with a savage skill for which battleball scouts would have paid millions. All Jennifer and Greenberg tried to do was roll out of the way of the battling behemoths.

A Great One who hadn't been disarmed slew a pair of Foitani from Odern. Then, all at once, he ceased to be. Jennifer closed her eyes against a terrible glare that had already struck and vanished—an antiship laser, fired now at a ground target. Another old-time Foitan sizzled into nonexistence. A voice from the research base, amplified to a volume that approximated divine wrath, bellowed a command.

The imperial Foitani seemed better at giving orders than taking them. Another Great One fired in the direction from which the laser had come. Jennifer didn't know whether he took it out. Another laser, from a different position, cut him down. That bolt flew much too close to her. She felt a blast of heat and smelled ozone as if lightning had struck nearby. Only a few meters away, sandy ground bubbled into glass.

The amplified voice roared again, louder than ever. This time, the Great Ones, those few left on their feet, spread their arms wide. The ones with weapons dropped them. Only a couple of Foitani from Odern were in any shape to keep fighting. Regardless of whether their foes had quit, they started to attack again. The voice from the base cried out once more, this time with different words. Reluctantly, the Foitani from Odern held back. One—Jennifer thought it was Pawasar Pawasar Ras—shouted what was plainly a protest. The voice from inside the base shouted him down.

More Foitani from Odern emerged. All of this group were heavily armed, with rifles similar to the ones the Rof Golani carried. An armored fighting vehicle also came forth from some concealed entrance and clanked toward the Great Ones. It carried a fat laser tube and a cannon whose muzzle seemed to Jennifer's frightened eyes to be about as wide as her head.

The armed modern Foitani advanced on the imperials who had come out of the Great Unknown. They were more than cautious but less than the bloodthirsty maniacs into which Pawasar Pawasar Ras's party had turned. Greenberg noticed that at once. "How come they don't want to tear the Great Ones limb from limb?" he said.

"The breeze is blowing from the base to us again," Jennifer answered. "Maybe they can't smell them any more."

"Maybe the Great Ones haven't had a bath in the last twenty-eight thousand years," he said.

Jennifer made a face at him. Taking advantage of the fact that nobody was going to point a gun at her for talking, she said, "Maybe they—"

The voice from the base boomed forth once more, this time in Spanglish. "Humans Bernard and Jennifer, this is Aissur Aissur Rus. I suggest you come into the base through the passage from which our soldiers have just debouched. They are ordered to let you pass through them. We would not want you to come to harm through staying too close to the *kwopillot* from the Great Unknown."

"The who?" Jennifer said at the same time as Greenberg

said, "The what?" The translator program had missed a word.
Maybe it didn't have a Spanglish equivalent, even an approxi-
mate one. That happened now and again with translator programs. Trouble was, when it did, the word that refused to
translate was almost always vitally important.

Aissur Aissur Rus didn't answer either Greenberg or Jennifer.
Neither of them felt like asking again—whatever *kwopillot*
were, he'd made it clear it wasn't safe to be anywhere around
them. The behavior of Pawasar Pawasar Ras had done a pretty
good job of that, too. Both humans hurried to pass through the
ranks of the Foitani from Odern. The big, blue aliens ignored
them, keeping eyes, attention, and weapons on the Great Ones.

The fickle breeze shifted again just as Jennifer was about to
go down into the underground research base. Behind her, the
Foitani from Odern bellowed in rage. A rifle began to bark, then
another and another. Aissur Aissur Rus was screaming for the
soldiers to stop shooting, but they wouldn't stop. The Great
Ones went down like ninepins. When they were all dead, the
soldiers rushed forward to kick and beat at their shattered bodies.

Sickened, Jennifer turned away. The kibbles she'd eaten sat
like a ball of lead in her stomach. She hoped they'd stay down.
"Back inside the radius of doom, the old-time Foitani treated
the ones from Rof Golan the same way," Greenberg said.

"I know," Jennifer said. That had been only yesterday. She
shook her head in disbelief. "I didn't like that, either."

"Neither did I. Let's get away from the Foitani with guns
before they decide we might make good targets, too."

She let Greenberg take her by the elbow and lead her down
the passageway. As soon as they were at the bottom, Aissur
Aissur Rus spoke to them in Spanglish once more. "Come immediately to the command center. The ceiling light will direct
you."

Following the moving light like a will-o'-the-wisp, they soon
came to the screen-filled chamber from which Aissur Aissur Rus
had spoken. He said, "I congratulate you on penetrating the
tower at the center of the Great Unknown, humans. But had I
known it was filled with *kwopillot*, I would have agreed with
Pawasar Pawasar Ras that it remain sealed forever. I thought

them merely the stuff of legend and modern depravity. Would I had been right."

"What *are* kwopillot?" Jennifer demanded. Bernard Greenberg opened his mouth, then closed it again. He'd evidently been about to ask the same question.

But before Aissur Aissur Rus could answer, Pawasar Pawasar Ras and Thegun Thegun Nug limped into the chamber. They were dirty and bloody and looked more like beasts of prey than intelligent beings. *"Kwopillot!"* Pawasar Pawsar Ras exclaimed. Had she not thought he'd tear her limb from limb, Jennifer would have kicked him.

Thegun Thegun Nug said something. Aissur Aissur Rus's translator turned it into Spanglish. "Filthy, reeking perverts! If the Suicide Wars were fought against them, suppressing them was worth the price."

"Aye, so it was," Pawasar Pawasar Ras declared. Aissur Aissur Rus didn't say anything, but he didn't look as if he disagreed, either.

"What are *kwopillot*?" Greenberg got the question out this time.

Word by word, the translator turned it into the Foitani language. That seemed to remind Aissur Aissur Rus and his colleagues that the humans were there. His answer, though, was less than helpful. "Never mind, human Bernard. They are practically extinct, and it is as well."

"No, they aren't," Greenberg said loudly. "Whatever they are, you may have murdered as many of them as came out of the tower in the middle of the Great Unknown, but how many do you think are still left in there? It's a big tower, you know, and it's awake or active or whatever you want to call it, thanks to us. What do you want to bet that more *kwopillot* will pop out of it soon?"

Aissur Aissur Rus, Pawasar Pawasar Ras, and Thegun Thegun Nug all bared their teeth at him. Thegun Thegun Nug growled something. Aissur Aissur Rus's translator turned it into, "What a terrible thing to say." Jennifer suspected the original had been rather more pungent.

Aissur Aissur Rus said, "Unfortunately, the human may well be right. We should make preparations on that assumption, at any rate. Those who came forth may have been *kwopillot*, but they were also Great Ones, with all the powers we have long believed the Great Ones held. If the *kwopillot* truly hold all the resources contained within the Great Unknown, how are we to resist them?''

''Better to ally with the Rof Golani than to risk such filth spreading through our sphere,'' Pawasar Pawasar Ras said.

Maybe he had just been indulging in rhetoric, but Aissur Aissur Rus took him up on it. ''An excellent suggestion, honored kin-group leader. Call them at once; we have already observed that they, too, know the proper response to this menace.''

''As you say, Aissur Aissur Rus.'' Pawasar Pawasar Ras went over to a communications panel and started talking into it. Before long, the image of a gray-blue Foitan from Rof Golan appeared on the screen on front of him.

''What are *kwopillot*?'' Jennifer asked. It was the third time the humans had tried that question, and they were still without an answer.

''They are disgusting,'' Thegun Thegun Nug said. ''I go to wash their reek from my fur.'' He stalked off.

Jennifer turned to Aissur Aissur Rus. ''Will you please explain what's going on, and why you've all started killing each other on sight?''

Aissur Aissur Rus made a noise that might have come straight from a wolf's throat. The translator rendered it with a sigh. Jennifer had some qualms about the translation; nothing that sounded so . . . carnivorous . . . had any business being merely a sigh. Aissur Aissur Rus said, ''This subject is not easy for us to discuss, human Jennifer. It is also one we never thought could arise—as the Great Ones were believed to be extinct, surely the degenerate *kwopillot* had to be gone. Sadly, this now appears not to be the case.''

''So what are *kwopillot*, and why do you keep calling them such nasty names?''

''Wait a minute,'' Bernard Greenberg put in, his eyes lighting up. ''This has to do with sex, doesn't it? Otherwise you wouldn't mind so much talking about it.''

''You are, as usual, astute, human Bernard,'' Aissur Aissur Rus said with another of those bloodthirsty-sounding sighs. ''Indeed, the matter of the *kwopillot* does turn on sex, or more precisely on gender.''

He paused, plainly not eager to go on without being prodded further. Jennifer looked at Greenberg in open-mouthed admiration. His shot in the dark had struck home—had it ever! If the Foitani were anything like most other species, they'd find sex worth fighting about no matter how technologically advanced they were. All at once, the Suicide Wars had a rationale that made some kind of sense.

Aissur Aissur Rus still stood silent. He looked big and blue and unhappy. Jennifer said, "May I ask, solely for the purpose of remedying my own ignorance, and with no desire to cause offense, what *kwopillot* do that other Foitani disapprove of?"

The variant of the trader's standard question paid off. Aissur Aissur Rus said, "You know that my race is unusual among intelligent species, in that we are born female and become male after our thirtieth year, more or less."

"You said so, once, yes," Jennifer agreed. "I didn't think much of it. We humans have found that intelligent races vary widely. Also—again I speak without intending to cause offense—Foitani are not sexually interesting to humans."

"The converse also holds, I assure you," Aissur Aissur Rus replied at once. He waggled his ears. "I thank you, human Jennifer. You have given me an idea so vile to contemplate that beside it the depravities of the *kwopillot* fade almost—not altogether, but almost—into insignificance."

Aissur Aissur Rus was the only Foitan Jennifer had ever suspected of owning a sense of humor. If he did, it was a nasty one, and he didn't bother with trying to speak inoffensively. She tried to match him irony for irony: "I'm glad I've given you something new and revolting to think about. Meanwhile, though, you'd started to explain what *kwopillot* were."

"I had not started yet," Aissur Aissur Rus said. "Indeed, I approach the task with considerable reluctance. You may perhaps have observed that we Foitani are somewhat reticent in discussing matters which pertain to the reproductive process. The Middle English term for such affectation of reticence, I believe, is *Victorian*, is it not?"

Jennifer stared at him. "That is exactly the word, Aissur Aissur Rus. I've thought it of your people myself. Now I have another reason for wishing you hadn't kidnapped me—I'd love to have seen the research paper you would have turned in. If you didn't outdo all the humans in my class, I'd be amazed.''

"As may be," Aissur Aissur Rus said. "That, however, is at present irrelevant. Rather more to the point, one of the reasons we are as reticent as we are concerning reproductive matters is that they are relatively simple to disrupt among us.''

"And *kwopillot* choose to disrupt them?'' Greenberg pounced.

"Exactly so, human Bernard. For unnatural reasons of their own, they choose through hormonal intervention in the egg''— this was the first Jennifer had heard of Foitani coming from eggs—''to produce creatures . . . monsters might be a better word . . . male from birth. Even more outrageously, those born properly female, again by means of hormones, opt to retain their initial gender. That is what it is to be a *kwopil*—to be or to have been of the wrong gender for one's age.''

"Why would anybody want to do that?'' Jennifer asked, though she doubted she would get a rational answer. When it came to sex and gender, few intelligent races were rational.

Sure enough, Aissur Aissur Rus said, "*Kwopillot* act as they do because, being afflicted with perversity themselves, they wish to have others with whom to share it.''

"Wait a minute," Greenberg said. "Suppose you have a male, uh, *kwopil*. What happens after he gets older than the age at which he was supposed to turn male anyway? Isn't he pretty much normal from then on?''

"No," Aissur Aissur Rus said. "For one thing, the hormone treatments which made him a *kwopil* leave their mark: he never smells as a proper Foitan should. For another, how could he be normal even were that not so, when he has spent all his previous life in a gender unnatural to that phase?''

"I see your point," Greenberg said slowly. So did Jennifer. No matter how refined the surgical techniques that changed them had become, transsexual humans were often pretty strange people. That might be an even greater problem for the Foitani, where the alteration was made before an individual ever saw the light of day, and where there was no natural equivalent of, say, a ten-year-old male.

She asked, "How do you know these things, Aissur Aissur

Rus? Are there still *kwopillot* among you? You said they were extinct.''

"Sadly, I overstated," Aissur Aissur Rus admitted. "Every starfaring Foitani world knows them, and many of those still sunk in planet-bound barbarism. The modification techniques, as I said, are far from difficult. Depraved and wealthy individuals, anxious only for their own degenerate gratification, generally create the first ones on a world. But once there are *kwopillot* on a world, they make more like themselves. In a way, it is understandable—who else but others of their kind would care to associate with them?''

Jennifer and Greenberg looked at each other. They both nodded. Humans made genetically engineered sex slaves every now and again, too. A year didn't go by without a holovid drama showing that kind of lurid story. Jennifer didn't know whether to be relieved or depressed that another race could act the same way.

Pawasar Pawasar Ras was talking to the gray-blue Rof Golani officer. He spoke too softly for Aissur Aissur Rus's translator to pick up what he was saying, but Jennifer heard one word she understood: *kwopillot*. When Pawasar Pawasar Ras said it, the Rof Golani Foitan's red eyes opened wide. So did his mouth, displaying his large, sharp teeth. *The better to eat you, my dear*, Jennifer thought. But where before the Rof Golani had wanted only to attack the Foitani from Odern, now this one listened attentively to everything Pawasar Pawasar Ras had to say.

"They both hate these *kwopillot* worse than they hate each other," Greenberg said.

Jennifer quoted the title of a Middle English novel: "The enemy of my enemy—"

Greenberg knew the saying from which it had come. "Is my friend. Yes." He turned to Aissur Aissur Rus. "Obviously the Great Ones knew of *kwopillot*, too. Did they feel the same way about them as you do?''

"There can be no doubt of it," Aissur Aissur Rus said. "Because we normally find it distasteful in the extreme to discuss such reproductive issues, the speculation is not published, but many, I think, privately believe the *kwopillot* problem to have been a possible cause of the Suicide Wars. I am one of those, and not the only one here at the base.''

"What's the point of thinking if you don't publish?" Jennifer said. What she was thinking of was her fruitless search through the Foitani records on Odern. She'd never so much as heard the word *kwopillot* there, not even from Dargnil Dargnil Lin, who was supposed to be helping her learn about the Great Ones. She made a mental note to give him a good swift kick the next time she saw him.

Before Aissur Aissur Rus could answer her—if he was going to—Pawasar Pawasar Ras broke his connection with the Foitan from Rof Golan. When he turned and spoke directly to Aissur Aissur Rus, the latter's translator caught his words and turned them into Spanglish: "The barbarians have agreed to parley with us. Even they know the extent of the *kwopillot* menace."

"Excellent," Aissur Aissur Rus said. "All the resources we and they both can bring together will be important in eliminating revenge-minded *kwopillot* backed by the technological power of the Great Ones."

"You have stated my precise concern." Pawasar Pawasar Ras went on, "Humans Bernard and Jennifer, your presence will be required at this parley. You had the greatest and most significant contact with the denizens of the tower."

"May we go back to my ship first so we can rest and wash?" Greenberg asked.

"Rest and wash here," Pawasar Pawasar Ras said. "If further trouble erupts from the Great Unknown, this base is the most secure place on the planet. We would not want you to be lost before you have provided us with the information we need."

"What about afterward?" Jennifer said. Pawasar Pawasar Ras did not deign to reply, from which she drew her own dark conclusions. Reluctantly, though, she admitted to herself that the Foitan administrator had a point. She wished the *Harold Meeker* were an armed and armored dreadnought instead of a thoroughly ordinary trading ship.

By Foitani standards, the chamber to which Aissur Aissur Rus led her and Greenberg was luxuriously appointed, which is to say that it had its own plumbing fixtures and a foam pad twice as thick as the one she'd enjoyed—or rather, not enjoyed—on her journey from Saugus to Odern. Aissur Aissur Rus took the door with him when he left, but Jennifer was sure the room was bugged.

Sighing, she walked over to what the Foitani used for a toilet. "Turn your back," she told Greenberg. "I hate this miserable excuse for plumbing."

"I know what you mean," he answered. "Still, given the choice between this and what the Great Ones had us do earlier today, I'll take this."

"Not my idea of a pleasant choice," she answered.

A little later, they both got out of their clothes and washed in the lukewarm washbasin water that was the only water they had. Greenberg shook his head as he examined his tattered coverall. "I should have insisted on going back to the *Harold Meeker*, for fresh clothes if nothing else."

"Too late to worry about it now." Jennifer scrubbed and scrubbed until most of the dirt came off her hide. She looked down at herself. Even clean, she was several different colors, most of them unappetizing. "With all these scratches and bruises and scrapes, I look more like a road map than a human being."

"A relief map, maybe. The terrain is lovely," Greenberg said. Jennifer snorted, not quite comfortably; even foolish compliments made her uneasy. Greenberg went on, "What do you think we ought to do now?"

She chose to think he was talking about the situation generally rather than the two of them in particular. She was too tired to worry about the two of them in particular. "Given the chance, I'd just as soon sleep," she said. "If we're going to be talking to the Rof Golani, we shouldn't be punchy while we're at it."

If he'd had anything else in mind, he didn't show it. He got dressed and lay down on the pad. Jennifer joined him a moment later. No sooner was she horizontal than exhaustion bludgeoned her.

"Wake up, humans!" The flat Spanglish from the translator was loud and abrupt enough to make sure they did just that. Jennifer found she'd snuggled against Greenberg while she slept, whether for warmth, protection, or no particular reason she couldn't say. The voice from overhead went on, "The delegation from Rof Golan has arrived. Your immediate presence at the deliberations is necessary."

"Yes, Thegun Thegun Nug," Jennifer said around a yawn.

A brief pause, then. "How do you know to whom you speak? The translator eliminates the timbre of individual voices."

"It doesn't eliminate personalities," she answered; let the order-giving pest make of that what he would. Whatever he made of it, he said nothing more. She asked Greenberg, "How long were we out?"

"A couple of hours," he answered after a glance at his watch. "Better than nothing, less than enough."

"Enough of your chatter," Thegun Thegun Nug said. "As I told you, your presence is required immediately."

Jennifer was fed up enough with his arrogance to tell him to take a flying leap, but a door opened in the wall just then. Behind it stood a Foitan with one of their nasty stunners. He gestured imperiously. "Charming as always," she said to the ceiling as she stood up. Thegun Thegun Nug did not bother answering.

The Foitan gestured again: *out*. He stepped back to make sure Jennifer and Greenberg could not get behind him. They followed a glowing ceiling light. He followed them. After a while, he rapped on a hallway wall. When the rap produced a door, he pointed through it. The two humans went in. The door vanished behind them.

Pawasar Pawasar Ras, Aissur Aissur Rus, and several other Foitani from Odern stood against one wall of the room. A smaller number of blue-gray Foitani from Rof Golan stood against the opposite wall. No one carried any weapons. From the way the two groups kept empty space between them, Jennifer got the feeling they'd fight with bare hands if they got too close together.

The Rof Golani turned their red eyes on the humans. Pawasar Pawasar Ras spoke; his translator passed his words to Jennifer and Greenberg. "Warleader, these are the aliens of whom I spoke. Humans, know that you face the Rof Golani warleader Voskop W Wurd and his staff."

Voskop W Wurd took half a step forward to identify himself. He looked like a warleader, especially if the war was to be fought with claws and fangs. When he spoke, his words had the howling quality Jennifer had heard before from Rof Golani. Pawasar Pawasar Ras's translator abraded emotion from them. "You are the creatures who effected entry into the Great Unknown?"

"So we are," Greenberg said. "Your soldiers did their level best to kill us while we were in there, too."

Several Foitani from Rof Golan snarled as that was translated. Jennifer was glad they were unarmed. Voskop W Wurd spoke to Pawasar Pawasar Ras. "You are soft, blue one. You allow the vermin more license than even a person deserves."

Aissur Aissur Rus answered for his boss. "And because of it, Rof Golani, we have learned more than we would have with our usual straightforward approach to non-Foitani intelligences."

Voskop W Wurd's wordless snarl told what he thought of that. But in his own way, he, too, was an officer and leader. "This is a parley, to seek information," he said, as if reminding himself. "Very well, creatures, inform me."

Having met Enfram Enfram Marf, Jennifer knew what the typical "straightforward" Foitani attitude toward other intelligent races was like. The Great Ones had shown it, too, so Voskop W Wurd's version was less irritating than it might have been otherwise. She merely wished him into the hottest fire-pit in hell before she began telling what had happened over the previous couple of days. She and Greenberg took turns with the story. They must have been interesting, for Voskop W Wurd eventually settled down and listened just as if they had been Foitani.

At one point, he asked, "What is the mechanism that creates a ring of insanity around the Great Unknown?"

"We do not know that," Pawasar Pawasar Ras answered. "We have been trying to learn for many years."

Again, a little later, "How is it that you creatures were able to enter the central tower and we True Folk not only failed but also failed to perceive the existence of an opening?"

"I don't know how that happened, either," Jennifer said. "The Foitani from Odern also couldn't see the opening; I do know that."

"It is so," Pawasar Pawasar Ras admitted. "Voskop W Wurd, when the humans went inside the central tower, our visual observations and the readings of our instruments reported that they were penetrating a wall which remained solid. Indeed, it did remain solid for your soldiers close by. The Great Ones seem to have mastered selective permeability of solid matter. How they did this, I cannot say."

"Selective is right," Greenberg said. "When we wanted to get out of the tower later on, the wall was solid for, or rather against, us, too."

"Tell me of the Great Ones," Voskop W Wurd said. As best

they could, Jennifer and Greenberg did. When they finished, the
Foitan from Rof Golan made a ripping-cloth noise the translator
rendered as a thoughtful grunt. "To think they truly have survived, to think their knowledge is available for hunting down."

"I see two problems with that," Jennifer said.

"You are not a Foitan. Who cares what you see?" Voskop W
Wurd said.

"If you don't, why are you asking me questions?" Jennifer
asked. Voskop W Wurd's lips skinned back from his teeth. Jennifer ignored him and went on, "First, now that the Great Ones
are awake again, they may be interested in hunting down what
you know, too. And second, they're *kwopillot*, so how do you
propose to deal with them?"

Voskop W Wurd turned to Pawasar Pawasar Ras. "There can
be no doubt they are *kwopillot*?"

"None." Pawasar Pawasar Ras spoke to the air. "Bring in
the evidence." A door opened in the wall opposite the one by
which Jennifer and Greenberg stood. Two Foitani from Odern
dragged in the torn corpse of a Great One. Pawasar Pawasar Ras
addressed Voskop W Wurd, "Judge for yourself."

Voskop W Wurd's nostrils flared. The snarl he had given Jennifer was as nothing next to the one he unleashed now. The
gray-blue Foitani from Rof Golan who were with him echoed
the cry. He said, "Aye, that is the harshest *kwopil* reek I've ever
had the misfortune to encounter. They were all thus?"

"Every one we encountered," Pawasar Pawasar Ras answered.

"Then every one needs to be tied down in the hot sun and
disemboweled. That's how we keep the menace of *kwopillot*
from spreading among us," Voskop W Wurd declared.

Jennifer gulped. She hoped the Foitani from Odern would
denounce Voskop W Wurd for the bloodthirsty barbarian he
was. But Aissur Aissur Rus said only, "We use lethal injections,
ourselves. Still, the principle remains the same."

Greenberg whispered, "I wonder what *kwopillot* do to ordinary Foitani when they're the ones in power."

"Nothing good, I'd bet," Jennifer whispered back.

"You Oderna are too soft with your aliens," Voskop W Wurd
said to Pawasar Pawasar Ras. "There they go, plotting who
knows what between themselves."

"Repeat yourselves, humans Jennifer and Bernard, loud enough for the translator to pick up your words," Pawasar Pawasar Ras said.

Before Jennifer could repeat herself, a Foitani voice started shouting from a ceiling speaker. The translator brought her the gist of the announcement. "Honored kin-group leader, radar reports the central tower of the Great Unknown has lifted off from the surface of Gilver and is performing as a spacecraft. We have visual confirmation as well. Please advise."

VIII

"A SPACECRAFT?" PAWASAR Pawasar Ras, Aissur Aissur Rus, and Voskop W Wurd said it in the Foitani language, Jennifer and Greenberg in Spanglish.

Voskop W Wurd recovered first. He shouted in the Foitani language. "Shoot the foul-smelling thing down," the translator said. "Your ships and mine together, Oderna. We can kill each other any time we choose. The *kwopillot* will not wait."

"That is a reasonable assessment of the situation," Pawasar Pawasar Ras said after a moment's pause for thought. He spoke to the ceiling. "All ships from Odern are directed to destroy the spacecraft which has arisen from the Great Unknown. Warleader Voskop W Wurd instructs Rof Golani ships to cooperate in this effort."

"Missiles launching," the ceiling speaker reported.

Voskop W Wurd bared his teeth. "This is not a proper headquarters, Pawasar Pawasar Ras. If I cannot bite the foe in person, at least let me see how my fellows' fangs sink in."

"As you wish," Pawasar Pawasar Ras said after another pause. "I do not think you or your followers would be in a good position to betray us." He rapped on the wall behind him, then hurried through the door he had called into being. Aissur Aissur Rus and his other aides followed. The Foitani from Rof Golan were right behind.

The Rof Golani did not bother making the doorway close after themselves. "Come on," Jennifer said to Greenberg. "If we follow them, we may get some idea of what's going on."

"We may get our heads bitten off, too—literally, if the Rof

205

Golani have anything to say about it," he answered. All the same, he went after the Foitani. So did Jennifer.

They had to trot to catch up with the bigger aliens, then to keep up with them. A couple of Rof Golani snarled at them, but otherwise left them alone. They hurried into the command post hard on Voskop W Wurd's heels.

The plan had been chaotic enough before the Rof Golani came in. Foitani from Odern ran here and there, shouted at one another and into headsets, pointed at screens and holovid radar plots. A couple of the dark blue Foitani turned in threatening fashion toward the gray-blue interlopers from Rof Golan. Pawasar Pawasar Ras said, "They are to become our cobelligerents against the flying tower. Furnish Voskop W Wurd with communications gear, that he may command his spacecraft to cooperate with us against the common foe, for *kwopillot* cannot be other than the enemies of all proper Foitani."

One of the Foitani from Odern gave Voskop W Wurd a headset. He screamed into it. Watching one of the radar tanks, Jennifer saw red sparks begin to move in unison with blue ones as both colors converged on a bigger white point of light.

Greenberg was watching the tank, too. He said, "The Rof Golani came here intending to smash up Gilver. They ought to be able to blow the tower into the middle of next week, no matter how big it is."

"Do we want them to?" Jennifer asked. "I know they say the old-time Foitani are evil and vicious, but as far as I can see, they're just acting the same way the modern ones do. And since when are aliens' sex lives any of our business?"

"I'd feel better about being neutral if we still had a way home in case the Great Ones wrecked the *Harold Meeker*," he answered. "As long as it's sitting outside this base, I'm for the Foitani from Odern and Rof Golan."

"Something to that," Jennifer had to admit.

She and Greenberg did their best to stay out from underfoot as Foitani hurried this way and that. Jumping clear was all up to them, for the Foitani would not change directions for their sake. Jennifer wondered if that was because humans were too small for Foitani to bother noticing, or just because they were non-Foitani and therefore not worth dodging. Whichever way it was—she suspected the latter—she quickly learned to grow eyes in the back of her head to keep from getting trampled.

A Rof Golani ship abruptly vanished from the radar tank. Voskop W Wurd screamed something that the translator rendered as, "How extremely unfortunate." A good deal of juice seemed to have been squeezed out somewhere.

More ships started disappearing. No matter what sort of Foitani perverts crewed it, no matter that it had been grounded for twenty-eight thousand years, the ship that had been a tower was a formidable killing machine. Voskop W Wurd made noises suggesting a wild animal with a leg caught in a trap. Pawasar Pawasar Ras sounded calmer—that seemed the way on Odern—but no happier.

After a dismayingly short while, the course of the battle grew clear: the Great Ones were mopping up everything the modern Foitani could throw at them. Pawasar Pawasar Ras ordered one of his few surviving ships to break off and head back to Odern.

Voskop W Wurd yowled a phrase that sounded as if it would have made a pretty good operations order for the end of the world. "A cowardly act," the translator reported bloodlessly.

"By no means," Pawasar Pawasar Ras said. "Suppose we are defeated and destroyed here. That will leave the *kwopillot* free to rampage through the Foitani sphere, with no one to know what they are until they come within smelling range. Our homeworlds must be warned. What I do is wisdom. Deny it if you may."

The Rof Golani warleader did not reply directly, but spoke into his headset. Before long, one of the red blips in the radar tank turned tail and boosted toward hyperdrive kick-in. Voskop W Wurd said no more about it. No Foitan Jennifer had ever seen was any good at admitting he was wrong.

"I just hope the Foitani sphere is all these revived Great Ones worry about for a while," Greenberg said. "If they have records of humans, they know where Earth is."

"They'd find out soon enough anyway, from dealing with the Foitani from Odern," Jennifer answered. It was not much consolation. One way or another, trouble was coming.

Trouble was, in fact, already here. The ship that had spent a geological epoch being a tower was still dreadfully efficient in its own role. Gallant to the end, the Foitani from Odern and Rof

Golan kept attacking long after they must have known they were doomed. Back on Earth, a long time ago, tribesmen had shown insane courage by charging straight at machine-gun nests. But for making them end up dead in gruesomely large numbers, their courage hadn't got them anything. Similar bravery served the Foitani no better now.

"Attack from space imminent," Pawasar Pawasar Ras called. "Prepare to resist to the end."

Jennifer was certain the Foitani would do just that. She was also certain the end had become quite imminent. She squeezed Bernard Greenberg's hand, hard. "I love you, too," she said. When the end comes, some words should not be left unspoken.

He hugged her. She hugged him, too. She did not care what the Foitani thought, not now. The only good thing she saw about being here was that the end would probably be quick. The Great Ones up there had overwhelming weapons and could hardly miss.

Voskop W Wurd said, "Get me a hand weapon, Oderna, that I may shoot at my slayers as they destroy me."

Jennifer watched the tower-ship in the radar tank. It hung overhead, an outsized sword of Damocles. Suddenly one of the communications screens lit up. A green-blue Foitani face peered out of it: a Great One. A technician spoke to Pawasar Pawasar Ras. "Honored kin-group leader, the, ah, Foitan Solut Mek Kem would address you."

Jennifer's heart leaped. Surely one did not seek to address a person one was on the very point of destroying.

Pawasar Pawasar Ras saw things in a different light. He said, "So you have called to gloat, have you, *kwopil*?" Jennifer's hopes plunged as far and as fast as they had risen. Pawasar Pawasar Ras could not help knowing his own species, knowing what its members did and did not do.

The Great One called Solut Mek Kem said, "By your murderousness, I gather your kind still exists, *vodran*." Jennifer felt like screaming at the translator program for falling asleep on the words that really mattered. Meanwhile, Solut Mek Kem went on, "We all hoped earthgrip would have taken you by the time we returned to the sphere at large."

But for once, the problem was not the translator's fault. Pawasar Pawasar Ras said, "*Vodran?* I do not know this word, Solut Mek Kem."

Voskop W Wurd echoed him, less politely: "Trust the stinking *kwopillot* to come up with a foul-smelling name for proper people."

"You've grown old in depravity, to think it the proper state for Foitani," Solut Mek Kem said. "I see the race has had time to degenerate physically as well as morally, else our sphere would not be plagued with such hideous specimens as you."

Voskop W Wurd told the Great One what he—or was it she this time?—could do to himself, in explicit anatomical detail. Jennifer did not think any of the suggestions sounded like much fun and did not think many were physically possible. Those limitations didn't bother humans in a temper, and they didn't bother Voskop W Wurd, either.

When the Rof Golani warleader ran down, Pawasar Pawasar Ras added, "You tax us with murderousness, yet outside this tower which is now a ship, you *kwopillot* wantonly slaughtered a great many Foitani, many of them unarmed and all of them mentally disabled by whatever means you employed to keep us from your precinct on Gilver."

"You are *vodranei*," Solut Mek Kem said. "You deserve no better. As I said, we had hoped our fellows would have exterminated you from the galaxy by the time we reawakened. Though I see it is not so, we shall join with the worlds of our kind and finish the job once and for all."

"What worlds of your own kind?" Pawasar Pawasar Ras said. "*Kwopillot* have no worlds. They merely plague true Foitani whenever a nest of them appears. This is so on every world where our kind survives, and has been so ever since the Suicide Wars cast our sphere down into barbarism."

"Lie all you like, *vodran*," the old-time Foitan said. "We could not have been destroyed in a few centuries."

Jennifer hurried over to Pawasar Pawasar Ras and tugged on the fur of his flank. "May I speak to the Great One?" she asked urgently.

Pawasar Pawasar Ras brushed her away, or tried to. She hung onto his massive arm. "Are you stricken mad?" he said. "Get away. This is not your concern."

Unexpectedly, Voskop W Wurd came to her rescue. "Why

not let the creature talk to the stinking *kwopillot*?'' he demanded. "Do *kwopillot* deserve any better?''

"There is some truth in what you say, warleader," Pawasar
Pawasar Ras admitted. Under other circumstances, Jennifer
would have been furious at the denigration inherent in what the
Rof Golani Foitan said and in Pawasar Pawasar Ras's agreement
with it. Now all she cared about was having this Solut Mek Kem
hear her. After a pause for thought that seemed endless, Pawasar
Pawasar Ras said, "Very well, human Jennifer, you may speak.
Here." He overturned a plastic container for her. "Stand on
this, so you will be tall enough for the vision pickup to notice
you. I shall stand close by, that my translator may render your
words into the speech of the Great Ones."

"Thank you, honored kin-group leader." Jennifer clam-
bered onto the container. She could tell Solut Mek Kem saw
her; the old-time Foitan's teeth came out. She said, "Honored Foitan—"

"So you *vodranet* consort with sub-Foitani, do you?" Solut Mek Kem interrupted. "We might have expected it of
you."

"*Will* you listen to me?" Jennifer said. "Your tower hasn't
been sitting on Gilver for a few centuries. You've been there
twenty-eight thousand of your years."

"It is amusing, *vodran*." Solut Mek Kem still refused to speak
directly to Jennifer. "But why should I listen to its lies any more
than yours?"

"I presume your tower or spaceship or whatever it really is
recorded Bernard and me when we went inside," Jennifer said.
"Check those records, why don't you? For one thing, you'll see
we have stunners that aren't like yours. For another, you'll see
one of your people comparing us to—I don't know whether
they're specimens or records of my kind back when we were
savages. You figure out how long it might take for a race to go
from savages to star travelers. And if I'm lying, then you can go
right on ignoring me."

The screen that had shown Solut Mek Kem went blank. Aissur
Aissur Rus said, "Well done, human Jennifer. You have made
the wicked pervert pause and examine assumptions, something
we did not succeed in accomplishing."

Bernard Greenberg said, "You ought to think about examining your own assumptions, Aissur Aissur Rus. Since when is someone who differs sexually from you necessarily a pervert—or necessarily wicked, for that matter?''

"*Kwopillot are* wicked perverts," Aissur Aissur Rus said.

Jennifer felt like banging her head against a wall; Aissur Aissur Rus not only wasn't examining his assumptions, he hadn't even noticed them. She asked, "What's a *vodran*?''

"We do not know this word, either," Pawasar Pawasar Ras said. "It is a piece of offal the *kwopillot* have appended to the pure and beautiful speech of the Great Ones, nothing more."

Just then, Solut Mek Kem reappeared in the holovid screen. "I will converse with the sub-Foitani creature," he announced.

"We call ourselves humans," Jennifer said pointedly.

The Great Ones, whether perverted or not, had all the arrogance of their descendants and then some. Solut Mek Kem said, "I care nothing for what you call yourself, creature. I have some concern, however, over your statements. It appears true that Foitani encountered your kind in the past. You were noted as being uncommonly brutish and scheduled for extermination. Why this failed to take place is a matter of some puzzlement to me."

Jennifer opened her mouth, then closed it again. Hearing that her species was going to have been killed off was not something she could take in at once. Into her silence, Aissur Aissur Rus said, "No doubt the Suicide Wars intervened and prevented the Foitani of that distant time from completing the protocol they envisioned."

"Suicide Wars?" It was Solut Mek Kem's turn to pause. Not even a Foitan could care for the sound of that.

"Suicide Wars," Aissur Aissur Rus repeated. He spoke to the command center's computer system. A holovid star map appeared in front of him. "This is the area the Foitani once inhabited, not so?"

"No. Wait. Yes, it appears to be," Solut Mek Kem said. "We customarily oriented our maps with the other direction to the top, thus my brief confusion."

"One more thing about the Great Ones of which we were ignorant," Aissur Aissur Rus observed before returning to the business at hand. "These are the known Foitani worlds now." The few points of light Dargnil Dargnil Lin had shown Jennifer back on Odern now sparkled in front of her. Aissur Aissur Rus said, "All other worlds within the sphere are devoid of our kind, or even of intelligent sub-Foitani life forms."

"More *vodran* lies, fabrications to confuse me," Solut Mek Kem said.

"If you will arrange a data link with us, we will supply you with documentation sufficient to change your mind," Aissur Aissur Rus said. "We could not have prepared this volume of information in advance to trick you, you will realize, because we had no idea we would discover you alive in the tower, and still less that you would prove to be *kwopillot*." More flexible than most of his kind, Aissur Aissur Rus managed not to affix a malodorous epithet to the term.

"Send your data," Solut Mek Kem said. "The *Vengeance* will refrain from destroying you until they are evaluated— you are no spacecraft, and cannot run. But woe betide you if we detect falsehood. It will only make your fate the harsher."

How could any fate be worse than destruction? Jennifer wondered. She did not speak her thought aloud. The Foitani might have had answers to questions like that.

"Did you notice the name of the ship?" Bernard Greenberg said. "The old-time Foitani who set up the Great Unknown must have figured their side might not win the war. I wonder if they figured no one would win it."

Jennifer thought about the map Aissur Aissur Rus had shown to Solut Mek Kem. She thought about the sphere the Foitani had once ruled, about the handful of worlds they still inhabited. She thought about how many other species the imperial Foitani must have destroyed, about the calm way Solut Mek Kem remarked that humanity was on their list. Softly, she said, "Maybe that's just as well."

"Maybe it is," Greenberg agreed.

The Foitani in the command center seemed to have forgotten about the humans again, now that Jennifer had bought them some time. That was typical of them, she thought, but she could not make herself angry. She only wished they'd never heard of her in the first place.

Solut Mek Kem came back on the screen after perhaps half an hour. He said, "Our computers have been analyzing and summarizing the information you are presenting to us. The problem does seem rather more complex than we may have envisioned."

From a Foitan, even so small an admission had to spring from profound shock. Jennifer realized that at once. She wondered if Pawasar Pawasar Ras or Voskop W Wurd would see it. To them, it might be taken as only a sign of weakness. Before either of them could speak, she climbed on the plastic box and said loudly, "Then you agree it's wiser to talk, Solut Mek Kem, than to try to fight off every starship from every Foitani world that still knows about spaceflight?"

Pawasar Pawasar Ras growled at her. Voskop W Wurd snarled at her and took a step in her direction. His clawed hands stretched greedily toward her. She felt like Miles Vorkosigan—much too small and extremely breakable. How would the Middle English SF hero have handled this particular mess? Audacity, that was his only way. She went on quickly, not giving any Foitan a chance to talk: "A peace conference seems the appropriate solution, don't you all think? None of the modern Foitani are likely to get any of the technology of the Great Ones without peace, unless the *Vengeance* shoots it at them. And you Foitani from long ago will only be hounded all through this sphere unless you come to some kind of terms with your modern relatives."

"Peace with *vodranet*? Never," Solut Mek Kem said.

"Talk with *kwopillot*? I'd sooner claw my own belly open," Voskop W Wurd said.

Jennifer glumly waited for whatever bellicose ranting Pawasar Pawasar Ras chose. But before the honored kin-group leader could get a rant in edgewise, Aissur Aissur Rus said, "Save over communicators, how can we talk with those on board the *Vengeance*?" Again, he had sense enough to keep to himself the slurs he was no doubt thinking. "If we and they come into the same room, their smell will make us want only to kill, and ours no doubt the same with them."

Jennifer felt like kissing him, no matter how repugnant he

might find it. *How* could be solved; *never* left little room for negotiation. She said, "If you wanted to meet face-to-face, as I can see you might, do you have nose filters to keep your two sides from smelling each other?"

"We would still know they were *kwopillot*," Pawasar Pawasar Ras said.

Voskop W Wurd put it more pungently. "I'd smell that perverts' reek if you cut off my nose."

Solut Mek Kem seemed no more enthusiastic. The *kwopil* said, "Better to exterminate all *vodranet* and begin to populate the sphere anew with Foitani who have not been altered to the point of degeneracy and decay."

"You are the altered ones, you *kwopillot*," Pawasar Pawasar Ras said.

Jennifer filed that away for further consideration; she had more pressing business now. She said, "Don't you think, *kwopillot* and *vodranet*, both sides have done enough exterminating here? Aissur Aissur Rus, call up those maps of how your sphere looked in the days of the Great Ones and how it is now."

Aissur Aissur Rus did as she asked. The few points of light that still glowed in what had been a great shining globe told their own story. Another round of war at that intensity might leave no Foitani of any sexual persuasion alive anywhere. The projection was plain enough for even the big aliens to get outside their ideologies and notice it.

Pawasar Pawasar Ras saw. He said, "You can destroy us here on Gilver, *kwopillot*, but I doubt you can destroy all our worlds without being slain yourselves in the attempt."

"Let's fight them now," Voskop W Wurd said. "The more damage we do to them, the easier a time the attackers who come after us will have." Some people, Jennifer thought, did not want to get the message. But even one of Voskop W Wurd's subordinates took the warleader aside and spoke urgently to him.

Solut Mek Kem said, "What a dolorous choice: the galaxy without Foitani or full of accursed *vodranet*. We shall have to consult among ourselves as to which alternative appears preferable." He disappeared from the screen.

"Talking with *kwopillot*!" Pawasar Pawasar Ras shook his

head in a very human gesture of bewilderment and dismay. "Who would have supposed it would come to that?"

"You know, one of the things Foitani really need to learn, if you'll forgive my telling you, is diplomacy," Bernard Greenberg said. "The Great Ones never seemed to have used it—they were always one people themselves, and other races were just there to be exploited or massacred. Then when they had this split into *kwopillot* and *vodranet*, the only thing they knew how to do with beings who were different was kill them. There are other choices. You Foitani from Odern and Rof Golan—and I suppose your other starfaring races—are starting to get the idea, because you have to deal with each other, and I suppose also because you have the old-time Suicide Wars as a horrible example. But none of you is what you'd call good at dealing with anybody from outside your own immediate group."

"He's right," Jennifer said. "Now you're all in a place where you can see that a big war isn't the right answer, but you don't have any other weapons—you should pardon the expression—handy with which to attack the problem."

"War is simple and direct. Its answers are clear-cut," Voskop W Wurd said.

"A writer of my species once said that, for any problem, there is always a solution that is simple, obvious—and wrong," Jennifer answered. Voskop W Wurd started to snarl at her, then stopped, looking as thoughtful as any Rof Golani Foitan she'd ever seen. She suddenly laughed. Here she was, doing exactly what the Foitani from Odern had kidnapped her to do—using her knowledge of human literature—even if not science fiction this time—to help them deal with the problem of the Great Ones.

Solut Mek Kem, who personified the problem of the Great Ones, came back onto the screen in front of Pawasar Pawasar Ras. The *kwopil* said, "We will speak with you, unless you would rather fight." By the way that came out in the Spanglish, and by the way he let his teeth show, Jennifer guessed he was half hoping for a battle.

"We will talk with you," Pawasar Pawasar Ras said. "War is the obvious solution; but for every question, there is an answer that is obvious, simple, and wrong."

"An interesting point of view," Solut Mek Kem said. Jennifer didn't know whether to be angry at Pawasar Pawasar Ras for taking her thought without giving her credit or glad he had listened to her. She got little time to think it over, for Solut Mek Kem went on, "In any case, we will also talk, I suppose. Do you possess nose filters such as the yellow-haired creature suggested? They might keep our two sides from fighting whether we so intend or not. The odor of *vodranet* cannot help but inflame us."

"I will put our technical staff to work fabricating filters," Pawasar Pawasar Ras answered. "We are similarly aroused—and not in any sexual sense, I assure you—by the way *kwopillot* smell. As for these non-Foitani, they are without a doubt ugly, but they have their uses."

From a Foitan, Jennifer knew, that was about as good a recommendation as she was likely to get.

Just when all seemed sweetness and light—or as close to sweetness and light as was practicable after ground and space combat between two groups each of which wished extinction upon the other—Voskop W Wurd reminded everyone that there were in fact not two groups involved, but three: "Nose filters? I don't give a putrescent fart about nose filters. I don't have to smell *kwopillot* to know they stink, either. Let them come after Rof Golan if they've the stomachs for it. We'll blast them into incandescent gas, and better than they deserve, too."

"Oh, shut up, you hotheaded fool," Aissur Aissur Rus said—hardly diplomatic language, but the most direct statement Jennifer had yet heard out of a Foitan from Odern.

Greenberg added, "Voskop W Wurd, think about this: suppose they blast your people on Rof Golan into incandescent gas instead? That sort of thing happened all the time during the Suicide Wars. Wouldn't you rather talk first and then fight, given the chance? Think of it in terms of tactics if you don't understand diplomacy. Before you start a war, you ought to learn about your enemies."

"I know they are *kwopillot*. What more do I need?"

"You might remember they're also Great Ones," Jennifer said. "And remember how many ships you just lost. You might even remember that if the Foitani from Odern do talk with them and you don't, they might make common cause and leave you out in the cold.''

"We would not do that,'' Pawasar Pawasar Ras and Aissur Aissur Rus protested in the same breath, so perfectly in chorus that the translator turned the two sets of identical words into a single sentence. Were less riding on this ticklish situation, it might have been funny.

However pious their protest, the two Foitani from Odern failed to convince Voskop W Wurd. "Of course you would, if you saw any advantage to it,'' he said. "You Oderna are like that, and what's more, you know it perfectly well. But if you think you'll make a deal with the perverts behind my back, think again. This creature has given me a good reason to enter into these talks: to keep you as honest as may be.''

"Congratulations,'' Greenberg told Jennifer. "You've just made this a problem with three sides instead of two. Now the Rof Golani are ready to take on the Foitani from Odern again.''

"Maybe there are three sides, but they're all going to talk,'' Jennifer answered. "When there were just two, they weren't talking. Sometimes even going backward is progress.''

"I'm sure the Foitani from Odern would have agreed with you, the way they blindly loved the Great Ones till they found this batch of *kwopillot*.''

Before Jennifer could answer, Solut Mek Kem said, "If we are to enter into these distasteful discussions, *vodranet*, let us begin. We will send down a flier to bring your representatives back here to the *Vengeance*.''

"Come up into your lair?'' Voskop W Wurd exclaimed. "Do you take me for a male altogether bereft of his senses? Treating with the Oderna is quite bad enough. Why should I tamely walk in and let you do as you would with me?''

"The wiser course would be for your envoys to come down to this research station,'' Pawasar Pawasar Ras said.

"That will not happen,'' Solut Mek Kem said at once. "We have already seen how you treat our kind when we approach this research base of yours. You merely seek the opportunity to dispose of our representatives quietly.''

"Your behavior toward the Rof Golani in the precinct of the

Great Unknown and toward the fliers of both sides in our recent dispute naturally leaves us suspicious of your good intentions,'' Aissur Aissur Rus said.

"We will not meet with you inside your station," Solut Mek Kem said.

"We will not meet with you inside your spaceship," Pawasar Pawasar Ras said.

"I wouldn't want to meet you *kwopillot* squatting over a waste-disposal hole," Voskop W Wurd added.

"These talks aren't off to what the diplomats call a constructive start," Greenberg observed.

Jennifer could only reply with a mournful shake of her head. If the parties allegedly negotiating couldn't even agree on where they would allegedly negotiate, the alleged negotiations looked anything but promising.

Then she said, "If the one side won't come down here and the other won't go up there, why don't you all come to the human ship, the *Harold Meeker*?"

"Yes, why not?" Greenberg chimed in. Under his breath, he added for her ears alone, "Anything to start this moving and give us a chance to get out of here." Jennifer let out a small, silent sigh of relief; it was his ship, after all, that she'd just proposed as a negotiation site.

"Come aboard the human ship for these discussions?" Pawasar Pawasar Ras said. "I would almost prefer bearding the *kwopillot* in their den." Jennifer blinked and wondered what the literal Foitani version was of the phrase the translator had rendered in that fashion.

"Go aboard a ship constructed by creatures?" Solut Mek Kem said. "We do not treat with creatures; we destroy them."

"You wouldn't be treating with us. You'd be treating with Pawasar Pawasar Ras and Voskop W Wurd," Greenberg said. "I might add, just so you know, we humans range across as much space as you Foitani did when your empire was at its height."

"You are telling me you are widespread and dangerous vermin," Solut Mek Kem said.

"I'm telling you we're widespread and dangerous, yes,"

Greenberg answered, "But to us, you are the vermin. You'd better bear it in mind."

Solut Mek Kem snarled at that. So did Voskop W Wurd. So did Pawasar Pawasar Ras, but not as loudly. Aissur Aissur Rus said, "Unlike others here, I have been into human space. They lack our race's straightforward character, but are not to be taken lightly. Success is the best measure of a species' true attributes; by that standard, their attributes are formidable indeed."

"They are small and weak and ugly." This time Solut Mek Kem and Voskop W Wurd said the same thing together. Neither looked happy at agreeing with the other.

Well, you Foitani are big and fuzzy and vicious, Jennifer thought. She kept it to herself. Studied insult of the sort Greenberg had given was one way of breaking through the arrogant contempt with which the Foitani viewed those who were not of their kind. Indulged in too often, though, it degenerated into name-calling of the sort five-year-olds used when they argued over toys.

"Just remember, the *Harold Meeker* is neutral ground," Greenberg said. Now he sounded calm and reasonable and persuasive: downright diplomatic, Jennifer thought—too bad the translator would wash all tone from his words. He went on, "Neither of you trusts the other's stronghold. If you can't trust my ship, at least all of you can distrust it equally."

"You are in the company of *vodranet*, creature," Solut Mek Kem said. "Before we would hazard ourselves, we demand the right to examine the proposed chamber for booby traps. *Vodran* treachery is notorious and despicable."

"Inspect all you like," Greenberg agreed cheerfully.

"We will have monitors present when the putative inspectors board your ship, human Bernard," Pawasar Pawasar Ras said. "Who knows what *kwopillot* might install under the pretext of removal?"

"That's fine, too," Greenberg said. "If both kinds of Foitani are going to be on the *Harold Meeker* at the same time, though, everything had better wait until you get those nose filters designed. I don't want anybody blowing holes in my cargo bay because he doesn't like the way someone else smells.''

"One other thing," Jennifer added. "Everyone should remember that ships from Gilver are on their way to Odern and to Rof Golan. They'll probably bring big warfleets back with them. It would be nice to have some sort of agreement by the time those fleets get here. If we don't, I think another round of Suicide Wars starts right here. Is this fight worth your whole species?''

After she asked the question, she realized all flavors of Foitani could be intransigent enough to answer *yes*. When no one—not even Voskop W Wurd—said anything, she counted that a victory. The modern Foitani still lived in the long horrid shadow of the Suicide Wars; they knew too well what another round of such insensate frenzy would do to their surviving worlds. As for the newly revived Great Ones, perhaps they were still in shock from learning what the rest of their race had done to itself while they lay dormant through the millennia.

Greenberg prodded everyone along. "Have we decided, then, to meet in the cargo hold of the *Harold Meeker* as soon as nose filters make it possible?''

Again, none of the Foitani said anything. Again, Jennifer counted that a victory.

Being back in the *Harold Meeker* was almost as good as being home on Saugus, at least when the alternative was the Foitani research base. The lighting felt right to human eyes, the plumbing fixtures were as they should be, the chairs were made for human fundaments—and, best of all, the Foitani kept out of the crew compartment.

They were and stayed busy down in the cargo bay. They moved around boxes and bales to create a clear space on the floor where they installed their own furniture and computer gear. The Great Ones cleared out bugs set by the Foitani from Odern. The Foitani from Odern, in turn, cleared bugs set by the Great Ones. The Foitani from Rof Golan took a turn clearing everyone else's bugs, and, presumably, planting a few of their own.

All the Foitani of whatever race who entered the cargo bay

wore a little silvery button in each nostril—"The better not to smell you, my dear," as Jennifer said to Greenberg. The nose filters seemed to work; at least, no fights broke out between *kwopillot* and *vodranet*. Greenberg manufactured a little silvery button of his own and left it on an out-of-the-way box. A suspicious Foitan from Rof Golan found it and took it away, either to destroy it or to glean from it what he could of human electronics.

"Good luck to him," Greenberg said when he discovered his little bait had been taken. "It's filled with talcum powder."

He and Jennifer got Foitani electronics to study: they persuaded Aissur Aissur Rus to give them each a translator. "I'm bloody tired of having Foitani talking all around me without the slightest idea of what they're saying," she said.

"True enough," Greenberg said, "but now that we are supposed to understand them all the time, they'll ask more from us. You'll see."

That hardly struck Jennifer as requiring the mantic gift to predict. Greenberg was proven right soon enough, too. All Foitani factions distrusted the humans and affected to despise the *Harold Meeker*. All of them, however, distrusted their furry fellows even more and actively feared the headquarters of those fellows. Thus Jennifer and Greenberg spent a good deal of their time keeping the Foitani from one another's throats. When the actual discussions started, all factions insisted that the two of them sit in as mediators.

To keep potential carnage to a minimum, only two representatives from each group went inside the trading ship's cargo bay. Pawasar Pawasar Ras and Aissur Aissur Rus spoke for the Foitani from Odern, Solut Mek Kem and a colleague named Nogal Ryn Nyr for the Great Ones, and Voskop W Wurd and his chief aide Yulvot L Reat for the Foitani from Rof Golan.

At the first uneasy meeting, all three sets of purported diplomats spent the first several minutes standing around and glaring. Voskop W Wurd let out a series of ostentatious sniffs. His nose filters must have been working, though, or he would not have been so restrained. Since the Great Ones and the Foitani from Odern seemed willing to ignore him, Jennifer did the same.

She said, "Let's start this off with an issue that I hope we can easily deal with. It doesn't involve any quarrel between the newly revived Foitani and their modern relatives. In fact, it concerns us humans. Solut Mek Kem, do you really have specimen humans aboard your ship"—she almost said, *your tower*—"or are they just images in your data storage system?"

"The distinction is not as clear as you made it, ignorant alien creature," Solut Mek Kem answered. "They are at present potential, but could be realized in actuality. Do you seek live copies?"

Jennifer gulped. She looked at Greenberg. He seemed shaken, too. Taking a pair of genuine Paleolithic people back to human space would set every anthropologist's pulse racing, and likely would be worth millions. But would it be fair to the poor Cro-Magnons themselves? Could they ever be anything more than specimens? How could they possibly adjust to twenty-eight millennia of changes?

"Do you seek live copies?" Solut Mek Kem repeated.

"Let us think about that. It's not something we have to decide right now," Jennifer answered. If the cave humans had been frozen so long in Foitani data storage, a little longer wouldn't hurt anything. She went on, "Tell me the meaning of a term you use, one our translator does not interpret: *vodran*."

"These are *vodranet*." Solut Mek Kem pointed to the Foitani delegations from Odern and Rof Golan. "They are depraved and disgusting."

"They call you *kwopillot*, and say you're perverted and revolting," Greenberg said. "We needed a good deal of work, but we finally got them to explain what *kwopillot* were. I'm not of your species; I make no judgments about what's right or wrong as far as your sexual habits go. But right or wrong, they're an important issue here, one the human Jennifer and I need to understand. Could you please explain to me what makes these Foitani *vodranet*?"

"Explain to us as well," Aissur Aissur Rus added. "This is not a word my people comprehend."

"Nor mine," Voskop W Wurd said. "What could be vile enough for a stinking *kwopil* to despise?"

"You could," Nogal Ryn Nyr told him. Aissur Aissur Rus at least grasped the concept of diplomacy, even if he didn't always use it very well. Voskop W Wurd hadn't a clue, and infuriated other people with his own aggressive lack of tact.

"Stay calm, everyone," Jennifer said, wondering how she and Greenberg could make the Foitani stay calm if they didn't feel like it when they were about the size and disposition of a like number of bears. She went on, "We're here to discuss your disagreements rationally, after all." She wished disagreements about sexual habits more readily lent themselves to rational discussion.

"Let's try again," Greenberg said. "Foitani from what is now the ship *Vengeance*, what are *vodranet*? We can't have any kind of discussion if we don't all understand what our terms mean."

"Discussing matters pertaining to reproduction is not our custom under most circumstances," Solut Mek Kem said—a view he had in common with Pawasar Pawasar Ras, though he didn't know it. "It is doubly unappetizing when attempting to evaluate manufactured monstrosities such as *vodranet*."

The Great One obviously bought tact from the same store that had sold it to Voskop W Wurd. The Rof Golani Foitan yelled, "You're the monster, *kwopil*!"

Greenberg yelled, too. "Enough!" Trying to outshout a Foitan was like trying to hold back a spaceship with bare hands, but he gave it a good game go. "Let Solut Mek Kem finish, will you? You can say whatever you want when he's done."

Fortunately, Aissur Aissur Rus supported him. "Yes, calm yourself, Voskop W Wurd. Gather intelligence before commencing operations." Advice set in a military context seemed to get through to the warleader. He snarled a couple of more times, but subsided.

"Solut Mek Kem?" Jennifer said.

But Solut Mek Kem, again like Pawasar Pawasar Ras, refused to go on. He gestured toward Nogal Ryn Nyr. *Let the flunky do the dirty work*, Jennifer thought—some attitudes crossed species lines. After a couple of false starts, Nogal Ryn Nyr said, "An unfortunate discovery made long ago is that the sexual physiology of Foitani is all too easy to alter."

"That is true enough," Aissur Aissur Rus said. "The problem of *kwopillot* would not exist were it otherwise."

"We, obviously, perceive it as the problem of *vodranet*," Nogal Ryn Nyr said. "And with greater justice, for, after all, *vodranet* represent a distortion of the original Foitani pattern, which is to say, ourselves."

Jennifer needed a second to grasp the implications of that. The Foitani from Odern and Rof Golan caught on quicker. The bellows of outrage they emitted, however, were so loud and so nearly simultaneous that they overloaded her translator, which produced a noise rather like an asthmatic warning siren.

Finally Voskop W Wurd outroared everyone else. "You lie as bad as you smell! We are the true Foitani, the true descendants of the Great Ones, not you wrongsex badstink perverts."

"Were you there in those days, *vodran*?" Nogal Ryn Nyr shot back. "How do you know whereof you speak? We can prove what we say, just as, regrettably, you appear to have proven to us the existence of the Suicide Wars and their long and painful aftermath."

"Who would believe proof from a *kwopil*?" Yulvot L Reat said. By all signs, his charm easily matched that of Voskop W Wurd.

"The suggestion is implausible on the face of it," Aissur Aissur Rus said, more politely but just as certainly. "How is it that all modern Foitani worlds are populated by normal Foitani—Foitani I would judge normal, at any rate—and *kwopillot* are universally reckoned aberrations?"

"The reason is painful to me but nonetheless obvious," Nogal Ryn Nyr said. "It appears that, insofar as the Suicide Wars had winners, those winners are *vodranet*. No doubt massacres on planets reduced to barbarism completed the overthrow of normality by—your type."

In her mind, Jennifer saw mobs of big, green-blue aliens rampaging through bombed-out cities, sniffing like bloodhounds for the hated scent of those different from themselves. Would there have been massacres at a time like that? By all she knew, the Foitani were appallingly good at massacres; they almost seemed the chief sport of the species, as battleball was for humans. The picture Nogal Ryn Nyr painted had an air of verisimilitude that worried her.

It convinced Voskop W Wurd, too; he said, "You deserve being massacred."

"We thought the same of *vodranet*, I assure you," Nogal Ryn Nyr said. "Our chief mistake appears to have been waiting too long before attempting to stamp you out."

"I will believe none of this without proof," Pawasar Pawasar Ras said. "Nothing impedes you from making any claim you like, simply for the purpose of improving your own position at these discussions."

Solut Mek Kem tossed a silvery wafer onto the table, then, after some hesitation, another one, the latter in the direction of Voskop W Wurd and Yulvot L Reat. "Here are the data," he said. "Shall we adjourn until you have put them in your computers and had the opportunity to evaluate them?"

"Let's wait one Gilver day—no more," Greenberg said. "Remember, fleets are on the way. You can start the fighting all over again, if you like."

Jennifer waited for Voskop W Wurd to say that was a good idea. But even the Rof Golani warleader kept quiet. He picked up the little data storage device as if it were a bomb. In a way, it was, for it seemed likely to blow away his misconceptions of his species' past. The four modern Foitani were quiet and thoughtful as they left the *Harold Meeker*'s cargo bay. When they were gone, the Great Ones left, too.

"Whew!" Jennifer sagged against a box which Greenberg had neatly labeled FOITANI ELECTRONIC WIDGETS. "Far as I'm concerned, the diplomats are welcome to diplomacy. Give me a simple trading run any day."

"You said it, especially when the people we're supposed to keep from each other's throats are as all-around charming as the Foitani," Greenberg said. "Right now, I would kill for a beer; Foitani kibbles and water aren't my idea of a way to unwind.''

Jennifer quoted Heinlein. "One more balanced ration will unbalance me.''

"I second that,'' Greenberg said, approving of the sentiment without recognizing the source. He went on, "The other thing is, I don't know whether we ought to be encouraging the Foitani to make peace with each other or to slug it out. If they do band together and have the technology of the Great Ones to use, they could turn into a real handful for the human worlds to deal with. But I can't say I'm eager to think of myself as the fellow who touched off the second round of the Suicide Wars.''

"I know.'' Jennifer turned and thumped her head against the box of widgets. "The trouble with the Foitani is, they have no notion of moderation whatever. Whatever they think, whatever they do, they think it or do it all out, and they're sure anybody who thinks or acts differently deserves nothing better than to have her world blown up. Still, setting them at each other's throats—''

"How could we look at ourselves in a mirror afterward?'' Greenberg walked over next to Jennifer and thumped his head, too. "The thing is, as best I can tell, getting them to slaughter each other will be a lot easier than making any sort of peace. And if they do have peace among themselves, how do we keep them from attacking all their neighbors? That seems to be the way they use peace among themselves.''

"From time to time, when I remember, I think I'd like to live through this, no matter how it turns out,'' Jennifer said.

"Me, too.'' Greenberg made the hair-pulling gesture he must have started using when he had more hair to pull. He said, "I'm going up to the living quarters and take a shower. Maybe once I soak my head, all this will make better sense. Somehow I doubt it, though.''

Jennifer rode up the lift with him. As usual, just being in an area designed by humans for humans cheered her up. Even the noise of the plumbing in the refresher chamber as Greenberg washed himself reminded her of other trading ships and of plan-

ets where she'd lived. The sound of Foitani plumbing reminded
her of nothing but kidnapping and fear.

Greenberg came out with a towel around his middle. "You
want a turn?"

"At what?" With a mischievous smile, she pulled down the
towel. When Greenberg reached for her, she skipped back.
"There, you'll see, the communicator will buzz just as we get
started." Her words didn't stop her from undoing the straps of
her coveralls.

Just as they got started, the communicator buzzed. Jennifer said something rude. Greenberg said, "You might as
well have had that shower." He sounded more resigned than
martyred.

Voice replaced the insistent chiming. "Humans Bernard and
Jennifer, this is Aissur Aissur Rus. I would like to consult with
you concerning the new information presented by the—" He
hesitated, plainly not wanting to call them either Great Ones or
kwopillot. "—by the recently revived Foitani from the Great
Unknown."

"Go ahead," Jennifer said, knowing perfectly well that he
would go ahead whether she invited him to or not.

"Although analysis can at this stage be only preliminary, the
data appear to possess validity."

"Do they?" Jennifer wasn't surprised. Solut Mek Kem
and Nogal Ryn Nyr had seemed very sure of themselves.
But if the Great Ones had originally been *kwopillot*, that
made a hash of everything the successor races believed about
themselves and their past. In an abstract way, she admired
Aissur Aissur Rus for being able to acknowledge that. He
had a lot of integrity, but he couldn't be very happy right
now.

He said, "As I stated, they appear to." He wasn't going to
concede anything he didn't have to, integrity or no. Jennifer
supposed she couldn't blame him.

"If they were *kwopillot*, how did you get to be *vodranet*?"
Greenberg asked. "Did a mutation spread through the species?"

"In a manner of speaking, yes," Aissur Aissur Rus said, and
said no more.

Having dealt with Foitani for some time, Jennifer suspected that abrupt silence meant he knew something he didn't care to let out. She tried to figure out what might make him reticent, and asked, "Was it by any chance an artificial mutation?"

More silence from the communicator. Greenberg drew his own conclusions from that and made silent clapping motions. Finally, Aissur Aissur Rus said, "If the records of the *kwopillot* are to be trusted, it was, yes." The translator was emotionless and Foitani from Odern didn't sound upset even when they were, but Jennifer knew he was anything but happy. He went on, "If they can be believed, our variety of Foitan was—engineered—for no better purpose than increasing the variety of sexual pleasure available to every individual."

"What's wrong with that?" Greenberg said, in spite of Jennifer's frantic shushing motions. With the Foitani attitude about sex, anything that had to do with sensual pleasure was automatically suspect.

Aissur Aissur Rus said, "I can conceive of no greater humiliation. How would you like it if your entire species had been deliberately redesigned, merely to allow a greater number of sexual opportunities to its members?"

Put that way, Jennifer thought, it didn't sound appetizing. It had to be all the more galling for the Foitani, who had spent the millennia since the Suicide Wars thinking their original configuration a horrible perversion.

"No wonder it is so easy to produce *kwopillot*," Aissur Aissur Rus went on. "They are, after all, merely a reversion to our former evolutionary pattern. If the Great Ones are to be believed, the origins of *vodranet*—our origins—sprang from the desire of some Foitani at the time to experience both male and female sexual pleasure, which are for us quite different in sensation. Others resisted the introduction of such a radical change into the germ plasm of the race, and the result—the result appears to have been the Suicide Wars."

Jennifer said, "Aissur Aissur Rus, of all the Foitani I've met, regardless of race, you strike me as the most adaptable. The new data from the Great Ones seem to have crushed you. What do the rest of your people think about what you've found out today?''

"Pawasar Pawasar Ras has gone into his quarters. He has spoken to no one. He has forbidden me to discuss this with any person. I have chosen to interpret that to include only Foitani. Our sexual difficulties and conflicts must be of merely academic interest to you humans.''

"Not if we end up getting killed on account of them,'' Greenberg said.

"Yes, that might affect your thinking to some degree,'' Aissur Aissur Rus admitted. "Nevertheless, although I have always been one to favor the expansion of knowledge by whatever means become available—as witness my recruiting the two of you to help enter the Great Unknown—I would, for the sake of my species' future, be willing, indeed eager, to see that no mention of what we have learned here ever reached Odern.''

"The only way to make sure of that would be to destroy the *Vengeance*,'' Jennifer said.

"Were it in my power, I would cheerfully do so,'' Aissur Aissur Rus said. "Unfortunately, however, the *kwopillot* are much more likely to destroy me. Perhaps the soundest course would be merely to string these discussions along until the fleets from Odern and Rof Golan arrive, and hope they can rid us of the *Vengeance*—and our problem—once and for all.''

"If it is, you've just given the game away,'' Greenberg pointed out. "Or don't you think the Great Ones are monitoring your radio traffic?''

"I say nothing they could not reason out for themselves,'' Aissur Aissur Rus answered. "They are depraved and perverse; they are not foolish.'' That was a distinction most humans would have had trouble drawing; Aissur Aissur Rus was able to be dispassionate even over matters that involved his passions.

"The other thing is, you don't think even full warfleets could beat the Great Ones, so you'd better talk with them,'' Jennifer said.

"You overstate the case,'' Aissur Aissur Rus said. "I am in doubt as to the likely outcome. The same must hold true for the *kwopillot*, else they would feel no need to continue discussions with us.''

''You may well be right about that,'' Jennifer said.

''You humans have sexual deviants; I read of them in some of the materials in your course, human Jennifer. How is it that you have failed to destroy yourselves as a result of this fact?''

''That's a good question,'' Jennifer said slowly. Aissur Aissur Rus had a knack for asking good questions. That was probably how he'd come to be a leader of the team investigating the Great Unknown. He'd even gotten answers to his questions there, though by now he wished he hadn't.

Greenberg said, ''One difference between Foitani and humans is that humans who differ sexually don't stand out in any obvious way like smell. When we fight, we fight about things like religion or politics or race, not sex.''

Jennifer had what she thought for a moment was a brilliant idea. Then she realized that if it were all that brilliant, the Foitani would have thought of it for themselves. She threw it out anyway, to let Aissur Aissur Rus shoot it down if he wanted to: ''Is there any chance that you and the *kwopillot* could put on perfumes that would keep you from going berserk at each other's odors?''

''There are no records of this succeeding,'' he answered. ''The pheremones are most distinctive and most different. In any case, we need to be able to perceive these pheromones if we are to function sexually.''

''Just a thought,'' Jennifer said, remembering that she had been about to function sexually before Aissur Aissur Rus called. She wasn't even angry at the Foitan; by now, she was used to getting interrupted.

For a miracle, Aissur Aissur Rus gave up about then and broke the connection. Grinning—he must have been thinking along with her—Greenberg stepped close. ''Shall we try again, and see who calls next?''

''Sure, why not?'' Then she asked, ''What all do you have in the cargo bay, anyhow? A proper science fiction hero—or even heroine—would be able to improvise his way out of trouble with something that had been sitting there all along, just waiting to be used.''

"You're welcome to look," Greenberg answered. "If you think you can improvise a way out of this mess with a bunch of trade junk, go right ahead and try."

"Maybe another time," Jennifer said. "Thing was, SF writers had the habit of putting things that would really help into cargo bays. I've got the feeling that real life isn't so considerate."

"The only thing real life has been considerate about is giving me the chance to fall in love with you. Even then, the damned Foitani keep calling at the wrong time."

"They aren't calling right now," Jennifer said softly.

"So they're not. Let's enjoy it while we can."

"What are you doing, human Jennifer?"

"Just examining cargo," she answered. Since the Foitan on the communicator had known her name, it was probably someone from Odern. Whoever it was, he had to have been monitoring her through some of the spy gear aboard the *Harold Meeker*. If she and Greenberg could sell that alone to one of the more paranoid human intelligence services, they would show a profit for the trip. The only problem there was getting the goods to the marketplace.

Armed with Greenberg's labels, with the computer to give her more details about what was in each crate or box or plastic bag, and with a pry bar, she wandered through the cargo bay, opening packages that looked interesting. A lot of them were interesting: pelts and spices and books and works of art and electronics. She knew she would have had trouble assembling such a rich variety of goods while keeping everything of high quality, as Greenberg had. He deserved his master rating. Somebody back in human space would be sure to want everything the *Harold Meeker* carried, and want it enough to pay highly for it.

Whether any of it would be of any use in keeping the next round of the Suicide Wars from breaking out was another matter. Maybe the Great Ones would admire some of the sculptures produced by a planet-bound Foitani race with which Odern traded, but that would not keep them from hating the artists as so many *vodranet*. Maybe the Foitani from Odern made marvelously compact and clever holovid scanners, but that would not keep them from loathing *kwopillot* or, if the claims of the old imperial Foitani got loose among them—as was very likely—from despising themselves as altered versions of the original Foitani plan they had been trying for so long to emulate.

Frustrated by her complete inability to find anything that might stop big, bluish aliens from massacring one another, Jennifer gave up and went back to the crew compartment. "Any luck?" Greenberg asked when she came out of the lift.

"None. Maybe a little less." She ran her hands through her hair, making tugging motions at it the way Greenberg did. "I should have known better. We don't have a writer stowing away a *deus ex machina* for us. We're going to have to do this ourselves, with our brains."

"Which haven't done us a whole lot of good so far."

"Isn't that the sad and sorry truth?"

Negotiations resumed the next day. The representatives of the Great Ones started things off by declaring in unison, "We have the solution to this problem."

"You and all your perverts are going to go and commit suicide so you don't bother decent Foitani any more?" Voskop W Wurd asked. From a human or an alien of different character, that would have been sarcasm. Jennifer thought the odds favored Voskop W Wurd's meaning every word of what he said.

Pawasar Pawasar Ras said, "Despite contemplation, I have not come upon anything that so much as approaches such a solution. I would be willing to hear one from any source, even a source as unreliable as *kwopillot*."

"Yes, tell us," Greenberg urged. "Jennifer and I haven't found anything that looks like an answer, either."

"Very well." Solut Mek Kem spoke for the old-time Foitani now. "The solution is classic in its simplicity. You have seen that *vodranet* are an unnatural alteration of the true Foitani way of being. Is this so, or not?"

"We see that the Great Ones appear to have been *kwopillot*, yes," Aissur Aissur Rus said. "Nevertheless, since the Suicide Wars we have built our own reality."

"What you say, though, *kwopil*, appears to remain in essence true, if bitter," Pawasar Pawasar Ras said. "If we are to have emulation of the Great Ones as our goal, we must bear this unpalatable fact in mind."

"Excellent," Solut Mek Kem said. "Then to solve the problem of strife between *vodranet* and proper Foitani, all modern Foitani must abandon their present distorted way of life and become as we are. As you have seen for yourselves, turning a *vodran* into a proper Foitan is easy—and no wonder, given that you are poor modifications of the true form. In a generation's time, the race can be whole again, and as it always should have been."

"I like the way I am just fine, and if any stinking *kwopil* has the brass to tell me my get or I would do better as perverts, we'll see how well he does radioactive," Voskop W Wurd said. Great Ones, Foitani from Odern, and Rof Golani had all installed weapons checks outside the *Harold Meeker*. Had it been otherwise, Jennifer was sure the blue-gray Foitan would have blazed away with everything he had.

Pawasar Pawasar Ras, as was the way of the Oderna, was more restrained but no less certain. "I fail to see how this proposal in any way benefits the Foitani now living within our sphere. We gain nothing from it save the commitment of the *kwopillot* not to attack. Buying safety with capitulation is always a poor bargain."

"On the contrary: you *vodranet* gain a great deal. Being as you are, you have lost the possibility for lifelong relationships between the sexes, the cornerstone of Foitani society since time immemorial," Solut Mek Kem said.

"He has something there," Jennifer whispered to Greenberg. Greenberg nodded. Maybe stable home life would be more likely to lead to a stable existence for the species than the serial relationships in which modern Foitani perforce engaged. On the other hand, the Great Ones, while stable among themselves, had wreaked unmitigated havoc on every other race they met. Human notions of right and wrong were anything but universal outside humanity.

Aissur Aissur Rus said, "Perhaps, *kwopil*, we lack the characteristic you extol. Yet can your kind claim to understand our race's whole nature, as we do? We give birth and sire, nurture and conquer, all of us together. Why should we give that up? If you put the proposition to our species on any surviving world of the sphere, few would choose it.''

"Then as I believed from the outset, there is no point to these talks,'' Solut Mek Kem said. ''We will have war.''

IX

FOR ALL HIS ringing proclamation, for all his departing from the *Harold Meeker* and flying up to the *Vengeance*, Solut Mek Kem did not commence battle at once. Jennifer took that for a hopeful sign—with how much justification, she did not know. Trying to provide more justification, for herself and everyone else, she called the Great One. There was, she knew, a real chance the Foitan would not deign to speak to her, she being, after all, a mere alien. In that case, though, she—and everyone else—would be no worse off than if she had not called.

As far as she could interpret Foitani expressions—which wasn't far—Solut Mek Kem was anything but delighted to get on the screen with her. But the Great One did not refuse. Again, she took that for a hopeful sign. "Thank you for being willing to listen to me," she said, wanting him to know she realized the concession was unusual.

"It is no inherent merit on your part, let me assure you." Like most Foitani, Solut Mek Kem did not waste politeness on beings outside his kin-group. "My willingness, as you call it, is purely pragmatic. I am forced to recognize that the situation in which I find myself is not that which I anticipated on returning to awareness. You are part of this new situation. I will learn what I can, then act."

From a Foitan, that was a miracle of moderation; had Jennifer had to devise a motto for the Foitani, she would have come up with something like, *Shoot first, then question the corpse.* She said, "I have two things I want to discuss with you. One, obviously, is the prospect of a second round of Suicide Wars."

"This, again obviously, has my interest, though many aboard *Vengeance* feel it would be worthwhile if it meant exterminating all *vodranet*."

"But isn't it as likely to result in getting rid of all you *kwopillot*, or maybe all of your species?"

"This prospect is all that has stayed our hands thus far."

"Wonderful." The Great Ones used little in the way of subterfuge. They'd had scant need of it; whatever they wanted, they'd simply taken. Jennifer could have done with more socially lubricating hypocrisy—facing up to such straightforward self-interest was daunting. She said, "The other matter has to do with the humans you hold in your data storage system."

"Here we may have room for discussion, assuming it can be completed before fighting commences. As I told you before, I am indifferent to their fate," Solut Mek Kem said. "I asked you once if you wanted live copies produced for you."

"I don't think of them as copies. I think of them as humans," Jennifer answered. "I don't like the idea of their being in your hands; they aren't experimental animals."

Bernard Greenberg came up beside her. "That's right. What would you do if some other race held Foitani just to find out how they worked?"

"Destroy that race," Solut Mek Kem answered at once, his own voice as flat as the Spanglish words that came from the translator. "It has happened before. With the contemptible popguns in your vessel, however, you do not enjoy that option. You exist here on sufferance, not through strength. Remember it."

"We're here because Foitani thought we could solve a problem that baffled them, and the *Harold Meeker* is only a trading vessel, not a warship. I suggest you remember that, if you ever go into human space. We're better able to protect ourselves now than when you kidnapped those primitive ancestors of ours," Greenberg said.

Jennifer clapped her hands. From all she'd seen, matching the Foitani arrogance for arrogance was the best way to make them act in a humanly reasonable fashion. They could be made to respect power. Weakness they simply trampled.

Solut Mek Kem said, "I repeat, this matter is subject to discussion."

"Then let us come up to *Vengeance* and discuss it," Greenberg said. "I might point out that if it hadn't been for us, your ship would still be a tower and you would still be sleeping and impotent inside it." *And the war on Gilver would have only two sides, not a good potential for three*, Jennifer thought.

"A race that relies on the gratitude of others to cause them to act on its behalf is well on the way to extinction," Solut Mek Kem observed. "Nevertheless, you may come—in your own ship, not one furnished by either race of *vodranet* with which we have had the misfortune to become acquainted. Make note that I do this from considerations of my own advantage, not out of sentimentality." The screen blanked.

Greenberg called the research base. "I presume you were monitoring our call to the Great Ones' ship. They've given us permission. If you start shooting at us, it might annoy them. You don't want that, do you?" To Jennifer, he muttered under his breath, "I know damn well I don't."

The Foitani needed a couple of minutes to reply. Finally, a translated voice came back to the *Harold Meeker*. "You have our consent to undertake this mission, but you shall not under any circumstances enter into agreements binding up Odern in any way."

"We won't, Thegun Thegun Nug," Greenberg promised.

Another pause. "One day I must learn how I am so readily identifiable."

"It's your charming personality, Thegun Thegun Nug," Greenberg said. "What else could it possibly be?"

"Undoubtedly you are correct," Thegun Thegun Nug said. "Out." Jennifer and Greenberg tried to hold it in, but they both started laughing at the same time.

Greenberg began talking with the *Harold Meeker*'s computer, making sure the ship was ready for space. Jennifer waited for a furious call from Voskop W Wurd. The Rof Golani knew how to delegate authority, however, for the furious call that came was from his aide Yulvot L Reat, accusing her and Greenberg of selling out to the perfidious *kwopillot* and threatening to shoot them down if they took off.

"If you do that, you risk starting the war with the Great Ones again," Jennifer pointed out. "Not only that, you might antagonize the Foitani from Odern. Besides, we're just humans, remember? Do you expect any self-respecting Foitani to take seriously anything we say?''

"Probably not," Yulvot L Reat admitted, "nor do you deserve serious regard.''

"Thank you so much, Yulvot L Reat," Jennifer said. "Out."

"You're getting to be able to handle them pretty well," Greenberg said.

"Bernard, I don't think that's necessarily a compliment. I just want to get into space again.''

"Me, too. Stuck on the surface of Gilver like this, I've felt like a bug with a shoe poised over it. Once I'm flying on my own power, at least I'll have the illusion of being a free agent again, even if I'll still be under the guns of *Vengeance*.''

The *Harold Meeker* lifted off a few minutes later. Jennifer watched the Foitani research base fall away. The screen's view expanded to pick up the Great Unknown. The precinct looked strange and incomplete without the central tower, as if all roads led, not to Rome, but to nowhere.

The sky quickly darkened toward black. Stars came out. Jennifer looked at the radar pickup. On the way in to Gilver, it had shown a hideously jumbled swarm of ships and missiles, their tracks and signals jammed to provide them the greatest possible protection. Now only one artificial object swung in space near Gilver: the *Vengeance*. On radar, it was only the palest of flickering ghosts.

"I'm just glad to see it at all," Greenberg said when Jennifer remarked on that. "If we couldn't pick it up, that would be bad news for human space.''

A Great One sent a peremptory signal. "Approach slowly and directly, or you will be destroyed without further warning.''

Jennifer acknowledged, then shut down the communicator and sighed. "They're such a charming race. I don't know what those Cro-Magnon people will do once we get them back, but we have to do it. The more I think, the more it looks like I couldn't live with myself if I just left them there in that Foitani data base.''

"I know what you mean," Greenberg answered. "At first, I didn't worry too much about it—they were in storage and weren't aware of anything that happened around them. But if the Foitani can call them up again and again, do what they want with them every time—test them to destruction if they've a mind to, which they probably do—I think we have to get a live copy back, and get the Great Ones to wipe the files so they can't make any more.''

"Sounds good to me," Jennifer agreed. She didn't know what sort of deal they would have to make with the Great Ones to accomplish that. Whatever it was, that price needed paying. Sometimes profit didn't count for everything.

The *Vengeance* might have been more or less invisible to radar, but before long it showed up visually in the *Harold Meeker*'s forward screen. It looked even bigger alone in space than attached to a planet . . . and no wonder. It wasn't the size of a spacecraft. It was the size of a baby asteroid—maybe even a toddler asteroid. It also bristled with weapons emplacements that hadn't been visible while it slept away the centuries on Gilver.

What worried Jennifer most was that the *Vengeance* was an artifact from the side that had lost the Suicide Wars. What sort of craft had the winners used? Whatever the answer, those ships were gone now, either destroyed in the war or turned on one another afterward. The *Vengeance* remained, huge and deadly and all alone, as if a last *Tyrannosaurus rex* had somehow been raised from the grave and turned loose in the jungle parks of modern Earth.

The abrupt voice came out of the speaker again. "Berth your vessel at the lock with the flashing amber light, non-Foitani."

Jennifer looked in the screen. The flashing amber light seemed bright enough to be visible down on Gilver, let alone from just a couple of kilometers away. She said, "They aren't crediting us with a whole lot of brains."

"We aren't Foitani. How could we have brains?" Greenberg answered. "They're giving us more credit than they think we deserve just by talking with us. For that matter, how smart are we? Here we are, going to dicker for specimens from our own race and for a way to keep the Suicide Wars from starting over, and what can we offer? What do we have that the Great Ones might want?"

It was a good question. As with a good many others lately, Jennifer would have admired it more had she had a good answer for it. She rocked back and forth in her seat, not so much concentrating as trying to relax and let her subconscious come up with one. In SF novels, inspiration was usually enough to let the hero make the story come out right.

Inspiration did not come. In any case, inspiration looked puny when set in the balance against the kilometers of deadliness of the *Vengeance*. A mammal in the jungle park might be more inspired than any *Tyrannosaurus rex* ever hatched, but that wouldn't keep it from getting eaten if the dinosaur decided to open his mouth and gulp.

A human in the jungle park, of course, would think about a weapon to use against a monster dinosaur. Put a character from a Don A. Stuart novel in that park and he would think of a weapon one day, build it the next, and eat *Tyrannosaurus* steak the day after that. The spacegoing *Tyrannosaurus* engulfing the *Harold Meeker*, unfortunately, had already thought of more weapons than any Don A. Stuart character ever born. The Foitani, whether ancient or modern, put a lot of effort into destructive capacity. If only they'd expended even a little more on learning how to get along with one another, they would have been much nicer people . . . and Jennifer wouldn't be coming aboard a spacecraft called *Vengeance*.

"If only . . ." Jennifer sighed. That was one of the ways old-time SF writers had gone about building a story. She wished it had more bearing in the real world.

The communicator spoke. "You may now exit your ship. You will find atmospheric pressure and temperature maintained at a level suitable for your species; at least, the specimens of your kind in our data store take no harm of it."

Jennifer's hands curled into fists. Those poor cave people were getting the guinea-pig treatment again, and then being— what? Killed? Just erased? She thought of the explorer in *Rogue Moon*, who died again and again as he worked his way through the alien artifact on the moon. She wondered if, like him, the Cro-Magnons in the Foitani data banks remembered each brief incarnation, each death. She hoped not.

"Atmospheric analysis," Greenberg told the *Harold Meeker*'s computer. It, too, reported that the air was good. Greenberg said, "I don't trust the Foitani any further than I have to." He cocked a wry eyebrow. "If they do want to kill us, I guess they could manage it a lot more directly than lying about the air outside.''

"I don't blame you for not trusting them," Jennifer said. "I don't, either. And they have something we want, too. I only wish we had something they needed."

"A way for them to live in peace no matter whom they go to bed with would be nice. You don't happen to have one anywhere concealed about your person, do you?"

"Let me look." Jennifer checked a pocket in her coveralls, then mournfully shook her head. Greenberg snorted. Jennifer said, "Shall we go see if we can get our own remote ancestors out of their clutches—and maybe even ourselves, too?"

"That would be nice," Greenberg said. He and Jennifer went through the air lock one after the other. They peered around. The *Vengeance* was so big that Jennifer didn't feel as if she were on a spacecraft; it was more as if the *Harold Meeker* had inadvertently landed in the middle of a good-sized town.

A green-blue Foitan with a hand weapon stood waiting for them. Jennifer was tired of aliens ordering her around with jerks of a gun barrel. It didn't stop happening just because she was tired of it. The Great One led her and Greenberg to a blank metal wall. He rapped on it. A door into a small chamber opened. He chivvied the two humans inside, then rapped on the wall again. The door disappeared, in the way Foitani doors had a habit of doing.

The guard spoke to the air. "The offices of Solut Mek Kem," the translator said. Jennifer felt no motion, but when the Foitan opened the doorway again, the small chamber was not where it had been.

Solut Mek Kem stood waiting. "Well, creatures, shall we get to the dickering?" he said. "What can you offer that might persuade us to give you copies of these other creatures of your kind, now maintained in our data store?"

"That's not all we want," Jennifer said. "Once we have these—copies—we also want you to erase the archetypes of the humans you have in your data bank, as long as you can do that without causing them any pain. Can you do that?"

"Yes, we can, but why should we?" Solut Mek Kem said. "I repeat, what will you give in exchange for this service? Be quick. I am not in the habit of bargaining with creatures. Were it not for the service you rendered in slowing the outbreak of a combat whose result is uncertain, I would not waste my time here, I assure you.''

"Oh, I believe it," Jennifer said. "Your whole species is like that. If only you were a little bit more easygoing—"

"What exactly do you want from us?" Greenberg demanded. "I can provide trade goods from Odern, and others of human manufacture. I can also give you information about what this part of the galaxy is like these days. Just how much, of course, is what makes a dicker."

"These things may perhaps buy you copies of your fellow creatures," Solut Mek Kem said. "They will in no way persuade me to clear our patterns in the matrices. Your kind, evidently, is a part of the galaxy about which we shall require a good deal of information. If you expect us to forgo it, you will have to do better."

"I've told you what we have," Greenberg said slowly.

Jennifer felt her face twist into a scowl. She didn't want to leave any vestiges of the Cro-Magnons in Foitani hands. "What would it take?" she said. "Do you want us to tell you how to live in peace with all the modern Foitani, who'd like nothing more than seeing every last one of you dead?"

"If you can tell us how to live in peace with *vodranet*, creature, you will have earned what you seek."

Jennifer looked down at her shoes. If only she were a Middle English SF hero, the answer to that question would have been on the tip of her tongue. Would Miles Vorkosigan or Dominic Flandry just have stood there with nothing to say? "If only . . ." she said softly, and then, a moment later, more than a little surprised, "Well, maybe I can."

"Go ahead, then, creature," Solut Mek Kem said. "Tell me how I shall leave in peace with beings for whom I have an instinctive antipathy. Instruct me. I shall be fascinated to imbibe of your wisdom." The *kwopil* used irony like a bludgeon.

"Actually, I can't specifically tell you how," Jennifer said. "But maybe, just maybe, I can tell you a way to go about finding the answer for yourselves, if you really want to." That was the rub, and she knew it. If *kwopillot* and *vodranet* wanted to fight, they would, and good intentions would only get in the way.

"Say on," Solut Mek Kem said, not revealing his thoughts.

"All right. You know by now that the Foitani from Odern brought humans—my people—to Odern because by themselves they couldn't safely enter what they called the Great Unknown—the area around your ship."

"We made sure prying *vodranet* would not be able to disturb us, yes."

"Fine," Jennifer said. "The reason the Foitani from Odern got me in particular is that I'm an expert in an old form of literature among my people, a form called science fiction. This was a literature that, in its purest form, extrapolated either from possible events deliberately taken to extremes or from premises known to be impossible, and speculated on what might happen if those impossible premises were in fact true."

Solut Mek Kem's ears twitched. "Why should I care if creatures choose to spend their lives deliberately speculating on the impossible? It strikes me as a waste of time, but with sub-Foitani creatures, the waste is minimal."

"It's not the way you're making it sound," Jennifer said. "Look—you know about military contingency plans, don't you?"

"Certainly," Solut Mek Kem said.

"I thought you would. If you're like humans at all, you make those plans even for cases you don't expect to happen. Sometimes you can learn things from those improbable plans, too, even if you don't directly use them. Am I right or wrong?"

"You are correct. How could you not be, in this instance? Of course data may be relevant in configurations other than the ones in which they are first envisioned. Any race with the minimal intelligence necessary to devise data base software learns the truth of this."

"Whatever you say, Solut Mek Kem. Do me one more favor, if you would: give me the connotations of the word this translator program uses to translate the term *fiction*."

The Great One paused before answering, "It means something like, *tales for nestlings' ears*. Another synonym might be, *nonsense stories*."

Jennifer nodded. A lot of races thought that way. With some, the only translation for *fiction* was *lying*. She said, "We use fiction for more things than the Foitani do, Solut Mek Kem. We use tales that we know to be false to entertain, yes, but also to cast light on true aspects of our characters and to help us gain insight into ourselves.''

''And so?'' Solut Mek Kem said. ''What possible relevance does a creature's insight into itself have to the truly serious issue of *vodranet*?''

''Bear with me,'' Jennifer said. ''More than a thousand years ago, back when humans were just starting to develop a technological society, they also developed the subform of fiction called science fiction.''

''This strikes me as a contradiction in terms,'' Solut Mek Kem observed. ''How can one have a nonsense story based on science?''

''Science fiction doesn't produce nonsense stories,'' Jennifer said, reflecting that Solut Mek Kem sounded like some of the contemporary critics of the genre. ''It's sort of a fictional analogue of what you do when you develop a contingency plan. Conceive of it as a method for making thought experiments and projections when you don't have hard data, but need to substitute imagination instead. You *kwopillot* don't have hard data about living with *vodranet*, for instance; all you know is how to go about killing each other. You need all the imagination you can find, and you need a way to focus it. If imagination is light, think of the techniques of science fiction as a lens.''

''I think of this entire line of talk as a waste of time,'' Solut Mek Kem said.

''Let me tell you this, then,'' Jennifer said quickly, before he could irrevocably reject her: ''The Foitani from Odern sought me out and brought me here specifically because I'm an expert in this kind of fiction.''

''The foibles of *vodranet* are not a recommendation,'' Solut Mek Kem said, and she was sure she had lost.

But Bernard Greenberg said, ''Consider results, Solut Mek Kem. Before Jennifer got here, you had been dormant for twenty-eight thousand years. The Foitani from Odern weren't close to getting into the Great Unknown, let alone into the *Vengeance* by themselves. Look at all that's happened since Jennifer came to Gilver.''

Jennifer put her hand on Greenberg's arm. It was completely in character for him to minimize his own role in everything that had happened so the deal could go forward.

Solut Mek Kem opened his mouth, then closed it again. Greenberg had managed to make him thoughtful, at any rate. At last the Great One said, "An argument from results is always the most difficult to confute. Very well; let me examine some samples of this alleged science fiction. If I think expertise in it might prove of some value to the present situation, I shall meet the terms you have set: copies of the creatures of your kind in our data stores, with the originals to be deleted."

Jennifer clenched her teeth. *Put up or shut up*, she thought. While she tried to decide which stories Solut Mek Kem ought to judge, she said, "May I please call Aissur Aissur Rus at the research base of the Foitani from Odern? He has a program that translates between your language and the one in which the stories were composed, one which we humans no longer speak."

"First scientific nonsense or nonsense science, I know not which. Now you haul in the *vodranet*," Solut Mek Kem grumbled. "Do what you think necessary, creature. Having stooped so low as to negotiate with sub-Foitani, how could *vodranet* befoul me further? Speak—your words are being transmitted as you require."

"Aissur Aissur Rus?" Jennifer said. "Are you there?"

The reply came from nowhere. "That is a translator's voice, so you must be a human. Which are you, and what do you need?"

"I'm Jennifer," Jennifer said. "Can you transmit to the *Vengeance* the program you used back on Saugus to read Middle English science fiction? You thought someone who knew it might be able to give you insights on the Great Unknown. Now the Great Ones hope its techniques may help them figure out how not to fight the next round of the Suicide Wars." She knew she was exaggerating the Great Ones' expectations, but no more than she would have in arranging a deal of much smaller magnitude.

"I will send the program," Aissur Aissur Rus said. "I would be intrigued to learn the Great Ones' opinion of this curious human discipline."

"You aren't the only one," Jennifer said.

Solut Mek Kem turned to glance at something—evidently a telltale, for after a moment he said, "Very well. We have received this program. On what material shall we make use of it?"

"I've been thinking about that," Jennifer said. "I'm going to give you three pieces. You know or can learn that humans are of two sexes, which we keep throughout life, just as you do. *The Left Hand of Darkness* speculates on the consequences of discovering a world of humans genetically engineered to be hermaphrodites."

"That is not precisely similar to our case, but I can see how it might be relevant," Solut Mek Kem said. "It is not the sort of topic about which we would produce fiction."

"Species differ," Jennifer said. Mentally, she added, *You might know more about that if you hadn't gone around slaughtering all the aliens you came across.*

"You spoke of three works," Solut Mek Kem said. "What are the other two?"

"One is 'The Marching Morons,' which looks at the possible genetic consequences of some of the social policies in vogue in the author's day. The events it describes did not happen. Kornbluth—the author—didn't expect them to, I'm certain. He was using them to comment on his own society's customs, which is something science fiction did very effectively."

She waited for Solut Mek Kem to say something, but he just looked at her with those dark green eyes. She went on, "The third story is called 'Hawk Among the Sparrows.' It warns of the problems someone used to a high technology may encounter in a place where that technology cannot be reproduced."

"Yes, that is relevant to us," Solut Mek Kem said. "Again, it is not a topic we would choose for fiction. I will consider these works. I will consider also the mind-set which informs them, which I gather to be the essence of what you seek to offer me."

"Exactly," Jennifer said, more than a little relieved the Great One understood what she was selling.

"Enough then. You are dismissed. I shall communicate with you again when I have weighed these documents. You would be well advised to remain in your ship until that time, lest you be destroyed by one of my fellows who has less patience with vermin than I do. The guard here will escort you."

Jennifer fumed all the way back to the *Harold Meeker*. The worst of it was that she knew Solut Mek Kem had been trying to help. The Great Ones simply had no idea how to deal with any beings unlike themselves. No wonder they had started fighting when the split between *kwopillot* and *vodranet* developed among them, and no wonder they kept fighting until they could fight no more.

The only glimpses she got of *Vengeance* were of the open area around the *Harold Meeker*, which she'd already seen. Just a couple of Foitani beside her guard saw her, which she soon decided was just as well. By the way they automatically took a couple of steps toward her, she was sure they would have attacked if the guard had not been with her. They probably assumed she and Greenberg were prisoners. By the way the guard acted, that was what he thought. She didn't care to find out what would happen if she tried going in the wrong direction.

The quiet hiss of the air-lock gaskets sealing made her sag with relief. Logically, it shouldn't have mattered. She was just as much in the power of the Great Ones inside the *Harold Meeker* as she had been outside. But logic had little to do with it. The barrier looked and felt strong, no matter how flimsy it was in fact.

"I have a question for you," Greenberg said. "Suppose you do manage to convince the old-time Foitani you've given them a way to work out how to exist alongside their modern cousins? The modern Foitani don't have that way. You need two sides to have peace, but one is plenty to start a war."

"You're right." She paced back and forth, as best she could in the cramped crew compartment. "I'll call Aissur Aissur Rus. He's had some actual experience working with the concepts I'm selling. If anyone can interest the others in them, he's the one."

"Not Voskop W Wurd?" Greenberg asked slyly.

She rolled her eyes. "No, thanks."

As it happened, Aissur Aissur Rus called her first. She explained to him the deal she had put to the Great Ones, knowing all the while that Solut Mek Kem or one of his aides was surely listening in. She finished, "You were the one among your people who thought someone used to the ideas of science fiction would be able to help you on Gilver, and you turned out to be right. Do you think that you modern Foitani can apply this same sort of creative extrapolation to the problem of living with *kwopillot*?"

"That is—an intriguing question," Aissur Aissur Rus said slowly. "If the answer proves to be affirmative, its originator would surely derive much credit therefrom." *You would derive that credit, you mean,* Jennifer thought. Aissur Aissur Rus continued, "If on the other hand the answer is in the negative, the Suicide Wars begin again shortly afterward, at which point no blame is likely to accrue, for who would survive to lay blame?"

"Then shall I send you the same materials I gave to Solut Mek Kem?" Jennifer asked. "Maybe you can use them, if not to change Pawasar Pawasar Ras's mind, then at least to open it a little bit."

"What materials did you furnish to the Great One?" Aissur Aissur Ras asked. Jennifer told him. He said, "I presently have all of those, I believe, save 'Hawk Among the Sparrows.' We kidnapped you before you gained the opportunity to discuss the literary pitfalls of overreliance upon advanced technology. Though alien, I find them most intriguing documents. 'The Marching Morons' presents a quite Foitani-like view of what constitutes proper behavior under difficult circumstances—not that we would ever have permitted culls to breed as they did to establish that story's background."

"Aissur Aissur Rus, I'm convinced you would have gotten an *A* in my course," Jennifer said.

"So you have said, human Jennifer. I shall take this for a compliment. My people have said repeatedly, in talks you have heard and in many more conversations where you were not present, that they could not imagine how they were to live with *kwopillot*. I still cannot imagine how we are to accomplish this. Nevertheless, perhaps you have furnished us a tool wherewith to focus our imagination more sharply on the problem. If this be so, all Foitani will be in your debt."

"That's not something you ought to tell a trader, you know," Jennifer said.

"Possibly not. Nevertheless, you are at present in no position to exploit my words. Will you send 'Hawk Among the Sparrows' to me now?"

Jennifer fed the piece into the computer for transmission to Gilver. She remarked, "You know, Aissur Aissur Rus, you may end up as Odern's ambassador to the Great Ones if you do manage not to fight. You're better with strange peoples than any other Foitan I've met. Thegun Thegun Nug, for instance, would have ordered me to send him that story just now, instead of asking for it.''

"He is an able male," Aissur Aissur Rus said stoutly.

"Have it your way," Jennifer said. "Out." She turned to Greenberg. "Now we wait to see what the Great Ones have to say.''

"I hope we don't wait too long," he answered. "I'd be willing to bet Odern's fleet is already heading this way, and I have no idea how far from Gilver Rof Golan is. For once, I wouldn't mind if the communicator interrupted us.''

"Is that a hint?"

"You know a better way to pass the time?" Greenberg asked.

"Now that you mention it, no," Jennifer said.

The communicator did not interrupt them. Like Greenberg, Jennifer almost wished it would have.

"You will report to me at once," Solut Mek Kem said, as abrupt as if he'd been Thegun Thegun Nug. Jennifer and Greenberg traded worried glances as they hurried out through the air lock. The communicator had been silent for thirty-six hours before that sharp order. Solut Mek Kem knew what he thought of the works Jennifer had given him. Whatever it was, he wasn't letting on.

A Foitani guard waited outside the *Harold Meeker*. Jennifer could not tell if it was the same one who had escorted her to Solut Mek Kem before. The guard said nothing and gave no clues, merely gesturing *come along* with his hand weapon. One of the nice things about human worlds, she thought, was that sometimes whole weeks went by without anyone pointing a gun at you.

She also could not tell if she and Greenberg went by way of the same moving chamber as they had the last time; one blank room looked much like another. Solut Mek Kem was definitely in the same office he had occupied before. The company he kept there, however, was a good deal different.

Some sort of invisible screen—possibly material, possibly not—kept the Cro-Magnon man and woman from either running away or attacking the Foitan. The two human specimens turned fierce, frightened faces on Jennifer and Greenberg as the guard led them into the chamber. They shouted something in a tongue as dead as the woolly mammoth.

"You have won your wager," Solut Mek Kem said. "The concept of extrapolation mixed with entertainment is not one we developed for ourselves, yet its uses quickly become obvious as we grow acquainted with it. I wonder how many other interesting concepts we have exterminated along with the races that created them." Jennifer had not imagined a Foitan could feel guilt. A moment later, Solut Mek Kem disabused her of her anthropocentrism, for he said, "Well, no matter. They are gone, and I shall not worry about them. The masters of these creatures—" He stuck out his tongue at the Cro-Magnon couple. "—are also now gone from our data store; I keep my bargains. The copies are yours to do with as you will."

Jennifer started to ask if there was any way for her to check that, then held her tongue. If the Great Ones wanted to cheat, they could; how was she supposed to thread her way through their data storage system? Besides, questioning Solut Mek Kem was liable to make him angry, and at the moment he was about as well disposed as a Foitan could be toward members of another species.

Instead of complaining to him, she turned to Greenberg. "I suppose the kindest thing we can do for these poor people is stun them and put them out of their sensory overload before they scare themselves to death." She wasn't sure she was exaggerating; half-remembered tales of primitive humans said they might do just that.

The translator carried her words to Solut Mek Kem. "I will take care of it for you," the Great One said. He rapped on the wall behind him to expose a cavity. From it he took a weapon smaller than the one the Foitani guard carried. He started to point it at the two reconstituted humans.

"Wait," Jennifer said quickly. She didn't know whether the Great Ones used the same stun beam as modern Foitani, but if they did, the Cro-Magnons wouldn't like waking up from it. She drew her own stunner from a coverall pocket, turned it on the man and woman from out of time. They slumped bonelessly to the floor.

"Let's take them back to the ship and get them into cold

sleep,'' Greenberg said. ''I don't want them awake in there and bouncing off the walls.''

''Sounds good to me,'' Jennifer said. She spoke for the first time to the guard. ''Honored Great One, could you please carry these humans to our ship? With your great size and strength, you can easily take them both at once.''

Flattery got her nowhere. The guard said one word: ''No.''

She appealed to Solut Mek Kem. She got four words from him: ''No. Carry your own.''

She and Greenberg went over to the Cro-Magnon couple. Whatever had kept them in their corner of the room didn't keep the traders out. Greenberg grabbed the unconscious man by his shoulders. Jennifer took hold of his ankles. He was hairy, scarred, flea-bitten, and smelly. He seemed to weigh a ton, and Jennifer was sure he would only get heavier as she toted him.

''Let's go,'' Greenberg grunted. Neither of them had much practice at hauling what was in essence deadweight. Having the Foitani guard alongside watching did nothing to make matters easier. Getting the limp Cro-Magnon into and through the cramped air lock of the *Harold Meeker* was a separate wrestling match in itself. Breathing hard, Greenberg said, ''Give him another dose, Jennifer. We want to make sure he's out until we can bring his mate back.''

''Right,'' Jennifer said. Thinking of all the trouble a primitive who woke up too soon could get into on a starship was enough to make her blood run cold and then some.

After the man was sent into deeper unconsciousness, she and Greenberg went back for the woman. She was just as dirty and smelly and flea-bitten as her companion, but, fortunately, a good deal lighter. Greenberg once again handled the head end. ''You know,'' he said, looking down at his burden, ''clean her up a little—well, a lot—and she might be pretty.''

''Maybe,'' Jennifer said. ''So what?''

''It makes life easier.'' After a few steps, Greenberg noticed Jennifer hadn't answered. ''Doesn't it?'' he asked.

''A lot of the time, all it does is make things more complicated,'' she said. She thought about it for a few more steps, then added, ''This one, though, will need all the help she can get. For her, I suppose, being pretty really is going to be an asset instead of a nuisance.''

The woman was starting to wiggle and moan by the time they got to the *Harold Meeker*. Greenberg stunned her again before he and Jennifer hauled her through the air lock. He said, "Let's put them into cold sleep as fast as we can, before they start getting frisky again."

The cold-sleep process was designed to go fast, so it could be activated in case of sudden emergency aboard ship. As Jennifer hooked the male of the pair up to the system, she said, "What *are* they going to do when we get them back to human space? Nobody's had to deal with human primitives for hundreds of years; it must be a lost art."

"I haven't the slightest idea what they'll do," Greenberg answered. "I'm not going to worry about it, either. Whatever it is, it has to be better than life as experimental animals for the Foitani."

"You're right about that," Jennifer said. Just as she was connecting the nerve-retarder net, the communicator buzzed. "No, damn it, not now," she shouted at it. "We're not even screwing!"

The communicator ignored her. The words that came from it were more like snarls than speech. The translator turned them into flat Spanglish. "Answer me, you pestilential sub-Foitani creatures. When Voskop W Wurd deigns to speak with you, you are to take it as a privilege."

"Oh, shut up for a minute," Jennifer said, enjoying the license given her by a good many thousand kilometers of empty space between herself and the Rof Golani warleader. When the Cro-Magnons' pod retreated into its storage bay, she decided to notice the communicator again. "Now, what is it you want, Voskop W Wurd?"

"Whatever documents you have passed on to the Oderna and the *kwopillot*," Voskop W Wurd answered.

"Oh," Jennifer said. "Yes, I can do that. I would have done it sooner, but it never occurred to me that you might want them, Voskop W Wurd. You hadn't shown much use for humans, you know." *You haven't shown much use for anything, you know*, she added mentally.

The warleader said, "If my potential allies and my enemies have these data, I should be privy to them as well. Explain to me why the Oderna and *kwopillot* are interested in these long effusions by sub-Foitani.''

"I love you, too, Voskop W Wurd," Jennifer said sweetly. But the more minds trying to find avoid a new round of Suicide Wars, the better, so she did explain to the warleader the concept of science fiction and its potential application here. Voskop W Wurd was vicious, but not stupid. Jennifer finished, "The books and stories are examples intended to turn your thinking in the appropriate direction.''

Voskop W Wurd remained silent for some time after she was through. At last, he said, "This new concept will have to be analyzed. We on Rof Golan write and declaim sagas of great warriors of the past, but have nothing to do with the set of organized lies you term fiction, still less with using it as if it were fact.''

"Let me know what you think when you've looked at the documents,'' Jennifer said. "You might also want to talk to Aissur Aissur Rus. He comes fairly close be being able to grasp another race's point of view.''

Voskop W Wurd switched off without replying—typical Foitani manners, Jennifer thought. But she remained more cheerful than otherwise. The Rof Golani hadn't dismissed the concept of trying SF techniques to extrapolate ways in which *kwopillot* and *vodranet* could live together in the same galaxy. From him, that was an excellent sign.

Greenberg said, "The primitives are down and freezing. Assuming we ever get to leave—and assuming we don't run into any more leftover weapons from the Suicide Wars—we shouldn't have any trouble getting them back to Saugus.''

"Saugus? Why Saugus?'' Jennifer said.

"For one thing, it's the planet you live on these days. For another, I assume the university where you're teaching is a good one.'' He waited for her to nod, then went on, "It ought to have some good anthropologists, then. I can't think of any people better suited to helping show our unwilling passengers how the world has changed since they were last around to look at it.''

"Makes sense,'' Jennifer said.

"Saugus also ought to have a merchants' guild hall.'' Again, Greenberg waited for a nod before continuing. "In that case, I can do a couple of things. First, I can recommend you for master status." He held up a hand to forestall whatever she might say. "You've earned it, you ought to have it, and you're going to get it. If we do manage to get out of this mess, it'll be thanks to your expertise. And we'll show a profit, and a good-sized one. You qualify."

"All right." The only thing Jennifer really wanted was to get back to teaching and research, but she'd learned that having something else to fall back on could come in handy. She said, "That's one thing. What turns it into a couple?"

Greenberg hesitated before he answered. "The other thing I was thinking of was transferring my base of operations to Saugus. That is, if you want to turn us into a couple once we're back."

"Oh." She felt her face twist into a new expression as the implications of that sank in. The expression was an enormous grin. "Sure!" She hugged him.

"I don't want you to leap into this, you know," he said seriously. "I'm not going to stop trading, which means we may be apart big stretches of time. And I know you'd sooner stay at the university."

She shrugged. "We'll do the best we can for as long as we can. That's all we can do—that's all anyone can do. Right now, I don't want to worry about complications, except the ones that are keeping us stuck in Foitani space."

"Sounds sensible to me," he said. "People who borrow trouble usually end up repaying it at high interest." He yawned. "I wouldn't mind going into cold sleep myself. I'm far enough behind on the regular sort that I guess that's the only way I'm likely to catch up. Shall we try to gain on what we can?"

"When going to sleep sounds like a better idea than going to bed, does that mean the romance is starting to fade?" Jennifer asked. Greenberg had just pulled his shirt off over his head. He bunched it up and threw it at her. She tossed it aside, undressed, and settled down on her foam pad. She didn't care about romance right this second, only about how tired she was. Greenberg told the computer to turn down the lights. Sleep hit her like a club.

The communicator hauled Jennifer and Greenberg back to life after about five hours of sleep—just enough to leave them both painfully aware they needed more. A Foitani voice roared from the speaker. "Answer, humans," the translator supplied.

"What is it now, Voskop W Wurd?" Jennifer asked, rubbing her eyes and thinking wistfully of coffee.

"This is not Voskop W Wurd. This is Yulvot L Reat. The warleader ordered me to evaluate your concept of scientific lying."

Jennifer wondered whether the translator was hiccuping or whether Voskop W Wurd had given that name to the Middle English literature as he assigned it to his subordinate. That didn't really matter. "What do you think of it, Yulvot W Reat?"

"To my surprise, I find myself quite impressed," the Rof Golani Foitan answered. "It serves to make extrapolation palatable, and by extension even speculates logically about the consequences of propositions known to be false, something I had not imagined possible."

"Then you think it might let you find a way to live with the *kwopillot* aboard the *Vengeance*?" Jennifer asked hopefully.

"It might let us look for a way," Yulvot L Reat said. "I take that for progress. So will the warleader Voskop W Wurd, since we never imagined—"

Yulvot L Reat's voice vanished from the speaker. A moment later, that of a different Foitan replaced it. "Humans, this is Solut Mek Kem. We have detected ships emerging from hyperdrive in this system. Your presence compromises *Vengeance*'s defenses, to say nothing of the fact that your drive energies could be used as a suicide weapon against us. You will leave immediately."

"Of course, Solut Mek Kem," Greenberg said. "I'll order the computer to—"

"Look in the viewscreen," Jennifer said. Greenberg did. His eyes got wide. There was the *Vengeance*, some kilometers away and visibly shrinking. When Solut Mek Kem said *immediately*, he didn't fool around.

"One of these days, I'll see if our instruments picked up any clue of how they just did that," Greenberg said. "Right now, though, I think the smartest thing to do is put as much distance between us and the *Vengeance* as we can."

Jennifer did not argue with him. The *Vengeance*, at the moment, was the biggest target in the Gilver system. No, the second biggest—Gilver itself was still down there. "Can we monitor traffic between the ship and the ground?" she asked.

"Good idea," Greenberg said.

The first signal the *Harold Meeker* picked up was almost strong enough to overload its receiver. "Solut Mek Kem aboard *Vengeance*, calling the base on Gilver. We will act for our own defense only for a period of two rotations of Gilver, in which time you are to persuade your newly arrived ships to break off combat so that we and your leaders may extrapolate ways in which we need not destroy each other. If they continue to attack thereafter, we shall fight as we see fit. Be informed and be warned."

"We did it!" Jennifer exclaimed.

"We may have done it," Greenberg said, less optimistically. "Let's see what Pawasar Pawasar Ras thinks of the offer."

The answer was not long in coming. "Incoming Foitani fleet, hold your fire," Pawasar Pawasar Ras said. "This is Pawasar Pawasar Ras on Gilver. I speak without coercion of any sort. Know that the Suicide Wars arose out of conflict between our sort of Foitani and *kwopillot*. Know also that if we and they fail to come to terms now, the Suicide Wars will return; earthgrip will hold sway over us all, and it shall be as if our race had never existed. Let us talk and explore other ways before we fight."

A louder, shriller voice followed that of Pawasar Pawasar Ras. "I, Voskop W Wurd, Warleader of Rof Golan, declare the time for fighting is not yet—and who would dare coerce a warleader? Hear me and obey, my breathren of Rof Golan!"

"Do you think they'll listen?" Jennifer asked.

"I don't know." Greenberg glanced toward the radar. So did Jennifer. The screen was full of ships. All of them were headed straight toward Gilver, or rather toward the *Vengeance*, which hung above the planet in a synchronous orbit that held it right above the precinct of the Great Unknown—and the Foitani research station. He looked at the radar plot again and shook his head. "I don't intend to wait around and find out, either. Computer, initiate hyperdrive acceleration sequence, vector exactly opposite that of those approaching ships."

"Initiating," the computer said.

If Greenberg had hoped to sneak out of the brewing fight while no one was paying attention to the *Harold Meeker*, that hope lasted less than a minute. A Foitani voice came from the communicator. "Human ship, this is Solut Mek Kem. Why are you abandoning this solar system? Answer immediately or face the consequences."

When a Foitan said *face the consequences*, he meant *dig your grave and jump in*. Greenberg said, "When you pushed us away from your ship, Solut Mek Kem, you left us sitting right next door to you as the modern Foitani head in on an attack run. We can't defend ourselves; this is a trader, not a warship. This isn't our war, anyhow. If you were in our position, what would you do?"

"Extrapolate, please," Jennifer added, knowing the only way Foitani usually put on other people's shoes was after those other people had no further use for them.

No answer came from Solut Mek Kem. Jennifer found she was grinding her teeth, made herself stop, then found she was grinding them again. *Vengeance* could swat the *Harold Meeker* out of the sky like a man swatting a gnat.

"Weapon homing!" the computer shrieked.

"It's not the *Vengeance*," Greenberg said after a quick look at the radar tank. "It's from one of the ships that just came into the system."

"Can we get into hyperdrive before it catches us?" Jennifer asked.

"No," he and the computer replied at the same time.

Jennifer went over to the radar tank and watched the missile close. Others trailed it, but they did not count; the *Harold Meeker* would hit hyperdrive kick-in velocity before they reached it. That first one, though . . . some Foitani pilot, not knowing what the fleeing ship was, had been fast on the trigger—too fast.

Then, without warning, the missile ceased to be. Greenberg shouted and pounded his fist against his thigh. "Human ship *Harold Meeker* to *Vengeance*," Jennifer said. "Thank you." Still no answer came. Less than half a minute later, the *Harold Meeker* flashed into hyperdrive.

Snow clung to the ground wherever there was shadow. The distant mountains were cloaked in white halfway down from their peaks; a glacier came forth from them onto the nearer plains like a frozen tongue sticking out. Musk oxen and the larger dots that were mammoths moved slowly across those plains.

Jennifer shivered. The synthetic furs and hides she was wearing were not as warm as the real things. Her arms were bare; gooseflesh prickled up on them as she watched. Her breath came smoky from her nostrils. "They'd better hurry up, before I freeze to death," she said, making a miniature fogbank around her head with the words.

"Maybe there's such a thing as too much realism," Greenberg agreed through chattering teeth.

On the ground a few paces away from them lay the two humans they had brought back from the Foitani sphere. The Cro-Magnons were just on the point of coming out of cold sleep. The anthropologists at Saugus Central University had gone to a good deal of effort to make them as homelike an environment as possible in which to awaken. Putting the temperature somewhere below freezing struck Jennifer as excessive. Still, in trying to bridge the gap between Pleistocene and starship, who could say what detail might prove crucial?

The woman stirred. A few seconds later, so did the man. "Here we go," one of the anthropologists radioed into the little ear speakers Jennifer and Greenberg were wearing. "Remember, you people are the link between this familiar—we hope—place and what they've gone through. When they see you here, they ought to get the idea that they aren't really home, or not exactly, anyway."

"We'll see soon," Jennifer answered. Getting through to the primitives was going to be as hard as any first contact with an alien race. They'd have to learn a new language from scratch; not even theoretically reconstructed _Ur_-Indo-European went back even as far as a quarter of the way to their time.

The man sat up first. His eyes, at first, were only on the woman. When she opened her eyes and also managed to sit, his face glowed with relief. Then he noticed Jennifer and Greenberg. He rattled off something in his extinct speech.

"Hello. We're peaceful. We hope you are, too," Greenberg said in Spanglish. He held his hands out before him, palms up, to show they were empty. That was about as old a pacific gesture as humanity knew. Nobody could be sure, though, whether it went back to the Paleolithic. Everything the Cro-Magnons did taught researchers something.

The man didn't return the gesture, but he seemed to understand what it meant. He stood up and took a couple of steps forward to put himself between the woman and Greenberg and Jennifer. Then he spoke again, this time in a questioning tone. Jennifer made what she thought was a pretty fair guess at what he was saying. *You were there in that strange place with those monsters. Now you're here. What's going on?*

"Time for that special effect we were talking about," she whispered, for the benefit of the anthropologists outside.

Without warning, a holovid projection of a Foitan sprang into being, a few meters away from the primitives. The woman let out a piercing shriek. The man shouted, too, fear and fury mingling in his voice. He looked around wildly for a stone to throw.

"You!" Greenberg said in a commanding tone, stabbing out his forefinger at the alarmingly perfect image. "Go away and never come back!" He struck a pose that proclaimed he had every right to order the big, blue alien around so.

The projection winked out as if it had never been. The man and woman shouted again, this time in amazement. Then they both hurried over to Greenberg, embraced him, and pounded him on the back. He staggered under the joyful blows. "They're stronger than they think," he wheezed, trying to stay upright.

"Congratulations," the anthropologist said into his and Jennifer's ears. "You are now a powerful wizard."

"Good." Greenberg turned his head. "Ah, I see the second part of the demonstration is on its way."

Four plates floated toward the humans. Each one carried a thick steak, a couple of apples, and some ripe strawberries. The primitives needed another few seconds to spot them. Then they started exclaiming all over again.

Jennifer intercepted two of the plates, Greenberg the other two. She passed one to each Cro-Magnon, then unhooked a couple of knives from her belt and handed them to the primitives, too. She drew one more for herself. Greenberg had his own. She cut a chunk from her steak, stabbed it, and lifted it to her mouth. Fancy manners could come later.

Neither of the humans just out of cold sleep had recognized the metal knife for what it was—they were used to tools of bone and stone. But they caught on quickly. The man grunted in wonder as the keen blade slid through the meat. He grunted again, this time happily, when the first bite went into his mouth. Jennifer knew just how he felt. After so long on Foitani kibbles, every meal of honest food was a special treat.

The primitives made the steaks vanish in short order. They inhaled the strawberries and ate the apples cores, stems and all. When they saw that Greenberg and Jennifer didn't want their cores, they made questioning noises and reached out for them. Getting no rebuff, they ate them, too.

"Hunter-gatherers can't afford to waste any amount of food, no matter how small," the anthropologist said.

The man kept trying the edge of the knife with his thumb. The woman said something to him, rather sharply. With obvious reluctance, he held out the knife to Jennifer. The woman held out hers.

Jennifer shook her head as she made pushing noises. "No, they're yours to keep," she said.

When the primitives realized what she meant, they whooped with glee and pummeled her as they had Greenberg. The man also reached under her synthetic fur and squeezed her left breast. She knocked his hand away. He didn't try twice. She gave him points for getting the idea in a hurry.

She pointed to herself. "Jennifer," she said.

"Bernard." Greenberg did the same thing.

The man's eyes lit up. He thumped his own chest. "Nangar," he declared.

He spoke to the woman. "Loto," she said, touching herself.

"I wonder if those are names or if they just mean 'man' and 'woman,' " an anthropologist radioed to Jennifer and Greenberg. "Well, we'll find out soon enough."

Language lessons went on from there, with parts of the body and the names of things close by. Nangar seemed to have an easier time picking up Spanglish words than Loto did.

"Maybe the tribe next door spoke a different language," the anthropologist suggested. "We think men traveled more widely through a tribal range than women, so he could be more used to using different words than she is."

After a while, Nangar pointed to the distant herds, which were actually holovid projections on a not-so-distant wall. With his own speech and many gestures, he got across the idea of hunting and then feasting. He gazed confidently at Greenberg all the while. Jennifer said, "After you got rid of that Foitan, Bernard, he figures you can do anything."

Greenberg grinned wryly. "No matter how big a wizard I am, I don't think I can put much nourishment into a projection. Maybe it's time to distract him again." He spoke as much to the waiting anthropologists as to Jennifer.

A few seconds later, a couple of the scientists came out from behind a boulder. They wore modern cold-weather gear. Nangar and Loto drew back in alarm. "Friends," Jennifer said reassuringly. She went over and smiled at the newcomers, patting them on the back. So did Greenberg.

The primitives remained dubious until one of the anthropologists reached into her backpack and took out several pieces of roasted chicken. When she passed them to Loto and Nangar, she found that the way to their hearts lay through their stomachs. Although they'd eaten a good-sized meal not long before, they devoured the chicken and gnawed clean the bones the anthropologists discarded.

The woman who'd given them the treat looked faintly appalled. "The way they eat, it's a wonder they aren't two hundred kilos each."

"The fact that they aren't tells you how often—or rather, how seldom—they get the chance to eat like this," her male companion answered. She thought it over and nodded.

Seeing that friendly relations had been established between the primitives and the people whose job it would be to guide them into the modern worlds, Greenberg and Jennifer strolled casually toward the boulder from in back of which the anthropologists had emerged. Several more anthropologists waited in the doorway the boulder concealed. They greeted the two traders with almost as much enthusiasm as Nangar and Loto had shown. One of them—in the crowd, Jennifer couldn't tell which one—let his hands wander more than they might have. Whoever he was, he didn't have Nangar's excuse for bad manners—he was supposed to be civilized.

Jennifer changed back into proper clothes with more than a little relief. Greenberg was waiting in the hall outside her cubicle when she emerged. "Do you want to hang around for a while and watch them work with the Cro-Magnons?" he asked.

She shook her head. "Do you?"

"No, not really," he said. "They do want us to stay on call for a few days, though, in case they run into trouble and need our familiar faces."

"I suppose that's fair enough." Jennifer sighed. "Still, what I'd like most would be just to start picking up the threads of my normal life again."

"Normal life? What's that? I gave it up when I decided to become a trader. But I will say that the time I spent in the Foitani sphere turned out to be even farther from normal than I was quite braced for myself." Greenberg smiled and set his hand on her waist. "Not that all of it was bad, not by a long shot."

Her hand covered his. "No, not all of it was bad. We wouldn't have ended up together if they hadn't kidnapped me, and I'm glad we did. But I'm a whole lot gladder to be back on a human world again and to feel fairly sure no one's going to shoot at me or fire a missile at my ship in the next twenty minutes."

"Amen to that," he said. "All the same, I can't help wondering whether the *kwopillot* and the *vodranet* decided to talk things over or just slug it out."

"I wonder, too," Jennifer said. "Still, you did the right thing when you got us out of there. We never would have found a better chance. But I would like to know what the Foitani ended up doing. I wonder if we'll ever find out."

"Hello, dear," Ella Metchnikova said as her path crossed Jennifer's on the edge of the university campus. "You must come over to my place before long. I have a marvelous new—well, old, I should say—drink that everyone loves. It's called a Black Russian, and you simply would not believe what drinking two or three of them will do to you."

"Set you up for a liver transplant?" Jennifer asked, not altogether in jest—some of Ella's concoctions seemed to have been invented by ancient temperance workers intent on demonstrating the evils of ethanol poisoning by horrible example.

Ella laughed heartily. Despite mixological experiments too numerous to remember, her liver was still intact—unless, of course, this was her second or third by now. She said, "They're not as bad as all that. And bring your Bernard by. Perhaps he'd be interested in the recipe as something he could trade to, ah, aliens."

To unsuspecting aliens, Jennifer thought, inserting a likely word into Ella's hesitation. Her friend meant well, though, so she said, "Maybe he would be—you never can tell. Still, I can't bring him by for a while; he set out on a trading run last week and he won't be back for a few months."

"Really? What an—interesting—arrangement. Do you plan on, ah, consoling yourself with someone else while he's off being primitive?" Ella's eyes went big and round.

"No," Jennifer said shortly. Ella Metchnikova wanted everything to be melodramatic. Jennifer had been in the middle of enough melodrama to last her a lifetime. But however volatile Ella was, she came through in a pinch. Jennifer said, "Thanks again for putting my stuff into storage when I disappeared."

"It was only my duty, dear," Ella said grandly. "Unlike some I could name but won't—Ali Bakhtiar, for instance—I was always sure you would come back."

"There were a lot of times when I wasn't," Jennifer said. Her kidnapping and spectacular return with Nangar and Loto had given her brief media fame on Saugus; she wasn't the least bit sorry it had finally started to wear off. She and Greenberg hadn't given the snoops all the lurid details of their adventures; that would only have made getting back to the ordinary course of day to day life harder.

Ella looked down at her watch. "Oh, dear, I'm late; I must fly. Call me soon, Jennifer—promise you will."

"I promise," Jennifer said. She was late, too, not a good thing to be on the first day of a new semester. Ella went on her way. Jennifer hurried across the campus. Out of the corner of her eye, she saw people stop and look at her. That had happened before the Foitani kidnapped her, too, but now about as many were women as men—a legacy of having had her face in the holovid tank a lot. She hoped that sort of attention would die down soon. She wanted no part of it. Aside from Bernard, all she wanted was to get back to work.

Even that wouldn't be easy. Almost in a trot, she went past the building where she'd lectured before notoriety came her way. No hall in that building was big enough to hold a class the size of the one she'd be teaching today. The enrollment was three times as big as she'd ever had before, which angered her more than it pleased her. She wanted students who would be interested in the material she presented, not in her as a curiosity.

She checked the time and swore. Five minutes late—that was disgraceful. But there at last ahead of her lay the second biggest lecture hall Saugus Central University boasted. The rear double doors were closed, which meant all the students were already inside. She swore again. They had to be thinking unkind thoughts about her. She fairly ran toward the special faculty entrance, which let her in right behind the podium.

She dashed up the steps onto the lecturer's platform. "I'm sorry, class," she began as she got her first look at this year's crop of students. "I—"

She stopped dead. She knew she shouldn't, but she couldn't help it. Better than three-quarters of the seats in the huge chamber were occupied by Foitani—blue Foitani from Odern, grayblue Foitani from Rof Golan, green-blue Great Ones, purple and brown and gray and even pink Foitani from worlds she'd never heard of. Hundreds of pairs of round, attentive, deeply colored eyes bored into hers.

They didn't kill each other off, she thought. *Good—I think.* She took a deep breath and started her lecture. Translators droned to turn her words into ones Foitani could understand. Somehow she got through it. "I'm sorry; I can't take questions today," she said when she was through.

She hurried out of the lecture hall, found a public phone, fed her access card into it, and checked the listings. Then she made a call. A man's face appeared on the screen. "Universal Protective Services," he said. "We're the best on Saugus."

"You'd better be," she told him.

ABOUT THE AUTHOR

Harry Turtledove is that rarity, a lifelong southern Californian. He is married and has three young daughters. After flunking out of Cal Tech, he earned a degree in Byzantine history and has taught at UCLA, Cal State Fullerton, and Cal State Los Angeles. Academic jobs being few and precarious, however, his primary work since leaving school has been as a technical writer. He has had fantasy and science fiction published in *Isaac Asimov's*, *Amazing*, *Analog*, *Playboy*, and *Fantasy Book*. His hobbies include baseball, chess, and beer.